WAYMAKER

BOOK 2
OF THE PEARLSONG REFOUNDING

A fantasy novel by

MICHAEL D. WARDEN

ASCENT BOOKS & MEDIA
A division of Ascent Coaching Group Inc.

WAYMAKER
by Michael D. Warden

www.thepearlsongrefounding.com

Published by Ascent Books & Media, 9901 Brodie Lane, Suite 160, Austin, Texas 78748. For reprint permission requests and other inquiries, email us at admin@ascentcoachinggroup.com.

This book is a work of fiction. Names, characters, places, and incidents are either products of the author's imagination or used fictitiously. Any similarity to actual people, organizations, and/or events is purely coincidental.

ISBN 978-0-6152-3792-3

Editorial Consultants: Karl & Lisa Lauffer
Cover Design: Josh Tilton, Grip Creative
Interior Design: PerfecType, Nashville, TN

Printed in the United States of America

"Death and Life are in the power of the tongue,
and those who love it will eat its fruit."

PROVERBS 18:21 NASB

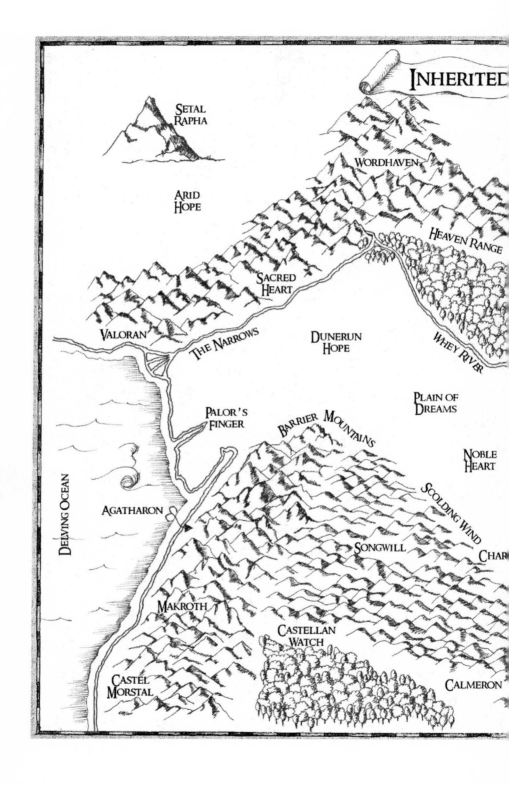

INHERITED

SETAL RAPHA

ARID HOPE

WORDHAVEN

HEAVEN RANGE

SACRED HEART

VALORAN

THE NARROWS

DUNERUN HOPE

WHEY RIVER

PLAIN OF DREAMS

PALOR'S FINGER

BARRIER MOUNTAINS

NOBLE HEART

SCOLDING WIND

DELVING OCEAN

AGATHARON

SONGWILL

CHAR

MAKROTH

CASTELLAN WATCH

CALMERON

CASTEL MORSTAL

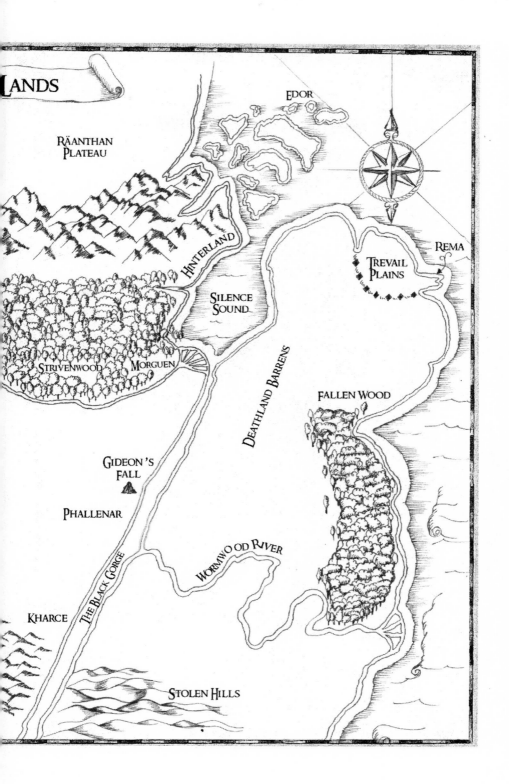

TIMELINE OF THE

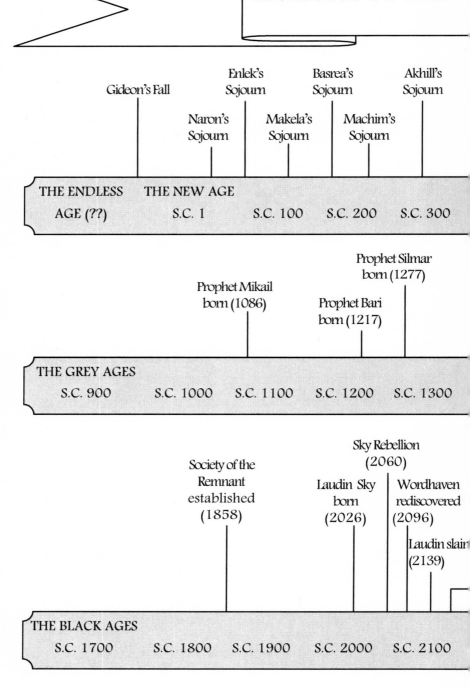

Gideon's Fall

Enlek's
Sojourn

Basrea's
Sojourn

Akhill's
Sojourn

Naron's
Sojourn

Makela's
Sojourn

Machim's
Sojourn

THE ENDLESS   THE NEW AGE
AGE (??)   S.C. 1   S.C. 100   S.C. 200   S.C. 300

Prophet Silmar
born (1277)

Prophet Mikail
born (1086)

Prophet Bari
born (1217)

THE GREY AGES
S.C. 900   S.C. 1000   S.C. 1100   S.C. 1200   S.C. 1300

Sky Rebellion
(2060)

Society of the
Remnant
established
(1858)

Laudin Sky
born
(2026)

Wordhaven
rediscovered
(2096)

Laudin slain
(2139)

THE BLACK AGES
S.C. 1700   S.C. 1800   S.C. 1900   S.C. 2000   S.C. 2100

INHERITED LANDS

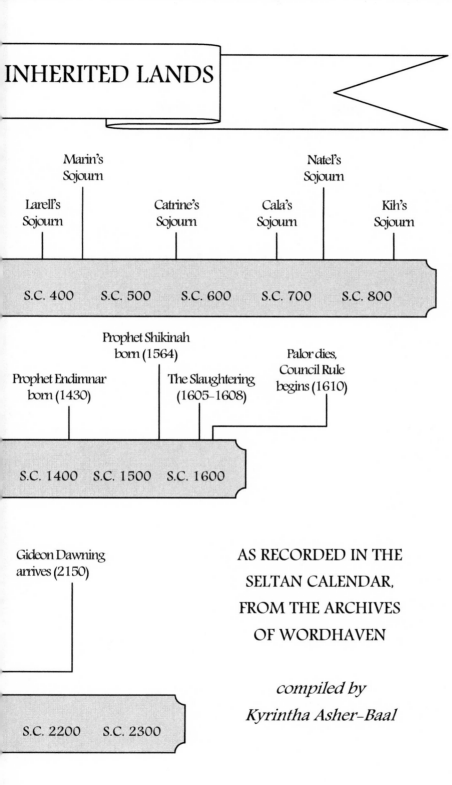

Marin's
Sojourn

Natel's
Sojourn

Larell's
Sojourn

Catrine's
Sojourn

Cala's
Sojourn

Kih's
Sojourn

S.C. 400   S.C. 500   S.C. 600   S.C. 700   S.C. 800

Prophet Shikinah
born (1564)

Palor dies,
Council Rule
begins (1610)

Prophet Endimnar
born (1430)

The Slaughtering
(1605–1608)

S.C. 1400   S.C. 1500   S.C. 1600

Gideon Dawning
arrives (2150)

AS RECORDED IN THE
SELTAN CALENDAR,
FROM THE ARCHIVES
OF WORDHAVEN

S.C. 2200   S.C. 2300

compiled by
Kyrintha Asher-Baal

PROLOGUE

To the Most Excellent Laytren Toole, Ward of the Guardian Legion, 37th Warcor, Tower Wall Regiment, Post I

From the Underlord Kyrintha Asher-Baal, seed and heir to High Lord Balaam and Lord Lysteria of the Council at Phallenar, composed by my hand this 21st day of the season of Shadows, S.C. 2150

My Dearest Laytren,

It is with all my hope and prayer that this letter finds you well and safe beyond the foul reach of my parents in Phallenar. If my instructions were properly carried out, then this missive comes to you directly from the hand of Mentor Spriggs, and he is standing before you even now. I ask that you not be too hard on him for what he has done. The plan to force you into hiding was wholly my own. The good Mentor is only following my explicit instructions regarding your safety, which I gave to him prior to my departure. I know that you could never abandon your post of your own volition, regardless of the obvious risk to all involved, least of all yourself. Indeed, I could never ask that of you. But neither could I bear to see you slain on my account. And so I have forced you to remain alive, and safe, and by that act made you as much a fugitive of the Council as I. Forgive me, Laytren. I know my actions are abhorrent to your soldier's heart. But what I have done, I was compelled to do out of love for our friendship. I hope in time you will see the truth of that.

It is for love as well that I write this now, for I want you to understand something of the larger tale which has now caught us both up in its grasp, and is carrying us unbidden along a shrouded and perilous path. You know some of the reasons that lead me to flee Phallenar and take my place among these rebels. But there is much of the story you do not know. It is my hope that in hearing the whole tale, you may come to better understand my choices. And in understanding, forgive.

Less than a year ago, the sojourner Gideon Dawning—you know him as Stormcaller—miraculously appeared in the Inherited Lands. No one knows where he came from or how he arrived. But all instantly recognized his power. Confronted by your fellow guardians on the Floor of Calmeron Sounden, he summoned a Storm of Deliverance—an act that has not been seen in over a thousand years.

The sojourner claimed no knowledge of the storm or how it came to be. But others knew. They recognized the signs, prophecies recorded centuries ago on those Worded black scrolls you always chide me for reading. This was no ordinary sojourner, Laytren. Whether his destiny was for good or ill I could not then say. Perhaps I cannot still. But I now know his coming to us is destined to challenge everything we believe, and will inevitably change us all.

I heard about the sojourner within the first few days of his appearance, despite the isolation of my prison cell, and soon discovered that his visitation caused an uproar among the Council Lords. The Council focused its full attention on retrieving this unusual stranger who had named himself Gideon—a title that of its own accord could begin and end wars in its sounding. Several warcor of guardians and vile riftmen were sent to find him. Most returned empty-handed, unable to locate the rebel Remnant who hid him. The one warcor that did find him never returned at all. The sojourner destroyed it. Thirteen hundred riftmen slain in a matter of moments—and still he claimed no knowledge of the act!

In spite of these dangers, the Remnant remained determined to keep the sojourner safe, at least until they could deliver him to Wordhaven, where the veracity of his insistent claims—that he was misplaced, that he had no knowledge of the Words, that he, in fact, hated our lands, and wanted nothing more than to leave them—could be properly tested.

Despite repeated efforts from the Council at Phallenar to destroy them, the Remnant eventually reached their goal. And there at Wordhaven (yes, it does exist!), the probity of the sojourner was tested nearly to the point of death. But even under the power of the Words—Words of *Dei'lo*, Laytren, not the foul *Sa'lei*—the truth would not come clear. All that could be determined was that his presence would change everything, which the prophecies alone had already affirmed.

The Remnant was at an impasse. Even among their own number, many hated Gideon Dawning; most feared him. The Council, especially my father, wanted to learn his power, then destroy him. Only a few of the Remnant believed the best, pushing the sojourner to fulfill the destiny of the prophesied Kinsman Redeemer, and overthrow the Council Lords. As for Gideon, who can say what he wanted? Having known him only a short while now, I could only guess at his deeper motives at the time. He seems an ordinary man in most respects, but focused in a way I've never seen. Formidable, daring, perhaps even reckless. But I am told he was not this way at first.

Not long after Gideon's testing, spies from the Remnant uncovered the long-sought location of the Book of *Dei'lo* in Phallenar. You have heard me speak of it before—a powerful tome containing knowledge of that ancient language as powerful as *Sa'lei*, but free of evil's taint. I know you hold *Dei'lo*—and the Book itself—to be nothing more than myth. But Laytren, hear me. I have now seen the Book with my own eyes! I have risked my life— I risk it still—to see it freed from my parents' grasp. Does this not convince you?

But back to the matter. It was decided that a team from the Remnant would travel in stealth to Phallenar and attempt to steal the Book from its warded chamber deep beneath the city. Despite their desperate pleas, Gideon refused to join them, and purposed in his heart to leave Wordhaven—and the Remnant—perhaps forever, so that he might seek out a destiny of his own choosing.

And now to the part of the story more familiar to you. Upon Gideon's departure, he was captured by the Council Lords Fayerna and Bentel, that perverse brother and sister who were sent by my father for this very task. But, against my father's explicit command they carried Gideon to Morguen sounden and concealed him there, intending to learn the secret of his power for themselves and use it to gain supremacy over my father and his fellow lords.

Not knowing what had become of Gideon, or of the sibling lords' betrayal of the Council, the Remnant was naturally overcome with urgency and fear. The Wordhaven team left with haste to find their way to Phallenar in the hope that they might recover the Book before Gideon could be forced to reveal their plan. What they did not realize—perhaps, what they failed to believe—was that the sojourner was made of nobler stuff than that. He resisted Fayerna and Bentel's attempts to break him. Enduring weeks of torment under the power of *Sa'lei*, the sojourner told them nothing...not even the Remnant's given names.

When the Council Lords at Phallenar realized they had been betrayed by their own, they sent a warcor of their most formidable guardians to Morguen sounden to destroy the errant Lords and retrieve their coveted prey. The warcor failed, but not before providing Gideon a chance to escape his captors. In time he rejoined the Remnant team and they continued their quest to Phallenar.

As you are aware, I knew of the coming of the team from Wordhaven the instant my parents learned of it. And I saw in their arrival a way for me to escape my prison in the Tower of the Wall, and perhaps exchange my strangled life for something better.

The plan itself I kept from you, not for lack of trust in you, but to keep you innocent of the scheme. Such secrecy hardly matters now, of course; the deed is done, and I suspect the news of it has already spread into the streets. I captured the Remnant team the moment they reached the Wall—never mind how. I told them I would assist them in their quest if they would take me with them when they fled. Naturally, they did not believe me. Yet with some persuasion, they agreed to my terms. In truth, I left them little choice.

Using my spies as guides, they delved deep into the heart of the earth, through leagues of tunnels that run the length and breadth of Phallenar, and there they found the Book they sought. And there they also found my father and his puppet lords, waiting. My plan was compromised, whether by betrayal or by some dark art of *Sa'lei* I do not know. But despite his power, my father was still denied his prize. Gideon used his great ability to hold the Council's power at bay, and in the confusion the Remnant snatched the Book and escaped. Gideon himself was captured, but soon regained his freedom with help from unexpected sources.

My own part of that story is far less glorious, and the dark grief of it still far too fresh for me to recount on these pages. In time, I promise, I will tell you everything, when the pain is not so near. Suffice for now to say that I was not in the caverns with the others—my task was elsewhere—and that I too was most horridly betrayed and nearly slain. But I survived, and was carried with the others as they made their escape from Phallenar. Now, some seven or eight days later—I lose count—I am restored to health in body, though certainly not in soul, and have taken my place with this group of rebels, for good or ill.

They say they will take me to Wordhaven in time. But for now that is impossible. The Council hunts us still, but it is more than only that. It seems this sojourner has taken on a change of sorts. A Raanthan is with him, hovering always by his side like a pale and silent shadow from the Barrens. He has told the sojourner something; they won't tell me what. They do not yet trust me. But whatever it is, it has put a reckless fire in Gideon's eyes, and forged within his breast a will of iron. And the rest of them have been inexorably sucked up in the draft of his determined course.

And so it seems I have as well.

Stay safe, Laytren. Stay hidden. I will send word again as I am able.

Your loyal underlord and true friend,
Kyrintha

THE ENDURANT

A Word is heard weeping in the plains,
"Make way for the Pearl!
Make clear the path of the Staff of Life!"
He wears a crown of black upon his head
And on his shoulders a mantle of deliverance has been laid,
For the sake of the Refounding Age
That he is called to preach as herald, as witness,
as the maker of ways.
      —From the writings of the Prophet Shikinah, in the year S.C. 1600

His legs were still bleeding.

From his perch upon the bowsprit of the Endurant, he probed the seeping divots along each shin, noting any deviance in color or swelling. In some places, the blood ran almost clear, but in most it was still red and sluggish. At least there seemed to be no evidence of infection. He took that to be a hopeful sign. Perhaps the scars would not be so bad.

His wrists were another matter entirely. The scars there were already beginning to build, smooth and pink like worms sleeping just beneath his skin. He found it odd that his wrists, torn so deeply by the rusted manacles in the dungeons of Phallenar, had scarred over much more quickly than the rat bites on his legs. The bleeding from his wrists had stopped after only a night, and, aside from a vague numbness in his fingers, there was little soreness. But the scars...those scars would mark him for the rest of his days. Every time he shook a hand, or waved goodbye, or held a staff.

It had become his morning ritual, this silent survey of his wounds, since he first boarded the Endurant over three days past. Both Ajel and Aybel had implored him to let them heal the lesions with Words, but he refused. He still wasn't sure why. He needed the pain; that's all he knew. The bleeding was his comfort. It reminded him he was still living.

As if to mock his reverie, the Endurant plowed through a cresting wave that sent a spray of stinging salt water across his legs. But he did not flinch. In truth, it was the water's stench, and not its sting, that tormented him most. He had tried to grow accustomed to it, as much as one can try to do such a thing. But every now and then a foul whiff of the stuff would rise from the waterline, and he would find himself lurched over the railing, offering his last meal to the black waters of the Gorge. That peculiar Captain Quigly insisted the water carried no foul smell at all, and grumbled that Gideon was far too much a "lander" to even be allowed at sea, much less darken the deck of a fine ship like the Endurant. But Gideon was not the only one aboard who'd lost his lunch to the stench. And if that stumpy little captain refused to admit his bulbous nose couldn't smell a pile of crap if it hit him in the face...well, let him have his fantasies.

In fairness, the Captain had called them all "landers" from the start— even Ajel, though somehow the term carried more respect when thrown his way. Ajel just smiled deferentially, of course, the way Ajel always did. But that was about the only time he smiled. When he wasn't pouring over the precious Book of *Dei'lo*, which was most of the time, he would quietly convene with Aybel, Kair or Kyrintha and talk in urgent, serious tones, or else calmly comfort Revel as he wept in grief over Paladin's death. At first he approached Telus as well, but soon grew weary of the effort and stopped trying. The Raanthan, it seemed, would not speak to anyone but Gideon.

Now Ajel was gone, and Gideon missed him already. He had teleported by Word with the Book of *Dei'lo* earlier that morning—back to Wordhaven, along with Kair. He had lingered on the Endurant only long enough to be certain the rest of them were safe, or at least relatively so, before giving his blessings and saying his goodbyes. Kair had said little to anyone before departing—nothing at all to Gideon. She alone had witnessed the horror of Paladin's death in Prisidium Square, and so Gideon did his best to believe it was her grief that made her manner so cold in recent days, much colder even than he had come to expect from her. But the way she glared at him even in her silence, you'd swear it was Gideon and not Lord Lysteria who'd burned their trusted leader to ash.

The role of Remnant leader—along with its title—now fell to Ajel. He had lost his uncle—a second father, really—as well as his trusted commander in one black night. But there was little grief to be seen on his face; at least, he never revealed it to Gideon. He seemed only a bit more serious. Determined, perhaps. He never spoke of Paladin's death; never shed one tear.

Well, *he* was Paladin now. Perhaps the time for tears had passed him by.

As the new Paladin, Ajel had wasted no time in issuing commands. After learning of Telus' announcement that Gideon was the Waymaker, he ordered Revel to remain with him and Telus, to travel with them wherever their path might lead. Gideon, for once, decided not to protest the decision. He doubted it would have made any difference in the outcome. And he had to admit that Revel would be a formidable ally and knowledgeable guide, and could even be a reasonably amiable companion, even if his hawk-like manner was a bit quirky at times.

At least Ajel didn't order Aybel to travel with him. That, Gideon would have refused, violently if necessary. She was a capable fighter, but Gideon cared too much for her to see her life endangered again on his account. Knowing him had cost her too much already.

Thankfully, Ajel assigned her to the underlord. Since Kyrintha did not speak *Dei'lo*, and therefore could not transport away to Wordhaven as Ajel and Kair had, Ajel instructed Captain Quigly to carry them to the Hinterland, where Aybel's people—the Kolventu—made their home. There, Aybel and Kyrintha would take their leave from the others, and travel by land across the Heaven Range to Wordhaven. It would be a long and perilous trek, especially with no horses, and with winter just a few months away. But at least on that route, their chances of eluding the eyes of their pursuers were much improved.

Revel, meanwhile, would remain on the Endurant with Gideon and his self-proclaimed protector, Telus, to aid him in his quest to fulfill his role as Waymaker...whatever that meant.

No matter. Telus told Gideon he would know the way when the time came, but he couldn't even think about that now, not with Aybel leaving soon and squads of black winged lions still shadowing them overhead.

Since the Endurant's escape from Phallenar, the guardians of the Council Lords had never been far off. Soon after Gideon boarded, three black-garbed riders on juron swooped in from the south. But they were careful to stay out of earshot, and after circling a few times, retreated back toward Phallenar. Ajel said they were merely scouts, sent to spy out their position. The attack, he surmised, would come in a few days' time, unless they could find a way to conceal their whereabouts. In the hours that followed, two more packs of juron were spotted, their guardian riders watching the Endurant from the distant safety of the skies. So, in the middle of the first night while Gideon slept, the Sea Folk captain sailed the Endurant deep inside a narrow fissure on the west side of the Gorge. The fissure could not be seen from the cliffs above, and was apparently hardly visible even from the water due to an excess of poisoned vines shrouding it like a curtain. No one besides the Sea Folk knew of that place, Quigly said. When morning came, it would seem as though the ship had simply vanished. If they were lucky, the guardians would believe the Endurant had been attacked by watery demons from the Barrens, and sunk sometime in the night.

Ajel did not believe the Council or their guardians would give up so easily; neither did Gideon. But for the next two days, they remained huddled in the slime-coated dark of that slender cave, and waited. Scouts were sent out several times, but no sign of guardians or juron were ever seen.

Not long after dusk on the third night, a dry air mass blew in from the south, and Quigly announced that if they were ever going to make a run for Silence Sound, they'd best do it now.

And so they did. Using long poles designed especially for the task, the crew poked and pressed against the fissure walls in unison until, at length, the Endurant began its silent backwards waddle out of the slender cavern and into open waters once again. It seemed only moments before Quigly and his bondmate had unfurled and trimmed all five of the larger sails, and turned the bow of the Endurant straight down the black center of the Gorge's gurgling throat.

Gideon slept after that, like a dead man. When he finally awakened at first light, he was told that the winds had held throughout the night, and still no guardians had been spotted in the skies or along the canyon rim on either side. With any luck, they would coast out of the Gorge within the hour.

"Has the Raanthan told you about the Sound?" Aybel's voice was unmistakable, but Gideon turned around anyway as if unsure of who was speaking.

"Huh?"

"The Raanthan," she repeated, glancing briefly at the silvery-skinned apparition who was never far from Gideon's side, "has it told you about the Sound?" She seemed hesitant to look at Telus. If Gideon didn't know Aybel better, he'd have guessed she was afraid to be near him. Or rather, to be near "it."

Gideon shrugged lightly. "As Raanthans go, I think he's a pretty quiet one. Not that I have much data on the subject."

"The Sound is Worded," said Aybel. "We must prepare before we cross the threshold."

"Prepare for what?" Gideon flung his legs to one side of the bowsprit and hopped down to the deck. The brown leather shortpants and jerkin Telus had given him allowed him to move much more freely than the robes he'd worn since his time in Strivenwood. But the jerkin still bore the white emblem of the Pearl on its breast, just as the robes had. Telus never said where he got them.

"The silence," Aybel replied. "Once we cross the threshold, we will not be able to speak again until we reach the shores of the Hinterland. All sound will cease."

"Are you saying there is no sound in the Sound?" Gideon laughed. "Now that's a good one!"

Aybel didn't seem amused. "It is no laughing matter, sojourn...Way.... What should I call you now?"

He thought a moment, then said, "Gideon. I'd like it if you called me Gideon."

She shook her head. "That is not a safe name. Many would slay you to hear you—"

"Sojourner, then! Whatever," Gideon quickly ran his fingers through the length of his curly black hair. "What about the Sound? Is it dangerous?"

"No," Aybel replied. "In some ways it is the safest place within the whole of the Inherited Lands—at least as far as Sa'lei is concerned. With no sound, the Words cannot be uttered within its borders. We cannot be attacked."

"Not with Words, anyway," Gideon corrected.

"Just so," Aybel replied with a nod. Her face and shoulders glistened wetly in the morning sun, like chocolate silk. Her hair, as white as the clouds, was still as short and brilliant as the day they met. He wondered when she found the time to cut it.

"What are you looking at?" she asked.

Gideon blinked, slowly. "Nothing," he said. "I just thought maybe I should get a haircut." His own black curls had grown wild and long in the weeks since he'd arrived in the Inherited Lands. Not that he'd had time to care. Not that he cared much now.

"There will be time for such trivial matters once we have traversed the Sound," she replied. "Besides, I think it suits you."

Gideon grinned in surprise. "Do you?" He playfully flipped a wind-blown lock away from his eyes.

Aybel shrugged. "It marks you. As many things mark you."

His smile faded to sarcasm. "Yeah," he snorted. "I suppose it does." He had been in the Inherited Lands only a few days when he learned that no other living soul had hair as black as his—the color of midnight. It had been one of the early signs that set him apart. And there had been many others since—the almond wood staff, the robe of the old Lords that mysteriously appeared on him in Strivenwood Forest, the prophecies of the Grey Ages. And, of course, the power.

Just then, a rogue gust shot across the bow from the cliffs to the west. The wooden masts creaked heavily under the strain, forcing the ship to heave far to starboard. Aybel grabbed Gideon's arm to keep from losing her balance, even as she shot a worried glance back toward the cockpit. Gideon's eyes followed hers. Captain Quigly was not at the helm, but his bondmate was, cursing the wind with a zeal that matched—or perhaps surpassed— her strained determination to hold the wheel on course. Like the captain, she was excessively squat, with a barrel-shaped torso and legs so short as to be almost nonexistent. But her arms were of normal length and as thickly muscled as any man's, and with them she latched onto the wheel and leaned her stumpy frame heavily to port. The curses continued unabated, but the wheel held steady.

Ajel had told him that the unusual physical traits of the Captain and his bondmate were common to all the Sea Folk, and uniquely suited them to life on the open sea. It might make them good sailors, Gideon had replied. But they should definitely steer clear of beauty contests.

A few seconds later the wind subsided, and the deck rolled quietly back to its former position.

"Well. That was weird," said Gideon, looking at Aybel.

Her hand lingered on his arm. When her eyes met his, they seemed full of questions, but not about the wind. "Gideon, there's something—"

"You must take your staff now, Waymaker." Gideon glanced over Aybel's shoulder to see Telus looming over them, thrusting the almond wood staff out toward the Waymaker like a scepter.

"What for?" asked Gideon. *She called me Gideon.*

"It was an ill wind," replied Telus. "*Sa'lei* has been spoken. I sense it."

"That wind was Worded?" asked Gideon.

Aybel released his arm and stepped toward the companionway. "Revel, Kyrintha," she called. "You're needed."

The Raanthan's sinewy silver-grey arm extended the staff toward Gideon a second time. "Take it," he said. "You may have need of it."

Gideon frowned. After Telus had freed Gideon from the dungeons of Phallenar and carried him to safety at Gideon's Fall, the Raanthan left him alone for a time while they waited for the Endurant to find them. When he returned, he carried with him the gilded almond wood staff, looking more like a flimsy twig in his overly-large hand, as well as a new set of clothes. Gideon took the garments, but refused to touch the staff. He did not ask how Telus knew where to find it or how he came by the clothes, nor did he wish to know how the Raanthan retrieved the items from Phallenar without being seen. He didn't care. He knew only that he did not want to be reminded of the staff right then. He didn't even want to look at it.

In truth, his strong reaction to the staff surprised him. He'd never been afraid of it before. Even when the power overtook him on the Plain of Dreams, where Lord Bentel perished in a flash of brilliant blue, it felt like the most natural thing in the world—just holding the staff as he did; and letting it hold him.

But now he knew too much to be so naïve. He was the *Waymaker*. He could no longer pretend that the staff of almond wood was merely a token of the world he'd left behind, a miraculous talisman endowed with power by some fluke of magic or circumstance he did not understand. It was—had always been, really—a symbol; a sign of the calling the prophecies of this world had ordained for him.

It wasn't that he had changed his mind about pursuing the course Telus had laid out for him. Far from it. From someplace deep within the dark pit of his soul, he knew it was more than simple choice that prompted him to say yes to his unlikely calling as Waymaker. It was *need*. He needed to walk out this path, to discover, for himself, where it might lead. He ached for the mystery of it and all the unknown perils it invoked. He craved it as a man might crave riches or a woman's touch...though he couldn't explain why, not even to himself.

Still, a part of him held back. Perhaps it was just his stubbornness, that fractious aspect of his character that instinctively grated against all attempts to steer him against his will. Or perhaps it was his reluctance to abandon all the practiced years of self-imposed isolation, to break out of that comfortable cocoon of familiarity that concealed his broken vulnerability from the world.

Ultimately, however, he realized neither of these things kept him from the staff. Instead, it was fear. Simple, selfish fear. For somewhere in the deepest part of his soul, he realized he did know one thing about the path ahead—it was a one-way trip. Once he took the staff in his hands again, somewhere a door would close forever. There would be no chances to change his mind after that, no room for barter or appeal. Once he took the staff, there would be no turning back.

Thankfully, Telus did not force the issue. But the staff had not left the Raanthan's steely grip from that first moment to this, and in all that time the Raanthan had not once left Gideon's side. And so the staff was ever before him.

"I don't even know how to use it," Gideon said finally.

"You will." The Raanthan smiled. Or perhaps he frowned. With that tiny sliver of a mouth, it was never easy to tell.

"Rollers Ho! Astern! Astern!"

It was Quigly, standing on the stern, gesturing angrily toward the waters behind them. "Man the spars, you landers, if you care at all for Quigly's boat," he bellowed. "Woman, secure that wheel and help me trim the sails!"

Everyone jumped into action. Revel and Kyrintha, having just emerged from the companionway, dashed to either side of the deck and unstrapped the longpoles secured along its borders. Aybel ran to midships, with Gideon close on her heels.

"What is it?" Gideon asked.

She flung her arm out toward the south. "Something comes." She snatched one of the longpoles from Kyrintha's hand and thrust it toward Gideon. "Take this. Man the starboard bow. Don't let them near the hull." She grabbed another pole, then spun back toward Gideon, who still stared at her in confusion. "Go!" she commanded. "And tell that silvery ghost of yours to either take a spar or be tossed overboard to fight them by hand!"

Aybel's tone made it clear that she would brook no further discussion on the matter. So Gideon took the spar, and a second one for Telus, then ran back to the foredeck where the Raanthan calmly stood, seemingly unaware that anything out of the ordinary was going on around him. "Take this," Gideon said, holding out the longpole. "Whatever's coming, Aybel wants us to keep it from touching the hull. You can watch the port bow. I'll watch the starboard."

The Raanthan's liquid bronze eyes stared down at the spar dispassionately. "I cannot slay them," he said. "It is not permitted."

"What?" asked Gideon. "What are you talking about?"

Telus blinked. "I cannot slay them," he repeated.

"You don't even know what they are! Wait, do you?"

"Even so, I cannot."

Gideon shook his head in frustration. "Fine!" he growled, thrusting the spar toward Telus' face. "Do you see any spear points on these? You don't have to kill them, whatever they are. Just keep them away from the ship." He threw the spar down on the deck, then turned to take his position along the railing just to the right of the bow. After a moment he glanced over his shoulder to see Telus slowly reaching down toward the longpole, fingering it dubitably as though the thing might rear up and bite him. *What is his problem?*

But there were more pressing matters now than unraveling Telus' odd reluctance to help. Once Gideon positioned his spar over the water, he looked astern to see if he could get some idea of what had inspired such a panic. Behind him, some ten feet or so, stood the underlord, spar in hand, looking something like a misplaced princess with her disheveled blond hair and her dark green gown, now torn along the side—the same gown she had worn since the night he first laid eyes on her in the dingy torchlight within the Wall. Beyond her stood Aybel, leaning anxiously over the stern like a huntress from the Amazon. But what was she hunting? In the waters beyond them both, there were no monsters that he could see.

There were only waves. Deep rolling mounds of blackish blue, smooth as glass, advancing toward the ship like lethargic torpedoes.

"Woman, what's the count of them?" Quigly barked from his perch at the wheel.

"A dozen at least," his bondmate called back, rather matter-of-factly it seemed to Gideon. "Maybe more."

"More," echoed Revel, who stood opposite Kyrintha at midships.

Captain Quigly grunted in disapproval. "And I s'pose you can tell us which ones are pregnant while you're at it, too." He spit. "Landers."

Gideon glanced over his shoulder. The Raanthan's back was to him, his waist-long fine spun hair swirling around him like a glistening silver shroud. But at least he was holding the spar now. And his eyes scanned the waters behind them, seemingly intent on the approaching threat.

"What are we running from?" Gideon called out. "All I see are waves."

"Sound Ho!" cried Captain Quigly. "Sound Ho! Hold your spars aready, my landers. My fine lady may yet save your arses twice this week!"

Gideon turned to look ahead. A half mile away, the red cliffs of the Gorge seemed to melt away, opening the horizon to a broad expanse of blue as deep and peaceful as the azure sky.

"Won't they follow us into the Sound?" asked Gideon.

"They don't like the taste of unsullied waters," replied Quigly. "I've never known a Barrens beast to swim beyond the cliffs."

"What 'Barrens beast'?" Gideon asked again. "What are they?"

"What matters in a name, lander?" Quigly snapped. "They'll eat my ship if given the chance, and swallow you with it! That's all you need to know. Stop jabbering and set your eye on the task."

Gideon grimaced. He didn't like not knowing what he was up against, even if it was just a name.

The underlord leaned in toward Gideon. "If you must know, sojourner, I believe they are viperon," she said, keeping her eyes on the water. She spoke with a blank tone and no expression, as if the events of recent days had not yet become real. "I've seen them on occasion on the plains from my perch within the Tower. Though I never thought I'd have the misfortune of encountering one up close."

"Come now, wind, come on," called Quigly, half grumble and half chant. "Kiss my lady's sails. Kiss 'em sweet, kiss 'em hard. That's how they like it." He spun his barrel shape toward the stern. "If you Remnant folk are so blessed with lordly powers, why don't you call a stronger wind to blow us on?"

"The Words have little strength so close to the Barrens," replied Aybel. "We must rely on what wind the Giver has provided."

Quigly spit again, and shook his head. "Let's hope the Giver put some secret strength in those spindly arms of yours, then. We'll need it."

"They come!" cried Revel. Gideon peered down the length of the ship. But the silken waves were gone.

"Where are they?" he cried.

"Get your spars down, landers!" barked Quigly irritably. "Get 'em down! It won't do no good to swat 'em like mosquitoes, will it? When you see the rainbows, stab 'em in the heart."

"Rainbows?" mumbled Gideon. "What rainbows?"

But them he saw them. About twenty fathoms down, directly beneath the hull—bursts of color, like prisms swimming in chaotic patterns. Suddenly, he heard an owlish screech behind him, and turned to see Telus reared back on his gangly heels, frantically thrusting his spar into the air, high above the water. The air before him flashed white and blue with hints of rust, like a mosaic of mirrored tiles slithering madly in the breeze. Then, just as it hit the water, Gideon caught a glimpse of its true form. A serpentine shape nearly as big as a whale, covered tip to tip in scales as smooth as glass.

The tremendous splash from the beast nearly knocked Gideon over the railing. But he held his footing somehow. And when he looked back, Telus was still standing too, his spar held high and defiant.

No sooner had he resumed his stance than the waters beneath the Endurant began churning on all sides. Gideon pointed his spar straight down. This time, he saw no rainbows at all. Only teeth. Rows and rows of shark-like teeth, spinning in circles like a top, and rising fast.

"Thrust 'em down, landers! Quickly!" cried Quigly. "Thrust toward the keel! They're aiming to latch on beneath us!"

With a fervor inspired by blind panic, Gideon pointed his spar toward the murky shadows under the ship and plunged it downward with all his might. Instantly, he struck something hard—and so solid the impact stung his hands. Even so, the hardness bucked against the stabbing force for only a moment before giving way.

"Again! Again!" cried Quigly. "We've nearly reached the Sound."

Gideon lifted the spar and plunged again, and again, each time striking something hard, each time pushing the mysterious creatures reluctantly away. His arms began to ache from the effort, and he cursed the shadows beneath the ship for obscuring the view. If only he could see them, he could aim the spar to stab their eyes. Provided they had eyes, that is.

A wave of stench-filled water knocked him momentarily off balance, forcing him to grab the railing for support. By the time he blinked the sting away, Captain Quigly was screaming.

"Strike it, lander! Are you daft? Strike it! Or you'll kill us all!"

Gideon looked up. Some ten feet above his head a mouth hovered, perfectly round and pulsing with multiple rows of razor-sharp teeth. There must have been hundreds of them. Thousands. Beneath them writhed a form suggestive of a snake, but ultimately lost in a torrent of glassy scales, each flashing its deceptive image in his eyes.

There wasn't time to think. Instinctively, he thrust the spar up toward the mouth, and jammed it hard right into the center. The pole went deep, and the mouth collapsed around it like a carnivorous flower sealing in its prey. The longpole lurched from his hands, and for a moment seemed to dance madly through the air, with nothing to propel it but a sinuous spout of mirrors. Then there was a crack, and the pole's protruding end splashed limply to the waves. The scales shimmered in the air a moment more, then whirled madly as the beast dove back beneath the surface.

"Grab another spar!" yelled Quigly. "The Sound is upon us. Don't lay back until you see me stand down from the wheel!"

Gideon slipped another longpole from the loops along the deck. Just before positioning it over the rail, he stole a quick glance around the ship. The beasts were everywhere, flying through the air like glassy serpents, churning the water's surface with rainbows left and right, and charging the hull like cloaked torpedoes. Spars were flying too. Poking, jamming, flinging madly at the prism lights wherever they appeared. But at least everyone was still accounted for. They were clearly tired, panicked perhaps. But no one had been lost.

Gideon turned to face the waters once again. Just as he did, a ferocious wave erupted from below, followed by a stream of colors hurtling so fast they bled together in a blur. A wall of scales that felt something like polished tin slammed him hard onto the deck. He heard a scream, and Captain Quigly cursed. And when he looked up, he saw a massive serpent coiling on the deck, mirroring the sunshine in its scales like the angel of death itself.

And at that moment, everything went silent.

BALAAM'S CHAMBERS

It seems incredulous to me now to think of Stevron as I remembered him in my childhood. He was bold even then, especially for an orphaned boy. But he was sensitive as well, and often seemed the first to notice whenever I felt tired or thoughtful. Being of a similar age we often found ourselves together—studying with the mentors in the Axis, or else performing the duties of state our office required. In truth, I considered him a friend. He laughed more easily than most, and never accused me of disloyalty when I would confess doubts about my parents' rule. But there was always a hollow place within him that my friendship could not touch. He often clung to private places, struggling with a sadness I could neither name nor comprehend. Looking back, of course I now know what it was. And I cannot help but think that he was more a victim of my parents' greed than I could ever claim to be.
—The Kyrinthan Journals, Musings, Chapter 13, Verses 48-51

Even from the anteroom, Lord Stevron Achelli could smell the vomit.

"I will see him. Now," he said.

The *mon'jalen* shifted nervously in her seat behind the expansive gilded desk. She was young, and obviously newly trained. Her eyes weren't even fully black. "As I mentioned, my Lord, the High Lord is currently indisposed," she said. "He asked me to bid you return later in the day, when his schedule is less constrained." She smiled weakly. "At dusk, perhaps."

Slowly, Lord Stevron placed a black-gloved hand upon the desk and leaned in toward the girl. His own steely blue eyes flared with quiet menace. "You do know the consequence for lying to a Council Lord, don't you, *mon'-jalen?*"

"My Lord, I am only relaying what the High Lord—"

"You do *know.*" he repeated, more quietly this time.

The *mon'jalen* pursed her lips. "Yes, Lord."

"Good," he whispered. "That's good." He leaned in farther. "Now, the High Lord summoned me here with his own Word this very hour. Summoned me from a task I did not wish to leave, a task that he sent me to do, and that now may very well be compromised by my forced departure. I dislike having to leave my work unfinished."

"My Lord," she stammered, her eyes flickering about to avoid his stare, "the High Lord is not well."

"I know," he said, suddenly smiling. "We both have noses, don't we?"

She returned his smile, sheepishly, clearly unsure of its intent. "I will check and see," she said.

"Yes," he replied. "Yes you will."

She smiled again as she rose from the desk, then quietly disappeared through the elaborate gold-laden doors that dominated the room behind her. A moment later, she returned, leaving the door ajar this time. "The High Lord bids you come," she said.

He said nothing, but walked passed her without a glance as though she were no longer there.

"Stevron, my son! How good of you to come so quickly." The High Lord waved him in excitedly, forcing a fleshy grin out of his pale, sweaty face, which otherwise reflected little else but pain. He lay awkwardly straddled upon a bed, his corpulent torso leaning forward upon a formidable stack of goose down pillows. His bare back was coated with strips of thin white cloth that reeked of fish oil, and which only poorly concealed the scores of open boils that lay beneath.

"It was not my goodness but your Word that summoned me, High Lord. So I am here." His tone was not half as warm as the High Lord's, but that was just as well. He wanted Balaam to know he was angry.

Balaam was about to speak when a servant abruptly stepped between them. Ignoring the lords, and with far less gentleness than one would expect, he began stripping back some of the bandages and sniffing at the oozing boils beneath. It was a wonder he didn't wretch right on the spot. In truth, it was a wonder they all weren't spilling the contents of their guts, given the stench that permeated the room—vomit and fish oil mingled with the sickly sweet smell of infection.

Balaam tolerated the interruption with a modicum of irritation and a considerable amount of pain, but he didn't try to stop it. *Probably ser'jalen,* thought Stevron, eyeing the servant. Many of the lords thought of their *ser'-jalen* as private pets, and as such, tended to indulge them too much, letting them get away with things that no ordinary servant would survive.

After a few moments, the servant silently pattered away, a wad of bloody bandages in his hand. Despite regular lancings and a continual regimen of foul-smelling ablutions from the healers, the boils had grown progressively worse since the night they first appeared, when that rebel slammed the cursed Book of *Dei'lo* against the High Lord's back. With each new day his condition grew increasingly grave...and all the lords knew it. But Balaam remained blithely unconcerned. *Does he care nothing for what has happened to him? For what will happen within the Council should he die?*

"I take it my summoning came before your task was complete?" Balaam asked, wincing slightly as he adjusted his position on the bed.

"Perhaps. Perhaps not," replied Stevron flatly. "I saw the viperon attack the craft, but was summoned here before the battle was done. From what little I did observe, it seemed the rebels' Words had little effect on the beasts, if they used them at all. I expect the creatures will have pierced the hull by now, though being here naturally makes it hard to report anything with confidence."

Balaam nodded, a hint of concern flashing across his brow. "Just so," he said. "Yet viperon are difficult to control, even for us. Your hold on them will not last long."

Difficult for you, perhaps. "With all deference, High Lord, I dislike leaving a task before it's done. Perhaps you could tell me why you have recalled me so unexpectedly?"

Balaam wiped a trickling bead of sweat from the top of his head. "To stop you," he said. "Though I now see my summons may have come too late."

Stevron blinked in disbelief. "To stop me? Why? The Stormcaller and his Remnant keepers must be destroyed—you said it yourself. And what of the item they stole? You cannot mean to let them keep it?"

"The Book of *Dei'lo* is no longer on the ship," replied Balaam dismissively. "We will have to look elsewhere to find it now. And as for the Stormcaller, there are ways that we can make good use of him yet. I do not want him harmed."

Stevron shot a furtive glance around the room. The servants and *mon'-jalen* seemed not to hear them, but he knew better. They would replay every word and gesture—later, among their fellows, when there were no lords around to cut out their tongues. It was the height of foolishness to announce the Book's existence within their hearing, much less that it had slipped beyond the Council's grasp. Besides, how did Balaam know the Book was no longer on the ship? "My Lord, perhaps we should speak further on this in private," he said.

"What...about the Book?" Balaam chuckled weakly. "They already know, son. Word of its theft spread across the city within an hour of dawn. Another day, and all the soundens will know of it too. But that is my concern. Yours is the Stormcaller—assuming he still lives."

The young lord straightened abruptly, clasping his hands behind his back. "That is not likely," he said.

Balaam lifted a shaky finger and wagged it at him briefly. The mere effort of it forced tears to drip from his ink-black eyes. Stevron watched him worriedly, his anger over being summoned battling against his growing concern for the High Lord's health. Every day since the attack—now four days past—Balaam's strength had dimmed a little more. How many more would it take before he faded to nothing?

In truth, it troubled him to see such obvious weakness in his High Lord. It seemed ill-fitting for one who'd always been Stevron's bastion of strength—his steadfast leader and trusted guide. Looking at him now left Stevron feeling strangely betrayed.

"Don't discount him too quickly, Stevron," said Balaam. "He is more capable than he appears, perhaps even more than he knows. He took the staff, did you know? Lysteria herself sealed it here in my chambers not long after the Stormcaller's capture. But within an hour of his escape, it was gone. I cannot fathom how he got to it, or even how he knew where it was."

"All the more reason to let me slay him," replied Stevron, "along with all those tainted by his influence."

Balaam shook his head slowly. His expression seemed suddenly vacant and troubled. "Not yet," he said quietly. His eyelids drifted halfway over his eyes. "That one's going places. He's got places to go, and you..." His eyes flew open suddenly. "You must follow him. Follow him, and tell me everything you see."

Cautiously, Stevron knelt before him and leaned in toward his sweaty face. The stench of infection lodged in his throat, but he defied the urge to back away. "That makes no sense, Father," he whispered intensely. He rarely used that word anymore—*father*—preferring the cleaner formalities of their assigned titles. But his feelings for the High Lord still ran deep, as deep as any young man's passion for the man who raised him, though they never formalized the familial bond. Every now and then—when need served—he allowed his feelings to show. "There is nothing to gain from letting the Stormcaller live," he continued, gently. "If you do, his status will only grow among the rebels *and* the soundens until he becomes a rallying point for every sick or bitter peasant who blames us for their woes."

As Stevron spoke, a calmness settled over Balaam's features, and he blinked as though he'd just awakened from a dream. "He will not live long, Stevron," said Balaam. "As you said, he may be dead already. If so, then that will end it. But if not, I would have you follow him a while, to see just where he goes."

"But why?"

Balaam looked into Stevron's eyes and grinned—the same slight grin he always gave when someone asked a question he did not like. Then he said, "I will summon you every sixth day, in the evening hours. Be ready."

Stevron stiffened. He regretted ever telling Balaam about summoning— a subtle form of cording in *Sa'lei* that gave one man the power to transport another into his presence with a simple phrase, then send him back at will. It seemed a small matter at the time, a boy's attempt to make his father proud. And Balaam had been pleased, that was sure. He slapped the young boy on the back and rubbed his hair and said well done. And then corded him with those same Words the very next day.

After that, Stevron was more cautious in sharing his discoveries with Balaam. Not that he wasn't grateful for all that Balaam had done for him— he was. The High Lord had been his secret tutor in *Sa'lei* since the earliest years of his childhood, from the time his father killed himself on the red cliffs of the Gorge. After that fateful day, the High Lord had taken him in, given him a home, and provided for his every need. In every way that mattered, he treated Stevron as a trueborn son. More than just a son, in fact—an heir. For Balaam also trained him in the ways of authority, and schooled him in the Council law. He meant for Stevron to one day take Balaam's place as High Lord.

What Balaam did not know was that Stevron had outgrown his mentor years ago. Though his proficiency in *Sa'lei* grew deeper with each passing year, he was careful not to share too much of what he knew, for fear that Balaam would turn the knowledge against him as he had before. Some of what he learned seemed simple, like how to keep his eyes from turning black so Balaam would not discover that he spoke *Sa'lei* aloud. But other nuances he had discovered locked within the Words— secrets of alarming power no one could suspect—frightened even him.

Over the years, Stevron came to understand Balaam's true intent in teaching him the Words so young. It wasn't really because Balaam loved him above all others or thought of him as particularly gifted or unique. The High Lord had done it entirely to serve his own personal ambition to create a legacy that would proclaim his greatness to all the generations that would follow.

Balaam's trueborn daughter, Kyrintha, had made it clear early on that she would not let the High Lord mold her to his will. So he locked her in the Tower, and simply selected another. The choice of Stevron was prompted more by convenience than any of the boy's intrinsic qualities. Stevron was orphaned, young and malleable. And so Balaam chose him.

Though Stevron knew all this, it didn't make him love the High Lord any less. How could it? He was a great man, the most powerful and cunning of the High Lords since Palor Wordwielder himself. He had been an excellent mentor for Stevron, and, in truth, the only father he had really ever known.

The servant returned with more bandages draped across his arm, so Stevron stood to let him pass. Balaam followed Stevron's movements, his face awash with an odd mixture of warmth and suspicion. Stevron smiled. "Every sixth day, then, High Lord. As you say."

"What were you thinking about just now?" asked Balaam.

Stevron shrugged lightly. "Childhood memories, my Lord. Nothing of consequence."

Balaam was about to speak again, but then quickly winced in pain. "Careful with those bandages, you clumsy lout!" he shouted at the servant. "I've got quite enough pain to tolerate without your fumbling ministrations!"

"Your pardon, High Lord," the servant replied, but then he kept at the task as if nothing had been said.

The High Lord sank back into his pillows, clearly weary from the sudden exertion. More tears fell from his eyes, but he seemed not to notice them. "You should return now," he said. "If your quarry survived, they're sure to be looking for someplace to hide and lick their wounds."

"If they survived, yes," agreed Stevron.

"And you won't harm the Stormcaller," he repeated firmly. "Just follow, and tell me where he goes."

"By your word, High Lord, he will live until you say otherwise."

"Good." Balaam sighed. His eyes drifted closed as he drew in a breath. Then his lips began to quiver weakly, as if unsure of what they were supposed to say. Finally, they found the Words to send Lord Stevron back to where he was before, and the whispering began.

I will let the cording remain intact for now, Stevron thought as he watched his High Lord fumble with the Words. *But if he is not more himself when I return, I will be forced to break it. And then, he will know.*

And Lord Stevron disappeared.

3

SILENCE SOUND

Little is known of the origins of the Wording that rests on Silence Sound. How was a Word placed over so vast a region? What phrasing of Words could create such a profoundly elegant, yet dreadful effect? Why were the Words spoken—for what purpose? Who spoke them?

What we do know is that the silence has rested on those waters for at least two thousand years—from long before the time of Palor or the Council Lords— and that it is the product of a particularly powerful Wording of Dei'lo, one that our best scholars have still yet to unravel.

The question as to why such Words were spoken over the Sound remains unanswered, and may be unanswerable. Yet I offer this personal account, which I believe may provide an anecdotal clue. On my travels with Gideon Dawning, I once spoke with a fel'adum of the Kolventu in the Hinterlands. He scoffed at my ignorance when I asked about the Sound, and said that everyone knew the Silence—which they call the Veil— was created out of an ancient pact between Wordhaven and the Kolventu. I asked him if he would teach me all he knew of this pact, but he grew angry at my request, and called me a fool for forgetting such a thing. He would speak to me no more on the subject after that.

—The Kyrinthan Journals, Chronicles, Chapter 6, Verses 130-140

I t was like passing from the waking world into a sea of dreams. A curtain, unseen, swept across the deck, and all sound simply evaporated into nothing—like a vapor, like a mist burned away by sunlight. It felt like going numb.

Gideon jiggled his jaw to pop his ears. He blinked wide, his jaw agape, and looked around suspiciously, as if searching for the blast that had stunned his ears into silence. But there had been no explosion. There had been no warning at all.

The prismatic beast still towered before him, swinging its circular mouth fore and aft across the deck like a radar dish in search of a target. Gideon could still smell the putrid stench of it, and even feel the heat of the sun reflecting off its scales. But it no longer seemed quite real, in the same way dreams don't seem real when they carry you in silence.

For all its threatening movements, the viperon was clearly hesitant to attack. In truth, it appeared to be confused as well. Its still gaping mouth swayed like a wrecking ball dangling from a crane, and yet it did not strike. Perhaps there were too many targets, and it didn't know which to choose. Aside from Gideon, the underlord and Telus were both in easy reach of the viperon's teeth, as were Revel and Captain Quigly. All of them, like Gideon, stood as still as stone pillars, staring at the deadly apparition with a combination of horror and wonder, perhaps to some degree enchanted by its swinging dance of teeth and liquid mirrors.

That's when Gideon realized the creature had no eyes. No eyes!

That's it, he thought. If the viperon had no vision, it must rely on other senses—sound and touch—to locate and track its prey. Within the Sound, the beast must be been running blind. That's why it wasn't striking any of the crew. It could not attack what it could not perceive.

Gideon dropped his spar and ran to the companionway leading down into the bowels of the ship. As he suspected, the beast seemed not to notice he had moved, preoccupied as it was with anxious searching for the smallest hint of vibration carried on the breeze. When he emerged from the cabin below a moment later with a silver blade sheathed beneath his sash, he did not remember where he had gotten it, or when he had decided to take this course of action. But that is the way of dreams, he supposed. Sometimes there was little point in making sense of them.

Within two strides he was standing on its tail. Then it was just a running leap to latch himself onto its scaly backside. The mirrored scales were hot like tin left in the sun, and sharp as glass, but he was used to bleeding by now. The beast must have had some sense of touch, for it instantly knew it was under attack, and began to fling its body madly like a cracking whip across the deck. But Gideon wedged his boots beneath its scales and let his fingers dig in deep. He would not let go now. The thrill of the cutting pain across his palms sent a shiver down his spine, and made him grin.

With each panicked whip across the deck, Gideon caught glimpses of the others standing below. Their faces were awash with horror at what he was doing, and he wondered what they would say to him now if only they could speak. "Have you gone mad, sojourner? Are you truly trying to die?" But they were silent as a tomb, like everything else, and set about striking the viperon with their spars to draw its focus away from his attack.

The tactic seemed to work. The beast stopped its whipping motion, and began to strike blindly at the air, first this way and then that, according to which spar had struck it last. The distraction gave Gideon the opening he needed. Slowly, almost gently, he pulled his body farther up the mirrored scales until at last he was within reach of the reddish rim of the gaping tooth-filled mouth. If the creature had a brain, he guessed it must be some- where on that end, close to the source of its protection and power. With hardly a thought, he slipped the silver blade out from his sash, and lifted the edge of a single mirrored plate. The skin beneath was pink and mottled like a pig's, and smelled of salt and dead fish. It wasn't difficult at all to pierce, and oozed a whitish fluid as he plunged in the blade—deep, all the way to the hilt. Suddenly, the beast froze in place, as if wondering what sort of wasp had wriggled beneath its scales to sting it. With both of his bloody hands, Gideon gripped the hilt and twisted it in the wound. The viperon shuddered momentarily. Then gracefully, as if through water, it settled its great bulk upon the deck and went to sleep.

It was Revel who offered a hand to help Gideon down, his golden hawk-like eyes alight with amusement and surprise as wide as his abundant smile. He seemed not to notice the blood on Gideon's hands as he gripped them, and once the sojourner was safe upon the deck, he slapped him on the back in congratulations. Gideon laughed in return, and was once again sur- prised to find no sound rumbling through his throat. He tried in vain to remind himself he wasn't dreaming. But he felt no pain at all.

There was another slap, this time on the arm, and Gideon turned to find Aybel standing no more than a hand's-breadth away, her dark brown eyes swimming in palpable fury. She launched a tirade at him, her lips moving like a blur upon her face, her eyes darting back and forth between his bloody hands and the shimmering corpse lying next to them on the deck. He couldn't hear a lick of it, of course. But he could make out a few words here and there by the way she formed them—Waymaker...foolish...purpose...pearl. Enough for him to get the message, as much of it as he cared to. She was most probably yelling, he realized. Purely out of deference to her anger, he tried very hard not to laugh.

Lucky for him her silent assault was cut short by a sharp prodding in Gideon's ribs. He jerked around to see Captain Quigly standing above them on the upper deck, with a long wooden spar clenched firmly in hand and pointed at him like a cattle prod. He quickly poked the others as well, then gestured angrily with his apish arms for all of them to get that stinking barrens beast off his fine ship's deck.

Gideon turned back toward Aybel and shrugged as if to say, "Hey, the captain has spoken; I guess you'll have to yell at me later." Yet, despite offering his most sincere smile, she did not seem the least bit amused.

Telus appeared bearing a bundle of longpoles in his arms, apparently suggesting that they use them to leverage the beast off the side. The idea seemed good to Gideon, but just as he reached to grab a spar, he felt a callused hand grip his wrist and pull him back.

It was Captain Quigly's bondmate. Her dark eyes looked up at him blankly, then she turned abruptly and yanked him toward the companionway. He had little choice but to follow. Her thick, fleshy hands, which were a fair bit larger than his own, gripped his wrist like padded steel. Gideon looked up questioningly at Captain Quigly as his bondmate started down the stairs, but he only stared back with a blank expression, and spit.

They went below, where she promptly pushed him down onto the bench next to the galley table. It was an awkward fit for Gideon, as was everything else below decks. The entire innards of the ship had been designed to fit the needs of the Sea Folk, with no regard whatsoever for their land-loving cousins. The seats and tables were all too small, the doors and ceilings far too short. It was like crawling through a children's maze just to reach his bed each night, and *that* was so short it would have been better named a crib. At least the beds were plenty wide, he reminded himself. With shoulders as freakishly broad as Quigly's and his bondmates, they had to be.

The Sea Folk woman turned her back to Gideon and fumbled with some unseen items on the counter beside the water barrels. She barely even looked at him when she turned his way again, but quickly cupped one of his bleeding hands in hers and swapped it off with a rag. She then produced a vial full of some sort of milk-white jelly, and scooped out a wad with two of her fingers and smeared it across the cuts on Gideon's palm.

He watched her curiously as she worked, and wondered what she must be thinking. No one on board even knew her name. It was forbidden, the way Ajel told it. The Sea Folk believed their given names held power—"the essence of the Sea Folk soul is wrapped up in their naming," as Ajel put it. To know a Sea Folk person's true name, and to speak it, was to have power over him or her. According to Ajel, outside of her immediate family, only a Sea Folk woman's bondmate was permitted know her true name. Not even her children could know it, since that would give them power over her.

The rules were somewhat different for Sea Folk men, though the effect was much the same. A man could reveal his true name to whomever he chose, and to do so was considered the highest gift of respect and honor any man can give. But the Sea Folk did not trust easily or quickly, even among their own kind. Beyond their siblings, the Sea Folk men typically revealed their names only to their bondmates and perhaps a trusted few others within their own clan. According to Ajel, no lander had ever known a Sea Folk person's name. He admitted that even Quigly's true name was a mystery to him, though he had known the Sea Folk captain since he was a young boy. "Quigly" was just his public alias, a label the Captain had given himself so people would have something to call him.

Gideon assumed the captain's bondmate also had a public name of some sort, but if she did, she had clearly chosen not to share it with any of them. It was anyone's guess as to why. The captain simply called her "woman," which seemed to work well enough for him, but hardly seemed an appropriate title for anyone else to use with her. So the best solution seemed to be to avoid talking with her at all, which is exactly what most of them did.

After applying the salve, the woman dug her hand into the pocket of her britches and pulled out a wad of sheer white cloth, which she unrolled then used her teeth to rip it into usable strips. She wrapped each of his hands in turn, securing the bandages with tiny fishhooks that she kept in her vest pocket.

When all was done, she leaned back and looked at him with an awkward sort of frown. Then, without the slightest warning, she reached out and slapped him on the head—not too hard, but enough to sting—and wagged a callused finger in his face. Once she seemed content that she had made her point, she waved for him to leave. He was all too happy to comply.

When he emerged from the companionway, Telus was there waiting for him, staff in hand once again. For the moment, Gideon ignored him—a difficult task at best, given the Raanthan's strength of presence and the intensity of his gaze, hot like molten bronze. But Gideon had learned something of his own strength since his brutal torture at the hands of Fayerna and Bentel. He was not so easily intimidated as he once was.

Scanning the ship, he saw that the beast was gone, leaving nothing on the deck but a pool of sticky, whitish fluid to mark its passing. Revel and Aybel were already washing the stain away with wooden buckets of water drawn from the Sound. The underlord was seated near the bowsprit, fumbling with a carving knife used for cutting fish, although she was using it to slice away the sleeves from her tattered gown. The silver sword, which Gideon had used to slay the viperon, lay precariously across her lap, all evidence of its recent violence wiped away.

Telus' gaze was unyielding. A Raanthan's face, Gideon had learned, was impossible to read. It had about it an all-encompassing quality, as though every expression there ever was or ever would be resided on it all at once. But there was an uneasiness to a Raanthan's face as well, a forced peculiarity, like when someone's trying very hard not to laugh, or the converse, trying not to kill you in a flood of rage. Looking at Telus was always like that. You could never tell what he was thinking, or what he was going to do.

With mild reluctance, Gideon finally turned his attention toward the Raanthan and slowly peered up into his eyes. Telus blinked, then extended the almond wood staff toward Gideon. At the same time, his free hand reached down and enveloped Gideon's own, cupping it carefully, as though he might crush it if he didn't take care. Gideon allowed the contact, watching carefully to see whether Telus' would try to put his hand on the staff. But he didn't. He only stared down at the bandage wrapped around Gideon's palm. His silvery mane danced and swirled about him like a drove of glistening sprites. He seemed to frown.

You are still hurt.

The voice was definitely Telus'. But it did not come to Gideon through his ears. Yet it wasn't only in his mind either. It was as if the Raanthan had spoken just a moment before, but Gideon was only now hearing what he said.

Gideon said, "Are you talking to me?" The air flowed passed his vocal cords, but no sound came.

Telus glanced at Gideon's mouth and shook his head. *You need not try to speak. I hear you.* He looked down at his hand again. *You are still hurt,* he repeated.

Gideon looked down at his bandaged hand, and wondered why he still felt no pain. *It's not that bad,* he reasoned to himself. Gideon tried to focus his thoughts toward Telus, but he suddenly felt his mind became a cacophony of echoes, questions and stray images. Were his thoughts always this jumbled?

Telus' voice sliced through the chatter like a scythe. *The cut to your hand is but a sign of the injury I mean. You are becoming reckless.*

Gideon drew his hand away. He felt heat rising in his cheeks. *I am becoming strong, Telus. There is a difference.*

No. You have forgotten Seer's words.

Seer? What does she have to do with anything?

You will remember.

Remember what?

But Telus did not respond. Instead, he smiled—a sad smile it seemed, a smile of pity—and extended the staff toward Gideon once again.

No, thought Gideon. *I'm not ready yet.*

You must. Telus' thoughts echoed forcefully in his mind. *We will have three days in this Sound before reaching the shores of the Hinterland. Revel needs that time to begin your training in the art of staff fighting.*

Staff fighting? How do you know Revel wants to teach me anything?

You will ask him. The words landed weightily in his mind. It was not a suggestion, but rather, a command.

I will not!

Telus smiled again. *If you do not, you will die. Choose, then, Waymaker, what you will do.* The Raanthan shook the staff before him like a threat.

How could you know that?

I know some things.

Not good enough, Telus. How?

Choose.

Gideon eyed the Raanthan angrily. This alien…whatever it was had saved his life in Phallenar. He owed him some respect for that, if nothing else. And Telus had known the others would come to rescue him on Gideon's Fall—more than that, he knew precisely when they would come, and how they were traveling. The creature did, in fact, "know things"— things that Gideon couldn't explain. But neither could he shake the feeling that he was being manipulated all over again—herded like a bleating sheep toward whatever fate others had ordained for him. The thought of it settled on his throat like a tightening noose.

Do not listen to your fear. You are free to choose, Waymaker. Remember that.

Stop listening to my thoughts! Gideon demanded. *I didn't ask for your opinion.* Then, before he could stop it, a question rose unbidden in his mind. *How is it you can you do that anyway? Have you been reading my mind all this time?*

The Raanthan know the Wording of this place.

You know the Words? You know Dei'lo?

Not as such. The Words are not for us. But we are familiar with their ways.

Gideon shook his head angrily. *I should have known better than to ask.* Then, with a sudden flash of his arm, he snatched the staff from Telus' grasp. Its warmth surged through him like a flood, wrapping itself around him like a comforting blanket of fire and peace. He tried not to let it show. He glared at Telus angrily, then turned and walked away.

You have chosen well, Waymaker.

What choice, Telus? Gideon shot back in his thoughts. *You say I either take the staff, or die. What kind of choice is that?*

The same choice that falls on all in their time.

Gideon paused a moment, then shook his head again, and stormed away in search of Revel.

THE HINTERLAND

For generations, the Kolventu cultivated a reputation as a secretive and intractable people. Their cultural isolationism and disdain for external trade effectively shielded them behind a curtain of conjecture and suspicion that stretched back to the founding of the New Age, over 2,000 years past. Before the coming of the Waymaker, what little was known about them had been largely gleaned from legend or from personal accounts of those precious few who dared to travel beyond their shores. However, in the first years after Wordhaven's rediscovery, scholars from the Remnant uncovered a few startling aspects of their history that had been lost. First, that the secluded stretch of swamps and fertile forests we now know as the Hinterland was originally a part of the Giver's Gift during the Endless Age—meaning that its people were at one time citizens of the Inherited Lands. In the beginning, they were known as the Miranti, a High Tongue name meaning "Wise Ones." Descriptions of the Miranti culture in the ancient texts match well what we know of their present-day descendants, the Kolventu: A tribal society, disciplined and well-ordered, but with a wary suspicion toward outsiders. The shift in title—from Miranti to Kolventu—is said to have come about some time after the arrival of the Pearl as a direct result of a dispute between Wordhaven and the Miranti people. The nature of that dispute is unknown, but it eventually resulted in the succession of the Hinterland, and perhaps even the subsequent Wording of Silence Sound. Only one somewhat cryptic clue remains as to the specifics of the conflict—the name change itself. "Kolventu" is derived from the High Tongue phrase meaning "Eyes Closed."

—The Kyrinthan Journals, Chronicles, Chapter 6, Verses 257-267

S ojourner..."

The voice echoed down through the clouds like rumbling thunder...

"Sojourner..."

...like the sound of trees falling in the forests of Wordhaven...

"Sojourner..."

....the ominous thrum of footsteps in the dark...bringing death in their wake.

"Sojourner, we must rise."

Gideon's body suddenly lurched in alarm. The spasm knocked his head squarely against the wooden bulkhead of the Endurant, sending spikes of pain shooting down his skull. "Shit!" he yelled.

With squinty eyes, he peered over his shoulder to find the source of his agitation. A pair of golden, hawk-like eyes peered back, looking pleasantly amused. "Revel," he grunted. He closed his eyes, and let his head drop to the pillow.

"Sojourner," Revel replied.

Gideon sighed. "What time is it?"

"Dawn is approaching," said Revel. "You must rise."

Suddenly, Gideon's eyes flew open at the reality of what was happening. "Hey!" He blinked. "I can hear you!"

Revel laughed. "Yes. And I you. We have crossed beyond the boundary of the Wording."

"Are we at the shore?"

"It is within sight," replied Revel. "That is why I must wake you. Aybel is anxious to depart. She has been up for some time, preparing."

Gideon nodded, then grunted several times in a rough attempt to clear his throat. His head throbbed dully from where it impacted the headwall of his berth. With beds this short, it's a wonder his head wasn't full of lumps by now.

With a sigh, he forced himself to sit up. "How long to do I have?" he asked.

"Long enough," said Revel. "Was your sleep restoring?"

"No."

"Hmm," Revel nodded, his face mildly surprised. "I, too, have not slept well these past five days. It will be good to be near trees again."

Gideon rubbed his head. "I'd have thought you'd had enough of trees, after Strivenwood," he said.

Revel looked thoughtful for a moment. Then he said, "I will see what remains to be done on deck." With that, he rose and walked away, bowing gracefully under the doorframe as he departed.

Gideon sighed. It *would* be good to be on solid ground again at least, trees or no trees. The weather had been frustratingly calm since they entered the Sound. As a result, the crossing had taken five full days rather than the typical three. But even with the slight wind that they had, the gentle rocking of the ship had turned his stomach more than once. There was something about moving through the sea in utter silence that seemed to heighten nausea's effects.

But now the silence was gone. The air that it had held imprisoned in its Worded grasp now echoed contentedly with a chorus of noises—the creaking of the bulwarks, the lapping of waves against the hull, the muffled sounds of voices overhead. Aybel's voice.

With forced determination, he rubbed the sleep from his eyes, then quickly went about packing the items he would need. There weren't many, really. A change of clothes, a knife or two, a cloth for washing the salt from his body, should he get the chance. He would take the staff as well, he decided, in the hope that he and Revel could continue his training during their time on shore. Despite his initial reluctance to Telus' suggestion, he had to admit he had enjoyed his recent lessons with Revel. The silence had proved no deterrent to learning the basic forms of staff fighting. In fact, it may have proved an advantage, for it forced him to lean on other senses beyond his hearing. In particular, he found—much to his own surprise— that he possessed a special gift for instinct, predicting where his opponent was about to strike. He'd yet to bring Revel to ground—it was much to soon for that— but he'd already managed to hold the warrior at bay for several minutes, which was longer than anyone would have expected.

He stuffed the items in a leather satchel, then dressed himself in his remaining fresh tunic, jerkin, and leather shortpants. The boots he strapped to the outside of the satchel, preferring to put them on once they reached the shore.

A few minutes later, he trudged onto the deck with his staff in hand and the satchel strapped snugly across one shoulder. There was no one else in sight, though he could hear their voices—her voice—echoing from the rear of the ship. He stood still for just a moment and let the morning air sink beneath his skin. He closed his eyes and breathed in deep. The air was moist, cooler than on previous mornings, and carried a surprising mix of smells—pine and swamp, and the scent of ocean.

But it was the noise that dominated both his senses and his thoughts. The creaking of the mast, the lapping of the water against the hull, the gentle roar of the breeze against his ears, the overlapping voices of the crew—all of it seem magnified a hundred fold beyond what he remembered. It was...unsettling.

He welcomed the return of sound to his world, but its sudden reappearance had come as a shock. He needed time to readjust—just a few minutes, perhaps—enough to bring his mind to some semblance of order again. Rather than head aft right away, he walked to the bowsprit, climbed to his perch and settled in.

He could not yet see the sun, but its yellow-gold hues had begun to filter through the clouds to the east, bringing a sense of promise to the sky. The Sound itself was blanketed in a low-lying mist, but even so it wasn't hard to find the land...on account of the trees. Thin spires of narrow trunks, huddled in clumps as if for warmth against the morning chill, rose from the mist like long-stemmed candles, each crowned with a torch of piney growth. It was like a forest on stilts, marking the shore in a wavy line from north to south as far as he could see.

He suddenly noticed that the ship was anchored much farther offshore than he would have expected, given their impending departure. He wondered if Quigly was waiting for the morning sun to sail them in closer.

"They're lovely, aren't they?"

The sound startled him. When he turned, he found the underlord standing on the deck below him. She held two plates, each dotted with a smattering of dried fruit and nuts and a few strips of dried meat. She extended one toward him. "I was asked to bring this to you," she said. "Aybel says we should eat before going ashore."

Gideon nodded his thanks as he took the plate. Then he turned his back to her again and began to eat. Kyrintha turned to leave.

"Are you going ashore with us this morning?" Gideon asked quietly, little more than a whisper. He did not turn around.

The underlord stood silent for a moment, then settled herself on the bench beneath the bowsprit. "Yes, of course," she said. "I'm told this is where Aybel and I will take our leave of you."

Gideon nodded. "Oh yeah," he said. "Heading to Wordhaven." He took a bite of some fruit—he couldn't recall the name. "It's a long trip," he added.

"So I am told," Kyrintha replied quietly.

An awkward silence followed. Gideon hadn't spoken much with the underlord since he came aboard—not at all in the past five days, of course. Honestly, he didn't know how to talk with someone like her. What should he say? *"So you're Balaam's daughter. Wow. That's gotta suck."*

Right. And what was he supposed to call her anyway? Underlord, Kyrintha, Underlord Kyrintha, Ms. Asher-Baal, my lady—what?

"What should I call you?"

"Huh?" asked Gideon, surprised.

"By what title would you have me call you?" asked Kyrintha.

Gideon grinned. The underlord wasn't the only one with a title now, he remembered. "Gideon is fine," he replied. But then he thought better of it. "Maybe 'sojourner' is better, when we're not on the ship anyway. Apparently the name 'Gideon' is a hot button with a lot of people around here."

Kyrintha blinked slowly. "A 'hot button'?" she asked.

"A controversial topic of discussion," he amended.

"Ah," she sighed with understanding. "Yes. Tell me, were you named for him?"

Gideon glanced down at her dubiously. "Who?"

"The High Lord Gideon Truthslayer, the one who betrayed the Pearl, and brought the Barrens to our lands." Her description sounded rehearsed and cool, like something she'd memorized from a book.

"No," replied Gideon firmly, shaking his head. "I didn't even know he existed until Ajel and Donovan told me about him."

"I see," said Kyrintha. "Who were you named for, then?"

Gideon looked down at her thoughtfully for a moment. Then he jumped down from the bowsprit and brushed the bits of nut and dried fruit off his jerkin. "Nobody special," he said, still inspecting his clothes for signs of breakfast. "A character in a book my mother used to read all the time. You finished?" He glanced toward her plate.

"Yes." She handed it to him, then stood and brushed out the folds of her gown. It was sleeveless now, and shorter as well. But mostly it was much less, well, *puffy* than it was at first. It was as if someone had gutted the thing and left only the skin behind. Aside from the dark green color, you'd never know it was the same dress at all.

"Thank you for dispatching the viperon," she said stiffly. "It was quite a brave act you did. I confess I have never seen one slain without the Words."

Gideon shrugged. "It's probably just as well I didn't know what I was doing," he said. "If I'd been thinking clearly, I would have never tried it. I just got lucky."

She smiled politely. "Perhaps," she said. "But still, I am in your debt."

Gideon gave her a quick grin and a nod, then ambled toward the galley with the plates. The way she looked at him made him edgy—like he was a stray dog she wanted to shoo away, but didn't for fear it might be crazed.

After leaving the plates in the galley, he returned to the deck and made his way aft. As expected, Quigly and his bondmate were there, as was Revel and Telus. But he didn't see Aybel anywhere.

"So you've decided to join the living after all, mighty Waymaker." Captain Quigly glared down at him from atop the rear deck house, where he could assess the preparations like an emperor appraising his troops. His tone was as contemptuous as Gideon remembered it, but for some reason he noticed a hint of a grin on the Sea Folk's fleshy lips.

"And the hearing as well it would seem," Gideon replied with a mild grin of his own. He glanced around curiously. "Are we about ready to go, Revel?"

"About ready?" snorted Quigly with a frown. "'About ready,' he says! I would have been free of the lot of you an hour ago if not for having to wait on you and that underlord! Get your gear in the launch."

"It's barely dawn!" Gideon protested.

But Quigly only grunted and shook his bulbous head. "May the Giver save me..." he muttered.

Quigly's bondmate waddled over and pulled the satchel from Gideon's shoulder. She patted him roughly on the arm. "Don't pay him any mind now, lander," she said. "He's taken a liking to you, that's all it is."

Gideon looked down at her in surprise. "Really?" he asked in disbelief. She nodded. He leaned down. "Tell me...exactly why does he like me?"

"'Cause you saved his precious ship from that barrens beast, a'course," she said. "Why else?"

"Oh, that," he said, still unsure whether she was serious. "Well, if this is his good side, I'd hate to see how he treats his enemies," he added under his breath.

She nodded, patting his arm a second time. "Aye. That you would."

"Where is the underlord?" asked Revel.

Gideon shrugged. "At the bow, I think. Where's Aybel?"

"Awaiting us in the launch," said Revel. "You may join her there. I will get the underlord. It's past time we were off."

Revel moved passed him and faded into the mist, which had in recent moments grown much thicker around the ship.

"This fog is a bad omen, I say," muttered Quigly. "It's no time to be sailing toward uncharted waters."

"Aybel knows this place," said Gideon, gesturing toward the line of trees he could no longer see. "This is her home."

"Was her home, or so I hear it," replied the Captain. "There's not much known about the Hinterland folk, but one thing is sure—they show little favor to deserters."

"Aybel's no deserter!" Gideon retorted.

"Aye? Then what is she, lander?"

And he suddenly realized he did not know. He never thought to ask her how she came to be in the Inherited Lands, or why she left her home in the first place. He didn't even know how long she'd been away. *There's still so much I don't know.*

Captain Quigly snorted, apparently satisfied that his point was made. Gideon could barely see him now. The fog was getting thicker by the second. At this rate, they might not be able to find the shore at all, especially at this distance.

"Captain, I was wondering, why are we anchored so far from shore? Is it a dangerous approach?" Gideon tried to make his voice sound harmless; he didn't want the little man to think he doubted his judgment.

"Dangerous, aye, but not from rocks or shallows," said Quigly, apparently unperturbed by the question. "No one dares sail near the Hinterland uninvited."

Just then, Revel appeared from out of the mist with the underlord in tow. "We should go now," he said, and headed for the rail.

"Won't the fog be a problem?" asked Gideon.

"Not to Aybel, sojourner," said Revel shortly. "Come. We must travel some distance over land before the sun rises too high."

"Why?" asked Gideon. "Where are we going exactly?" But Revel did not answer. So Gideon trailed after him. Once at the railing, Revel helped the underlord step down onto a rope ladder, which dangled flimsily over the side.

"I don't see anything," said Kyrintha.

"The launch is there," Revel assured her. "Aybel awaits below." He held her hand a moment longer, then gestured for Gideon to follow. He took one step toward the railing, then turned back toward the Raanthan, who had stood silent since he first approached.

"Aren't you coming, Telus?" Gideon asked.

"No," came the stoic reply. "I cannot travel in the Hinterland."

"Why not?" asked Gideon.

"We are not welcome there," said Telus.

"So?" said Gideon. "From what Captain Quigly says, we may not be welcome there either."

The Raanthan's thin lips smiled faintly. "It is not permitted for me to go, Waymaker. Besides, my presence would only prove a detriment to your cause."

"The Raanthan can remain aboard the Endurant, sojourner," said Revel. "It's already been agreed."

"He spoke to you?" asked Gideon incredulously.

"No," said Revel. "To the captain. Come now, we must leave. You will see him again soon."

"Huh," said Gideon hesitantly. "Okay, then." It wasn't that he would miss the Raanthan's presence. If anything, taking a break from Telus' ever-present gaze upon his back would be a relief. Still, the Raanthan's refusal to go left him feeling unsettled. It seemed a bad omen, like the fog.

But the decision had been made, and there seemed little point in arguing it further. With a curt nod toward Telus, Gideon stepped over the railing onto the rope ladder below. As he did, Revel turned to Quigly—who was now just a dim shadow in the mist—and asked, "You will wait for us?"

"I make no promises to landers," the captain grumbled in response. "But your Paladin was a good man—a friend, if there could be such a thing between your folk and mine. On his account, I'll wait a while, a week at most. Provided there's no danger to my ship."

"We could not ask for more than that." There was a sorrow in Revel's tone that wasn't there a moment before. But his expression showed no hint of it. "We are in your debt."

"That you are, lander," said Quigly. "And don't think I'll forget it."

With the staff clutched under his arm, Gideon descended the ladder. The mist obscured everything. He couldn't tell he'd reached the launch until both feet rested firmly on its planks. And even then, he could barely see it.

"Please sit down, Gideon Dawning."

"Hello, Aybel," said Gideon into the mist. "It's good to hear your voice again."

"Your satchel is safely stored with the others," she said.

"Good. Thanks," he replied. But her tone confused him. "Are you excited about going home?" he asked.

"Excited," she replied flatly. "No. That is not the word."

Revel's form appeared and stepped gingerly into the launch. Immediately, he grabbed hold of one of the oars, and directed Gideon to take the other. A moment later, the two lines securing the smaller boat to the Endurant, tumbled into the launch. Kyrintha, who sat aft of Gideon and Revel, quickly began to coil one line, while Aybel, who sat at the bow, did the same. With a gentle push of his oar against the Endurant's dark hull, Revel sent them quietly off into the grey nothingness of the mist.

"Veer to port a half-quarter moon, then straight," instructed Aybel. Gideon guessed a "half-quarter moon" meant forty-five degrees, but he tried to follow Revel's lead, just to be sure.

"Once in the trees, we should not speak," continued Aybel, "so listen carefully, and heed me."

Gideon squinted into the fog. Though she sat only a few feet away, her face was shrouded in mist as if by a veil. He could not read her expression. But her voice sounded strained.

"I am...I was once a woman of high standing among my people," she said. "But that was many years ago. My people are suspicious of those who leave these shores, even if the cause is just. I cannot say how I will be received. We must be cautious. None of you should speak. Especially you, underlord. Though your heart may not be in league with the Council, your accent will betray your origins."

"I understand," said Kyrintha.

"When we arrive on shore, we must move with haste. There will be a wooden path not far into the trees. We must follow it, quietly, but with speed, to reach the Kalmath'ar."

"What's that?" asked Gideon.

"A waiting circle," she replied. "Once there, we must lay our weapons outside the perimeter, then move within it and sit in silence. My people will come to us there."

"How will they know we are there?" asked Gideon.

"They will know," said Aybel. "There is one other matter. The Words—any Words—are forbidden in the Hinterland. To speak even one, even a whisper, will condemn us all to death."

"But why do they fear *Dei'lo?*" asked Revel.

"They do not know of *Dei'lo*, Revel," she replied. "And they would not recognize the difference in any case. The Words are the Words."

"What do we tell them about who we are, then?" asked Gideon. "We obviously can't say we're with the Remnant."

"We will tell them what truth we may," said Aybel. "But no more. We are friends, refugees, fleeing the tyranny of Phallenar. We seek only a few days of sanctuary and supplies for our journey ahead, nothing more."

"Won't they force you to stay with them?" asked Kyrintha. "I understand your people do not let their own go easily."

"I cannot say with certainty," said Aybel. "After so many years, they may consider me a reprobate."

"Then why go this way?" asked Kyrintha. "Surely we could follow another route to Wordhaven, one that holds less risk for you!"

"All other routes hold more risk for both of us," replied Aybel. "Only through the Hinterland and the Heaven Range beyond can we hope to elude the eyes of Phallenar. And even then, it will be a difficult journey. Winter will soon arrive in the mountains; there will be little game, and the passes will be bitter with snow and storm. This is why we need to get supplies here, from my people, before we attempt the journey."

The underlord considered Aybel's response for a moment. Then she said, "What of your parents, your family? Do they still live? Won't they vouch for you?"

"Do yours vouch for you, underlord?" Aybel snapped. Kyrintha did not respond. A moment later, Aybel said, "Pardon, Kyrintha. I mean no disrespect. But the ways of my people are not like yours. Even if my parents live, they will have little say in how I am received, either for good or ill."

"The trees draw near," said Revel quietly.

Gideon saw them too. Thick lines of velvet green emerged above the mist to the west, supported on spindly stilts of moss and wood. Here and there the tips glowed vibrant and bright, kissed by the first light of the sun. But below the canopy of pine, the fog still reigned. He could not discern the shore.

"Once in the trees, speak little," said Aybel. "If you must speak, whisper."

"Why?" asked Gideon, half-whispering already.

"Just heed me, Waymaker," said Aybel. "Please." Her voice sounded almost pleading.

Gideon nodded. "Sure," he said. "Whatever you say."

Upon entering the first line of trees, Revel let out a heavy sigh. He said nothing, but turned to Gideon and smiled broadly, as if reacting to a joke that no one else could hear. The water quickly turned from blue to bright lime green, and Gideon could now see it stretched some distance into the woods. The matchstick trunks were everywhere, but he still could not find the shore. As they moved deeper inland, the smell of mud and rotting leaves flooded his nostrils, and whatever breeze there was had died away. At least the fog was thinner in the trees, he thought. A little farther in, and it would be gone for good.

As if by instinct, both he and Revel began to paddle more quietly, taking care not to stir the waters any more than necessary as they moved. As it was, each stroke brought up a slimy film of green upon the oars, making their motion sluggish and stirring up the pungent smell of the place even more with every row.

After several minutes, a line of brown at last appeared across the limey green. A forest of ferns grew up from it, forming a misty landscape all its own that reached as deep into the woods as far as he could see. And through its center, directly ahead, a path of brown was cut, winding its way through the trunks until it disappeared several hundred feet into the woods.

The fog was all but gone now. But it didn't make the place seem any less disturbing.

"There," whispered Aybel, pointing to jutting patch of brown just left of the path. Gideon and Revel obeyed. Moments later, the hull scraped quietly onto a mound of pine needles, and slid to a stop.

Aybel exited first, pulling the launch more firmly onto the bank. The others grabbed the packs and tossed them to her, then followed her onto dry ground. It was then that Gideon noticed they all already wore their boots, except for the underlord, who wore slippers that looked something like ballet shoes. He quickly fumbled with his satchel to untie his boots and put them on.

"There is no time, sojourner," whispered Aybel scoldingly. "Come!" Without waiting for a response, she turned and lead the others toward the path. Gideon grimaced in frustration, but then quickly gave up the task, and fumbled after them barefoot.

It turned out not to be a problem, anyway. The pine needles that covered the ground did not hurt to walk on. And within a few seconds, they were on the path. It was forged of wooden planks, laid at right angles to the course and tightly seamed together, like a bridge. The border on each side was lined with planks as well, and the whole thing was lifted several inches above the forest floor. The wood was weathered to a mottled green, and coated here and there with leafy moss. But it was solid, and seemed to merge into the forest floor as though it were a part of it. It had clearly been there a long, long time.

They moved at a pace just shy of running, and wasted no time looking about. The air was cool, but so thick with moisture that their clothes soon felt sluggish from the weight of it, and their faces glistened with a chilling sweat. From the beginning, Revel touched the tree trunks as they passed, apparently sensing for danger in the woods. But it wasn't until several minutes into the trek that he grabbed Aybel's arm and whispered, "We are being watched."

She nodded, but said nothing, and turned to continue on their course. It was as if she had expected it. Gideon scanned the trees for any sign of movement, but could see nothing.

"Eyes front," Aybel whispered. She shot him a reproachful glance, then continued on ahead. With some reluctance, Gideon obliged. *I wonder what is making her so afraid*, he wondered.

Suddenly, the forest became a blur of white. Shapes, like great white birds, descended rapidly on them from the trees, swirling passed them in a silent fury. From each of their talons came a tendril, something like a whip perhaps. Gideon couldn't tell. No sooner had he spotted it than it enwrapped his torso like a vise, and forced the air out from his lungs. An instant later, another coiled around his ankles and yanked him harshly off his feet. His body struck the wooded planks with a helpless thud. The impact jolted his grip on the staff. He watched as it bounced noiselessly across the ground.

When he looked up, he saw the others in a similar state—lying helpless on their backs or sides and bound with viney cords just like his own. He looked at Aybel's face, and saw the horror on it. He opened his mouth to speak, but she quickly glared at him in fear and shook her head no.

5

WORDHAVEN

The answers to our deepest questions never come to us in the season we deem best, nor in the respectable ways we imagine they should. Instead they come quietly and out of time, in ways both absurd and offensive to our souls. The true test of the human heart, then, is not in proving we are worthy of the answers we seek, but whether, when they come, we will be humble enough to surrender ourselves to their call.

—The Kyrinthan Journals, Musings, Chapter 7, Verses 33-34

His eyes, like the eagle's, sweep across the meadows that lie below the tower where he stands. The wind he sees makes those lower grasses bend and bow and swirl, so that they dance to music that in its purer moments all life knows by heart. The eagle knows this dance as well, but his is different, strong and smooth and brazen in its freedom. He is not aware of fear. The mighty breezes of the heights are but gentle hands that hold him, and through surrender he bends them to his desire. His song echoes off the morning cliffs like sunlight, and in his wake a fury calls to all that lies beneath his talons and his wings. He knows there is no challenger who can match the glory of his flight.

He sees the man and turns his way without a thought. His yellow beak hangs open, and draws a breath in preparation of the whispered warning to come.

"Abaddon is near!"

Ajel Windrunner stumbled backward from the window in shock. In that instant, his connection with the bird was severed; he knew not whether it was by him or some outside power. But his thoughts recoiled from the encounter as if from a snake. *Where did that voice come from?* he wondered. *Eagles do not know the words of men.*

He watched the bird a moment longer as it soared westward toward the cliffs, innocent and strong. Soon it floated out of view.

"May I enter?" The voice came from the door behind him.

"Yes, Kair. Of course," said Ajel. He did not sense her coming, but then that hardly surprised him. His thoughts had grown so distracted in recent days by all that must be done. There was so little time.

After lingering at the window a moment longer, he turned to face her. She wore the fighting garb of Wordhaven—brown leathers with a sash of forest green bound at the waist. Everyone in the Remnant wore them now, regardless of the day or duty, by Ajel's command. It was but one small way to help shake them of the stubborn belief that Wordhaven was and forever would be far removed from war. Already, three of the Council Lords had managed to find them. In time, the others would as well. And when they did, they would come against Wordhaven with all the combined forces of Phallenar.

Kair took only a few steps forward and paused. She cradled in her arms a tablet full of parchments, no doubt the first reports from the Remnant teams he'd sent out to the soundens upon his return to Wordhaven. He wondered how news of the Book's return had been received across the lands—in particular, he wondered how many would believe it.

"The Remnant has convened," she said. "They await you in the Servants Hall." Her grey-blue eyes looked quiet and peaceful, as they always did. But her thoughts were mostly closed to him.

"Is it time already?" he asked. Had he been communing with the bird for so long? But she gave no answer. "Are you well, Kair?" he asked. "Your thoughts are sealed away."

She pushed a wayward lock of auburn curls from her cheek. "It is nothing, Ajel," she said. "I am feeling sad today. The loss of Paladin Sky is still fresh upon my mind."

Ajel quietly crossed the chamber and laid his hand upon her arm. "I know," he said, smiling gently. "I cannot sit in this chamber and not think of him. It was his study for so many years. It is still." He looked around. Despite removing his uncle's personal items from the room and replacing them with a few of his own, the chamber still did not feel his. The scent of Paladin Sky was everywhere. It lingered around the furniture, and wafted through the walls. At times it even flowed in through the window, as if the whole expanse of Wordhaven's valley had become unmistakably marked by the great man's comings and goings over the years.

"It is your study now, Paladin," said Kair. She emphasized the last word. "Your uncle would be proud to have it so."

Ajel smiled. "We must give it time, I think," he said. "For now, however, we should go."

Kair quietly nodded, then turned to leave. Ajel trailed after her. For such a diminutive woman, he nevertheless found it difficult to keep up with her anytime they walked together through the Stand. She moved with the single-minded purpose of an arrow speeding toward its target.

"Are those the reports from the Remnant teams?" Ajel asked as they hurried down the winding corridors toward the Inner Hall.

"They are," she said. "I just received them from Donovan. So far, seven of the soundens have agreed to your proposal."

"What of Makroth and Shabar?" asked Ajel.

Kair nodded slightly. "Curiously, their elders were among the first to say yes. The teams report that they've already begun to gather volunteers."

"That is a wonder," said Ajel, "and a great relief." In truth, he doubted those two soundens would ever agree to cooperate with the Remnant, even in the clandestine way that he proposed. To do so might draw the eyes of Phallenar; and among the soundens, Makroth and Shabar feared the wrath of the Council more than most. He wondered what had swayed them. "What news of Morguen sounden?" he asked.

"Not good, I fear," replied Kair. "Their elders will not consent to hear the Remnant team in open council. So far the team has spoken only to a few of the elders, separately and in secret. The sounden is still in shambles from the battle between the Council Lords. They are a shaken people. They say they are simply too close to Phallenar to take the risk you suggest."

"To close in distance, or in heart?" Ajel snapped angrily. He shook his head in frustration. "It is precisely because they are close to Phallenar that we need them! They must be made to see that."

Kair glanced toward him questioningly. "You mean to extend the Sacred Path within the Wall?"

"It is already done," he said. Stepping out from the corridor, they emerged into the expansive brightness of the Inner Hall. The rapid cadence of their footsteps echoed off the walkway and down all seven stories of the massive ivory atrium, but there was no one below to notice the sound. By now the entire Remnant—all two thousand of them—were seated in the Servants Hall.

"How could the Path come to Phallenar—and so quickly?" Kair whispered the question pensively, as though she were afraid someone would overhear.

"That would take some time to explain," sighed Ajel distractedly. "And I'm finding it difficult to focus my thoughts. I must prepare for what I am about to say to the Remnant." He thought a moment, then added, "But it seems we are now indebted to Underlord Kyrintha Asher-Baal for far more than just our escape from Balaam's grasp."

Kair's stride slowed momentarily, as if pondering whether to press the matter further. But she didn't, and soon her pace resumed its usual briskness. Ajel felt quietly relieved. He was tired, and his thoughts seemed jumbled, but it wasn't only that. Though he normally enjoyed talking with Kair, since their return to Wordhaven she had seemed much more closed and resistant to him than before. Their recent encounters had the flavor of those early conversations with Gideon Dawning, when the sojourner had first arrived at Wordhaven, full of suspicion and fear. It troubled Ajel that Kair would choose to shield her thoughts as the sojourner had—even if her motivation truly was simply to keep her grief private.

Still, he did not feel it right to question her about it. After all, she was the only one with his uncle the night he was slain. She alone stood with him against Lord Lysteria, and faced the horror of that brutal combat. And when Paladin Sky faltered and fell, it was Kair alone who fought to save him, and found that she could not. That must have been a terrible blow to her heart.

Perhaps it was best after all that she hold her grief in private, he reasoned. Perhaps that's what she needed—at least for now. In time, she would open her heart to them again, when she was ready.

They continued the rest of their walk in silence. When at last they stepped through the triangular doors of the Servants Hall, the rumbling voices in the room immediately fell to a hush. Ajel paused a moment at the doorway and surveyed the vast chamber. Its high, pyramidal walls, glistening with flecks of black and gold, reflected off the anxious faces that crowded the floor, their eyes all watching him. He could not help but feel the weight of it.

Like almost every other location within the Stand, the light that filled the Servants Hall seemed to filter in from nowhere. But it had always been strongest along one corner, the one closest to the Chamber of the Pearl. And so that spot became the place his father had built the Servants Call so many years before—a simple, long wooden table, where the other leaders of Wordhaven now sat.

Donovan stood stoically behind them like some Council Lord's *mon'-jalen*, his hands clasped behind his back, his black-orbed eyes relentlessly scanning the crowd for any sign of danger. Ajel grinned nostalgically at the sight of him. His overprotective nature had always proved a source of endless amusement to both him and Revel, who taunted the big man relentlessly on account of it. But soon enough, Ajel knew, Donovan's wary instincts might prove to be the salvation of them all.

Leaving Kair at the door, Ajel glided toward the center seat behind the Servants Call. He nodded briefly toward the other leaders as he passed—old Teram and Katira, the eldest of the leaders at Wordhaven and among the first to flee from Phallenar with Ajel's father at the time of the Sky Rebellion so many years before. It had been good to speak with them in recent days as they studied the Book of *Dei'lo* together. They were peace-filled people, a comfort to be around. And they carried many stories of his father that he still had never heard.

Next to them sat Saria and Seer Sky, the two elder sisters of Ajel's uncle. They were mirror images of each other in many ways, both possessing a gift for prophecy and dreams, which had been awakened by the learning of *Dei'lo*. But while Seer's visions often carried warnings of a threatening darkness, Saria's were more hopeful, reflecting the power of goodness that yet remained within the Lands. In truth, they could hardly stand to be in the same room together. Yet, with the passing of his uncle, they were now the only family Ajel had left in the world—except for Revel, of course, whom he had always loved as a brother for as long as he could remember.

With a quiet sigh, he took his place behind the Call, and surveyed the crowd once more. He wished that Revel were with him now. His brother's presence at his side always made him feel stronger and more brave than he could ever be alone.

"Who convenes here?" he asked in a commanding voice.

"The servants of the Pearl," came the booming reply, the voices of all those in the chamber speaking in unison. "Like the servants before us, our mothers, our fathers, our sisters and brothers, so we now serve. Like those of true heart who stood as Guardians on these grounds, so we now stand. Like those of noble wisdom who spoke as Lords in service to life, so we now speak, one heart in honor of one name."

"What name?" asked the Paladin.

"We speak in the name of the Pearl, in the memory, and the power. We convene in that name."

"Let our hearts, then, speak true, for the sake of the Pearl."

"For the sake of the Pearl," they echoed.

Ajel slowly lifted his gaze toward the center of the chamber. "*Adoni'far logaras veojo centreem*," he whispered. Light massed together in the air above the Remnant, and coalesced into a rotating image of the Book of *Dei'lo*. A ripple of murmurs floated through the crowd. He raised his hand to return them to silence. "A war is coming," he said. "A war like none has ever seen within the borders of these Lands. A war...over this." He gestured toward the Book.

"There are two languages of power in the Inherited Lands," he continued, "*Dei'lo* and *Sa'lei*. They are terrible and fierce in their power, and can do such things, perform such wonders, as I have never dreamed to see, and in some cases dream to never see again. Like light and darkness, like creation and destruction, so too these tongues stand in opposing corners of the world. They are opposite. But they are not equal. It has been this way from the beginning. And so it is now."

He looked up toward the Book and smiled. "We have the Book of *Dei'lo*!" he yelled. A cheer rose up from the crowd. "It is ours!" he yelled. And the crowd replied in kind, "It is ours!"

"It is ours!" he yelled again.

And the crowd replied, "It is ours!"

He allowed the excitement to linger in the echoes of their cheers. Then he said, "Already we have begun to study the Book, unlocking once again the teachings of the Pearl buried in the earth so long ago, hearing once again its Words singing through the open air. Until now, we have been children, fumbling with a language and a power we could barely understand. But here," he pointed commandingly toward the image overheard. "Here is the teacher and the key to understanding. Through this, we shall no longer be children, but shall be transformed into the true men and true women the Pearl meant for us all to become."

Another cheer erupted, but Ajel lifted his voice above the crowd. "Remnant!" he cried, "This Book is for you—each one of you! In the days to come, all of you, each and every one, will study what this Book has to teach. You will learn it as though your life depends on it...Because it does!"

Upon hearing Ajel's words, the crowd gradually settled once again to silence. "A war is coming," Ajel repeated. "The Council knows we have the Book. And even now Balaam sits in his chambers laying plans for war against us. Our sources tell us that, contrary to our fears, neither he nor the Council yet knows the true location of Wordhaven. But I believe it will only be a little time before he does. And when he does, the full might of the Council Lords and that of every warcor in Phallenar will fall mightily on Wordhaven."

He took a breath and let his words sink in. "Our time is short," he said. "And I know that we are all still deep in grief over the loss of Paladin Sky. I myself have been no stranger to sorrow in these days. But there is much to be done, and we cannot wait."

He scanned the crowd a moment, then asked, "Where is Brasen Stoneguard?"

"Here, Paladin," replied an eager voice from the rear of the chamber. The young man took a step forward to make his location more clear.

"Come forward," said Ajel. Then, looking behind him, he said, "Donovan, come and introduce the Keeper."

Donovan nodded, and immediately stepped forward to stand next to Ajel. "Since the Book's return to Wordhaven," Donovan began as Brasen approached, "the servants here before you have not rested in their study of its contents. Among the treasures they have already gleaned is the Wording to open the portals scattered throughout the Stand." A rumble of delight flittered through the crowd. "As some suspected, they are gateways to other places," continued Donovan. "We do not yet know all the places they can take us, but we have found several that lead to the soundens scattered throughout the Lands.

"Four days past, teams from the Remnant were sent to seven of the strongest soundens. Their task was to issue an invitation for all who are willing to leave their homes and their way of life and come to us at Wordhaven—so that they might study the Book along with us, and learn its ways, and fight side by side with us in its defense."

As the young man reached the Servants Call, Donovan paused and nodded briefly toward him. He returned the greeting, then turned and faced the Remnant. "We cannot say how many will say yes. But to those who are willing to answer our call, we have promised to provide safe and secret passage to Wordhaven. But this in itself is no easy task. As you know, the soundens are widely spread across the Lands. Most are several days' journey from here. And the Council's reaction to the loss of the Book has been swift. Already the guardian presence within most of the soundens has increased. The eyes of Phallenar are everywhere.

"To accomplish this task, the Paladin and I have laid the designs for what we have named the Sacred Path—a network of warrior guides chosen from among our number, who will link the soundens one to another through paths not known to the guardians and lords, and lead the willing from their soundens safely to the gates of Wordhaven."

Donovan lifted his hand toward the young man. "You see before you Brasen Stoneguard, whom many of you know. Since the day he joined the Remnant some twenty years past, he has proven himself an eager student in the Words and ways of war, and despite his youth, has in more recent years established himself as a trustworthy leader among our fighters. Because of his unique history in the Lands and his obvious talents, the Paladin and I have appointed him the task of overseeing the work of the Sacred Path. Under his title as Keeper he will help forge and direct the web of secret routes linking us with the soundens. It will also be his task to train and command its watchers."

Donovan glanced down at the young man before him. "Brasen, have you words to share?"

Brasen looked back toward Donovan and nodded respectfully then turned to face the Remnant. "I am a man of few words," he said. "All I can say is that I am honored by the confidence that both Donovan and Paladin

Windrunner have placed in me. I will not fail them. And I will not fail you." His voice echoed strongly through the chamber, and carried in its tone the hopeful sense of both his youthful confidence and his passion. Despite himself, Ajel felt a twinge of envy at the sound of it. How long had it been since he had felt such passion in his heart?

"The gratitude of the Remnant rests on you, Brasen," said Ajel. "Your task will not be easy. But you will have our full support in every way we can supply it."

Brasen acknowledged Ajel with a nod then moved to join Kair near the door of the chamber, where she still stood.

Ajel looked back toward the crowd. Two thousand faces, two thousand souls, looking anxiously to him to help them find their strength. And if the Sacred Path proved true, there would soon be many more. He felt a mighty weariness rise within his breast. Instinctively, he fought to deny it.

"Already, we are transforming ourselves," he said. "Under my uncle, and my father before him, we became a community, a family, a people all our own. Our common belief in the existence of *Dei'lo* provoked the Council to hunt us down like mindless beasts. When we could fight back, we did. And when we could not, which was more often the truth of it, we became adept at hiding—in order to preserve the knowledge of *Dei'lo* for a future time.

"That time has come. The days of hiding in this fortress are now past. Where once we were a band of rebels, now we will become an army. The future of our people—indeed, our world—depends on this transformation.

"We have the Book. The task to make it known has fallen to us. A war is coming. And the hope of the Inherited Lands rests on our shoulders."

Suddenly, a lone voice rang out from the crowd. "What of the Waymaker?" Ajel did not recognize the voice, and scanned the sea of faces to find its source.

"Who speaks?" demanded Teram Firstway, who struggled to his feet in indignation in spite of his advanced years. "Who speaks out of turn?" he repeated.

There was no answer.

"Be at peace, Teram," said Ajel soothingly. "It is all right." With a huff, the elder Wordhavener retook his seat. But his steel grey eyes still glared angrily at the crowd.

Ajel lifted his hand to his forehead a moment, to think of what he should say, and was surprised to find it damp with perspiration. "It was I, along with Kair of the Songtrust, who brought testimony to you that Gideon Dawning has been named the Waymaker," said Ajel. "It was a Raanthan who named him so, the same Raanthan who rescued him from Balaam's clutches in the dungeons of the Axis, and delivered him to us as we made our escape from Phallenar...the same Raanthan who travels with him now wherever it is his path may take him.

"As you well know, many among us hoped that Gideon Dawning would prove to bear a different title—that of Kinsman Redeemer, of whom many prophecies have been written and in whom many good-hearted souls have placed their hope for the future of our Lands. But it seems that we were wrong." He glanced at Kair, but upon meeting his eyes she quickly looked away. "As for the Waymaker," he continued. "I cannot say who he is, or tell you with certainty what role he may play in the events of these critical days we face. The prophecies concerning that title are few and cryptic, and, truth be told, little studied. Still, this much I believe—that the sojourner's heart is true, and worthy of our allegiance. That is why I have sent with him my own brother, Revel Foundling, to watch over him in his course and lend what wisdom he can to the sojourner's cause."

He sighed deeply. The weariness made his breathing seem constricted, like a stone upon his chest. He felt a tingling in his fingertips that he could not explain. "From the beginning," said Ajel, "the ways and purpose of Gideon Dawning have remained a mystery to us. And the same holds true today. The truth is that we do not know where he is. We do not know even whether he lives. We have had no contact with him or with those of the Remnant who travel with him, since the morning I left them all on a Sea Folk ship bound for Silence Sound. I know only that my brother still lives, for we are linked in soul, and if he were to perish I would surely know it..."

Just as those final words spilled from his lips, Ajel felt a sudden dizzying darkness sweep across his eyes, and before his thoughts could make sense of what was happening, he lost hold of consciousness and collapsed to the floor.

6

THE HINTERLAND

All tribes of the Kolventu forbid travel beyond the borders of the Hinterland. Even so, a small number in each generation are stricken with a wanderlust to see the outside world, and actively seek release from the edicts of their tribe. Such desires are dealt with harshly among the Kolventu, and most who express them eventually repent of their ambition to leave. But a few refuse to be swayed. In accordance with their laws, these are condemned as kreliz'adum—"haters of lore"—and are sent away, banished from the Hinterland forever.

In the Spring of the year S.C. 2113, a young Kolventu warrior named Tyrenon received just such a condemnation. He was the eldest son of Celedriel, who was at that time the Shal'adum of the Kolventu's most-southern tribe, the Arelis. And so Tyrenon departed from the Hinterland a condemned soul, with his heart intent on the Inherited Lands.

But Tyrenon's younger sister, Aliel, the first daughter of Celedriel and heir to her title as Shal'adum, was unwilling to be separated from her brother, for they were very close. So soon after he departed, she fled her father's house in secret to find him.

Aliel of Celedrial was only nine years old when she crossed out of the Hinterland. And though she could not know it at the time, she would not see her home again for thirty-seven years.

—The Kyrinthan Journals, Chronicles, Chapter 6, Verses 320-332

The feathered beings carried them, gagged and strung on poles like slaughtered game, a full day's journey into the wooded swamp. Not once did they speak to one another, nor would they permit any sound, not even a groan or sigh, to escape their prisoners' throats unpunished. Ironically, it was Aybel who made this latter point abundantly clear, for in those first few hours she repeatedly grunted an appeal to have her gag removed, only to be lashed each time with a wooden switch, exactly once for every sound she uttered. One time Gideon yelled as well, infuriated as he was by the sound of Aybel's torment. But they only whipped her more because of it, and then turned their switches on him. Thankfully, she eventually gave up trying, but whether it was from pain or frustration Gideon had no way to tell.

That their captors were human became evident to Gideon only after they finally emerged from their treetop perches and walked on the ground like ordinary men. But they adorned themselves like no human men he'd ever seen. Across their backs and arms and along their shins, their Nubian skin was fused with a mass of brilliant feathers, a cohesive plumage as white as their hair, and equally as long and flowing. They wore no covering other than that, except for a small white cloth bound at their waists, whose function seemed less concerned with decency and more with securing the coiled vine whips that hung at their sides. Their eyes were the most interesting thing of all. Some, like Aybel's, were brown and clear, but most were more exotic and strange—amethyst, magenta, or the color of lilacs. A few—the most unnerving by far—were the color of blood.

As dusk approached, they arrived at a clearing that bordered a vast open pond. The shallow water there was blue and clean, unlike the green slime of the swamps, and smooth like a mirror. Scattered across its surface were dozens of impressive multi-tiered structures, rising out of the placid waters like ancient wooden ziggurats, and linked to one another by an intricate maze of dangling walkways.

The buildings all looked like pyramids, reminiscent of Mayan temples Gideon had seen back home—only these had black sloping roofs topping each level, with overlapping slabs of slate extending a foot or more beyond each of the outer walls. Most of the structures were three-tiered, though some of the larger ones rose five levels or more, towering well above the tallest trees. The entire complex hovered a few feet above the surface of the pond, supported by a system of dark pillars, which were surreptitiously placed to make them difficult to spot, making the entire complex seem to hover above the water's surface.

Gideon closed his eyes and let his head fall back. The muscles and tendons in his neck and arms screamed in protest from the tortuous hours of hanging he'd endured. But worse than that, the old wounds on his wrists and ankles burned as if on fire from the aggravation of the rough-hewn bindings, reminding him that they were not nearly as healed as he wanted to believe.

Still, these things were of little concern compared to the larger problems they now faced. Aybel had seemed uncharacteristically anxious about their trek into her homeland, but the look of shock and horror on her face when they were captured told Gideon she had never expected something like this. If these were her people—and that was still an open question—they were certainly not behaving the way she would expect. Before that morning, he had never seen such naked fear shine through her eyes, not even when battling the Council Lords in Phallenar.

As the last light of the sun faded, a foreboding gloom fell over the swamp, spreading outward from the trees like a chilling mist. The feathered men took no notice of it—or if they did, it certainly did not slow their pace. For quite some time, they tracked along the pond's perimeter, until at last they came to a bridge that led out over the water. To Gideon's surprise, however, they did not take that route. Instead, they turned back toward the darkness of the wooded swamp.

Once in the trees, Gideon found it impossible to see anything at all, and so he simply closed his eyes to await whatever fate his captors had in store.

After a short while they stopped, and for the first time since they'd hoisted him up on the pole that morning, Gideon felt his overarched back settle against the ground. The pole was removed, his bonds and gag were checked and resecured. Then two sets of unseen hands lifted his aching body and tossed it unceremoniously through what seemed to be a gate, though it was far too dark to know for certain. He landed on his side upon a swath of pine needles, and immediately felt the silken fabric of the underlord's gown slip between his fingers. Reaching out, he touched her leg, which moved a little in response, assuring him at least that she was conscious enough to note his presence next to her. He patted her gently, then rolled onto his back. A moment later, he felt Revel's callused hands brush across his face, then fumble with the knot at the base of his neck where the gag was bound. Recognizing what he was trying to do, Gideon obliged by shifting onto his side. The knotting must have been complex, for it was several minutes before Revel finally loosened it, and Gideon felt a tingly rush of blood returning to his lips and jaw. He pulled the gag away and tried to swallow, but his mouth was dry as ash.

He knew better than to speak. Though he had heard nothing since they'd dumped him on the ground, the men were likely standing guard nearby. Quietly, he rolled over and felt around until at last he found the knot for Revel's gag. Untying the blasted thing was slow going—not so much because the knot was intricate, though it was, but because his fingers were all but numb from lack of blood, and the tightness of the bindings made it difficult to get any sort of leverage on the cords. When at last he succeeded, he quickly tapped Revel on the head to let him know, then rolled onto his back, exhausted.

A second later, Revel's hoarse voice cut into the darkness. "Sojourner, are you well?" he asked.

"Shh!" warned Gideon angrily, surprised that Revel would be so foolish as to speak aloud.

"It is all right," said Revel. "The fel'adum have gone."

"How do you know?" whispered Gideon sternly, assuming he was speaking of the guards. "They could be listening!"

"They are far from here, sojourner," Revel assured him. "I do not feel their presence anywhere in the wood."

"You didn't sense them before, when they captured us," Gideon retorted, still whispering.

"Yes, I did," replied Revel flatly. "Now, let me loose these bonds so we may more easily free the others."

Gideon said nothing, but extended his hands toward Revel's voice. The Wordhavener immediately grabbed them and went to work. The action surprised him. "Just how well do you see in the dark?" he asked.

"Well enough," said Revel.

Gideon looked over his shoulder, though it was a pointless act. "Can you see the others?" he asked. "How are they doing?"

There was a moment of silence, and then, "They are awake, and listening," said Revel. "Aybel looks angry about the eyes." He chuckled lightly.

"Where are we?" asked Gideon.

"I do not know," said Revel. "Our journey took us northwest into the wood. I do not know what tribe of Kolventu lives here. Though I suspect these are not Aybel's people."

"Hhn-nnn," grunted Aybel.

"There, you see?" said Revel. "Not Aybel's people. Ah, there." The binding on Gideon's wrists fell slack and slipped away. Immediately, he turned to reach for Kyrintha's gag.

"First my bindings, sojourner," said Revel. "Four free hands will be quicker than two."

"Yeah, okay," said Gideon, turning back to face him. He fumbled for Revel's bindings, then set to work, trying to ignore the tingly fire rushing through his blood-starved hands.

"The knot is hidden beneath the cords," said Revel. "Between the wrists. Yes, there."

"Why did those—what did you call them?" asked Gideon, pulling awkwardly at the rough-hewn vines.

"Fel'adum," said Revel.

"What do they want with us?"

"I do not know."

Gideon glanced back over his shoulder. "Aybel, do you know what this is about?"

"Hhnn...hhn," said Aybel.

"Perhaps we will learn more once we loose her gag," said Revel, chuckling again.

Gideon returned the quip with a sarcastic snort, but said nothing more, and redoubled his efforts on the knot. When at last he gained success, they turned their attention to the women. A short while later, they were all unbound, and sat conversing quietly in the darkness.

"They were not of my mother's house," said Aybel wearily, referring to the men who captured them. "They bore no markings of allegiance I could see, but I know the settlement that lies nearby. It is Ki'Mahdwin."

"Are the Mahdwin friends to your tribe?" asked Revel.

"There are no friends among the tribes of the Kolventu," said Aybel. "But the Mahdwin have long been our neighbors to the north. There has always been an uneasy respect between us."

"Then why did they capture us?" asked Kyrintha.

"The better question is why their fel'adum would set an ambush in the stakehold of my tribe," said Aybel. The anger in her voice was palpable.

"Why?" asked Gideon. "What's important about that?"

At first, Aybel didn't answer. Finally, she said, "I can think of no other reason."

"Reason for what?"

"For why they are here, sojourner!" Aybel snapped sharply. Then she sighed. "I fear we may have stumbled into a war."

THE HINTERLAND

Aliel of Celedriel was quick and cunning despite her youth, and managed to track Tyrenon's course all the way to the gates of Phallenar. But once there she lost his trail, and was soon captured by a ser'jalen belonging to a minor lord of the Council.

Rather than reveal her to his master, the ser'jalen decided to garner profit by selling Aliel as chattel to the leader of a band of Roamers with whom he often dealt. The girl endured harsh treatment at the hands of the Roamers for several months before finally escaping them on the outskirts of Chara sounden. Aware that she could not return home, and afraid to return to Phallenar for fear of being recaptured, she fled northwest across the Plain of Dreams for several days, wandering without purpose, until at last she came upon some members of the Remnant on sojourn to Wordhaven. Seeing she was a child alone, lost and with no home, they took her in and treated her as one of their own. In time, she came to view the Remnant as her own people, and even accepted the new name by which they came to know her—Aybel Boldrun.

—The Kyrinthan Journals, Chronicles, Chapter 6, Verses 333-341

D espite their exhaustion, they slept only a little that night, choosing instead to spend the quiet hours of darkness debating what course of action they should take now that they were captured. That they could escape their cage quickly became obvious. Though its wooden frame and bars were hard and thick, they were no match for the Words that either Aybel or Revel could throw to break them down. And yet Aybel adamantly advised against such an action, explaining that doing so would only lead to their deaths at the hands of the fel'adum, no matter how fast or far they tried to run. The wiser course, she said, was to appeal to the shal'adum of the tribe that held them, and make her believe that they were not a threat to her Ki.

Revel disagreed. His special abilities in wooded lands, he said, would allow them to travel unhindered and undiscovered all the way back to the Endurant, which he reminded them would only wait a few days before returning to the relative safety of the Sound. They would find no help among Aybel's people. And they should leave.

The underlord sided with Revel in the argument, though for reasons of her own. She knew nothing of Revel's abilities; in fact, she openly doubted they were real. What she did know was that she was an underlord of Phallenar imprisoned by the sworn enemies of the Council. If they so much as suspected her true identity, they would not hesitate to slay her on the spot.

In the end, however, Aybel and Revel deferred to Gideon to make the final decision—much to his surprise. He was the Waymaker, after all, Revel said. The quest was his, and he alone must decide their course.

Gideon reluctantly agreed. And though he had come to count Revel as a friend, and to trust his instincts in matters of survival such as this, he could not bring himself to openly defy Aybel's wishes. They would stay, he decided, at least long enough for Aybel to speak to the shal'adum and plead their case. If that failed, they would take the first opportunity to escape and make their way back to the Endurant.

When the fel'adum returned at daybreak the next morning, Gideon and the others were still in their cage, still awake, and waiting. Several feet behind the fel'adum walked another sort of man—an older man, still strong and formidable like the fel'adum, but without feathers fused to his skin. He wore a pure white cloak, and carried himself with the air of a king.

As best she could in the cramped space of the cage, Aybel stood and faced the feathered men. "Where is the shal'adum?" she demanded. Her tone was clearly angry. "I wish to see her. I will not speak to this...*man!*" She gestured toward him flippantly, but refused to look at him directly.

"Then you will not speak to anyone," replied the man smoothly as he moved to stand in front of her. "For I am all there is. Shal'adum Melindra is away on tribal business. I am Kaiba, Melindra's First." He bowed his head slightly. "If I am not of sufficient status for your liking, then we can leave you here until the shal'adum returns."

Aybel looked vaguely disgusted, as though she'd just taken a whiff of a drink she found questionable. "You seem young for a First," she said.

Kaiba smiled slightly. "The shal'adum is vigorous," he said. "The elder members of her ward cannot maintain her pace for long. And I am not so young as you may think. I, too, am vigorous." He seemed proud of the claim.

"When will your shal'adum return?"

Kaiba frowned. "I do not know. A week, perhaps two."

"Where has she gone?"

"Do I take it that you are willing to talk to me, then?" asked Kaiba.

Aybel nodded diffidently, then said, "Answer me."

"You seem a woman of standing," said Kaiba coolly. "I have told you my name. Are you ashamed to tell me yours?"

"Watch your tone, First," snapped Aybel, "or when your shal'adum does return, I will have her cut out your tongue."

Kaiba noticeably stiffened at the remark, but whether from fear or anger Gideon couldn't tell. Perhaps some of both. When he spoke again, however, his tone was softer. "If we are to speak together," he said, "introductions are called for."

Aybel glared at him a moment, as if debating whether he was worth her time at all. At last, she said, "I am Aliel of Ki'Arelis, first daughter of Celedriel and heir to the shal'adum of my tribe. If we are to speak together, as you say, then release me from this cage and welcome me to your Ki with the honor due a woman of my standing."

Kaiba stepped forward to get a closer look at Aybel's face. He tapped his chin thoughtfully. "Aliel, you say? Of Ki'Arelis?" His brow furrowed. "I seem to recall a story of an Aliel from your tribe," he mused. "But you cannot be her. She was lost from her father's house decades ago. Did she run off with her older reprobate brother? Yes, that was it. She was later declared kreliz'adum herself as I understand. Your tribe's shal'adum dis-owned her."

"I didn't realize Melindra would choose as her First a man so given to the pettiness of gossip," said Aybel. "You clearly know little truth regarding my tribe...or my history."

"Indeed," said Kaiba. "Then perhaps you could enlighten me. Why have you brought these strangers into the Hinterland?"

Aybel grabbed the wooden poles of her cage and pulled her face toward his. "No, you answer me now, First! Why were your fel'adum in the stake-hold of my tribe?"

Kaiba raised an eyebrow in surprise. "For the first daughter of Celedriel," he said, "you certainly know very little of the happenings in your Ki."

"Any man with the sense of a krell can see that I have been away," snapped Aybel. "I bring strangers with me from another place, do I not? What do you think, that I just found them wandering in the swamps?"

Kaiba seemed undaunted. "The people of the Hinterland do not go 'away,' as any true first daughter would know."

"I will not argue with you," she said flatly. "Answer my question."

Kaiba considered her for a moment. At last he said, "I doubt very much that you are the first daughter of Celedriel," he said. "But given the current madness we are in, I suppose anything is possible. I am willing to lay aside my doubt—for the moment."

"My question," repeated Aybel impatiently.

"Celedriel is dead," said Kaiba with a wave of his hand. "Ki'Arelis is all but destroyed. My fel'adum were in your stakehold at the request of your tribe. They were searching for her assassin."

If Aybel was stunned by the news, she didn't show it. "You test my patience, First," she snapped. "My mother is not dead. You speak nothing but mockery and lies!"

Kaiba chuckled. "Oh, she is quite dead. The story goes that she was blown apart not three weeks past, right where she stood along the border of Soulsbane, along with half of her fel'adum. Your people are shattered."

Aybel took a step back. Her hand, unbidden, rose to cover her heart. "How...how could that be?"

"It was a Lord from Phallenar or so it claimed, drunk with rage and the madness of the Words, as they all are." Kaiba spewed the description as if it left a rancid taste on his lips. "We don't know why it came, but when your fel'adum discovered it, it went berserk. The creature wreaked a great deal of havoc as I understand."

Aybel did not respond. Stumbling backward into the cage, she slowly let her body slump to the ground, and stared numbly at her feet. "Mother..." she whispered.

Revel immediately reached out to comfort her, while both Gideon and Kyrintha instinctively stood to block her from Kaiba's view.

"You are lying," said Kyrintha.

Kaiba looked down at the underlord, his eyebrow raised in apparent disdain. Then he sighed and looked away. "This is perplexing to me," he said to no one in particular. "My reason tells me you are in league with the lord who attacked Arelis. All facts point to this. But to see the lady's reaction to the news of Celedriel's death..."

"We are not in league with the Lords of Phallenar," said Gideon firmly. "We are running from them. We came here with...Aliel, to get help from her tribe. There is nothing more to it than that."

Suddenly, one of the fel'adum stepped forward. "Be silent!" he commanded. "You are not Kolventu. You will not speak to the First."

But Kaiba waved his hand dismissively. "It's all right. They are reprobates. We cannot expect them to be civil."

"We serve Aliel," declared Revel from his seat behind them. "Our lady is clearly distraught over the news you bring, great Kaiba. We speak only what we know she would have us say."

"Perhaps, perhaps not," said Kaiba. "For all I know, she is your captive. That, at least, seems a more plausible explanation."

"I am no captive," said Aybel suddenly. Her voice was firm and strong again. But she did not rise. "I have been away on a mission for some time. Its nature and purpose are none of your tribe's concern. But my bondman speaks the truth. Like you, I am an enemy of the Council. They hunt me, and I have returned to my stakehold for their help."

"Then it seems you may have brought the Lords with you. How sad to think you may be to blame for the tragedy that has befallen your Ki. Tell me, was this mad lord searching for you?"

Revel jumped to his feet and glared menacingly at the First. His yellow-gold eyes sparkled with the threat of danger. "Have you no heart?" he whispered harshly. "Whoever this invader wanted, it had nothing to do with us!"

But Gideon wasn't so sure.

Kaiba took in Revel's threatening gaze a moment, then waved his hand dismissively. "I have no time for this," he said, then turned toward the feathered men behind him. "See that they have food and water." He sniffed the air suspiciously. "And get them cleaned up," he added. "I will return for them at midday."

"What are you going to do with us?" Gideon demanded. But the First ignored him, and strolled away.

WORDHAVEN

Brasen Stoneguard came to the Remnant in the Spring of his twenty-first year, a lone fighter bent on revenge against the guardian regiment responsible for the execution of his parents, who were both outspoken insurrectionists against the Council in Agatharon sounden. By the time of his arrival, he had already lived more than a decade in the solitude of the wild places in the Lands, and had learned the ways of stealth and survival, becoming both a formidable warrior and a master of wood-lore. His knowledge of the hidden byways and havens within the Lands became invaluable to the Remnant in the years of their hiding from the Council Lords. And when the time came at last to establish the Sacred Path, Brasen was, despite his youth, the natural choice to lead it.

—The Kyrinthan Journals, Chronicles, Chapter 15, Verses 220-225

rasen Stoneguard watched impatiently as the curtain of light from the morning sun inched its way down Wordhaven's western cliffs. The cold air of morning made his brown leathers stiff, and sent wave after wave of chills through his bones. But he ignored the urge to move.

Even though he knew he was early, he eyes still frequently glanced toward the playful golden lion engraved on Wordhaven's massive inner gates. He felt anxious to get on with the morning's affairs. Soon the golden doors would swing open, bringing another small band of sojourners from the soundens, coming to learn the Words and take their place as soldiers in the battle to come.

This was the seventh such welcoming since the Sacred Path was opened just a few weeks past. In that time, close to fifty new recruits had arrived from the soundens. But though Ajel and Donovan said they were pleased with the initial response, the numbers didn't come close to satisfying Brasen. There were still hundreds, perhaps thousands of willing souls yet to find and bring safely through those gates. If Wordhaven and the Remnant had any hope of facing the challenge to come, they would need every last one of them. And they would need them soon.

Autumn had arrived early in the mountains this year—far too early for Brasen's liking. His trackers—all twenty-five of them—were good at their jobs, even if most were younger and less experienced at warfare than he would have hoped. But their time was short. Soon the autumn chill would spread like a blanket over the lowland plains and forests and the hills of Scolding Wind. Winter would follow quickly on its heels. Once the first hard snow hit the Heaven Range, the Sacred Path to Wordhaven would be cut off from the lowlands until the Spring thaw. And by then it would be too late to matter.

Hearing footfalls in the distance, he glanced over his shoulder to see Donovan Truthstay's imposing form approaching from the Stand. In deference to his superior, he turned to face him. "Donovan," he called out, bowing his head slightly in respect, "I've been waiting for you."

The big man's breath formed thick clouds in the chill air as he strode forward, but he did not respond. His pace was smooth and relaxed, but there was always a hint of threat in his stance, as if his body were a tightly coiled spring that could be unleashed at the instant of his choosing. The fact that Donovan stood nearly a foot taller than Brasen only served to magnify his intimidating effect. Brasen felt like a mere boy next to the warrior—a sense that automatically challenged him to demonstrate otherwise.

"I see that you are early as usual, Keeper," Donovan rumbled as he strolled up next to him. He glanced toward the east. "It will be some time before the sun's warmth reaches us."

"About twenty minutes," Brasen nodded, ignoring the urge to step away from the big man. "I like to be here in case they arrive early."

Donovan nodded in approval. But then he sighed and said, "I've come to tell you that you are to hold the recruits here until Seer arrives."

"Seer?" Brasen asked in surprise. "Why does she wish to come out here? She's never taken an interest in my work before."

Donovan breathed a cynical sigh. "Oh, she's interested," he said. "She won't allow a single one of your volunteers to so much as hear a Word of *Dei'lo* until she's personally peered into their souls." He shook his head. "It's a wonder they haven't all run fleeing back to their soundens."

"Our trackers are careful," said Brasen, feeling more defensive now as news of Seer's coming sank in. "I trained each one myself! The guardians have yet to hear a word of our passing among the soundens. Does she not trust us?"

Donovan thought a moment, then said, "She is...passionate for Wordhaven's safety."

"So are we all," said Brasen indignantly.

Donovan nodded. "Just so," he agreed. "Only she is more passionate, or so she believes." He looked at the ground a moment, then shook his head as if to banish a thought. "It is not your concern, Keeper. I think it is me she doubts, not you or your trackers."

"But why..." Brasen started, but then thought better of it. He could feel Donovan's tension rising...as well as his ire. Whatever struggle the big man had with the prophetess, they were his own concern. Instead, Brasen chose a different question. "Why does Seer want to see the recruits here?"

"She has had a troubling dream," Donovan explained. "She would not say what it was. Only that she needed to see the recruits at the inner gates, before they came too close to the Stand."

"She must suspect subterfuge," offered Brasen.

Donovan only shrugged. "You can ask her herself if you like," he said. "I sense her coming."

Brasen peered around Donovan's bulk and scanned the road. There she was, a diminutive figure cloaked in white from head to foot, plodding purposefully forward with her staff in hand. Though she was still a long way off, she seemed in no hurry to reach them.

Just then, Brasen heard a faint rustling sound, like wind blowing through tufts of fur, and turned just in time to see the golden doors of Wordhaven's inner gates part, and swing slowly open.

A young woman appeared in the space between. She was fair-skinned and childlike, with hair the color of honey, and eyes as deep brown as the bark of *bian'ar* trees. Like all able-bodied members of the Remnant, she wore the fighting garb of Wordhaven—brown leathers and a sash of green—with the added touch of a bow and quiver strung across her back.

Her cheeks were smudged with dirt, a fact she didn't seem to realize. Taking one look at Brasen, she smiled and bowed her head lightly. But her grin quickly vanished once she recognized the big man standing next to him. "Donovan Truthstay," she said, bowing her head again, deeper this time. "You honor me."

"It is you who honor us, Jessa Greenbearer," said Brasen. "Welcome home to the Stand. How many have you brought from Makroth sounden?"

"Four," she replied, somewhat apologetically. "Though more will follow in a few days time. And not all of mine are of Makroth."

"Indeed?" said the Keeper, curious. "Well, let's have a look at them."

Jessa gestured toward the darkness of the passage beyond the golden doors, and from it there emerged four weary-looking travelers—their eyes wide with wonder, and more than a little shock.

"You did warn them of Wordhaven's effects," said Brasen.

Jessa nodded. "Yes, Keeper. But it is not an easy thing to explain."

Brasen chuckled. "Just so," he said. "I'm not used to it yet myself, and I've been here more than twenty years." He glanced at Donovan to share the joke, but the warrior's expression remained cold as stone.

Awkwardly, Brasen cleared his throat, then took a step toward the new arrivals. They seemed completely oblivious to his presence, overwhelmed as they were by the sudden infusion of life from the valley. But that was to be expected.

"Greetings, brave hearts," he said loudly. "I am called Brasen Stone-guard, the Keeper of the Sacred Path. You are welcome in the valley of Wordhaven."

As if on cue, Jessa stepped toward one of the recruits and touched his arm. He was a tall, ruddy young man with bright red hair and freckled skin, and eyes the color of mint leaves. "Keeper, Head of Arms," said Jessa, "may I present Tomas conMeredith of Makroth sounden."

"Meredith?" interjected Donovan doubtfully. "That is not a father's name."

"His father was slain in a guardian raid before either he or his twin sister was born," explained Jessa. "I am told the father was an active opponent of the Council Lords. The children took their mother's name to conceal their blood bond to him." She reached past Tomas and touched the arm of the girl next to him. "This is his sister twin, Rachel." The girl stood several inches shorter than her brother, but bore the same eyes and coloring, with bright red hair that hung straight past her shoulders.

"This is wondrous!" exclaimed Rachel, looking at the cliffs that ringed the valley. "I've never experienced anything like it."

"We should have forced Mother to come with us," added Tomas, his own eyes lost in the grandeur of the place.

"Tomas, Rachel!" said Jessa harshly, shaking their arms in unison. "You stand before the Keeper, and the Head of Arms of Wordhaven!"

"It's all right, Jessa," said Brasen calmly. "Give them a moment. Who else do we have here?"

With a nod, Jessa stepped toward another young man—shorter than Tomas, but of such similar complexion they could have been brothers. "This is Corin conFrey, also of Makroth."

"Keeper Stoneguard," said Corin with an excited nod. He seemed ready to explode into a run at any moment. "Thank you for letting me come. I'd always heard stories of this place—as a boy, you know—but I never dreamed...It is so grand."

"Indeed it is, Corin conFrey," said Brasen. "And there will be time for you to explore every hill and crevice. That is what you long for, isn't it?"

Corin nodded excitedly. "Yes, Keeper," he said smiling. "I would like that very much."

"So I gathered," said Brasen. He looked at the last traveler. "And who is this fair traveler, Jessa?" He grinned. "She does not look to be from Makroth sounden."

The young woman stepped toward Brasen and extended her hand daintily. "My name is Sarla," she said smoothly. "Sarla Ferin." She bowed lightly toward the Keeper, causing her brown shoulder-length hair to tumble loosely around her eyes.

With a harshness that took Brasen by surprise, Donovan marched forward and snagged the young woman's chin, lifting her face toward his. He stared at her suspiciously with his black-orbed eyes. "Ferin is not a sounden name," he said. "From where do you come, girl?"

Sarla's eyes grew wide with sudden shock and fear. "I...I come from

Phallenar, sir. Escaped from Phallenar, actually. Ferin is my master's name. I...I do not know my own."

"My apologies, Donovan," Jessa interjected. "Sarla's story bears some explaining. I should have told you before I introduced her."

Donovan looked at the tracker with an unreadable expression, then slowly released the young woman's chin. "Very well. Explain."

"She is a just a bondmaid, you big ox!" A woman's voice, aged and shaky but with an edge of iron, echoed from behind them,.

Donovan did not turn around. "Seer," he said with a sigh. "The tracker was just introducing the Keeper and me to our new recruits."

Brasen watched as the old prophetess hobbled up beside them. She looked as small and harmless as a kitten standing next to the big warrior. But, as Brasen knew full well, such appearances were deceiving.

"There's no need to terrify them, Donovan," Seer chided with a caustic grin. "After all, that's my job, isn't it? Or so you tell everyone." She snorted in feigned disgust. "If you took the time to sense her thoughts, you'd know she is just a wayward soul, escaped from Phallenar months ago if my guess is right."

Sarla nodded hopefully.

"We found Sarla on the lower heights of Heaven Range," offered Jessa. "She had found a cave there, and made herself a home of sorts. She was completely unaware of our passage. I would not have been aware of her if not for the fire she used to warm herself."

"She is a servant fled from Phallenar then," said Brasen.

"I am, Keeper Stoneguard," said Sarla. The fear in her voice was obvious. "My master is...was a merchant. A harsh and brutal man." Her gaze drifted to the ground for a moment, and her face grew hard. "I had long planned my escape from him, even if it meant death, which I fully expected it would. But I could not live that way anymore."

Images of beatings and horrendous abuse flashed through Brasen's thoughts, but only for an instant. "How did you escape him?" he asked.

Sarla swallowed, then said, "He often took me with him when he traveled to the soundens to sell his wares. Some months ago—I forget how long—our caravan was raided by Roamers as we made our way to Chara sounden. In the confusion, I saw my opportunity. I broke away from him and fled."

"And you have been living on your own ever since?" asked Donovan.

Sarla nodded. Her dark brown eyes immediately filled with tears, and Brasen could feel the waves of her loneliness wash over him. "I was lost," she said shakily. "I did not know where to go, who I could trust. I have been a servant all my life, sir, or at least as long as I can remember." She bit her lower lip absently for a moment, as if to compose her thoughts, then continued. "I stayed clear of the soundens for the most part, stealing in at night to take only what I needed to survive. No one ever saw me come or go. A servant knows how to be invisible when needed. Eventually I found myself in the Barrier Mountains, and then, eventually, here in the Heaven Range. There are all kinds of sweet berries here, if you know where to look. And the air is cool and fresh. I thought perhaps I might live here in peace."

"You did not pass through Dunerun?" asked Donovan.

"No sir," she replied shakily. "I traveled along the shores of the Delving Sea."

Donovan looked unconvinced.

"It is possible to avoid the deathstorm if you don't mind extended swims through the surf, Donovan," said Brasen. "I have traveled that route many times myself."

"It is a dangerous path," said Donovan. "A path for the shrewd and strong."

Brasen smirked. "And Dunerun Hope is not?"

Donovan shook his head. "Few know it, Brasen." He turned toward the young woman. "Regardless of how you got here, you must have known you could not have survived in the cave through the winter," he said. "You are hardly dressed for autumn as it is."

Sarla shrugged lightly, and lowered her head. "I realize that now, sir. I am...grateful that Jessa found me, and convinced me to come. It's..." she glanced shyly around at the glades and cliffs. "It's quite wondrous here."

"You *convinced* her, tracker?" asked Donovan angrily. "Do you bring stragglers through our gates who have no interest in our cause?"

"Oh, but I do, I do," said Sarla excitedly. "Jessa told me about your war, and I want to help. I bear no love for the Council Lords. In truth, they disgust me as much as my master. It was they who forced my father's family into servitude while I was still a child. If it had not been for the Council, well, perhaps I could have been..." She bit her lip once more, then bowed her head and said nothing more.

"Is this all of them, Keeper?" asked Seer suddenly. "I expected more."

Brasen nodded. "Jessa says another group will follow in a few days," he said.

Seer nodded thoughtfully, then said, "I will come and meet them here as well. See that they do not approach the Stand until I arrive."

"Of course, Seer," said Brasen. "As you wish."

"Have your dreams not turned out as you expected?" asked Donovan, with just a hint of sarcasm.

"My dreams remain, Donovan Truthstay," Seer snapped. "But they are not an easy matter to discern. Above all virtues, they require patience. The message they hold will come clear in time."

"Perhaps if you told us the dream, we may be able to help," said Brasen.

Seer shot him a suspicious glance. But then she grinned. "When you have aged another sixty years or so, perhaps, young Brasen" she said. "For now, you will simply have to trust my word. You *and* this stubborn ox." She slapped Donovan's arm dismissively. He did not react. "I fear that danger will come through those gates," she continued. "I cannot say how or in what form. But I believe its time is near." She pointed a weathered finger at Brasen. "You must be vigilant to see it does not slip past you unawares."

"I am no stranger to vigilance, Seer," said Brasen coolly.

If Seer sensed the affront, she did not show it. "It's far too cold for an old woman like me to out at this time of day," she said, pulling her robe tight around her narrow shoulders. "I'm going back inside."

"I'll walk with you," said Donovan unexpectedly. "Keeper, you'll see them to their chambers?"

"Of course," replied Brasen.

"They'll need time to rest. We'll begin their training in the morning." With that, both he and Seer turned to go. As they departed, Brasen noticed Donovan offering Seer his arm for support. She accepted it without a word.

"As you say, Donovan," said Brasen. *Theirs is a strange relationship*, he thought as he watched them go. He doubted he would ever make sense of it.

"Are we free to enter the Stand now?" asked Jessa.

Startled, Brasen turned to face her. "Of course," he said. Then he smiled. "You can tell me of your journey as we walk. And I will tell you what's happened to the Paladin while you were away."

"Paladin Windrunner?" asked Jessa worriedly. "He is not harmed, is he?"

"He claims he is well enough," replied Brasen with a shrug, "but some of those closest to him are not so certain." Suddenly, he glanced toward Sarla and the others. For a moment, he had forgotten they were there. "I apologize for this strange welcome you've received," he said to the recruits. "These are difficult times for all of us. I hope you'll understand."

"Of course," said Tomas. "It's just so...overwhelming. All of it, I mean." He nodded toward the valley ahead. Apparently he hadn't heard Brasen's comments about Ajel; or, more likely, pretended not to hear.

Brasen grinned. "You'll get used to Wordhaven's effects over time—well, more or less. And you'll find your welcome far more gracious in the Stand."

"Come," added Jessa, also smiling now. "A bath and some rest will do us all good."

The group headed quickly down the road, with Tomas leading the way, followed by Brasen and Jessa and two of the others. Sarla, however, trailed behind them slowly, apparently still in shock from the sudden rush of awareness and life that Wordhaven brought. Brasen looked back toward her with a frown of concern. This must be especially overwhelming for her, he thought. She had been in isolation for so long, and now to be flooded with the thoughts of so many people all at once—to say nothing of the other forms of life that filled the valley.

He considered waiting for her to catch up, but then decided to leave her be. Perhaps she needed time to be alone. As if sensing his thoughts, Sarla looked back toward the Keeper, and nodded her thanks.

And somewhere, hidden deep within her mind, she smiled.

THE HINTERLAND

Even once I began to walk with him along his chosen course, I was not quick to trust in Gideon Dawning, or to see within him any of the noble qualities I would typically ascribe to greatness. In those first days with him, we rarely spoke—primarily by my own choice. I thought him an abrasive man, reckless and immature, not at all the sort that I deemed worthy of my respect or curiosity. In the beginning, of course, I did not know he had been named the Waymaker. The Remnant did not trust me with that knowledge until later. But even if I had known, I doubt it would have made any difference in my opinion. As I look back on it now, I realize the problem was not in Gideon's manner, but rather in my own arrogant blindness to the truth. For the glory was there all the while, wrestling just beneath the surface of his brokenness.

—The Kyrinthan Journals, Songs of Deliverance, Stanza 2, Verses 19-21

They called them krell. Or krellin or krellis, Gideon couldn't remember. They looked something like ostriches, only bigger, with larger heads and more menacing eyes and beaks—both black as coal. But their feathers were the most brilliant sort of white Gideon had ever seen, large and whimsical, and glistening with the iridescence of water fowl.

Gideon had asked if his had a name, but Kaiba just glared at him like he was crazy. Apparently, the Kolventu didn't stoop to such sentimentality. Not that it mattered, as things turned out. The creature hardly noticed Gideon was there at all, perched on its back though he was. It certainly didn't respond to any of his attempts to control its movements. It just raced along on its long stony legs, chasing the others through the trees like a bird in heat. Still, for all the wildness of the beast, it gave a smooth ride overall. Far smoother than a horse, anyway.

They had been traveling for several hours, heading north as best Gideon could tell, though in a round about way due to the swampy patches that dotted the woods, and the trees themselves, which presented a maze of obstacles all their own. The woods were different here, more thinly spaced than along the coast, but still thick enough to force the fast-moving birds along zigzag trajectories to avoid the moss-covered trunks and drooping branches. There was little for Gideon to do but hang on to the krell's spindly neck, and try to take in the scenery as it blurred past.

There had been little talk since their journey began, even though for some unexplained reason Kaiba had decided not to gag them as his fel'adum had done the day before. Still, just prior to departing Ki'Mahdwin, they had learned a little more about what was happening to them—thanks mostly to Aybel, who had somehow managed to regain her indignant inquisitiveness by the time Kaiba returned with the white-feathered beasts in tow.

They were heading to a place called Kiki, which, as Gideon understood it, was something like the equivalent of a United Nations for all the tribes of the Kolventu. It was located on an island called Edor, in neutral territory off the northern coast of the Hinterland. Apparently, all of the shal'adum of the Kolventu tribes were already there, convening in response to the Council Lord's murder of Aybel's mother and the attack on her tribe. According to Kaiba, the shal'adum were debating how they should respond to the attack—and even considering a declaration of open war on the Inherited Lands.

Kaiba had decided that his prisoners should be present for these important proceedings—though in truth he seemed mostly interested in Aybel, whom he begrudgingly admitted might actually be telling the truth about her identity. If she were the first daughter of Shal'adum Celedriel, he said, that would make her the heir as shal'adum of tribe Arelis—in which case, it was his duty to see her safely to the isle of Edor.

Perhaps it was his fear that Aybel truly was Celedriel's daughter that caused him to behave more agreeably toward them than he had at first. In addition to not gagging them for the journey, he had actually gone so far as to return their weapons—which included Revel's bow and quiver and Aybel's battle rod, and most important of all, Gideon's almond wood staff.

It felt good to hold it again, really good, in a way that he didn't fully understand—but that fact seemed to bother him less and less as time went on. The heat of it sent chills up his arm as he gripped it, and radiated in ripples of warmth down into his chest. It even made his scalp tingle. The staff's effect on him was getting stronger, that much was certain. It was beginning to feel a little like the *ja'moinar* bread Mara had given him so long ago in Calmeron—only fiercer, angrier. Gideon felt powerful holding the staff, dangerous, like he could take out Kaiba and his feathered goons with ease if he chose to. But he held back, and decided to keep quiet about it all for now. He didn't even tell Aybel. There wasn't really an opportunity anyway.

They had discussed trying to escape again, of course, during the hours they waited for Kaiba to return for them. But Aybel had remained adamant that doing so would accomplish nothing. They needed supplies, both for the Endurant and for Aybel and Kyrintha's long trek back to Wordhaven. And to get them, Aybel maintained, they had to speak with a shal'adum. Any shal'adum would do, she claimed, though she seemed to think Melindra would prove more reasonable than the others for some reason.

The discussion was heated, especially between Aybel and the under-lord, who clearly believed her life would be forfeit the instant any Kolventu began to suspect her true identity. But Gideon continued to trust Aybel's judgment in the matter. These were her people after all. She knew the dangers, what to expect of them. And when he finally voiced his opinion, the discussion quickly faded to silence. Apparently, being the Waymaker did have its perks.

Suddenly, Gideon was shaken from his thoughts by a loud squawk echoing through the trees. He turned just in time to see one of the Krell take off in a frenetic dash toward the front of the pack. Revel sat atop the wild beast, leaning heavily on its neck, but otherwise seemingly unperturbed by the bird's sudden charge. It was as if he actually knew how to control the thing.

Kaiba and the two fel'adum with him reacted instantly. Their krell quickly slowed to a halt and turned to face Revel's charge. Gideon's own krell, as well as Aybel's and Kyrintha's, followed Kaiba's lead, slowing to a walk within only a second or two of seeing Kaiba stop, and began plodding subserviently toward him.

Revel's bird, however, continued its crazed run toward Kaiba. For the next few seconds, it looked as though Revel might actually try to plow right over the First and his guards. But then, some thirty feet or so away, Revel's bird abruptly skidded to a stop, and absently began pecking at the ground as if nothing had happened.

"You did not tell me you knew how to guide a krell, bondman," said Kaiba threateningly. "That is dangerous information to conceal."

Revel bowed his head respectfully. "In truth, great Kaiba, I did not know how to guide the beast before today. And I would not have bothered to learn if my need was not so urgent."

Kaiba smiled. "Well, at least one matter is settled, bondman. You do know how to lie. It takes weeks to learn how to guide a krell. But no matter. What need is so great that you would charge us so?"

"We are being followed." Revel kept his head bowed slightly as he spoke.

Again, Kaiba smiled. "Really."

"You should listen to him, First," Aybel broke in as her krell lumbered closer. "My bondman possesses skills in woodlore that no Kolventu can match. If he says we are being followed, then it is so."

Kaiba hiked his eyebrows in a look of mock surprise. "Indeed? More skilled than a fel'adum? Tell me, bondman, who follows us? How many? Where are they hiding?" He looked around as if looking for a child playing Hide and Seek.

"I believe there is but one, great Kaiba," said Revel. "And he is on foot."

"On foot!" exclaimed Kaiba incredulously. "He must be very fast to keep up with krell, don't you think?"

"Yes, he must."

Kaiba leaned back and let out a heavy sigh. "You are both a liar and a fool, hawk face. I can't see why a first daughter would ever keep you in her service." He leaned toward Aybel with a mocking grin. "Then again, perhaps you chose him for his body rather than his brain." He laughed.

"The only fool I see here is you, Kaiba," said Aybel. "You ignore Revel's warning at your own peril—and ours. I tell you, his abilities far exceed your own."

Kaiba flashed a sarcastic grin. "We shall see." He looked up toward the canopy above and let out a long heavy breath. "It's just as well we stopped, anyway," he said. "Even krell need rest. And I for one am hungry." With an air of nonchalance, he raised his hand and snapped his fingers in the air, then quickly followed it with a hissed command—something like "sh'-teek...sh'teek." The krell, all seven of them, immediately folded their legs beneath them and settled to the ground.

"I suggest you walk about while you can," said Kaiba. "We still have far to go before nightfall."

Gideon watched as the First slid off the bird's white back and strolled off into the trees. The two fel'adum did the same, wandering off together in a different direction entirely.

"They don't seem very concerned that we'll run away," Gideon quipped under his breath.

"I think they realize there is nowhere for us to go," observed Kyrintha quietly as she strolled up next to him from behind. "There is nothing but these swamp-infested woodlands for leagues in any direction."

"Probably so," Gideon agreed. Throwing his legs to one side, he slid off the krell's feathered back and stomped his feet on the moss-covered ground. "But like he said, it's a good thing we stopped anyway," he added. "My legs were starting to go numb." Leaning on his staff, he shook each leg in turn to get the blood flowing.

"Your friends seem concerned about our alleged pursuer," said Kyrintha, nodding toward Aybel and Revel, who stood whispering excitedly some distance away. Just as Gideon noticed them, he saw Aybel hold up an angry hand in front of Revel's face, then storm off into the woods in the same direction Kaiba had gone. Revel did not watch her go, but only stood with his hands on his hips and stared down at the ground.

"They have reason to be," said Gideon. "I know something of Revel's abilities, and if he says we're being followed, then we're being followed."

The underlord looked up at Gideon dubiously. "But his abilities do not come from *Dei'lo*." It sounded like an accusation.

Gideon shrugged. "Not from what he tells me. But then, I'm hardly the guy to ask about such things."

The underlord let out a derisive snort.

Gideon chose to let the reaction pass without comment. Instead, he looked down at the underlord's tattered gown, which was now more brown than green from all the mud stains that coated it. "I guess that dress is getting pretty uncomfortable by now, isn't it?" he said.

Kyrintha absently brushed away a fleck of dried mud from her skirts. "I shall have to remember to dress more appropriately the next time I escape from prison," she said curtly.

"We could ask Kaiba if he brought something less cumbersome you could wear," Gideon offered.

Kyrintha scoffed at the suggestion. "The less attention Kaiba pays me, the better," she quipped.

"Suit yourself, underlord," said Gideon.

Kyrintha flashed him an angry glare. "Have you gone mad?" she whispered. "Do you mean to have me slain?"

Gideon rolled his eyes. "Don't worry," he said. "They can't hear us."

She let out another snort. "Even so, I will thank you to call me Maywin."

Maywin was the name Aybel had suggested she use. Apparently, it was a common name among the lower classes of the Kolventu, especially the servant caste. Aybel said the name might help the underlord pass as her bondmaid. Gideon doubted it would make any difference, however. Aside from the obvious questions raised by the gown, the woman was simply too full of herself for anyone to believe she had been raised as a slave. She carried herself like a princess, and spoke with the aristocratic manner of a woman who was used to being obeyed. As far as Gideon was concerned, her best hope for anonymity was to stay in the background and keep her mouth shut.

Luckily, Gideon was saved from having to continue the conversation, for at that moment Revel walked up to join them.

"What's Aybel so upset about?" Gideon asked as Revel approached.

"Aliel, sojourner," chided Revel. "Call her Aliel. It is her given name among the Kolventu."

"I'm aware of that," replied Gideon sardonically. "What was she so upset about?"

"We are being tracked," said Revel. "My sense of him is strange. But I know he is there, sometimes very close."

"Is he close now?" whispered Kyrintha.

Revel shook his head in frustration. "I do not sense him now," he said. "But a few moments past, I would have sworn he was right on top of us."

"You know it's a 'he'?" asked Gideon.

"I am certain of that at least," replied Revel. "His movements, when I sense them at all, are brutish and heavy. He lacks the grace of a woman."

"A *mon'jalen*, perhaps," said Kyrintha, still whispering. "A gift from my parents, most likely."

Revel nodded hesitantly. "It may be. But it may also be a Council Lord...perhaps the same one who attacked Ki'Arelis."

Kyrintha shook her head. "I don't believe that is so. It makes no sense that my father would send a lord where a *mon'jalen* would suffice."

"Perhaps he does not believe a *mon'jalen* will suffice, Maywin," replied Revel. "He underestimated the sojourner's ability once. It's doubtful he will make that mistake again. But if it is a lord, which one would he send? And why would he attack Ki'Arelis?"

The underlord pursed her lips worriedly as she pondered the question. After a few moments, she nodded to herself, and let out a whisper. "Stevron..."

"I am not familiar with that lord," said Revel.

Kyrintha brushed a wayward lock of blond hair from her eyes. She suddenly looked tired. "He is Sarlina's replacement, raised to the Council shortly after her death," explained the underlord. "Stevron is..." She paused and let out a sigh. "I've known him for years. He's my father's prize pupil...the child my parents never had." Her tone carried obvious contempt. "If my father were to send a lord, it would be him."

"What will he do if he finds us?" asked Gideon.

"I don't know," replied Kyrintha. "Perhaps try to capture us. Perhaps slay us. I don't know."

"He has already found us," said Revel firmly. "Whatever his mission, he is waiting for the right opportunity to carry it out."

"What does Ayb...Aliel think?" asked Gideon.

"She has gone to demand that Kaiba take us back to Ki'Mahdwin," said Revel. "With all of the shal'adum convened in one place, they are vulnerable to attack. If we continue to Kiki, she fears that we will lead the pursuer there and so put all the tribes of the Kolventu at risk."

"Kaiba won't believe that," exclaimed Gideon. "He doesn't even believe there's anyone tracking us!"

"That is what I told her as well," said Revel with a shrug. "But her concern for the shal'adum compels her."

Gideon felt the warmth of the staff circulating through his hands, like a living weapon aching to be the summoned to battle. Something about this whole scenario didn't sit right with him, but he couldn't quite name what it was. "I still don't see why a lord—or a *mon'jalen*, for that matter—would attack Ki'Arelis," he said finally. "We weren't anywhere near there at the time of the attack."

"At that time, we were still on route to Phallenar," agreed Revel. "Indeed, the matter is puzzling."

At that moment, Aybel came storming out of the woods, her face still fixed in the same angry glare she had when she went in. Kaiba strolled out casually behind her, looking smug. Aybel took one look at Gideon and the others and quickly shook her head no.

"It is as I feared," said Revel quietly. "Kaiba would not hear her."

"It is as you expected," corrected Gideon. "We can't hope for any help from these people, Revel. They're blind to anything that challenges their own sense of superiority. If an ambush is coming, we're the ones who will have to be ready for it." The heat in his staff seemed to pulse excitedly as he spoke.

"Yes," said Revel. He glanced at Gideon's staff, and let out a sigh. "At least the First has returned our weapons," he added. "I believe it will not be long before we need them."

"If our pursuer is an agent of the Council," said Kyrintha, "your weapons will do you little good."

"You're not much of an optimist, are you?" asked Gideon sarcastically.

Surprisingly, however, Revel laughed. "A weapon's power does not rest in the weapon, my lady," he said. "but in the one who wields it. And the best weapons of all are not the kind we carry in our hands."

Kyrintha scoffed. "If you're referring to *Dei'lo*, then I don't—"

"Return to your krell!" called Kaiba in a commanding tone. "We're leaving."

Revel leaned toward the underlord with a mischievous grin on his face. "I'm referring to Gideon, my lady," he whispered. Then he winked at Gideon, and strolled off toward the krell.

As he departed, the underlord raised her eyebrows and observed Gideon as if she were asking herself a question she didn't care to speak aloud. Finally, she said, "It seems the Wordhaveners have placed a great deal of faith in you, sojourner." She paused, then added, "I hope it is deserved."

This time, it was Gideon who laughed. "You and me both, Maywin," he chuckled. "You and me both."

A few minutes later, the entire group had returned to their krell, which had remained motionless throughout their entire respite. But as Gideon scrambled up the stunted white-feathered wings, he was distracted by a sudden prickly feeling that danced along his spine. Instinctively, he looked toward Revel, and watched with worry as the hawk-eyed Wordhavener stared uneasily into the shroud of leaves directly above their heads.

10

PHALLENAR

See, a storm of Words
Will burst out in wrath,
A whirlwind swirling down
On the heads of the wicked.
"Are not true Words like purging fire?" says the prophet.
"And like a hammer that shatters the arrogant rock?"

—From the Writings of the Prophet Mikail, in the year S.C. 1103

Lord Stevron Achelli winced instinctively as he felt it coming.

It began as it always did—with the tingly electric shimmering of the air around his eyes, quickly followed by the prickly feel of a thousand ants swarming on every inch of his skin. And then, a stifling fade to darkness, like a blanket falling on the universe.

It lasted only a moment, he knew. But it never seemed that way, no matter how he braced himself. The summoning Word carried the unmistakable stench of death.

When the next moment finally came, and the stifling dark was lifted, Stevron breathed in deep, and looked about. The mossy branch on which he'd been standing was gone, replaced by limestone blocks, smoothly cut and perfectly fitted across the ground beneath him. The dark of early evening was chased away by a hundred pillars of golden light, which stood like sentries along the expansive street that stretched before him, forming a chain of glistening gold that linked the Axis to the Memorial Wall. *Phallenar...*

The air, he noticed, was suddenly dry, and smelled of urine.

"Stevron, my son! Welcome home this fair eve."

When Stevron turned toward the booming voice, he could hardly believe his eyes. For there was High Lord Balaam, standing tall and strong in the open air, right in the center of Palorsfall Road, his hand resting idly on a gold and crystal monument honoring Palor's victory at Morguen. Lord Lysteria stood gracefully his side.

"High Lord!" exclaimed Stevron. "You are...you are well!"

"Of course I'm well," chuckled Balaam, slapping his abundant belly as if to prove the point. "How else would I be? Come now, walk with me and my lovely bondmate." He winked at Lysteria. "There's something I'd like to show you."

Before Stevron could say another word, Balaam grabbed him by the shoulder and yanked him along as he and Lysteria hastened up the road. In the flurry, Stevron tried to shoot a questioning glance toward Lord Lysteria, but she kept her eyes averted.

"How fair our quarry?" asked Balaam jovially.

Stevron cleared his throat before replying. "Well enough, High Lord. The Kolventu have carried them as far as the mainland's northern shore. I think they mean to ferry them to one of the islands, though I am not sure why, or even how it will be done."

"Really?" said Balaam happily. "Interesting."

"High Lord, if I may...how have you recovered so quickly?"

"Recovered?" Balaam asked. He seemed genuinely confused by the question.

"The High Lord is as strong and virile as always, Lord Stevron," said Lysteria smoothly. "Though it is kind of you to be so concerned for his well-being." She still wouldn't look at him.

"Lord Lysteria, I—"

"Ah, what a wondrous night!" proclaimed Balaam loudly, giving his bondmate a quick bear hug that nearly lifted her right off her feet. "It's a fine night for a celebration, wouldn't you say?"

"Yes, Balaam," replied Lysteria. "The night is lovely." Her words sounded practiced, as if she'd rehearsed them.

"Where are we going?" asked Stevron.

"There, of course," snapped Balaam, pointing toward the vast Memorial Wall ahead of them. "I told you that already."

"Your pardon, High Lord," replied Stevron, "but you did not."

Balaam wagged a pudgy finger in Stevron's face as they walked, but didn't deign to look at him. "Don't contradict me, boy. You think I don't know what I said? Pay attention."

Boy? He hasn't called me boy since... "My Lord, are you sure you're well?"

Balaam pulled up short and grabbed Stevron by the arm. "Why do you keep asking me that?" he demanded. "I've told you I'm well. Now let that be the end of it! You didn't endure the searing pain of those boils on your back, did you? You didn't wretch every day at the stench of infection and that cursed fish oil ointment those buffoons kept lathering on my seeping flesh? I am well, I tell you! You have no place to question me!"

The High Lord's overgrown fingernails dug through the fabric into Stevron's arm, but the young Lord chose to let the grip remain—for now. "I do not mean to offend, High Lord." He forced his voice to sound even and calm. "But it appears that you—"

"Balaam," Lysteria interrupted quietly. She wrapped her hands gently around the High Lord's arm. "We should keep going. Your men are waiting for us." At that moment, she flashed an angry glare at Stevron and shook her head no, careful not to let the High Lord see it.

Instantly, the grip on Stevron's arm fell limp. "Ah, yes," said Balaam. "My men." He lifted the hand off Stevron's arm and swapped a dollop of sweat from his forehead. "Nearly twenty thousand strong. Did you know that, Stevron? It will be the largest Word-wielding force assembled since the days of Palor."

"No, High Lord. I did not." He tried to catch Lysteria's eye again, but failed.

Balaam laughed. "Oh, it's quite a sight to behold. You'll see."

"The High Lord will commission them soon," said Lysteria lightly, her face now a perfect reflection of calm. "The rebels will have little hope of escape, even with their precious Book." Her behavior seemed nearly as erratic as Balaam's. Yet, in her way, perhaps she was trying to help Stevron understand.

"You know where the Book is?" asked Stevron.

"Of course I do, son," said Balaam. "The Book is at Wordhaven."

"And do you know where Wordhaven is?"

"Yes."

"How did you uncover its location?"

Balaam looked pensive a moment, then said, "How indeed? Now, that is the question, isn't it?" He seemed to think on it a moment longer, then said, "How is Kyrintha?"

"She seems well enough," replied Stevron, trying to keep up with the High Lord's erratic line of thought. It wasn't the first time the High Lord had suddenly averted a question he didn't like, of course. Perhaps he simply didn't want to reveal how he learned of Wordhaven's location. "She travels side by side with the rebels, but I do not believe they yet trust her."

"See that she is not harmed," said Balaam. "She is a foolish girl. Takes after her grandmother, I think. But she is still my blood."

"As you say, High Lord," replied Stevron.

"Has she spoken much?" asked Lysteria, her eyes still focused off in the distance. "I mean, have you overheard her saying anything?"

Stevron shook his head. "Most times I am not close enough to hear their conversation, Lord Lysteria" he said. "But they are not speaking much in any case. They ride the krell from first light until well after dark. By the time they stop, they are too weary to do much else but sleep."

Lysteria nodded thoughtfully, but said nothing.

"They did speak of escaping at one point," added Stevron. "But for some reason they have decided to remain with their captors."

"The reason is obvious enough," mumbled Balaam. "They need a shal'adum."

"A shal'adum?" asked Stevron. "But why?"

"They need supplies, Stevron," replied Balaam. "To get them, they must appeal to a shal'adum."

"Why did they not appeal to the one in Ki'Mahdwin?" asked Stevron.

Balaam grinned. "Obviously because she is not there."

Stevron smiled. This was the High Lord he remembered. "I should not remain gone for long, High Lord," he said. "If they take to the water, it will be difficult to trace their route."

Balaam gave him a quick pat on the shoulder. "Don't worry yourself, son. I know where he's going."

He...He means the Waymaker. "Where, then?"

"Why do you suppose we didn't simply transport ourselves to the Wall, Stevron?" asked Balaam. "Why walk, hmm?"

The question took him by surprise, but he was getting better at this game. And it was a game, he decided. It had to be. "I suppose, High Lord, to show your strength."

Balaam nodded in approval. "Just so," he said. "Very good. The Council needs to be reminded that I am fit. And unafraid. I can just imagine the whispered plots they have concocted against me in the shadows of the Axis in recent days." He laughed, but it sounded forced.

Stevron still wanted to hear just how the High Lord had become "fit" so quickly. But he knew better than to ask again. "It will do their hearts good to see you strong, High Lord," he said. "I know it does mine."

Balaam nodded. "The Council has little love for you, my son, you must know that. They realize I mean to make you my successor, whatever their thoughts on the matter." He wiped a wayward stream of sweat from his eyebrow. "Such a thing has never been done, of course. And under normal circumstances, even I could not do it. But war brings certain advantages. Certain powers to my office."

Lysteria's eyes widened in alarm, but Balaam didn't see it. "Surely such an act would not come for many years yet, my dear," she said with a forced laugh. "Any 'war' with these rebels will certainly end long before that."

"Yes," Balaam replied. "Of course it would. Of course." But he sounded unconvincing.

Until then, Stevron hadn't noticed the emptiness of the streets. Though it was still early evening, not a soul had crossed their path since the walk began. He wondered if Balaam had ordered the streets cleared, or if the people simply stayed away out of fear. But what was even more peculiar; he hadn't seen a single team of vigils. And not one *mon'jalen.* They must be somewhere nearby, he reasoned. In the shadows along the alleyways, perhaps, well-hidden from view. But why conceal themselves?

He had so many questions. But in Balaam's present frame of mind, he doubted he would get any answers. So he contented himself to walk along quietly for now, and trust that the explanations he required would come in time.

After several more minutes, they came to the final and grandest monument that graced the intersections along the road between the Wall and the Axis. It was the memorial depicting Palor's Fall—the one for which the street had been named. The High Lord stopped at the base, and gazed up at the resplendent gold and crystal dragon that towered arrogantly before him, glistening like stardust under the light of the glowood pillars nearby. Its expansive wings spread wide in triumph as its sinuous neck arched toward the heavens in a defiant screech. In its mouth, the limp form of Palor Wordwielder dangled like a broken puppet, his face contorted in the agony of his own bitter defeat and the knowledge of his coming death. The failed king's mouth hung open, and his golden lips were shaped in a peculiar way—as if he were trying to say something, but couldn't find the words.

Though it was the most celebrated monument in the city, and Balaam's personal favorite, Stevron had always secretly despised it. He saw no value in memorializing Palor's weakness as a leader, or his failure to master *Sa'lei* as he should have. The man was a fool. When Stevron's own memorial would be erected some day—and he knew that it would—it would be the dragon, and not him, that would lay broken and writhing in its own bitter defeat.

Just then, he noticed a tear dripping off of Balaam's pudgy cheek. He remembered the tears that spilled unbidden from Balaam's eyes during their last visit in his chambers. He thought perhaps the High Lord still bore some pain he meant to conceal.

"High Lord, forgive me, but...are you well?"

Balaam didn't look at him, and didn't wipe the tear away. "I wonder," he whispered, "what he knew that compelled him to craft his own destruction. How desperate his darkness must have been."

"Balaam, dear, we must go in." Lysteria produced a kerchief from the folds of her gown and gently dabbed the tear from the High Lord's face. He seemed not to notice. "Come now," she whispered. "The Council will wonder why it's taking so long." With considerable effort—she was less than half his size—she pulled him away from the monument and hurried him down the street. The High Lord seemed lost in a daze. And though Lysteria's bony face seemed calm enough, every now and then a look of worry flashed across it. And possibly, fear.

Stevron followed dutifully behind them. Whatever Balaam claimed, he was definitely not fully well. But what worried him more was the fact that the High Lord seemed oblivious to his condition.

"Lord Lysteria, the High Lord, understandably, has much on his mind just now. But I find I'm still quite curious about where we are going." With the High Lord's behavior so uncertain, he wanted to be ready to cover for him in whatever circumstance was coming.

"Isn't it clear, Lord Stevron?" she replied without turning around. "We're going to commission the army that will raze Wordhaven to the ground."

"I see," said Stevron. "That's outstanding." Normally, he would be thrilled at such news. But Balaam's current state dampened his enthusiasm. "How did you rally such a force so quickly, High Lord?"

"There will be plenty of time for questions later," Balaam replied. He seemed more himself now. "I want you to sit next to Lord Lysteria on the dais. Make a show of it. Look arrogant...not that you need any encouragement for that. Let the Council Lords see that I have chosen you. I want tonight to remove any doubt regarding my intentions."

Stevron bowed his head deferentially. "As you say, High Lord. Thank you."

"Don't thank me!" Balaam snapped angrily. "You may find you don't relish the role as much as you believe."

Stevron bowed again, deeper this time, but thought it best to say nothing more.

When they arrived at the main portal, a core of *mon'jalen* were there waiting for them. They quickly ushered the lords through the doors and down the expansive main stairs leading to the central colonnade below.

Once they reached the lower level, another *mon'jalen* approached carrying a jewel-encrusted sword and belt. Without comment, Balaam lifted his arms and the *mon'jalen* knelt to fasten the sword around the High Lord's abundant waist.

"Leave me," said Balaam, glancing toward Lysteria and Stevron. "Take your places upon the dais. I will follow in a moment."

Suddenly, Stevron felt Lord Lysteria's wrinkled arms entwine themselves around his. "Come, Lord Stevron," she said. "I'll show you the way."

"I know the way, Lord Lysteria," he said pleasantly. But he wasn't smiling.

They walked along a dark hallway lined with guardians and *mon'jalen* who bowed deferentially as they passed. The lords did not speak; they dared not among the soldiers, who would quickly pass on to their fellow guardians whatever snippet of gossip they might hear. But the questions burning in Stevron's mind spurred him to quicken their pace to the dais. Perhaps there they would have time to talk a moment before Balaam arrived.

Stepping through a small portal to their right, they emerged from the darkness into a vast light-filled chasm erupting with the energy and chatter of close to twenty thousand voices. The roar of it engulfed them as they moved across the platform toward the two gold-inlaid chairs Balaam had prepared. There would be no seat for High Lord, of course. He would stand before his fighters as a sign of his respect—and as confirmation to the Council that he was far from frail.

After seeing Lord Lysteria to her seat, Stevron mounted the footstool and took his place beside her. Before him stretched a long, narrow sea of black-garbed bodies, writhing and churning some fifty feet or so below the dais. The air was heavy here, hot and thick with anticipation. He liked the sense of power it evoked, and imagined how intoxicating it would feel on the day he stood before them as Balaam's successor.

There were three such colonnades within the Wall. But this was the largest, stretching a quarter league or more from end to end, and lined with imposing stone columns that spanned a hundred feet from crown to base. Even so, the horde before him could barely fit into the narrowness of the space. And the echo...the echo was deafening.

"Lord Stevron, we have little time, so listen closely." Lord Lysteria spoke over the noise of the crowd. She didn't look at him, pretending instead to be preoccupied with the folds of her gown. "The High Lord thinks himself well, but he is not. I have managed to conceal his sickness from the Council so far, but I can no longer do it alone. I need your assistance." There was a hint of desperation in her tone.

"What's happened to him?" asked Stevron, mimicking Lysteria's non-chalance. "He was so weak the last time I came."

"That cursed Book, of course!" she snapped. "I don't have time to explain it all. He will defeat this sickness. I know it! He is a good, strong man. He just needs time to recover himself. But time is one luxury we do not have. And I am losing my ability to keep him safe."

"What do you need of me?"

"The sickness has him obsessed, Stevron—with the man you follow, this...Waymaker. He speaks of nothing else. His every waking moment is spent reading those cursed black scrolls, trying to solve some archaic riddle. He reads them himself now, Stevron! Can you believe that? I can hardly stand to be near those vile documents, but he handles them—with his own hands, he opens them and reads them aloud! It's lunacy."

"What do you want me to do?"

"Slay the Waymaker." Her voice was cold and sharp. "We must end this obsession at its source."

"I cannot do that, Lord Lysteria," Stevron replied. "The High Lord has commanded me not to harm him."

"The High Lord is not well!" she retorted. "And I fear he will not recover until he gets away from those scrolls. The Book may have brought on this illness, Stevron, but it is the scrolls that are holding him there. He must stop reading them. But he will not stop reading them so long as the Way-maker lives. You must slay the Waymaker. Put an end to this. It is the only way."

"Why don't you simply hide the scrolls?"

"Don't you think I already thought of that?" she snapped. "He will not let me near them. He's warded them in his private chambers and set his *ser'-jalen* as guards. I think he suspects my intent."

"Lord Lysteria, I cannot disobey the High Lord. I will not."

Her hands balled into fists upon the arms of her chair. But her posture remained calm. "If you have any love for Balaam," she said, "any love at all, you must do this! Some members of the Council already suspect he is not truly well. I do not know how much longer I can protect him. I only mean to protect him, you see that don't you?"

"Of course," said Stevron. "Your love for the High Lord can never be doubted, especially by me. But..."

Suddenly, Balaam stood in the center of the dais, appearing out of nothing. Immediately, a roar of applause erupted from the floor of the colonnade, so deafening it was all Stevron could do not to cover his ears. The High Lord nodded respectfully to the throng, waving his hand in acknowledgment of their praise. Though his back was to him, Stevron could clearly see the glistening beads of sweat dripping from the High Lord's scalp. He wondered if the guardians below could see it too.

After a few minutes, Balaam raised his hands to silence the crowd, and his speech began. The High Lord's oratory prowess had been a key strength of his leadership since the beginning of his rule. And even now, it did not fail him. His words carried the sort of passionate accolades and bold pronouncements of power that caused warriors everywhere to love him and swear fealty to his cause. Balaam was a master in the language of *Sa'lei*—second in ability only to Stevron in all the Inherited Lands. But when it came to speaking the common tongue, the High Lord had no equal.

Perhaps it was the eloquence that dulled Stevron's thinking. For it wasn't until the end of his speech several minutes later that Stevron actually realized what the High Lord had said.

After Balaam's final words, the throng erupted in a roar so full of bloodthirst and raw passion that Stevron wondered if the massive columns of the colonnade would crack under the sheer strain of it. Dumbfounded, he forgot to stand, and had to be reminded by a gentle touch from Lysteria, who made it appear as though she was only straightening her gown. Her face positively beamed with practiced delight as he rose to join her in applause. She gave no indication that she'd heard anything amiss in Balaam's speech. But then, she wouldn't dare. Stevron, however, was not so practiced in the ways of politics. He forced the muscles of his face to forge a mild grin, but even that small show at pretense filled him with contempt. At least he had no trouble clapping. For the next several minutes as the horde continued to roar, he slammed his hands together with such heat and ferocity that his palms stung with heat, and the rings he wore cut into his palms.

When the cacophony finally died away, Balaam quickly departed the dais alone to convene with the Firstsworn and his chosen commanders, leaving Lysteria and Stevron to endure the sickly pleasantries of the other Council Lords, who swept in on them from the ramparts where they concealed themselves while Balaam spoke. As each lord came and went, Stevron smiled and bowed as he was trained. But he didn't remember a word they said, or even what he said in return, if anything. All he could think about was Balaam's final charge to the guardian throng.

I myself will lead you, then, to the hidden gates of Wordhaven. Together we will topple its defenses and drive the spear of our united voice into its ancient beating heart. No one shall stand before us. And once it is defeated, we will make it once again the throne of Lords!

The High Lord had no intention of destroying Wordhaven. He meant to reclaim it as the seat of power within the Inherited Lands! But such a goal was not merely foolish; it was impossible. Surely Balaam knew that! No lord of *Sa'lei*—however strong—could purge that fortress of the taint of *Dei'lo* that had filled its halls for so many generations. Not even Stevron, and he was stronger than any who had come before. The place would act as a slow poison in Balaam's veins if he tried to rule from there. There would be no way he could survive for long.

Unless...

No, he stopped himself. *It couldn't be that. The very thought is ridiculous.*

He had no further opportunity to speak with Lord Lysteria that evening. Balaam rejoined them on the dais just as the last few lords finally flittered off into the night. The High Lord looked haggard, but his black eyes gleamed with the hot fever of his own ambition.

"I'm glad you heard this for yourself, Stevron, directly from my lips," he said. Absently, he swapped the perspiration from his brow. "It was important to me to have you here. There are vital days ahead for us. I look forward to the time when you can be at my side once again."

"High Lord—"

"The hour is late," he continued. "You should be getting back to your quarry. When you return, travel to the Isle of Edor. That is where you will find him."

"The Isle of Edor?" asked Stevron in surprise. "But why would they take him there?"

Balaam tapped his temple coyly. "It's all up here, son. All up here. He'll be held in a somber-looking castle on the southern tip. The Kolventu call it Kiki. Hear all that you can, but do not interfere. I'll summon you again in six days' time."

Stevron was about to protest, but suddenly felt Lord Lysteria's bony hand grip his arm like steel. "I hope you'll remember to keep yourself safe...as we discussed," she said softly.

The distraction proved just long enough. For the curtain of darkness had already begun to cover his eyes.

11

THE ISLE OF EDOR

I never expected the road to my freedom would be easy or swift. I knew difficult times awaited me beyond the city gates. I even knew that I might be struck down on the way, and never truly succeed in reaching my goal. I was prepared for all of that. But what I did not know, and what very nearly destroyed me, was how quickly I would forsake my own true desire, and yearn once more for the shackles of my imprisonment in the tower—in secret, and in shame—and for no better reason than that I might have a dry set of clothes, a warm meal, and be left to my studies in peace.

—The Kyrinthan Journals, Songs of Deliverance, Stanza 14, Verses 101-103

It appeared to him from the mists like an image conjured from a fairy tale. A castle, vastly tall and more ancient than the sea, jutted from the blackened, wet cliffs of Edor like a weathered horn of mortar, slime and grey stone. It was stark, windowless, and foreboding to look upon—a tombstone marking the grave of a powerful giant from an age long forgotten.

Even so, the air of the place hung thick with memory, and with sorrow. The weighty blankets of mists resonated with it, like the echo of a million voices crying out a warning from a past too distant to be discerned. The feel of it gave Gideon the chills.

93

"Ah, the mists of Edolore."

Kaiba filled his lungs with the cold, prickly fog that swirled around their small boat. "Have you ever felt its like?" Gideon yanked the blanket Kaiba had given him up around his shoulders. He thought it best not to answer.

"You should consider yourselves privileged, bondmen," Kaiba prattled on. "No one outside the Kolventu has traversed these waters for more than a thousand years. The isles of the Hinterland are a wonder few behold."

That much was true, Gideon admitted. The islands had been incredibly beautiful. In the two days since they'd boarded the canoe on the mainland's northern shore, they'd glided past four of the impressive emerald jewels, each more stunning than the last. But the mists grew thicker the closer they came to the Isle of Edor. If they passed any islands after the fourth, Gideon never saw them.

"It will be good to see the Holding again," said Kaiba.

"The Holding?" asked Gideon. "What's that?"

"I believe the First refers to Kiki, Gideon," said Revel quietly, gesturing toward the towering horn before them. The Wordhavener sat hunched on the floor of the canoe at Gideon's feet, looking something like a disgruntled owl hunkering down in a vain attempt to stay warm and dry.

"In the common tongue, it is translated as the Domain of domains," continued Kaiba. "The one place within the Hinterland belonging to no tribe of the Kolventu, and to all." He glanced over Gideon's shoulder toward the rear of the longboat. "You should have some memory of this place, yes?"

"It was a long time ago," responded Aybel tersely. "But yes, I do remember it."

"Then you must know which direction the stone docks lie," said Kaiba.

Gideon turned to look at Aybel—slowly, so as not to upset the delicate balance of the jittery craft. She had draped her blanket over her head like a hood, peering out worriedly through its creases toward the hazy cliffs ahead. The underlord sat at her feet, equally bundled and clearly miserable from the cold.

"Testing me in this fashion is pointless, First," she said quietly. "I was a mere child when last I saw these shores. I can hardly be expected to remember such an insignificant detail."

Gideon turned back toward Kaiba, who was smiling. "You cannot evade the truth for long, my lady," he said. "When we reach the Holding, there is one who will know in a breath whether what you claim is true."

"And who is this discerning prophet?" Aybel asked with mild disgust.

"Your father," replied Kaiba with a mocking wave of his hand, "if you are who you say, that is."

"Kaligorn?" said Aybel. "Kaligorn is here?"

"Does the thought of it frighten you?" asked Kaiba.

Aybel remained silent for a moment. But then she said, "Yes, First, it frightens me. But not for the reasons you suspect."

"For what reasons, then?" asked Kaiba. But Aybel would say nothing more.

Kaiba's fel'adum guided the longboat toward a rocky peninsula west of the tower. Though the mists remained thick, Gideon could eventually make out the stony platform that rested there, and the stone-carved stairs that wound their way up the cliffs to the base of the castle wall some three hundred feet above. The water had been relatively calm so far this day, but it turned to glass the closer they came to shore. When at last they reached the dock, even the sound of the distant waves had faded to nothing.

As the fel'adum secured the craft, Kaiba hopped ashore and said, "Take them to the southern anteroom. I will go and find Kaligorn. We will meet you there, and determine at last whether this journey has been a waste of my time."

"What of their weapons?" asked one of the fel'adum.

Kaiba waved his hand dismissively as he marched away. "Let them carry them. I will not have it said I treated the daughter of a shal'adum as a common interloper," he called. "But if any of them make an ill move, slay them all save Aliel." He paused a moment, then added, "Beginning with the bond-maid. Her accent stinks of Phallenar." He resumed his march up the stairs.

"Get out," commanded the fel'adum. "Leave the blankets."

The four of them complied without a word. As they hiked up the stairs toward the cliffs above, Gideon clutched his staff close to his body—in part for the warmth it provided, but also to try and conceal it from the fel'adums' view. Despite Kaiba's command, he worried that they might try to take it from him. If they did, he knew he would fight them to keep it. And a fight was the last thing they needed right now.

Once they reached the cliffs, they formed a single file upon the narrow stairs, with one fel'adum in the lead, followed by Revel, Gideon, the underlord and Aybel, and the second fel'adum bringing up the rear. Though the route was strenuous, it felt good to Gideon to work his legs after being cramped up in a boat for so many days. His view was limited largely by Revel's back, who plodded on ahead of him as silent and somber as he had been since his confrontation with Kaiba in the forest some days' past. Whether his reticence was from anger or simple resignation, Gideon didn't know. But whatever sense Revel had of their mysterious pursuer had been lost the moment they left the trees of the mainland. If they were still being hunted, there was no way Revel could know it. That alone was probably enough to prod the Wordhavener into his irritable silence.

Several minutes later, they reached the final stair, and the fel'adum led them through a small but thickly fortified doorway at the base of the castle wall, which towered another hundred feet or more above them. The door opened to a windowless, firelit chamber constructed of dull grey brick walls and a high, vaulted ceiling. A few tapestries clung to the walls here and there. But after seeing the glorious tapestries of Wordhaven, these simplistic versions seemed a mockery of the art form. Whatever depictions they bore of the Kolventu's history were lost in the dim light. Beneath the cloths, a few benches were arranged on the floor in a seemingly haphazard fashion. The whole place smelled of mold.

"Sit," commanded one of the fel'adum. And so they did. "When our First returns with the First of Arelis," the fel'adum continued, "remain where you are and do not speak. If you do, I will slay you, beginning with the bondmaid."

The underlord cringed visibly at the pronouncement. But it was Aybel who spoke. "The First of Arelis is my father, fel'adum," she said. "Keep that in mind the next time you decide to threaten us."

"It was no threat, *my lady*," he replied scornfully. "And even if you are the daughter of Celedriel, then you are cursed as kreliz'adum. Your tribe would thank me for bleeding you dry."

At that moment, a thud echoed through the room, and the doors on the far end of the chamber creaked open. Kaiba appeared, followed by a man whom Gideon could only assume was Kaligorn.

He wore long robes of white draped over a full-length black tunic. His hair, too, was white, like all the Kolventu, but his was long, and his thick beard hung down from his jaw rather comically, like a bib. His hands were covered with rings of silver and gold, and across one shoulder hung a woven sash of black and silver thread embroidered on a field of white. The sash displayed a silver flame encircled by some kind of script, but they were in a language Gideon didn't know.

He was of a similar height to Kaiba, but far older—at least twenty years, perhaps more. The dark brown skin of his face and hands was riddled with the hard-earned creases of age and trials. His eyes, that same translucent brown of Aybel's, were wet with sorrow.

"Who dares to mock me at a time like this?" Though his words were threatening, his tone lacked the force to back it up. His voice quivered with weakness, perhaps of age.

Aybel stood quietly. With her head bowed, she whispered her response. "Do I address the First of Arelis?" she asked.

He moved to stand before her. Then, in a curious gesture, he leaned forward and sniffed her hair. "Do I address his daughter?" he replied.

"You do, sir. I return from my long journey to bring a warning of danger from beyond our shores."

He snorted and licked his lips. "You come too late! The reprobate has already come to slay the mother of Arelis." Tears welled in his eyes as he spoke.

"And the love of your heart," she whispered. "I am sorry for your loss. And mine."

The old man closed his eyes. "I have had three such loves in my life," he said. "Two were lost to me on the borders of Soulsbane—one of late, and one many years ago. Now only one remains."

"Three?" asked Aybel. "I have a sister?" She still did not look up.

He slapped her. "Do not mock my grief!" His voice trembled with the rage of sorrow.

Aybel bore the violence with uncharacteristic placidity. "I do not," she said calmly. "I am Aliel, First Daughter of Celedriel by Kaligorn. I have come home, father, at a dark and dangerous time."

With wrinkled fingers, he lifted her face by the chin. Her eyes met his, and they stared into one another for several tense moments. At last he said, "If you were my daughter, I would know you."

"Then look, father. And you will see that you do."

His hand dropped to his side. Shaking his head, he turned his back to her and stepped away. "My eyes are old. I no longer trust them. You are an interloper, come to take advantage of a simple man in his grief."

"I am not," said Aybel imploringly. "Look in your heart, father. You will see the truth."

"Do not speak to me of heart! What does the heart have to do with truth?" asked Kaligorn harshly. "It is the mind that guides our way. It is the mind that empowers a ruler to lead. A ruler cannot be swayed by the trifles of the heart."

"But faith is of the heart, father. A ruler who deadens his heart has no true faith, neither in himself nor in his calling. How, then, can his people trust him?"

Slowly, Kaligorn turned to face her. "Your voice sounds like hers."

Aybel's gaze fell to the floor. "I can barely remember it."

"Tell me true," he said. "Are you my daughter, Aliel?"

"I am."

Gently, quietly, he reached up and brushed his withered hand across the short-cropped whiteness of her hair. He sniffed it again, then let his hand drop. "Leave us!" he commanded.

Kaiba protested. "They are my tribe's to ward, Kaligorn," he said. "I will not leave them alone with you unguarded."

Kaligorn turned. "To discern the truth of her claims, I must ask her questions that you cannot hear! Nor your fel'adum. Every tribe has its secrets, Kaiba. You may not hear ours. Please, leave us."

"What if they attempt to harm you, or to flee?"

"I am too old to care for my own safety anymore. And as for fleeing, where will they go?" retorted Kaligorn. "The boats in which you came are locked away by now, yes? And you have no doubt set guards at the door. They aren't going anywhere."

"I will take their weapons, at least," said Kaiba.

"They hardly need them to slay me if they wanted," Kaligorn said in exasperation. "Just leave, will you? I will summon you shortly."

Kaiba bristled visibly at Kaligorn's tone. But he held his tongue. With a nod to his fel'adum, they opened the door and left.

As soon as the door thudded closed, the old man visibly slumped, and rubbed his arms through his robes. "Sit down," he said. "I'm too tired to be standing so long in this drafty place." Aybel complied. Kaligorn took the bench across from her. His eyes looked profoundly sad.

"Why have you come back?" he asked.

"You believe it is me, then, father?" she asked.

"Yes." His voice sounded pained. "Why have you come back?"

Aybel took in a long breath. Her sorrowful eyes darted across the floor, as if she were sifting through the possibilities of what she might say. "The evil that fell upon Arelis has not yet passed," she said finally. "The reprobate may now be here. The shal'adum of all the tribes are in great danger."

"Perhaps the reprobate sits with us now—here in this room," he scoffed.

Abyel folded her hands gently upon her lap. "These are my friends. You have no enemies here."

He snorted. "I have enemies everywhere! They are mad for power, these shal'adum. Not one of them is truly grieved to see my sweet Celedriel fall—though she gave her life to save their borders! It has always been that way with Arelis. We face the southern darkness spear to Word, while they rest easy in their feathered hammocks. Now all they want is to slice up our stake-hold—and me along with it!"

"What happened. . .to Mother?"

Instantly, Kaligorn's eyes fell closed at the memory. "You do not want to know that," he said. "No one should have to know such a horror."

"Who did it?"

"Who—or what?" he muttered. "No one leaves Soulsbane once they step through the dark veil of its limbs. But she did. Stepped out of the forest like it was her longtime home."

"She?" asked Aybel. "You mean Mother?"

"No!" he exclaimed. "Celedriel was no fool. She never came within a league of that cursed forest if she could help it. No. The reprobate—the crazed Lord of Phallenar. She's the one I speak of." He sighed as if his words were weights he could barely lift.

Aybel looked at Revel, who quickly shook his head. "Our pursuer is a man, Aliel," he said. "I know it as I know my own breath."

She mused a moment. "Then perhaps there are two," she said.

Slowly, Kaligorn rose to his feet. His hands were shaking. "There is no time for this!" he exclaimed, his voice suddenly tremulous again. "Your presence changes everything. I must think! I must think!" He shuffled back and forth across the floor licking his lips, his hand nervously stroking his bib-like beard. "Celedriel, help me!" he cried. "What should I do?"

Aybel stood. "What is the problem, father?"

"Haven't you been listening, girl? They want to turn Arelis into a ward of the tribes. It's just a veiled way of saying they want to unmake the tribe and portion it out like a carcass for them to feast upon."

"But Celedriel has another daughter!" said Aybel.

"Alielis, yes," muttered Kaligorn. "And a son as well—my Tyragorn— for what it's worth. But they are both too young to rule."

"Yet you are Celedriel's First!" exclaimed Aybel. "You stand as ruler in her place until her daughter comes of age."

Kaligorn nodded. "So it is written. But the shal'adum think me unfit for the task. And none of Celedriel's other bondmates carry enough status in the tribe to take the feathered shawl. I always was her favorite, you know, though why I could never fathom."

"They cannot remove you from your place, father," said Aybel. "Each tribe is its own to rule."

"No, they cannot," he agreed. "But they can declare war on me—and take my tribe by force."

"Not if you defend it!" Aybel's voice grew angrier with each exchange. "Arelis has always been strong. Is it not still so?"

Kaligorn nodded. "The tribe is strong, daughter. Your mother saw to that. But I, on the other hand...I have seen too much bloodshed for one lifetime."

"What are you saying?" exclaimed Aybel. "You *can* fight back, but will not? You would rather just let them decimate the tribe?"

Kaligorn nodded pensively for a moment, then said, "Perhaps there is another way, now that you are here."

Immediately, Aybel stepped back. She shook her head. "I am kre-liz'adum, father. I left our borders years ago without my mother's blessing, or yours. I have no place among the shal'adum. They would likely rather slay me than even look upon my face."

"What if you were taken?" he mused aloud. "Tyrenon—your renegade brother. What if he took you against your will?"

"But he didn't!"

"They might listen to you then. They might lift the curse. You could take your mother's place as shal'adum of Ki'Arelis."

"No, father. I am not made to rule a tribe."

"Who are you say what you were made for?" snapped Kaligorn. "You are the First Daughter of Celedriel, heir of the shal'adum of our tribe. Do not tell me you were not made to fill that role!"

"But Tyrenon did not take me against my will."

"Every tribe has its secrets, daughter," said Kaligorn. "What's one more? Especially if it can save the tribe from being lost." He took a step toward her and once again brushed his hand against her face. "Consider what I am asking, daughter," he said. "Perhaps you have come back to us at just such a time as you are most needed. Perhaps the Giver still has a thread of mercy for us after all."

She seemed to melt at his touch. But her voice remained firm. "You will surely hate me for telling you this, father. But I must, because of what you ask of me. I no longer believe in the way of the Kolventu. I have forsaken the Ancient Pact, for I have found a different path. I have joined with a new tribe now. These before you are some of its members." She gestured toward Revel and Gideon.

"What are you saying?" asked Kaligorn incredulously. "Have you changed your blood? Do you claim you are no longer my progeny?"

"Your daughter I am still, but—"

"Then you are yet Kolventu, whatever tribe you traffic with. There is no undoing what has been done, you know that. The Endless Age is less than a memory; its time is passed. And we haven't time for this foolishness!"

She wrapped his hand in hers. "I cannot lead others to follow a way I no longer believe, father."

Kaligorn licked his lips, and withdrew his hand from her grasp. Turning away from her, he said, "What do I care what you believe?" he asked quietly. "What does anyone care? You are Kolventu—and Celedriel's First Daughter. Your path is set. Your beliefs cannot change who you are."

"Yes they can, father," she said firmly. "They have changed me. They cannot help but change me, for they are rooted in truth greater than any tribe."

His eyes softened. "Your words sound almost hopeful" he mused. "Tell me, can this truth of yours take away the grief of a weak old man?"

She laid a hand on his shoulder. Her eyes teared as she spoke. "More than that. It can transform your sorrow into strength."

Kaligorn wept. As if by reflex, he reached out and clung to Aybel with a fierceness that belied the fragility of his aged limbs. Aybel returned the embrace, but Gideon couldn't see whether she was crying too. After a few moments, Kaligorn gently pushed her away and bowed his head. "Perhaps you are right, Aliel," he said. "Perhaps there is yet a small hope—even for a man as lost in bitterness as I." He looked up at her. "Forgive me, daughter. I am trying to thrust on your shoulders a weight that is mine alone to bear." He passed a withered hand across his eyes, and took in a shallow breath. "I will do what I can to help you," he said. "Whatever is within my power, while it is yet mine to wield." He straightened. "I am still the First of Ki'Arelis, am I not? Tell me what you need."

12

KIKI

In my training as an underlord in Phallenar, I had of course been taught about the Kolventu. I knew something of their government, their culture and traditions, and the peculiar social customs of their matriarchal tribes. But none of that prepared me for the reality I encountered on that day I appeared before the summit of the shal'adum on the Isle of Edor. In breadth of experience and the palpable weight of human cunning, the shal'adum were every bit the equals of the Council Lords in Phallenar. That was my first surprise. The second was this—that they, too, were brimming with arrogance, and just as blind as any lord of Sa'lei I had ever known.

This latter revelation created a problem for me. For I had always blamed the evil taint of Sa'lei for the corruption of my parents' hearts. But here the corruption lived as well, in a land where Sa'lei was forbidden. I began to wonder if Sa'lei was not actually the source of corruption and destruction in the world, but rather merely its tool. That at least would explain how evil could reside in the hearts of these shal'adum, who did not speak Sa'lei. But if that were true, what were the implications for Dei'lo? Is the Tongue of Life the source of true, holy power, or merely its conduit? And if its conduit—where, then, does the true power reside?

—The Kyrinthan Journals, Musings, Chapter 13, Verses 73-82

The words of Aybel's father had been sweet toward the end—earnest and compassionate, almost fatherly in their zeal. But when they dropped Gideon in his spartan "guest quarters" some time later, the old man still ordered a guard be posted at the door. No food had been brought to him, and no water either, though Kaligorn must have known none of them had had anything to eat or drink since before dawn. When Gideon finally asked the feathered guard about getting something for him, the man remained as motionless and silent as a rock.

He laid on a small wood-framed cot, his legs loosely covered in a moth-eaten blanket, and his staff resting warmly across his ribs. Whatever daylight that had crept into the dusky chamber through ventilation shafts above had faded hours before. But Gideon couldn't sleep. Or rather, he didn't want to sleep. He was too busy worrying.

It began as a vague feeling in his gut—a familiar sensation, one he'd known for years, and nurtured as an essential survival skill in his former life of secret rages and suppressed memories. He'd nearly forgotten how it felt—that subtle sense of someone pretending to be something they weren't, of them trying to manipulate you toward their own ends.

But this is Aybel's father! Her long-lost dad! Why would he want to deceive her? You're probably just being over-protective.

Still, why had he placed them all in separate chambers? And why post fel'adum at the doors? If they were really guests and not prisoners, as Kaligorn had claimed at the end, why did Gideon still get the feeling he was a captive?

Aybel's request of Kaligorn had been fairly simple, though certainly bold—a two-week supply of food and water, and a seaworthy boat capable of carrying the supplies back to the Endurant, which she hoped was still waiting for them in the waters beyond Ki'Arelis' shores. In addition, she asked for safe passage for Maywin and herself to the Kolventu's western borders. She did not explain why she and the underlord wished to go a different direction from the rest, and, to his credit, Kaligorn didn't ask.

Nothing she asked for seemed to shock Kaligorn in the least. He said he would take Aybel's request to the shal'adum, and pass along her warning that a reprobate lord may still be in their midst. As for her lineage, Kaligorn would say nothing unless he were asked, and then would say only that Aybel was a member of his tribe on a special mission sanctioned by Celedriel years before, and that as such, she and her party enjoyed Ki'Arelis' full protection and endorsement. The shal'adum would likely not press him further on the matter, as none of them wished to set a precedent for exposing tribal secrets to competing shal'adum. Each tribe had plenty of secrets of its own that it didn't want exposed.

The only wild card in all this was Kaiba. Aybel had told him her true name, and even though he clearly doubted the veracity of her claim, if the First decided to pass that information on to his shal'adum, Melindra, there could be trouble.

Kaligorn didn't say when he would come back for them. Only that he would return when a decision was made. Still, something about his whole demeanor didn't seem—

"I could slay you at any time I choose."

The voice was guttural and wet, and thick with loathing. Gideon tried to lift his head to see who was speaking, but he found he could not move. The staff instantly grew hot upon his chest.

"Who's there?" Gideon demanded.

"I cannot fathom why he wants you alive," the voice continued. "To follow you? Where? As far as I can see, you haven't the slightest notion where you're going. All you seem to be good at is getting yourself captured and being led around by the nose. By savages, no less." The shadow of a man loomed into view.

"Guard!" yelled Gideon. "There's someone in here!"

"The fel'adum cannot hear you, *Waymaker*." He spat out the title with vain disgust. "Can't you sense the Wording of *Sa'lei*?"

The staff was pulsing hotly now. "Who are you? What do you want?"

"What do I want?" the voice chuckled darkly. "Yes, what I *want*. Now that would take some time to answer. But you are hardly intelligent enough to comprehend it."

"Try me," Gideon replied. He strained against his unseen bonds. If he could just touch his staff...

"What I do not know is what the High Lord wants," said the voice. "I confess, his tactics elude me. I mean, look at you. You are nothing, a fleeting puff of smoke from an ember of rebellion that will soon fade from memory. But my fire is growing...will grow...until it scorches the sky itself— and you, when the time comes."

"Who are you? Why are you following us?"

"What is it he wants with you, Waymaker?" The voice turned sharp and grating, like a knife scraping stone. "Why not just slay you and be done with it?"

A flash of memory came to Gideon—something the underlord had said about the Council Lord she suspected was on their trail. "Maybe he's looking to replace you," offered Gideon. "Maybe he's not as pleased with you as you believe."

The invisible bonds tightened, and Gideon began to choke. "Mock me again," said the voice, "and I will end your life now."

Gideon tried to say something in reply, but the bonds choked his voice to a gurgle.

"I'll ask you once more...and only once. What does the High Lord want from you?"

The bonds relaxed slightly—enough for Gideon to speak. "I don't know," rasped Gideon. "Why don't you ask him?"

"He won't tell me," the voice replied, suddenly thoughtful. "He's always been that way. Even after all these years together."

"I guess he doesn't trust you," said Gideon. "Does he even know you're here, talking with me now?"

"You are a pathetic fool!" spat the voice. "It is a test, you see. He wants me to prove myself, show him that I am worthy of my calling as his successor."

"Really," said Gideon. "How's that working out for you?"

The voice chuckled darkly. "Oh, such bravado! The tiny mouse has the roar of a lion. Still...there's an energy about you. Yes. It's here, the infamous staff." A shadowed hand emerged from the dark slowly reaching for the staff that rested on Gideon's chest. "There's something unfamiliar about it." The hand began to tremble, as if the man was having to strain to move it closer. "What's this? It resists me!" He sounded almost amused at the thought.

Suddenly, sounds of heavy footfalls echoed down the halls outside, accompanied by the low rumble of voices. Instantly, the bonds holding Gideon to the bed dissipated, and by sheer instinct he snatched the staff high in his hand and bounded to his feet.

But the heat in the staff had fled.

The man was gone.

The chamber door creaked open to reveal four fel'adum. Gideon noticed they bore on their loin clothes the same insignia he had seen on

Kaligorn's robes—a silver flame encircled by some foreign script. "Come," one of them said, "the shal'adum require your presence."

It seemed pointless to mention the visitation from the Council Lord. The fel'adum would not believe him, and even if they did, they could hardly do anything about it. So he simply nodded and followed them out of the chamber. Wherever they were headed, he guessed Aybel and Revel would be there as well. Perhaps he would have a chance to tell them what had happened.

They led him through a series of narrow halls, each one more dank and cave-like than the last, until they finally arrived at a set of massive wooden doors set beneath an arch of dull grey stone. Upon their approach, the doors swung wide, revealing an expansive chamber within. It was the first sizeable room Gideon had seen since entering the castle, and the first one with a decent amount of light.

Revel was there, along with the underlord in her tattered green gown. They watched his approach, but offered no gesture of recognition or greeting. The chamber itself was blockish and tall, with rows of wooden benches filling most of the space, and a simple stage of stone set at one end. The mood of the place felt somber and suspicious, despite the warmth of dozens of torches burning along the walls. The air was heavy with must and oily smoke.

Upon the stage sat nine women in simple chairs, their arms folded stiffly across their laps. They were of various ages and sizes, but all were dressed in the same simple black robes. No doubt, the shal'adum. An empty chair sat at one end.

"Bring in the trespasser." The voice came from one of the women.

Gideon was quickly prodded forward to join Revel and the underlord, who stood off to one side near the stage. A moment later, Aybel was ushered through the doors by six fel'adum. They, too, bore the emblem of the silver flame. But Kaligorn was not with them.

She looked tired. Her hands, which usually carried such grace in their movements, jittered awkwardly at her sides. She glanced at Gideon as she came forward, but only for a second. Her eyes seemed most interested in the row of faces on the stage before her, scanning them like a cat cornered by a pack of rabid wolves.

They led to a spot a few feet shy of the stage, and left her there.

"You are Aliel, the First Daughter of Celedriel," one of women declared.

Kaiba told them!

"Where is the First of Arelis?" demanded Aybel. "Where is the head of my tribe? You have no right to question me in his absence!"

"You are kreliz'adum," replied a second woman. "It is you who have no rights before this summit!"

"With all respect to Shal'adum Melindra," said Aybel, nodding to one of the older women on the stage, "her First has no right to place a name on me. Kaiba is not of my tribe, and does not know me."

"Who speaks of Kaiba?" replied the older woman defensively. "My First has nothing to do with these proceedings. We did not learn your name from him."

"Who, then, lays this name upon me?" demanded Aybel. "The First of Arelis will speak for me. Ask, and he will tell you I am on a mission for my tribe—a long journey commissioned by Shal'adum Celedriel herself many years ago. Why is he not here?" She sounded defiant, but there was a hint of desperation in her voice.

"I have heard enough," said one of the women blandly. "If she had owned her name, perhaps there would have been hope. But her mind has become clouded by deception. She tries to deceive us even now."

"You have brought down a double portion of disgrace on your mother's head, and on your tribe," snapped a rotund woman on the end. "If Celedriel were here, she would condemn you herself!"

The words clearly stung Aybel to the heart. Despite her defiant stance, tears welled in her eyes. "You do not understand," she said. "There is an enemy among us, but it is not me. You are all in danger."

"See how she worms around her shame," declared on of the younger women. "She tries to throw the scent off her trail with talk of danger from another. Of whom do you speak, kreliz'adum? Is it your father you wish to shame now? Is it one of these interlopers you have brought unwanted to our shores?" The woman's eyes flashed down the line of matriarchs. "What further proof do we need of her guilt?"

The older woman—Melindra, if Gideon's guess was right—stood and glided to the lip of the stage. She looked down her nose at Aybel dubiously as if inspecting a questionable piece of meat. "I want to hear her say it," she said. "It is the least we can do for the memory of her mother." She sniffed the air in front of her, as if sampling Aybel's scent to verify her identity.

"Melindra, please..." said Aybel.

"I knew you as a child," said Melindra. "You were spirited then, I recall. Headstrong. But your mother believed such traits would serve you well when you took her place in the Ki. How it would sadden her to see what you've become. It is better that she is dead than to be forced to deal with such a shame."

Suddenly, a fire blazed afresh in Aybel's eyes. "I knew you as well, Shal'adum Melindra of Ki'Mahdwin. I know my mother had no great love for you, nor you for her. She told me that your dealings with my tribe were always two-faced! With one hand you pronounced a blessing on her house while the other stole the bread from off her table. Who are you to speak for my mother's heart?"

Melindra raised her eyebrows in mock surprise. "You admit it, then? You are her daughter?"

Aybel lifted her gaze to meet Melindra's. The fire in her eyes forced the shal'adum to step back a pace. "I am Aliel of the tribe Arelis," she said hotly. "First Daughter of Celedriel by Kaligorn, and heir to the shal'adum of my tribe. And I have returned to the Kolventu to tell you that your lives are all in danger. The reprobate lords that killed my mother have tracked my steps since I first laid foot on the Hinterland's shores. They have followed me here, and are likely listening to your prattle even now. I am no danger to you, but they have the power to slay you all with a single Word!"

"The Council Lords have not dared to cross our borders in two thousand years!" declared one of the women. "The Ancient Pact keeps us free from the taint of their influence, and their Words. You speak madness to save your own hide!"

"Then how did my mother die, Shal'adum Shamel?" Aybel cried. "If not by a Council Lord, then how?"

"We believe it was not a lord," said the woman. "It was likely one of their minions. A soldier, perhaps, gone mad from the Words."

"I tell you true, these new lords know nothing of the Pact," said Aybel. "While you've been sealed away in these Hinterlands these two millennia, clinging to your tribal arrogance and your reason like children afraid to grow up, the world beyond your shores has plummeted into a darkness greater than you can imagine. The Pact is forgotten! And you have little hope of surviving this age unless you will lay down your pettiness and listen to me. I am not your enemy! Ask my father! He will tell you."

Melindra sighed. "Your father, yes." She wandered idly passed her chair to the rear of the stage. "Kaligorn, have you been listening to this?"

"I have." The First of Ki'Arelis emerged from a narrow door at the rear of the stage, wearing the same black robes as the shal'adum. His face reflected a man in torment. But his voice had lost the shakiness of his earlier encounter with Aybel. "I have heard it all."

"What is your decision, then, First of Arelis?" asked Melindra. "What should we do with this renegade daughter of your house?"

He looked down at his hands. They were shriveled and old; all but dead. "She...she should be slain," he said. "For the sake of the tribe, and my Celedriel's memory." Slowly, he looked down at Aybel, but it was as though he didn't see her at all.

"So be it," said Melindra. "The summit will leave it to you to plan the particulars." Kaligorn nodded absently. "But it must be done before we leave this isle. That is the wish of the shal'adum. Is that understood?"

"Yes," said Kaligorn. "So be it."

"Remove her," said Melindra. The fel'adum immediately stepped forward to drag Aybel away.

"Wait a minute!" exclaimed Gideon. "Where are you taking her?"

"Don't fret, bondman," said Melindra. "You, too, will share in her fate."

Gideon lifted his staff in defiance and marched toward the stage. "You idiots!" Gideon yelled. "She's trying to help you, can't you see that? Are you blind?"

"You dare raise a weapon toward the shal'adum?" asked Melindra. "And in our own court?"

"Sojourner, no!" Aybel yelled, her eyes pleading. "Lower your staff. Do nothing."

But the deed had already been done. Fel'adum began to descend on Gideon like vultures swarming on a carcass. Instinctively, he lifted his staff high overhead and spun it defensively, simultaneously rotating his body in the fashion Revel had taught him. The action would hold back the fel'adum for only a few seconds, but it was time enough for Gideon to choose his first mark. With a seamless sweep of his arm, he let the staff flow down to strike one of the guards at the knee. There was a pop, and the man collapsed to the floor like a puppet whose strings were cut. With no loss in momentum, he swung the staff high to resume the spin, and chose another soldier to strike down. The effort was flowing, powerful, and it filled Gideon with a heady exhilaration he had never experienced. But in the back of his mind, he wondered why the staff was not warm.

Suddenly, Revel slipped into the throng. In a single move that defied description, he gingerly snatched the staff out of Gideon's hands and placed it submissively on the floor. Raising his palms in a sign of surrender, he said to the guards, "Be at peace, fel'adum, and do no harm. The bondman has forgotten himself in his grief. He did not hear the lady's command. Forgive him, please. Forgive us all. We will go with you peacefully."

"Revel, what are you doing?" asked Gideon angrily. "We can't let them do this to her!"

With a steely grip, Revel seized Gideon by the arm. But he did not answer him. Instead, he turned to the shal'adum. "Call off your guards," he commanded loudly. "We wish no dishonor on this summit, or our lady's name."

Melindra glared down at them. The outrage in her eyes was palpable. The fel'adum watched her too, waiting for the nod that would release them to kill. After a moment, she spoke. "It seems, Aliel, that you have acquired at least one bondman with the sense of a man. But even if he saved your lives today, it is only for a short while. Your end is sealed. Take them out of our sight!"

The fel'adum obeyed. Revel released Gideon, and began to gently pat him on the arm he had gripped. But Gideon angrily knocked it away. "Get your hand off me!" he snapped. He couldn't understand why Revel had intervened. If they would only use the Words, they could walk out of this place without a man or woman left standing to oppose them. They could be free to gather the supplies they needed and return to the Endurant in peace! Every day they delayed lessened the chance that Quigly would still be there waiting for them. Didn't they realize that? Why did they still insist on holding their tongues? Surely they could see by now that there was no other way out!

As the fel'adum dragged him roughly from the chamber, Gideon called to Aybel, trying to get her attention. But she did not acknowledge him, or even turn her head. He had to find a way to tell her about the Council Lord.

He had to tell her, because he believed that would convince her. He was sure of it. Whatever her reason for withholding *Dei'lo*, knowing *he* was here would change her mind. It had to.

Once they left the chamber, the fel'adum dragged them along a narrow corridor, then down several flights of stairs. The air grew more dank and laden with moisture. The smell of seawater and stale fish permeated the walls. And there was little light.

Their weapons had been taken, carried off to some other place by other fel'adum. But Gideon still thought they might have a fighting chance to break away. There were only seven of them. He knew Aybel and Revel could take down at least two apiece—*far more if they would use the Words!*—and he felt angry enough to believe he could take on that many as well, and maybe a third with the underlord's help. But they would not look at him. They seemed resigned to let the story unfold however it would.

Even if it means we die?!

A few moments later, they arrived at a holding cell, though it obviously hadn't been used in years. The bars were coated with a greenish slime. Even in places where the iron still showed, it was plagued with rust. The door creaked in protest as the fel'adum swung it wide. They tossed the four of them inside, and slammed the door until it clicked. And then left.

Gideon could hardly hold his tongue long enough for the footfalls of the guards to fade. "What just happened in there, Aybel?" he said at last. "Why are you allowing this?"

But it was Revel who spoke. "You disgraced Aliel in front of her people, sojourner!" he said angrily. "You acted impetuously. Have you learned nothing?"

"Me?" snapped Gideon. "*I* acted impetuously?" He couldn't believe what he was hearing. "Have you both gone mad? They're going to kill us unless we do something!"

Revel didn't respond.

"Aybel," Gideon implored, "help me out here. What is going on? Why won't you guys use the Words? We have to get out of here, you know!"

Suddenly, the underlord slapped him on the arm. "Have some decency, would you?" she said. "Aybel was just betrayed by her father, condemned to death by his own word in the presence of all the shal'adum. Or did you miss that whole event?"

"I heard it," argued Gideon. But really, he hadn't. In the anger of that moment, he never thought to consider the impact Kaligorn's words would have on Aybel. He felt a hot wave of shame rush over his cheeks.

"Be silent, both of you," said Aybel. Her voice sounded tired, but there was still steel in her tone. "I must think."

Gently, Revel reached out and stroked her arm. "I am sorry, Aliel," he said. "But perhaps there is a reason your father acted as he did. Perhaps his appeal to the shal'adum failed, and now he means to rescue us in secret."

But Aybel only shook her head. "Aliel is dead." Angrily, she wiped the tears from her eyes. "She died a long time ago. What is it to me what my father thinks of her? He does not know me now."

"He may yet prove true," said Revel.

She looked down. "Do you not see, Revel?" Her face looked bland, expressionless. "He has struck a deal with the shal'adum. And I am the price. I am betrayed."

"What sort of deal?" asked the underlord.

"It doesn't matter!" Gideon broke in. "The point is, if Kaligorn has betrayed us, then there's no reason for us to hold anything back anymore." He leaned toward Aybel. "Let's blow this joint! Get back to the Endurant." *If it's even still there.*

"I will not use the Words against my own people," said Aybel softly.

Gideon rolled his eyes and sighed heavily. "Then use them to protect your people!" he exclaimed. "That Council Lord who's been following us is here now, Aybel! He came to my cell not an hour ago. The longer we stay here, the greater the risk to your people."

"Stevron came to *you?*" asked Kyrintha in shock. "What did he say?"

"Silence!" whispered Revel suddenly. "Someone approaches."

There were at least two of them, but their footfalls were at once too quick and too noisy to be fel'adum. A few moments later, they emerged out of the darkness and stood in the dim light just beyond the bars.

They were children. The older one, a girl, locked her gaze on Aybel.

"I understand that you are my sister," said the girl. "I thought we should be properly introduced, so that I can determine whether you will be allowed to live."

13

WORDHAVEN

What Wordhaven attempted in those days was unprecedented. Since the founding of the New Age millennia ago, no human soul had ever been permitted to learn the more powerful Words of Life without first enduring extensive tests and training of the heart, mind and body. Dei'lo, after all, is a language of indescribable power, capable not only of creating new life but also destroying life that already is. One does not place a weapon of such magnitude in the hands of any soundenor on a whim, no matter how earnest his motives may be. And yet that is precisely what the Remnant leaders had chosen to do. Their fear of attack from Phallenar seduced them to forget one of the core tenets of the Tongue: That to speak it well requires not only pure motive, but also great wisdom of heart—a quality that cannot be fostered quickly, or without significant personal cost.

—The Kyrinthan Journals, Chronicles, Chapter 17, Verses 208-211

Paladin, here is the manifest you requested."

A small scroll, tightly bound, appeared before his eyes. He took it without missing a stride. "Which hold?" he asked.

"Outer Hall North," the voice replied.

Without thinking, he handed the scroll to Kair, who walked beside him. She already held four similar scrolls bundled under one arm. "What of the other holds? Are the supplies coming in on schedule?"

"Yes, Paladin," said the voice, whom Ajel now noticed belonged to one of the new recruits. *What was her name? Rachel?* "With the Giver's help," she continued, "we expect all nine holds to be at full capacity before the first major snow."

Ajel frowned slightly. "It's snowing now," he said.

She flushed with embarrassment. "Yes, Paladin," she said. And in his thoughts, he heard, *Rachel conMeredith, Paladin, of Makroth sounden.* She smiled faintly, and walked away.

Ajel closed his eyes in frustration. The voices were getting to be too much. Too many new minds within the Stand, all chattering at once, seemingly without end. He was having trouble separating them out from his own musings, which in recent weeks had taken on a heavy dissonance of their own. There was such a thing as too much communion, he decided. And some of his thoughts of late, particularly the darker ones, were best kept to himself.

He glanced briefly at Kair as they continued their march down the crowded atrium of the Outer Hall. Her gaze remained fixed on the shadowless white marble floors. If she was listening to his thoughts, she gave no indication. In truth, she had become the one person in the Stand that Ajel could tolerate being around for any length of time. Her thoughts were a placid lake—calm and, for the most part, silent. At first the reticence of her heart had been a source of concern for him, thinking it a sign of some dark trauma related to her witnessing his uncle's murder at the hands of Council Lord Lysteria Asher-Baal. But now he found her quiet mind refreshing. Her stillness gave his own heart room to breath...at least a little.

Sifting through the bustling maze of bodies, they made their way to the main antechamber of the Stand. Donovan would be expecting him on the training fields shortly to observe the progress of the newest recruits under his charge. It had become a part of Ajel's weekly routine, along with a hundred other new responsibilities that demanded his attention as Paladin, not to mention the long hours of private study and practice of the Book of *Dei'lo*, which he did in the predawn hours each morning without fail. Such a frenetic pace placed a relentless drain on his soul. But, slowly, he was learning to master it, keeping his heart centered and still regardless of what his mind and body was required to focus on from hour to hour. It was the only way to maintain a sense of himself in the onslaught of his new role, and stave off another humiliating collapse like the one that came over him in the Servant Hall a few weeks before.

As they walked past the ancient statue of the Pearl and through the main doors beyond, he unconsciously whispered to himself the Words to strengthen his body and center his thoughts. That, too, had become a part of his daily practice. He couldn't afford to let his weakness get the better of him again.

The Remnant council had fretted over him relentlessly for several days after that regrettable event in the Servant Hall—especially Seer, who worried that his black out was due to some malevolent work of the *Sa'lei* lords in his mind. But it was merely exhaustion, pure and simple. The battle in Phallenar, the momentous loss of Paladin Sky, and the burden of his new role as Paladin's successor on the eve of war—all of these had taken their toll. Added to that was the conspicuous absence of his brother Revel, whose presence by his side had always lent him a added strength he could not seem to muster on his own. A part of him now regretted sending Revel with the sojourner Gideon Dawning, though he still believed it was the best decision for all concerned. Still, perhaps there was a way to reforge that connection with his distant brother. If not through the new Words he was learning, then perhaps through the gateways that now lay open throughout the Stand. He would have to explore that possibility, when there was time.

As he and Kair made their way across the courtyards just south of the Stand, he noticed with relief that the snow had stopped. The air was crisp, but not yet so cold as to be uncomfortable. The thin blanket of white upon the meadows would not cling for long, especially here in the valley where the abundance of thermal vents continually warmed the earth and stone throughout the winter months. But they could not keep the snows from clinging to the mountains beyond the gold and silver gates. Winter was coming, and once it arrived, the Sacred Path would be closed until Spring. Time was short.

As they neared the training fields, Donovan naturally noticed their approach, and moved to greet them. "I see you decided to walk," he said to Ajel, quickly nodding a greeting to Kair.

"I thought it would do me good," Ajel replied. He had been using the Words to get around too often of late. For some reason, it seemed an abuse of the power.

"You are looking better," said Donovan. "I am pleased to see it."

"Thank you, kinsman," Ajel replied. "How fair our new soldiers?"

Donovan grunted in frustration. "See for yourself." He gestured behind him. "Their thoughts are unbalanced, as are their bodies. It is no easy work turning farmers and craftsfolk into warriors."

"Just so," agreed Ajel, smiling. "But they could not hope for a more capable teacher."

Donovan took the compliment without comment, and led Ajel and Kair toward the formation of students gathered on the field before them. They numbered nearly two hundred, perhaps a little more. *Far too few*, worried Ajel silently. But he was careful to keep the thought shielded from the others. The recruits wore the fighting garb of Wordhaven, and each held a focus staff before them in a standard defensive stance. The Keeper, Brasen Stoneguard, stood before them, barking out commands, guiding them through the various movements and Words of the Warrior's Way. It was clear the postures were as foreign and unwieldy to their bodies as the Words were to their hearts. And yet, through the mystic bonds that Wordhaven allowed, Ajel could sense a deeper reality as well. Their hearts were willing—stout and determined to stay the course. That, he reminded himself, was the most important element of all.

"They will master the Way in time," he said to Donovan. "Their hearts are true."

"In time, perhaps," agreed Donovan. "But time is not our ally in this battle."

Ajel laughed lightly. "I am learning a few things about time myself, my friend," he said.

Donovan arched an eyebrow his direction. "Indeed?"

"It is a maleable reality," said Ajel, "one that we are free to hold in any way we wish. I am finding it is best to engage with time in a way that serves your heart on the path you are called to walk. If you don't, you will quickly find yourself its slave."

Donovan stood silent a moment, as if pondering Ajel's words. Then he said, "I do not understand, kinsman. Time is time. There is no making it more or less than what it is."

Ajel laid his hand on Donovan's shoulder. "There is time enough for what is needed. Even now."

Donovan brushed a calloused hand through his long nut brown hair. Despite the cool, it came out dampened with sweat. "I trust that you are right," he said. But he didn't sound convinced.

"Would you care for a drink, Paladin?"

Ajel turned to see a young woman holding out a cup of water. She was small and lovely, fair of skin, with long brown hair that matched her dark, brooding eyes. She bowed her head slightly as she held the cup aloft. Her gaze shifted nervously as if she were afraid to look at Ajel straight on.

"Greetings," said Ajel. "I don't believe we've met." He wondered why he did not sense her presence earlier.

"I am called Sarla Ferin," said the young woman nervously. "Thank you for welcoming me to Wordhaven."

"She arrived with one of the groups from Makroth sounden," said Donovan by way of explanation. "Though she is not of Makroth herself."

Ajel noticed a faint tension in Donovan's heart. "Where do you hail from, Sarla?" he asked, accepting the cup of water from her hands.

She bowed her head even lower, so that her hair all but covered her face. "I am just a servant escaped from Phallenar, Paladin," she said. "The tracker Jessa found me on her return journey from Makroth. I am sure her kindness has saved my life."

Ajel watched her a moment. Her words were soft and humble, but her soul was a blank canvas.

She glanced up at him worriedly. "Have I offended, Paladin?"

Ajel quickly shot her a reassuring grin. "Not at all." Another pause, then, "Tell me Sarla, are you well?"

The question seemed to startle her at first, but she recovered quickly. "Actually, sir, my stomach has been somewhat troubled of late. It's merely a trifle." She smiled faintly. "Just the excitement of finding myself here, I suspect."

"Just so," said Ajel, still smiling. There was definitely something curious about this young woman. He pressed on. "I'm curious, Donovan," he said. "Why have you not invited Sarla to join in the training?"

"That's none of my doing," said Donovan bluntly. "It is her own wish."

Ajel looked surprised. "Indeed?"

Sarla's lip began to tremble noticeably. "It's just..." she hesitated. "I am but a servant, Paladin," she said shakily. "It is all I have ever known. These matters," she glanced toward the soldiers in the training field, "the Words, they are too grand for me. I wish only to serve in the way that…suits my station. Now please, excuse me. There are others who require water." She quickly gathered up the water bag at her feet, and scurried off toward the soldiers as timidly as a frightened mouse, glancing back at him several times as she fled.

"She is very closed, and fearful," commented Ajel as the young woman made her retreat.

"Just so," muttered Donovan gruffly. "Something in me does not trust her."

Ajel laughed. "I would expect nothing less from you, my friend." Still, something in his own heart agreed with Donovan's suspicions. "Tell me, what do you sense?"

Donovan's brow furrowed as he shook his head. "I cannot say, exactly. She seems…indistinct to me somehow, as though she were merely an illusion of my own mind. And yet a part of me finds her familiar, as though I should know her, but cannot recall where or how."

"She is too young for you to have known her in Phallenar," said Ajel. "And she was a servant there in any case."

"True," Donovan agreed. "But I cannot shake it. Her soul is disturbed, that much is clear. She has remained closed since she first set foot within the gates. She is often sick, and keeps to herself most of the time. And as you heard, she has stubbornly refused to study *Dei'lo*, insisting that she is not worthy of it. Seer put her to work in the kitchens, and spends time with her when she is able."

"Seer has approved her, then?"

Donovan sighed, "Yes," he said. "She had declared her a simple bond-maid from Phallenar. Nothing more."

Ajel nodded thoughtfully. "There was another stranger who came through those gates not that long ago, a man with a troubled soul much like hers." *And our arrogance nearly destroyed him, and Seer as well.* He patted Donovan on the shoulder. "Perhaps we should not be so quick to suspect her heart. Let us give her time to show herself to us."

"As you say, Paladin," responded Donovan. "But she should be watched, all the same."

"You are too quick to jump to judgment, Donovan," said Kair suddenly, and with more than a little edge. "If you are not careful, it will be your undoing." The two men turned. Ajel had forgotten Kair was with them. She always had a way of disappearing into the background when she wished it— a talent that on more than one occasion had led to her inclusion in conversations Ajel would have preferred kept private. "Even in Wordhaven, we cannot know what lies in someone's heart," she continued. "Not truly. Our time with Gideon Dawning has taught us that, at least."

"You now believe in the sojourner's heart?" Ajel was surprised to hear it. Kair had been raised as a member of the Songtrust in Songwill sounden, just as her father had been. That particular sect was renowned for its condemnation of the prophesied Kinsman Redeemer. He knew full well that Kair had wished Gideon Dawning dead on more than one occasion.

"He is not the Kinsman Redeemer," she replied. "You declared it yourself. I have no thought of him beyond that."

"I see," said Ajel. "Then you no longer condemn him."

"As I said, I have no thought of him."

"He now calls himself the Waymaker," added Donovan.

"That is unfortunate, but what of it?" Kair shrugged with obvious disdain. "The prophecies of the Waymaker are few and obscure. Even if he is what he claims, I think it is of little consequence in the story of the world. And I doubt he is in any case."

"If he is the Waymaker, then his role in these times may have more consequence than you suspect," countered Ajel. "Have you not read the passages in the Book of *Dei'lo* that speak of him?"

"There has not been time to study the Book, Paladin," she said sharply. But then, apparently realizing she was sounding harsh, she softened her tone. "Not as much as I would wish. My duties to you are more important." She smiled. And Ajel suddenly realized he had not seen her do that for a long time. "My point is simply that we should not judge the woman," Kair continued. "Perhaps she carries secrets in her soul she does not wish us to see. But that alone does give us cause to condemn her."

"As you condemned Gideon Dawning?" Donovan quipped.

Kair rounded on the big man without blinking an eye. "You speak to me of condemning Gideon Dawning!" she exclaimed angrily. "Who was it that concealed a blade within the folds of his tunic at Calmeron, Donovan? You believed him to be a guardian spy before you even learned his name!"

"Enough," said Ajel gently. "These are arguments for the past. Our focus is here, now. And on the winter to come." He looked up to the sky. The clouds of snow had passed. But though sun was now shining in the West, the force of it was weakening by the day. "Kair is right in this at least. We will give the young woman time, and anyone else among these recruits whose heart is closed from us. We will not make the same mistake twice."

He looked up at Donovan and smiled. "Your heart is true, Donovan," he said. "And your work is good. I know the soldiers will be ready when the time comes."

The big man seemed to soften a little, but he said nothing.

"Come, Kair," Ajel continued, turning his focus to her. "We have a little time before I meet with the council. I want to study the portals a while. They may provide a way for us to travel among the soundens even after winter comes." *And*, he added silently, *perhaps they will show me a way to reach my brother.*

As he walked away, he quietly poured the water from his cup upon the grass.

THE AXIS

He has made darkness his hiding place,
His canopy around him.
From the brightness before him
Passed his thick clouds of triumph and Words of fire.
The dark heavens thundered
At the utterance of his voice.
And the broken souls were laid bare at his rebuke.

—From the writings of the Prophet Shikinah, in the year S.C. 1600

H e what?"

"He has banned the convening of the Council. He didn't even tell me he was going to do it!" Lysteria looked haggard. She clung to Stevron's arm tiredly as they strolled along the balustrade on the upper levels of the Axis. "I am losing him, Stevron. I can feel it."

Lord Stevron sighed in frustration. He had just returned from yet another week of traipsing after the fool Gideon Dawning, and wanted nothing more than a warm bath, a soft bed, and several hours of undisturbed sleep. He was on his way to his private chambers when Lysteria accosted him in the walkway, latching onto him like a long lost son. "The High Lord makes many decisions without consulting any of the lords—even you, Lord

Lysteria," said Stevron. "Besides, canceling a meeting of the Axis is hardly an unprecedented act for any High Lord."

"You don't understand," she whispered. "He has halted all convenings of the Council—indefinitely!"

Now that *was* unusual. "What is his reason for this?" asked Stevron.

"How would I know?" she said, clearly exasperated. "He hardly speaks to me anymore."

Stevron shrugged. "The Council can overrule him if they wish," he said.

"Not without a majority vote," said Lysteria. "And he has seen to it that that cannot happen. A few days past, he summoned four of the most influential lords to his private chambers. Within a few hours, they were each on their way to different parts of the Inherited Lands."

"Who?" asked Stevron.

Lysteria frowned in distaste. "That witch Varia for one, and her dull-witted bondmate, Mattim. The other two were Lords Elise and Sed, I believe."

"He sent them beyond the Wall?" asked Stevron, surprised. "For what purpose?"

"He claims he commissioned them to search out Wordhaven's true location," she said. "He gave them barely enough time to pack a change of clothes. They travel in secret, with only a small detachment of their personal *mon'jalen* to accompany them. They hadn't been gone more than a day when Balaam announced that the Council was forbidden to meet again until he summoned us." She patted her grey-haired bun nervously. "I don't know what he's thinking. If he's thinking at all."

"But Balaam already knows Wordhaven's location," said Stevron. "He told me of the discovery himself!"

Lysteria nodded impatiently. "But now he tells the Council that he is not certain," she said, "and will not permit the guardians to march until the route is sure."

Lying to the Council Lords is a dangerous move, father, thought Stevron. *If you are found out...* "Where has he sent them?" he asked Lysteria.

She fluttered her hand dismissively. "Remote regions, I don't know. Agatharon, perhaps. Makroth. Anywhere far from civilized life, it seems."

Stevron stopped and rested his hands upon the balustrade. The city spread out before him like a blanket of brilliant white under the harsh light of the sun, dotted here and there by the greenery of gardens and trees. The people, small and insignificant, went about their mundane business as they always did, oblivious to the powers at work above their heads.

Those powers had dwindled in recent weeks, thanks to the Waymaker and his rebel following. First Sarlina, then later Fayerna and Bentel—all perished at the rebels' hands. More recently, in the caverns beneath the city, the Waymaker's power ripped the life out of Lords Vallera Kappan-Mati and old Baurejalin Sint. The Council had gone from thirteen to nine in a matter of weeks—it would have been eight if not for Stevron's raising. And now with four of the Lords gone from Phallenar, and Stevron himself wasting the bulk of his time following after the Waymaker on his quest to nowhere, only four Council Lords remained in the city. With the rebels in possession of the Book of *Dei'lo*, that seemed a foolish strategy at best.

Still, whatever Lysteria claimed, Stevron refused to believe that Balaam's reason was slipping. There must be a logic to his actions. But what was it?

"He's expecting you soon, isn't he?" She asked, releasing his arm at last.

Stevron nodded. "He summoned me, yes. But I mean to rest a while before I go to him. I have questions of my own to ask, and I doubt he will relinquish the answers easily. I need to be ready."

Unexpectedly, Lysteria nestled her body gently next to his. The feel of her motherly form so close to his repulsed him, but for the moment he resisted the urge to move away.

"What news of my daughter?" she asked softly, looking up into his eyes.

Does she mean to seduce me to gain news of Kyrintha? "The underlord is imprisoned by the shal'adum, along with the rest of her new friends," he said. "They are condemned to die before the week is done." He turned to her and smiled, deftly shifting his body away from hers in the process. "It seems you will have your wish after all, Lord Lysteria. The Waymaker will soon be dead."

To his surprise, however, she was visibly agitated by the news. "They mean to slay my daughter?" she whispered harshly. "But how?"

Stevron shrugged. "What does it matter? Drowning, hanging, driving a spear through her heart, it all leads to the same end."

"It most certainly does matter!" Lysteria snapped. "That girl is a misery to me, I will not deny it. But that does not mean I wish her life brought to a sudden end at the hands of savages!"

Stevron smiled. "You could have slain her yourself when you had the chance, m'lady. I'm curious. Why didn't you?"

Lysteria's back stiffened noticeably at the question. She looked up at him slowly, her pitch-black eyes unreadable and cold. "You are not yet so mighty a lord as be questioning my choices, young Stevron," she said. "I have treated you with more familiarity of late because of our shared concern for Balaam, but do not think that makes you my equal. Remember your limits."

Stevron chuckled lightly. "I am not so limited as you imagine, Lord Lysteria." He turned back toward the city view. "Still, keep your secrets. What does it matter to me what plans you hold for your daughter?"

Lysteria produced a kerchief from the folds of her gown and patted her cheek nervously. "I'm surprised you do not wish to save her yourself, Lord Stevron," she said. "After all, she is betrothed to be your bondmate."

He turned his gaze back toward the city. "She has forsaken you, Lysteria," he replied flatly. "She has forsaken Balaam. She is of no use to me now." He brushed a thick lock of blond hair from his eyes. It felt greasy to the touch. He wondered tiredly how long Lysteria would delay him from his bath. "In truth, I cannot fathom what usefulness you still see in her."

An awkward silence followed. For a moment, Stevron thought he might seize the opportunity to break away. But when he saw the uneasy expression on her face, it was clear that she was far from done.

"I wish to see her," she said at last. It sounded curiously like a confession.

Stevron snorted sarcastically. "Indeed? Whatever for?"

"That is not your concern," Lysteria replied, obviously put off by his reaction. "I wish to see her before she is slain."

Stevron shook his head. "There is no way, as you well know. You've never been to the Hinterlands. You cannot transport there by Word."

She laid a hand on his arm. "There is a way," she whispered. She glanced furtively down the hall before continuing. "Come to my chambers before you depart. I will have a gift for you."

"The High Lord sends me back at his whim, my lady," he said. "I cannot guarantee that I will see you before I leave."

"Then come to me before you go to see him!" she snapped. "But you must do this for me." She squeezed him arm with urgency.

Firmly, he laid his hand upon hers, and forcefully removed her grip. "If there is time and opportunity, my lady," he said, "I will come."

He released her hand, and she pulled it protectively to her bodice. Her expression suddenly became flat, unreadable. "Very well, then, Lord Stevron," she said. "I will look for you then." She turned and marched away, her shoes clicking angrily upon the marble floor as she went.

"*A gift for me*" *indeed*, he mused as he watched her go. *She probably means to bond me to her will somehow. Or worse, seduce me.* He shuddered at the thought. *Well, it doesn't matter either way. Let her try.* Despite his deep respect for Balaam, he'd never felt much of anything for Lysteria beyond a mild repulsion. Her feelings toward him were much the same, or so he had always imagined. They had tolerated each other over the years on Balaam's account, but neither had pretended there was anything more to it than that. *Until now, it seems.*

At that moment, a figure appeared from a shadowed portico nearby. The movement startled him, and he instinctively summoned a Worded shield around him as he fixed his eyes on the suspicious form.

"Poor, poor Lord Stevron Achelli," said the voice. The tone was feminine and alluring. "It must disgust you to have that old wench fondling you as she does." Lord Rachel Alli stepped out of the shadows and glided toward him slowly. She rested a delicate finger on her breasts as she walked, tracing the line between them absently as they disappeared beneath her low-cut burgundy bodice. Her lips formed a bemused grin as she looked him over. "Still, one can hardly blame her."

"Lord Alli," said Stevron. "I did not realize my private conversations were of interest to you."

She smiled. "There is much about you that interests me, Lord Achelli," she said. "In fact, you've interested me for some time, even before you were raised." She stepped closer, but was careful not to breach the perimeter of the defensive sphere, which she could not see but no doubt knew was there.

"You walk alone," he noted. "That seems imprudent, don't you think?" Stevron had never bothered with the annoyance of having *mon'jalen* trailing after his every step in the Axis, as most of the lords did. As powerful as he was, he hardly felt the need for them. But he was surprised to find Lord Rachel Alli coming to him unguarded. *Perhaps she does not consider me much of a threat.*

She sighed playfully. "There are some things better done in private, wouldn't you agree?" She smiled as she casually strummed her silky brown hair. "I wanted to speak with you freely, without the worry of *mon'jalen.*"

"You do not trust your own *mon'jalen?*"

She laughed. "Hardly any of the lords do now, after that brute of Lysteria's went berserk. It's hard to know who to trust anymore. Perhaps because you've been away, you do not see it."

Stevron looked at her thoughtfully. She was young for a Council lord, not much older than Stevron himself. And she was attractive in her way— with her round girlish face, rich brown hair and womanly shape—though certainly not stunning by any account. Still, she came from a strong blood-line, and rumor claimed that she was one of the few lords still capable of bearing young.

"Forgive me, Lord Alli," he said at last. "But I am tired from my journey, and in need of rest. What is it that you want of me?"

She walked to the balustrade slowly, carefully avoiding the sphere without appearing to notice it was there. "I am taking a risk in coming to you, Lord Achelli," she said smoothly. "I know your love for the High Lord runs deep. As it should, of course. But things are not well among the Lords. They are beginning to suspect what you obviously already know."

"Really? And what is it that you believe I know?" he asked.

"That the High Lord is not well," she replied simply. "That both his leadership and his reason are faltering."

Stevron felt his face flush with anger. It was bad enough having to listen to Lysteria voice doubts about his High Lord. But she was his bondmate, and as such, could be allowed a certain latitude in her words. He was not prepared, however, to tolerate such talk from another. "You are treading on the edge of a knife, Lord Alli," he said sharply. "You have no basis for such an accusation."

"Do not be upset," she said soothingly. "I mean the High Lord no harm. But Lysteria has not been able to shield his illness as effectively as she believes. The High Lord's actions are becoming less and less rational. He is clearly not himself. Surely even you can see how that puts us all at risk."

"I suppose you believe you are better suited for the role than he," quipped Stevron.

She laughed lightly. "Oh, by the Words, no! I have no desire to be named High Lord. I would sooner wish the title on an enemy than take it on myself. Who needs the stress?" But then her tone turned serious. "However, I do care for the Council, Lord Achelli. I care for its integrity, and its longevity.

She ran her finger lightly along the railing. "Order within the Council is slipping. Our numbers are dwindling; the balance of power has been upset. Factions among the bloodlines are beginning to resurface, ancient feuds that have been held at bay for decades by the High Lord's strong hand. Without that strong hand, I fear what remains of the Council will break apart. And sooner than you might suspect."

"Forgive me, Lord Alli," replied Stevron coolly, "but I find it odd that I have heard nothing of this infighting from Lord Lysteria. As you so cleverly overheard, she and I do not hide many secrets from one another."

She rolled her eyes—a curious expression for one with only black where pupils should be. "Lysteria is consumed with concern for her bondmate," she said. "She spends all of her energy trying to shield his behavior from the rest of us, unsuccessfully I might add. She has allowed little time to take notice of much else."

"And where is your allegiance, then?" asked Stevron. "Which of these factions in the Council do you follow?"

Lord Alli smiled. "None," she said. "I want only for the Council to survive this crisis, whole and united. I believe you are the key to that goal."

Stevron raised his eyebrows in surprise. "Me?" he asked. "But I have been a Council lord for less than a season." In truth, he found the suggestion perfectly reasonable. But he questioned her motives, and wondered for a moment if she might know more about his abilities than she let on.

"It's true you are new to *Sa'lei*," she said, nodding. "Your eyes have not even turned. But clearly, you are a fast learner." She gestured lightly toward the invisible shield around him. "And more to the point, you are the logical choice. The High Lord means to name you as his successor; we all know it. A transfer of power from him to you would insure that the Council would remain intact. That is all I want."

"Indeed," he said, doubtful. "And what do you ask in return?"

She smiled coyly. "Only your trust," she replied. "Any move to seize power from Balaam will be difficult, even for you. You will need to know who your friends are within the Council if you hope to succeed."

"Are you claiming to be my friend, then, Lord Alli?"

"Perhaps not yet," she replied playfully. "But I wish to be. And perhaps...even more than that." She traced a finger across her breast again to emphasize the point.

"I will not challenge the High Lord's right to rule," said Stevron quietly. "Besides, I am not yet convinced that he is unfit for the task."

"He will be challenged, Lord Stevron," she said. "And soon. If not by you, then by another. And when he is, he will be removed as High Lord. Even he is not powerful enough to withstand the forces that are mounting against him. All I am saying is that it would be better—for the Council, for all of us—if the change of power came from within his own house. Everyone knows he loves you as his own son."

Stevron glared at her coolly. "Then you must realize what you're asking of me. You want me to betray the only father I have ever known."

"I'm asking you to be the leader that the High Lord has raised you to be," she replied calmly. "I'm asking you to consider what is best for the Council, and for all of the Inherited Lands, above your own personal feelings for the High Lord."

She began to step toward him, but then stopped short. The presence of his shield was proving to be an effective hindrance to her advances. "If you do this, Lord Achelli, you can be assured of one thing. I will support you."

"Indeed?" said Stevron suspiciously. "And what favor would you ask of me in return for such allegiance?"

But she only smiled. "In time, sweet Lord, "she said. "Trust, after all, goes both ways. Just think on what I've said." She began to walk away slowly, but then turned. "Should you wish to speak of this further, you are welcome to come by my chambers anytime," she added with a grin. "I would relish a visit with you...without the shield." With that, she glided away.

Stevron spent the rest of the afternoon—what was left of it—in his private chambers. He needed rest before facing Balaam, but he realized there'd be none of that now. New questions had arisen about what he should do, and they now plagued him right along with those he already carried. He knew that Balaam would quickly grow frustrated by his failure to appear, and would likely send his *mon'jalen* to find and retrieve him before long. But he wasn't ready to face him just yet. He needed time to think!

Tossing his cloak upon the bedstand, he quickly issued commands in *Sa'lei*, forging wards around the chamber's perimeter to alert him of people nearby and prevent any entry without his permission. He then took to pacing the floor irritably, noting with casual disgust that the room was not at all to his liking. It was too small, for one thing. And its furnishings were far too soft and feminine—a legacy of the chamber's previous inhabitant, that simpleton Sarlina Alli. The whole place stank of cats.

In a flurry of frustration, he vaporized it all—every couch, every chair, every frilly pillow and pastel-colored rug—all pulverized with Words into dust so fine it could not be seen. With the lamps destroyed, the room immediately fell into shadow, illumined only by the failing light of the afternoon sun filtering through narrow stained glass windows that lined the upper reaches of the eastern wall. But he did not care. At least he had room to walk.

As he paced, he reviewed what he knew of Lord Rachel Alli. She was the elder sister of the dead Lord Sarlina, and so might have some personal motive for exacting revenge against Balaam, since he was the one who sent her to her death. But that chance was slim at best, for it was commonly known that Rachel had never held her sister in high esteem, believing her mental disability to be a disgrace to the family name—and more importantly, to her own standing within the Council. If anything, she'd be grateful to Balaam for getting rid of her.

And then there was Lord Baurejalin Sint, the old bag of a man whom Rachel was known to dally with from time to time. He had been slain during the confrontation with the Waymaker in the tunnels beneath the city. Could she have motive against Balaam on that account? Perhaps, but her sexual trysts with Baurejalin seemed hardly romantic, and were most likely pursued by Rachel for political advantage in the Council rather than love.

And what of Rachel's story of mounting factions within the Council? Those were likely true, given Balaam's distracted behavior of late. But why, then, hadn't Lysteria noticed? Or if she had, why hadn't she mentioned it when she accosted him earlier?

Eventually, Stevron's questions led him to the one that shadowed them all, the one he did not really want to face. Should he warn Balaam of Lord Alli's plans, or keep them to himself?

When the *mon'jalen* finally arrived at his door a half hour later, he still didn't know what his answer would be.

THE AXIS

Then the channels of water appeared,
And the foundations of the darkness were laid bare
At his Word,
At the blast of the power of his voice.
Who can stand in the flow of Bright Water and not be utterly revealed?
There is none. Not peasant, not prophet, not priest. Not even a king.
—From the writings of the Prophet Shikinah, in the year S.C. 1600

The walk to the High Lord's chambers did little to clear Stevron's thoughts. The *mon'jalen* kept pace several strides behind him, clearly aware of his resentment at being escorted through the Axis like an errant child. He had tolerated such condescending treatment from Balaam for years for the sake of keeping his secret safe. His humble subservience to the High Lord's every whim had long kept him safe from suspicion. But enough was enough. He was a Council Lord now. And more than that—the most fluent speaker of *Sa'lei* who had ever lived. One way or the other, the days of his belittlement would soon end. He had had enough of playing the weakling.

Upon reaching the High Lord's chambers, the *mon'jalen* suddenly grew nervous and distracted. After depositing Stevron at the closed door leading to Balaam's study, they wasted no time turning on their heels and disappearing through the foyer without so much as a word. *They are corded to the High Lord,* Stevron reminded himself. *They sense that something is not right with him.*

But even with that warning, nothing prepared him for what he saw when he opened the door.

Balaam's chamber was in utter disarray. Furniture lay strewn across the floor like a child's toys, some tossed haphazardly on their sides, others smashed into piles of splintered rubble. Pilings of clothes—some obviously several days old—trailed around the debris like discarded memories. The air was ripe with the stench of old sweat.

And over everything, there were scrolls. Stevron recognized many of them from his studies as an underlord—scrolls of history and of law, scrolls of journals from past lords, even accounting scrolls from the Sea Folk merchants and Roamers. But there was one type of scroll he'd never seen before, though the churning in his stomach immediately told him what they were. The forbidden scrolls. *Black scrolls.*

Balaam was reading one of them. He was seated at his desk, which aside from the chair on which he perched, was the only piece of furniture still upright in the whole room. The High Lord hovered protectively over the silver script before him like a man possessed. His bald head gleamed with perspiration, as did his portly body, which was bare from the waist up. He was whispering to himself, and did not seem to notice Stevron had entered.

"Have you gone mad, Balaam?" The words spilled softly out of Stevron's mouth before he had a chance to stop them. *What's happened to you?* The aberration seated before him was not—could not be—the High Lord he knew.

The High Lord blinked several times as if waking from a dream, then looked up. But when he saw Stevron he merely frowned and went back to reading. "You're late," he grumbled absently.

Shocked by the wretched image of his High Lord, Stevron began to move slowly toward the desk, but then stopped short as he felt the churning in his stomach worsen. "High Lord," he said, "what is happening to you?"

Balaam did not look up. "You're too late now!" he replied. "Go away. I'm too busy to see you now. You should've come earlier." His fat fingers traced the lines as he continued to read.

"How can you handle those?" asked Stevron incredulously. "They are tainted with the memory of *Dei'lo!* You must get away from them." But the High Lord seemed not to hear him.

Balaam Asher-Baal was the only man in the world Stevron respected. The only man he believed worthy of commanding him, of guiding him into the fullness of his power. But now some dark influence had reduced his mentor to nothing more than a filthy, babbling fool. The sight of him sitting there, half-naked, with sweat dripping from his corpulent frame like a Barrens' slug, repulsed him. The shame of it was too much for Stevron to handle.

Feeling a sudden rush of panic rise in his chest, he pointed to the scroll in Balaam's hands and yelled, *"Damonoi kirisecht nat!"* A blackness, like a fluid blanket of night, spilled from Stevron's hand and flowed sinuously toward the scroll. But when it touched the edges of the parchment, a shock like lightning surged through Stevron's body. The blackness instantly dissolved, and Stevron crumpled to the floor in pain.

Balaam, however, shot to his feet. "Fool!" he yelled. "It could've killed you!" There was a pause. And then, almost jovially, "You have to be careful with these scrolls. They're not for the faint of heart."

Stevron looked up. The sting was already fading, but the nausea continued to grow. "Can't you see what they're doing to you?"

Balaam licked his lips nervously. "Oh yes," he said. "Dangerous business. But I'm getting closer! I can feel it."

Forcing himself to ignore the churning in his gut, Lord Stevron rose to his feet and forced himself to look at him. "Closer to what, High Lord?" he asked.

Balaam's eyes narrowed a moment, as if the question were meant as a trick. At last, he said, "Tell me, son. How fair our quarry?"

Stevron ignored the question. "What is so important about these scrolls?" he repeated, more firmly this time.

Balaam's black eyes went wide—whether from anger or surprise Stevron couldn't tell. "You answer my question, young Stevron," Balaam said quietly, "and I'll answer yours."

Stevron felt his own anger surge. *No more games, father!* "You will be pleased to learn that your precious Waymaker will soon be dead!" he snapped. "The shal'adum have condemned them all as 'haters of lore' and locked them away somewhere in that fossil of a fortress where they meet. They will likely be slain before first light tomorrow."

THE AXIS | 135

Balaam slammed his fist on the table. "Then you must return immediately!" he shouted. "The Waymaker must not be slain!" His bulbous cheeks twitched erratically as he spoke.

"No, father!" Stevron declared. "I will not go back! Not until I know what is happening to you. Why do you care if the Waymaker dies? He is nothing!"

"Nothing! Nothing?" Balaam exclaimed. "And who is this who is so wise and powerful that he instructs me—*Me!* The High Lord of the Inherited Lands!—about what is nothing?" He gestured toward Stevron mockingly. "I'll tell you what 'nothing' is. You were nothing, boy. When I found you, you were nothing. You would be nothing today if not for me! Do not presume to tell me my business."

Stevron felt his blood run cold. Unbidden, he could hear *Sa'lei* rumbling in the back of this mind, willing itself to be spoken. "Don't do this, father," he warned quietly.

But Balaam did not seem to hear. He pointed his stubby finger at Stevron's face. "The Waymaker must not be slain," he repeated firmly. "You will go back, and you will see that he is set free from his bonds and sent on his way."

"You are not yourself, High Lord," said Stevron. "I see now that Lysteria is right. You are not well."

To Stevron's surprise, the High Lord threw back his head and laughed so hard his belly jostled with the force of it. "You think I don't know that?" he said. "I haven't slept in days. I can't keep food down. I sweat constantly like a pig in heat. I'm ill, Stevron, not stupid!" He stepped around the desk and moved toward Stevron excitedly. "That's why you must go back. The Waymaker, Stevron, he's the key. He must not die—not yet!"

Stevron was surprised to find tears welling up in his eyes. "But why, father?" he asked quietly. "What does he have that you need? And why spend time with these vile scrolls? Tell me what is wrong, and *I* will help you."

"No. No," replied Balaam nervously, shaking his head. "You cannot help me. Only the Waymaker. The scrolls are clear to me now. Well, not fully. But I know enough to know he is the one. It takes time, you see. It takes intelligence. Endurance. Fortitude. You have to know where to look, how to weave the pieces together. It's like a tapestry, you know. Very interesting tapestry." As if taken by the thought, he turned back toward the scroll on his desk and licked his lips. "A treasure," he whispered.

"Those scrolls are making you insane," said Stevron coldly.

But Balaam only chuckled. "You are an arrogant fool," he muttered. "You know nothing. The Waymaker, Stevron. He was there at the beginning of my struggle. And he is its end."

"If he is truly the cause of this, then I will bring him here," said Stevron. "Whatever he's done to you, I swear he will undo it!"

"No!" Balaam yelled. "Haven't you been listening? He must be set free!" The High Lord wiped the sweat from his brow and flung it absently to the floor. He shook his head with a sigh. "I'm too weary for this, son. I will send you back now. Do as I command. If what you say is true, there is little time."

Without thought, Words spilled from Stevron's lips as smoothly as molten bronze. "*Lusifen vadestro ak corredict suminaris Balaam et mios entrit,*" he said quietly.

"What was that?" Balaam asked. "I didn't understand it." He looked down at his body nervously. "What have you done to me?"

"You know, High Lord," Stevron replied calmly. "You feel it, as do I. I have severed the summoning cord you placed on me so long ago."

"Severed it? That's madness!" said Balaam. "You can't sever a cording once it's set. Not without destroying the one corded."

"Actually, *you* can't," said Stevron. "I can. And that is only the beginning of what I can do."

The High Lord looked at him suspiciously. "You are well trained, yes. I saw to that. I taught you, remember."

Stevron gazed at him defiantly. "I stopped learning from you years ago, father," he said. "Not long after you corded me, as it happens." He took a step toward the High Lord. "You should be proud of me. I have become everything you wanted me to be. And far more."

A fresh wave of perspiration sprang from the pores on Balaam's forehead, but he did not look away. "What is this?" he said incredulously. "You can speak the Tongue more fluently perhaps—that much I'll grant you. That was my aim from the beginning. But you cannot know Words I never taught. Who else could teach you more? No one in the Lands knows *Sa'lei* better than I!"

Stevron stepped closer. "Look at my eyes, High Lord. They are blue, not black. Yet I have spoken *Sa'lei* out loud and unhindered since my seventeenth year. It has become my native Tongue, just as you wished."

"Impossible!"

"At first, it was like stumbling in the dark," continued Stevron, proud at last to be telling his mentor the truth, "haphazardly piecing together odd phrases and forms without knowing what they meant, if they meant anything. But through trial and error, I learned. Slowly at first. But in time I discovered what you have never understood—that for the truly willing heart, *Sa'lei* becomes its own instructor. It *wanted* me to know, father! It *yearns* to be spoken. The Tongue itself taught me how to speak it. Within a few years I had already learned more than any Lord on the Council knew of the Words—including you."

"But how could you speak it aloud all those years without being discovered?" asked Balaam incredulously. "I would've sensed it. And your eyes! The eyes mark those who know the Tongue." He shook his head emphatically. "Whatever you say, you have not spoken it for long."

"The Words can do many things that even you have not imagined," said Stevron. "It is a small matter for them to conceal the evidence of their effects—in some cases, for a very long time." He reached out slowly and laid his hand on Balaam's sweaty arm. "Let me show you what I can do," he said, suddenly pleading. "I can help you, father. Test me, and I will prove it! Just tell me what he did to you, and I swear I will undo it. Then I will make him pay like no man has ever paid!"

"No, Stevron—No!" The High Lord knocked his hand away. "Do not harm him! If you have any love for me at all, you must let him be." He gestured emphatically toward the scroll. "He is the key, the *only* key to what I need! To what I must..." He stopped short, as though suddenly afraid to say more.

Stevron grabbed his arm again, harder this time. "Must *what?*" he demanded.

The High Lord stared at him a moment, his expression vacant and confused. But when at last he glanced down to see Stevron's hand upon his arm, he flew into a rage.

"Get out!" he shouted, jerking his arm free of Stevron's grasp. "You've distracted me long enough. You have your instructions. Now carry them out. You're wasting my time!" He fumbled back behind the desk and plopped down heavily on the chair. He stared blankly at the black scroll for a moment, then looked up. "Well, what are you waiting for?" he snapped. "Go!"

Sweat from Balaam's arm coated Stevron's hand like a sheen of dirty oil. He looked at it thoughtfully for a moment. Then slowly, purposefully, he reached down and wiped it off on his pants leg. "I will go," he said. "But not because you command it. I go because I now see what I must do." He turned to leave.

"Wait!" cried Balaam. "What do you intend?"

"Don't worry, father," he said, continuing his march toward the doors. "Everything will be all right. *You* will be all right."

With that, he stepped into the night.

16

KIKI

The "Adum," or Lore of the Kolventu formed the cornerstone of their society and defined the way they interpreted the world. Its most fundamental tenet held that the Tongue of Power was not actually real—but was rather simply an illusory concoction created by small-minded fools too afraid to believe in themselves. The true power of life and death, the Kolventu maintained, rested exclusively in the human spirit and intellect, and not in any mystical tongue. In their view, the Words were merely a crutch that trapped weak-minded people in self-delusion, preventing them from accepting the truth—that they, in fact, were the source of the power they wielded.

—The Kyrinthan Journals, Musings, Chapter 13, Verses 88-92

Five days had passed since their imprisonment in the bowels of the ancient citadel of Kiki. There had been no sign of Kaligorn, and whatever hope there was that he might free them had faded with the days. Word had come from one of the fel'adum that their execution was scheduled for the following morning. They would be drowned in the icy waters of the northern sea at first light, he explained, and left as food for the sea dragons.

And still, Aybel refused to use the Words.

Gideon believed he would have convinced her if the children hadn't come along. Alielis and Tyragorn, daughter and son of Celedriel by Kaligorn, younger sister and brother to Aybel. With Celedriel dead, by tribal tradition Aybel was now their mother. But tribal law had turned the tables. With Aybel condemned by the shal'adum, it was Alielis who now held the power their relationship. Apparently, it was she who would determine their fate, even though their father knew nothing of her involvement in the matter.

Aybel's spirits revived considerably upon meeting the children. She had always known she had other siblings—perhaps as many as twenty or more, she claimed, though Gideon found that hard to believe, even for a people as long-lived as those he'd met in the Inherited Lands. Apparently a shal'adum like Celedriel had many husbands—her Ward, as Aybel described it—whose primary duties included insuring that the shal'adum's bloodline continue for generations to come. But Aybel never suspected any of the new children born would be conceived through her father. He was already old by the time Aybel arrived. And his seed had been weak from the time of his youth. Aside from her, Kaligorn had fathered only one other child—her elder brother Tyrenon, who had disappeared years ago somewhere within the gates of Phallenar. She loved him so deeply she still could not speak of him without crying.

But now she had a new brother to love, and a sister as well. Her conversations with the children these past five days had been, for the most part, unremarkable. But even with the stiff wall of Kolventu formality dividing them, it was clear that Aybel would do anything to see that her siblings' futures were not threatened. Apparently, even if it meant that all of them must die.

Absently, Gideon picked at the scars on his legs and wrists. It had been barely a month since his escape from Phallenar, but already it seemed like a lifetime ago. And yet, here he was again, captured, locked away in a dungeon of sorts, wondering whether tomorrow he would live or die. What he wouldn't give for a visit from Telus now. But something told him the Raanthan would not be making an appearance this time.

Aybel and Kyrintha lay sleeping beside him, while Revel sat on the mucky floor as he did, knees to chin, staring off into nothing. The day, such as it was, was passing too slowly for Gideon's taste. If they were going to be killed, he'd rather just get it over with.

Aybel, of course, believed otherwise. She remained stubbornly confident that her sister would eventually recognize the injustice of their imprisonment and set them free. It did little good to remind Aybel that her sister was only twelve, that she had no real authority at all among the shal'adum, or that she had come to Aybel without the approval or knowledge of her father. All of that only seemed to shore up Aybel's confidence in her. It proved she was a leader, Aybel said. As the future shal'adum of Ki'Arelis, she would make up her own mind regarding their fate.

Well, even if the girl could deliver them from the shal'adums' judgment, she would have to do it soon. Time was definitely running out.

"Well," sighed Gideon, "I guess the good news is that the Council Lord hasn't shown up to scorch us all to death."

"Just so," replied Revel, grinning slightly. "Though, in truth, I cannot fathom why he hasn't. As it is, we are easy prey."

"Only because you won't blow the door down," muttered Gideon sarcastically.

Revel shifted his gaze lazily toward Gideon. "Must we have this conversation again?" he asked.

Gideon closed his eyes. "No," he said. There was no point.

The cell door had been a topic of heated debate many times over the past several days. Gideon had used every tactic he could think of to get Revel or Aybel to use the Words. But they refused. Or rather, Aybel refused, and Revel would not dishonor her decision by using the Words himself. After Gideon told them about the visit from the Council Lord, Kyrintha eagerly joined him in his efforts to convince them to escape, but even with her considerable powers of persuasion, it had no effect.

As Aybel told it, if any of them exposed their knowledge of *Dei'lo* to the shal'adum, the shame that would fall on her house would be extreme. Retribution would be exacted on her entire bloodline. Her father would certainly be slain. But more importantly, so would her newfound siblings. And that was a cost she was unwilling to pay—even if it meant that she must die.

"What about the rest of us?" Gideon had asked her angrily. "You're condemning us all to die, you realize that."

"That will not happen," Aybel replied firmly. "My sister will free us."

"What about the Council Lord?" Gideon retorted. "The longer we remain, the greater the risk to everyone here."

"If he was going to attack the shal'adum, he would have done so by now," she said. "He has had ample opportunity to slay us as well. I do not know why he follows us. But perhaps murder is not his objective. Perhaps he means only to track us for some purpose we cannot yet perceive."

And so the argument went, time and again, with subtle variations here and there that only grew more tedious with each repetition. But the outcome was always the same. Aybel and Revel would not use the Words. They would remain in the cell, and quietly await their rescue at the hands of a little girl who had so far promised them no such thing.

"What are you thinking about?" Gideon asked.

Revel continued to stare at the bars. "My brother," he said. "I hope he is well."

"He's safe at Wordhaven," said Gideon. With a sigh, he recalled the amazing beauty of the shimmering black and gold fortress with its shadow-less halls, and the comforting effects of the Words that permeated the entire valley. "He's probably reading that Book right now, laughing with glee at all the new tricks he's learning." He grinned at Revel, but the red-haired man wasn't smiling.

"He is preparing for war," he said. "I doubt very much that he is laughing about that."

Distant rumblings of thunder echoed over their heads. "Sounds like the storm is back," said Gideon.

Revel nodded slightly. "It never left," he said. "The rain has not ceased since our first night in the cell."

Gideon listened intently to the walls for a moment, but heard nothing. Even outside the forest, Revel's senses were the sharpest he'd ever seen—that is, unless you counted anyone living at Wordhaven.

"I just thought of something," said Gideon. "Couldn't you just transport to Wordhaven using *Dei'lo*? I mean, we've been here long enough now that you could transport back to the cell afterward, couldn't you?"

Revel closed his eyes. "I have thought of little else these past two days. I'm sure Ajel is wondering what has become of us."

"Then why not go see him? He might even be able to help us get out of this mess."

"There is nothing Ajel can do for us here," said Revel. "In any case, any contact with him will have to wait until we leave these shores."

Gideon snorted sarcastically. "If we leave these shores at all, you mean." He could understand Aybel's desire to not endanger her family, but at what cost? Did she really expect the rest of them to lay down and die just because she said that's how it must be? The very notion seemed ridiculously arrogant.

Suddenly, Revel's ears perked up. He listened in silence for a moment, then turned to Gideon. "We must awaken them," he said. "Alielis and her brother are coming. And this time they are not alone."

A few moments later, Gideon could hear the footfalls echoing distantly down the narrow corridor. Aybel and Kyrintha had stirred when he shook them—although somewhat reluctantly—and were now doing what they could to erase the signs of weariness in their eyes. Neither of them had slept much in recent days. The underlord, he noted in particular, looked thinner and far more gaunt in the face than when he'd first encountered her in Phallenar. She still had an attitude of pomposity that Gideon disliked, but he couldn't help but feel sorry for her all the same. Her freedom from Phallenar had certainly not turned out to be anything close to what she had imagined.

When Alielis and Tyragorn arrived at the cell, they were accompanied by two fel'adum, one of whom carried a long bundled cloth under his arm.

"I have a made a decision," announced Alielis proudly. She paused to make certain she had everyone's attention, then continued. "I have decided to spare your lives."

Aybel let out a heavy sigh of relief. "You have our thanks, sister," she said, smiling broadly. "I never doubted—"

Alielis quickly raised a finger to silence her. "Let me be clear," she continued, looking directly at Aybel this time. "I do not do this because I believe you are innocent. If anything, I am convinced that you are guilty of far more than even the other shal'adum may suspect. But my father has capitulated far too much in this matter. I will not have it said that the tribe of Arelis grovels like a dog to the will of other shal'adum, nor betrays the members of its own stakehold so flippantly, however contemptible their actions may be. Under my mother, Arelis was always independent and strong. I will not allow my father's fear of the shal'adum to undo that legacy."

Aybel positively beamed in reaction. "You will make a fine shal'adum for our tribe, sister," she said.

"I hardly require your approval, Aliel," said Alielis. "The fact that we are blood kin does not change the reality that you are kreliz'adum. I do what I do for the sake of the tribe. Not for you."

Aybel nodded compassionately. "I understand," she said. "What will you have us do?"

Alielis nodded to one of the fel'adum, who promptly lifted the bundled cloth and slipped it between the bars. "Your weapons," Alielis explained. "You must keep them hidden for now."

Revel took the bundle from the guard and set it gingerly on the floor. He did not open it.

Alielis pointed to the other guard. "In a few hours, this fel'adum will return with your evening rations. He will not speak to you, so do not ask him any questions. He will hand you the food through the bars as before. I have arranged for a double portion to be given to you this evening, as it is presumably your last meal. I suggest you do not eat it all at once. You will likely need it for the journey ahead. Just before the fel'adum leaves, he will unlock the gate. You will wait half an hour, then you will leave your cell quietly and travel down this corridor." She pointed farther down the narrow passage that continued beyond their cell. "It will lead you to the Eastern waterfront. You will find a small canoe there, concealed beneath the dock that has been prepared for your execution. Take it, and head east at least a day's journey into the open sea. From there, go wherever you wish, so long as it is far from here."

Gideon was at a loss for words. The girl's plan might get them out of the castle easily enough, but piling four full-grown adults into a small canoe and sending it out into the open ocean at night seemed more like suicide than escape. If the boat didn't sink right away, which was likely, it certainly wouldn't survive the first big wave to hit them in the open sea. The girl was incredibly poised and well-spoken for one so young—but she was obviously still just a child, with a child's grasp of the harsh realities of life in the real world.

"Forgive me, Alielis," said Aybel. "But what about you? The shal'adum will surely learn of what you've done. You could be in great danger."

"The shal'adum have no say concerning the matters of my tribe," said Alielis assertively. "That is something my father seems to have forgotten of late. I will make certain he does not forget it again."

Aybel bowed her head respectfully. "I do not know what to say, Alielis. Your kindness is beyond words."

"Say that you will never return, Aliel," said Alielis. "That is the only thanks I require."

Aybel nodded sadly, but said nothing.

Alielis turned to go, but then paused. "There is one thing I will tell you, Aliel. Perhaps you will consider it a gift. Even after betraying Mother the way you did, after all the years of pain you caused her by running away, she never lost hope that you would return. She did not understand how you could do what you did to her. But she never hated you for it."

Aybel nodded, tears forming in her eyes. "Thank you."

Aybel didn't say much for the next few hours, so neither did anyone else. Kyrintha cried a little, but whether her tears were for Aybel or for herself was impossible to tell.

Gideon considered voicing his concern about the canoe, but ultimately decided not to bring it up. It wasn't like they could really do anything to change it, anyway. He hunkered down in the corner of the cell and occupied himself with polishing his staff, and wondering how he could learn to access its power at will.

Revel, also, focused on the weapons the fel'adum had brought. After inspecting his arrows and the string of his bow, he passed his focus staff on to Kyrintha, whom he said might be able to use it as a weapon should the need arise, even though it was really meant as a focusing tool for the Words. Aybel took her own focus staff without comment, and promptly concealed it beneath her legs. She stared at the ceiling most of the time, as if trying to see the thunder that echoed continuously far above their heads outside.

At last, the moment arrived. The fel'adum came alone, bearing a tray piled high with dried fruits, a skin of water, and several small loaves of bread.

He never looked at them. After slipping the food through the bars, he stood and stared pensively up and down the corridor. After a moment, he reached inside his crotch and pulled out a key.

Just as he was about to slip the key into the lock, a boom of thunder shook the castle with such ferocity that it rattled the dust on the bars of the cell. The air itself seemed to vibrate with the electricity of it, and the fel'adum quickly slipped the key back into his feathered tights and scanned the corridor anxiously. He glanced back at the lock, then back at the corridor again. He seemed uncertain what to do.

"It's just the thunder," said Gideon. "It's just thunder."

But then there were screams. Drifting down the corridor, they sounded like the distant howling of wolves.

"It's just the storm," said Gideon, more anxiously this time. "That's all it is!"

But the fel'adum was already running by then—charging back up the corridor and out of sight.

Gideon ran to the bars and shook them. "Wait!" he yelled. But he knew the fool wouldn't come back.

Suddenly, Revel was standing beside him. "That is no storm, sojourner," he said. "The castle is under attack."

"All he had to do was unlock the stinkin' door!" exclaimed Gideon.

"Who is attacking?" demanded Aybel. She sounded personally offended by the suggestion.

Revel shook his head. "I hear explosions, walls crumbling," he said. "These are not the sounds of a battle among tribes of the Kolventu."

"It is Stevron," said Kyrintha. She spoke with a calmness and certainty that belied the fear in her eyes.

"How close?" asked Aybel.

"I cannot be certain," replied Revel, still listening. "Not close. Not yet."

Gideon slammed his staff against the bars. "We have to get out of here," he declared. "We don't have a choice now. He's coming for us." Gideon walked over to Aybel and grabbed her by the shoulders. "Aybel, we have to get out of here!"

She nodded. "I agree, sojourner. The Council Lord is forcing our hand. But with the Giver's help, we may at least stop him before he slays too many."

"Stop him?" said Kyrintha, incredulous. "You can't stop him! He is a Lord of *Sa'lei!*"

"He is newly-raised," snapped Aybel. "You've said so yourself! He cannot yet be that strong in the Words. We have defeated stronger Lords before."

"You mean *I* have!" exclaimed Gideon angrily. "With this!" He thrust the staff up in her face. "But I don't know how it works, Aybel! I don't know how to make it work!"

"Then what would you have me do, Gideon?" yelled Aybel. "Would you have me run away, and leave them all to die at his hand? Is that what you want me to do? You are the Waymaker—You decide!" She raised her hands in surrender. "What should we do, Waymaker? Save our own precious lives or fight for the lives of my kin? He would not be here if not for us!"

Her crystal brown eyes glistened with tears as she glared at him. He could see her pain so clearly, written there on her face and in her eyes. The agony of knowing that she had brought this terror on her people—the very people she meant to protect—simply by coming here. Simply by being who she was.

In that instant, Gideon understood. He was no stranger to that kind of horror. He knew what it was like to try to protect the ones he cared about by isolating himself from them. And he knew the despair of realizing—time and again—that it never really worked.

"What are you waiting for, Aybel?" said Gideon, grinning to hide the pain. "Open the door. Let's not keep the Council Lord waiting."

"This is insanity!" exclaimed Kyrintha. "You cannot possibly think you have a Barrens' chance against him!"

But Aybel was already at the door. She laid a hand on the bars and spoke to them gently. "*Jeo 'epathera.*" The lock clicked, and the door swung lazily open.

"Finally," said Gideon with a sarcastic grin.

Aybel seemed not to notice his attempt at levity. She led them into the corridor, where they scanned the distance for any sign of approach. There was none, but the screams were much closer now.

"Go to the boat and wait for us, underlord," said Revel. "You cannot help us in this fight."

To Gideon's surprise, the underlord shot him a look that would melt stone. "Do not to presume to tell me how I can or cannot help you, Word-havener," she growled. "I have experience with Stevron, which is more than I can say of any of you. If you insist on confronting him, then you will need me there. I may be able to persuade him not to scorch you on the spot."

Revel laughed. "Let us hope so, then, underlord," he said. "I do not much like the notion of being set ablaze."

"Don't worry yourself," said the underlord, brushing past him in a flurry of aggravation. "You'd most likely be dead before you hit the floor." She stormed on up the corridor in a fury. Aybel followed close on her heels.

"What's got her so riled?" asked Gideon.

Revel grinned. "I believe I made the mistake of telling her what she could not do."

Gideon grinned in understanding, then the two men took off up the corridor after the women.

"What do we do when we find him?" asked Gideon as they jogged.

"Whatever we can," said Revel simply.

Gideon rolled his eyes. "Well, that's brilliant," he mumbled. "If Donovan were here, he'd knock you flat just for thinking that."

"Donovan plans too much," Revel grinned.

They caught up the women around the corner, where the corridor continued its slow upward ascent into the darkness. But the women had stopped moving forward.

"The explosions are closer now than before," said Aybel quietly. "And more frequent. Revel, can you discern their direction?"

Revel perked his head to the side. Gideon listened too. As Aybel had said, the rumbling booms were getting louder, and seemed to be coming at regular intervals, as if someone above were setting off a timed sequence of bombs. But he no longer heard any screaming.

"The blasts are moving toward us," Revel said, "from that direction." He pointed into the darkness ahead of them.

"He must have learned our location," said Kyrintha. "He's coming for us."

"If he has, then he believes we are still in the cell," said Aybel. "We may yet have the element of surprise. We need only to conceal ourselves for a moment until he passes."

"Where?" said Gideon. "There's no cell but ours, and no other rooms as far as I can tell along this entire corridor."

Aybel looked at Revel. "Perhaps the Words," she said.

Revel shook his head. "The corridor is too narrow. He will walk right on top of us."

"That may be," she admitted. "But I see no other option."

Revel nodded in assent, then quickly grabbed Gideon by the shirt. "Put your back against the wall, sojourner. Here, next to me."

Gideon obeyed, pressing his shoulders and legs as hard as he could against the slimy stone. Down the way, Aybel and the underlord did the same. Then the two Wordhaveners spoke, almost in unison.

"*Jeo 'haaven.*"

The Word of Hiding, thought Gideon. He remembered it from the Dunerun Hope, when Ajel used it to hide them from the juron.

"What if he can see through it?" whispered Gideon.

"He cannot," replied Revel. But something in his voice made Gideon think he wasn't sure.

Just then, an explosion thundered down the corridor, followed almost immediately by a gust of wind and a flurry of dust. In the distance, Gideon could hear someone yelling. But it wasn't like the screams he'd heard before. This was just the cry of one man. And he sounded angry.

"*Satanis edibrasht shon ak barrir! Satanis edibrasht shon ak barrir!*"

The voice carried over the deafening sound of the explosions like the piercing cry of an eagle over the mountains. In the shadows ahead, the corridor exploded outward, one section after another, the wave of it moving inexorably toward them like a tsunami of wind and stone. And in the middle of it all walked the Council Lord, passing through the haze and rubble as if it wasn't even there.

Gideon froze. It was Stevron, the same one who had assaulted him in his room alone.

The Council Lord spoke again, and another section of the wall exploded outward in all directions. It suddenly occurred to Gideon that even if the Word of Hiding worked, it would not stop the walls from crushing them to death as the Council Lord passed. They would have to make a move, and soon.

But then, to Gideon's surprise, the Council Lord stopped. He stood motionless about twenty yards away, staring intently down the walkway as if waiting for the dust to settle.

It didn't take long for Gideon to realize he was looking right at him.

"What have you done to him?" Stevron screamed. "Tell me! Tell me now!"

Gideon said nothing. Maybe the Council Lord couldn't really see them. Maybe it was a bluff.

But then, he spoke again—harsh and grating—and invisible hands grabbed Gideon by the throat and lifted him to the center of the passage. Gideon clutched his staff desperately, holding it like a shield between him and his attacker. But to his despair, he felt no heat in the wood.

Stevron stepped toward him. "You will tell me, now!" he growled. "What did you do to him?"

"Nothing," rasped Gideon. "I don't know what you're talking about."

Suddenly, Revel appeared at Gideon's side and wrapped his arm around the sojourner's legs. He called out something in *Dei'lo* and a shield sizzled to life around them both. The stranglehold on Gideon's neck was instantly broken, and he tumbled heavily to the floor.

Stevron yelled in frustration. "Do not interfere, rebel! I will have my answer, or I will destroy you all!"

"The only answers we have are to questions you are unwilling to ask, Council," yelled Revel. "Leave this island now, and we will let you go in peace."

"Damonoi barriris nietan et sic suffarat'el!"

A sheet of black appeared over the shield surrounding Revel and Gideon, oozing across its surface like a second, oily skin. There was a sound of buckling, like the breaking of glass, and within a moment the shield shattered into a rain of sparks. From the remaining canopy of black above them, streams of glistening darkness poured down onto Revel's shoulders, quickly coiling themselves hungrily around his neck and arms. He began to choke. Gideon tried to grasp the oily strands and pull them from Revel's neck, but they only slipped like water between his fingers.

Suddenly, Aybel stepped forward, calling out Words to produce a new shield around them. But though the shield appeared, strong and illuminant blue, the black strands were not hindered by it. They reached for her as well, coiling themselves like snakes around her waist and neck. She tried to call out again, but could not for lack of air.

"Stevron, stop this!" screamed the underlord from somewhere behind them. "What is this madness that has possessed you?"

If the Council Lord heard her at all, he gave no indication. Instead, stepped toward Gideon. "Tell me," he said. "Tell me, and I will let them live."

Heat instantly surged through the staff like river of fire. "Let them go!" Gideon demanded.

Stevron took another step forward. "I will not say it again."

"Neither will I!" yelled Gideon. On instinct, he thrust the staff with all his might into the heart of the dark canopy above them. Blue light erupted like a torch upon its end, burning through the sheet of black, consuming it outward in an ever-expanding circle of flame. The darkness let out a defiant alien scream as it retreated, but quickly lost the power to maintain its hold on Aybel and Revel. They struggled to their feet, gasping, as the strands, one by one, dripped lifelessly to the floor.

"TELL ME!"

The Council Lord's words struck them all like an impregnable wall of solid air, hurling them tumbling down the corridor twenty paces or more. Clouds of mold-laden dust clogged Gideon's throat as he tried to get his bearings. He coughed at the taste of it, and tried to see Stevron through the haze.

"There is nothing to tell, Stevron," said Gideon raspily. "Don't you get it? I don't know what you're talking about."

Silence.

Gideon peered through the dust, but he couldn't tell if Stevron was still there.

But then he spoke. "Very well," said the Council Lord. "If you will not tell me, then you will die.

"Damonoi soladestro shon ak rabelein sic atros vulcaricht orbisht!"

A blazing orb of fire filled the corridor. So intense was the its heat that the moss-laden walls surrounding it instantly charred black, and even the dust that yet lingered in the air ignited, the particles flaming out like miniature fireflies as they drifted dead to the floor.

Upon appearing, it began to spin, and within an instant hurtled itself like a cannonball of lava toward them.

Without thought, without even awareness, Gideon leaped directly into the fireball's path, and thrust his staff toward it like a spear. "No!" he screamed, and blue lightning, like water, poured down through the ceiling and onto his head, saturating his body like a cloak of illuminant power. It flowed through his limbs and into the staff, and from it, a wall like a waterfall appeared. The fireball hit it with the force of a meteor and the sound of a thousand peals of thunder. But the waterfall stood firm, absorbing its heat with crackles and sparks and bursts of blue lightning, until all that was left of the raging fire was a sizzle and a fading wisp of smoke.

"Run!" yelled Gideon to the other behind him. "Get to the boat!"

"We will not leave you!" cried Aybel.

"I'll follow!" yelled Gideon angrily. "Now go!"

They obeyed. But just as the sound of their footfalls faded off down the corridor, he heard the Council Lord repeat the vile Words again.

"Damonoi soladestro shon ak rabelein sic atros vulcaricht orbisht!"

Again, the orb appeared. Again it spun and sped toward him, hungry like death. Thunder and lightning sounded as the fire railed against the waterfall shield, shaking the foundations of the castle, rattling the walls like an old man's bones. But once more, it sizzled and sparked against the wall to no avail, and faded into smoke.

Gideon took a tentative step backward. The waterfall followed him. He stepped again, careful to keep the staff held high. Again, the waterfall moved.

"I will bring this fortress down on your head!" yelled Stevron.

"Go ahead!" yelled Gideon. "You'll kill yourself too."

Stevron screamed in frustration. "I will have you!" he yelled. "I will not be denied!"

"Give it up, Stevron," said Gideon, taking another step back. If he turned to run, would the shield disappear? He wasn't sure he could take the chance. But he knew he couldn't stand there forever.

Surprisingly, Stevron smiled. "You obviously don't know me very well," he said.

Suddenly, an eruption of Words spewed from his mouth, faster and more eloquent than anything Gideon had ever heard. Fireball after fireball after fireball appeared, hurtling toward the waterfall wall in rapid succession, pounding it with fists of solid blaze, each with the size and fury of a missile. The sheer force of the impacts knocked Gideon stumbling backward. But though the waterfall moved with each successive strike, it did not buckle.

Still, Gideon wondered how long it could last. The power he felt surging through him was immense. But Stevron's power seemed at least equally as potent, and possibly more so. Even if the wall held indefinitely, Gideon's arms would eventually give out. He had to do something.

Just as two more blazing orbs shattered against his shield, he turned and ran, being careful to keep his staff raised high behind him as he went.

Thankfully, the waterfall followed him.

But so did Stevron.

Rounding the corner, Gideon ran desperately back toward the cell. Explosions of fire of followed close on his heels, battering the shield relentlessly like a sledge hammer as Stevron continued to scream out the Words. The shock of the blasts nearly toppled Gideon more than once as his ran, but somehow, he managed to keep his balance and keep the staff pointed high behind him.

The girl had said the passage beyond the cell would lead to the Eastern waterfront. Hopefully, the others were already there, preparing the canoe that would deliver them to the open waters—if it didn't sink first. Or if Stevron didn't blow it to bits with *Sa'lei* the instant he laid eyes on it.

He tried to think of some other option for their escape. Some other way to save all their lives. He remembered how the power of the staff had destroyed Bentel in a flash. But he didn't know how to make that happen now. And even if he did, somehow he knew the power wouldn't obey.

Plunging deeper and deeper into the narrow passage, he followed its twists and turns with a desperate but fading hope. Even if he made it outside, the Council Lord would surely follow. Even if he made it into the canoe, there'd be no time to row away before Stevron reached them. For all he knew, Stevron could turn the water to ice, and hold them in place as he pummeled them into submission. Who knew how long the shield would last? Surely even its power had limits.

If it weren't for the heavy rain, he wouldn't have noticed when he finally emerged from the passage and stepped into the night. The sky was starless and black as pitch. If not for the lightning, he would have had no idea which way to go. But the flashes revealed a mottled path over the rocks down to the small dock at the waters' edge, and the hands of his friends waving him into their tiny canoe.

As the shield emerged from the passage, its edges extended into the night, creating a translucent cocoon of blue that encompassed not only him, but also the others at the dock below. Boulders of fire continued to burst from the passage, with each collision propelling Gideon farther down the hill. A moment later, Stevron emerged behind him. His face was grinning, alive with madness. The Words still spilled from his lips like a merciless mantra that bore a life of its own.

"Damonoi soladestro shon ak rabelein sic atros vulcaricht orbisht!. . .Damonoi soladestro

shon ak rabelein sic atros vulcaricht orbisht!...Damonoi soladestro shon ak rabelein sic atros vulcaricht orbisht!..."

The fireballs continue to rail against the shield, and as Gideon stepped onto the dock, he realized the cocoon of luminescent blue was shrinking. Fearful that it would not last much longer, he ran to the boat. With the others already seated inside, there would barely be enough room for him to fit.

"We don't have much time," he said, still holding the staff aloft behind him. "How can we get this thing moving?"

As if on cue, Revel and Aybel began speaking to the canoe in *Dei'lo*. From their Words, a sail appeared, about two meters square, glowing eerily white like a squarish full moon as it hovered over the craft. Lines of light extended from its corners down to the hull, latching themselves onto the bow as if tied through holes that weren't there.

Suddenly, a blast of fire struck the dock, splintering it instantly into an exploding cloud of debris. The concussive force of the blast against Gideon's shield knocked him headlong into the boat. He landed partly on top of Kyrintha, who screamed in pain from the impact, but his lower half dangled precariously in the water to the side. He could feel the cold pull of the current dragging him in. But he didn't care about that. His only thought was not letting go of the staff, which now dangled unsteadily from this hand off the opposite side of the canoe. Instinctively, he gripped it tight once more. If he let it go, somehow he knew the shield would dissolve for good.

"I will see you die!" cried Stevron from the hillside above. "I swear you will not live through this night."

It was too dark to see exactly where he was. With the underlord's help, Gideon struggled to pull his legs into the canoe, and once more raised his staff overhead. The waterfall shield, which was now more of a bubble than a wall, glistened around them like a shimmering fountain. It was smaller now, encompassing only the canoe and those aboard, but it still seemed as solid and strong as when the onslaught began.

Revel and Aybel ignored Stevron's Words, and continued to focus on the Words of *Dei'lo*, repeating the same phrases over and over. Despite the obvious terror of their circumstances, both of their voices were even and calm, even musical in their way. Quietly, the sail of light began to fill with a breeze, and the tiny, overloaded canoe started moving slowly out to sea.

"Can't you give it more juice than that?" asked Gideon.

"Not yet, sojourner!" snapped Revel. "Too much too fast, and we'll topple the boat."

But then, once more, the vile sound of *Sa'lei* screamed into the night. Gideon couldn't hear the Words clearly above the thunder and the pounding of the rain upon the waters, but it didn't take long to figure out what it was meant to do.

Behind them, not fifty feet from shore, the surf began to rise in a rushing fury, forming a growing wall of water that quickly towered over their heads like a tidal wave frozen in time.

They had only a second to act.

"More wind—now!" yelled Gideon.

As if of one mind, Aybel and Revel joined in chorus together, spilling the Words from their lips in unison like a fevered, desperate prayer. Instantly, the wind erupted into a gale that billowed the sail and lurched the small craft farther out to sea. The force of it knocked all four of them to their backs, and once again, Gideon almost dropped the staff.

At that same moment, the mighty wave descended, toppling toward them from above like the lid of a giant coffin. Even with their greater speed, the wave was far too large for them to outrun. The best they could do was brace themselves, and hope Gideon's shield would soften the blow.

But just as the leading edge of the wave reached them, the shield transformed. Erupting into a fury of fire, it boiled the water away into steam as it toppled down upon them. Not even a drop made it through.

But the danger was not over. For the impact of the massive wave on the waters around them instantly created a backlash swell that shot the tiny canoe high above the sea line, lifting it to the crest of a second, equally massive wave. But this one apparently wasn't controlled by Stevron, for the force of it propelled them further out to sea, and farther away from Stevron's malicious voice.

Balancing precariously upon its crest, Revel and Aybel stoked the winds once more, and with Gideon's shield finally fading at last, they rode the little canoe out into the darkness and storm.

17

THE NORTHERN SEA

Vaganti, or more commonly, the Vag, has been the principal home of the Sea Folk since the time of the Endless Age. No one beyond the Sea Folk themselves knows much about the city's size, its population or architecture, and even less about its ancient origins. All we know with certainty is that the Vag drifted into the waters of the Eastern Sea sometime before the rise of Palor Wordwielder. Shortly thereafter, Sea Folk ships began appearing at various ports along the Gorge, bearing items for trade from distant cultures previously unknown to the Inherited Lands. The Sea Folk have remained with us ever since.

Before the Wayamker came, no outsider had ever stepped foot in the Vag. And to this day, no ship—except those belonging to the Sea Folk—has ever been able to find it.

—The Kyrinthan Journals, Chronicles, Chapter 18, Verses 60-64

The only buckets they had on board were their hands, so they used them, they all used them, bailing the water from the canoe one cupped handful at a time. They did this continuously—minute after minute, hour after hour—with the kind of mechanical desperation that comes from knowing you're going to die soon, but trying to stay alive anyway.

Within minutes of their flight from Edor, they let the sail dissolve into the night. Gideon wished they could have kept it, if only for its light, but it was obviously too dangerous to use in the storm. The winds had not been overly fierce when they first got in the canoe, but the gusts quickly turned shifty as they moved into open water. Both Aybel and Revel tried to direct the winds using *Dei'lo*, but it soon became apparent that neither of them was strong enough in the Words to do it with any consistency. Eventually they just gave up and let the sail go, and hoped that the storm wouldn't push them right back to Stevron's waiting arms.

Sometime around midnight, the rain stopped. The winds, however, blew on. The icy water drummed the sides of the canoe with a dull and maddening cadence, replacing every handful of seawater they bailed with one or two more just like it. No one said anything about the canoe going under. There was nothing to say. They just kept bailing, holding back the inevitable sinking of the boat for one more minute, and then one more minute after that.

It went on like that for hours.

Occasionally, the underlord would stop bailing and lean back on Gideon's chest, clearly exhausted from the strain. He would stop too, and lean back to rest on Revel, past caring what the Wordhavener might think of it. But then he could the feel the icy water climbing up his ankles, so he'd gently push Kyrintha off of him and they'd start the whole process all over again.

Despite their exhausting efforts, when the sun finally did creep above the waterline the next day, Gideon half expected to see the Isle of Edor still hovering right next to them, lurking in the mists like a nightmare that wouldn't go away. And Stevron would be standing there, grinning with that mad look in his eyes, and they'd all have a good laugh together before he burned them alive.

But that wasn't the way it happened. When the sun came up, the island was gone. But, to everyone's amazement, the Endurant was less than a hundred feet away.

"Ah, what a sad sight to come on first thing in the mornin'!" called Quigly from the deck. "You look like a bevy of drowned rats!"

Gideon stared at the ship in disbelief. How in God's name did the Sea Folk captain find them here?

"Still I s'pose I can't say I'm overly surprised," continued Captain Quigly. "What with that demon you cursed me with, may the Giver smite him! I say, are you living down there, or am I just talkin' to the dead?"

Gideon waved his hand. "We're okay!" he called. "How'd you find us?"

"Not from lookin', I'll say that much." The sea folk Captain spit into the water. "But here you be, so I guess we'll bring you aboard—despite my better judgment. Woman!"

Quigly's bondmate appeared on the deck, took one look at them, and instantly frowned.

"Throw down the ladder," ordered Quigly.

"Really?" she snapped angrily. "'Cause I was thinkin' of letting them drown."

"Well, you wouldn't be the first," said Quigly with a laugh.

"Just mind the jib," she grumbled. "You don't want to run them down before we save their sorry hides." With a snort, she trudged over to the rail and hefted the rope ladder over the side. It splashed into the water about thirty feet away.

"You just get one shot so don't waste it," called Quigly. "There's no wind to carry me around for a second pass."

"It doesn't sound like he's all that happy to see us," muttered Gideon.

"I think there's a story to be told here," agreed Revel. "It's unlikely the Captain came upon us by chance, yet it sounds as though he did not come willingly."

Once the ship was close enough, the foursome abandoned the canoe and swam to the ladder one at a time. Kyrintha went first, followed by Aybel, Gideon, and finally Revel. The water was icy cold, but they were all past caring about such things. Their only thought was getting on board. Quigly's bondmate lingered at the top to help them up on the deck, but she said nothing as they struggled up the ladder, and once they were all safely on deck, she just walked away.

"Peace unto the ship Endurant," said Revel to Captain Quigly. His voice lacked its usual strength. "Our thanks for welcoming us once again on the timbers."

"Thank me not, lander," said Quigly from the upper deck. "This was that Raanthan's doing, not mine."

"Where is Telus?" asked Gideon.

"Locked away in the hold, may he rot there," the captain replied. "He'd be dead by now if I knew how to slay him."

"What has he done?" asked Revel.

Captain Quigly stared down at them with disgust. "Let me tell you something, lander. There's two things you never do to a Sea Folk captain. You never meddle with his woman, and you *never* meddle with his ship. I'll give you one guess which one that silver demon of yours has done."

"How has he meddled with your ship?" asked Gideon.

"Blast it if I know!" Quigly shouted. He leaned over the upper railing and glared down at them menacingly. "Listen, I have sailed these waters for one hundred and twenty-two years. And in all that time, I have never once— once!—missed my mark by more than a single fathom. But in the last seven days I have five times set sail for the Vag, and five times I have found myself back in these waters by the time the sun kissed the horizon." He slapped the railing angrily. "It's a dark art that one carries! It'll be a happy day when I'm rid of him—and all of you along with him! Now get your arses below! The woman'll be wanting to get you cleaned up."

"Yes, Captain," said Kyrintha. "And thank you again. I apologize for the trouble we caused you."

Quigly ignored her, and shuffled back to the wheel in a huff.

"Isn't it possible he just got lost?" Gideon whispered to Revel as they walked toward the galley.

"Their people have a saying," replied Revel quietly. "'The Wondrojan heart was carved by currents.' The Sea Folk do not get lost at sea, sojourner. They cannot."

When they stepped down into the galley, they found Quigly's bondmate had already set out a blanket and towel for each of them, and was in the process of preparing a meaty soup with thick-crusted bread and flagons of wine. But her expression was far from welcoming.

"The water's nearly gone, so it's wine or nothing," she said without looking up. "I may have a suit of clothes long enough for the underlord, but the rest of you will have to settle for blankets until your garments dry. There's no water to rinse them of the salt either, so don't ask."

"Thank you," said Revel.

"You've provided more than we could ask," added Kyrintha.

Quigly's bondmate grunted, but still didn't look up.

The foursome collected their blankets and towels and walked past the woman without further comment. She was clearly not in the mood for conversation.

They moved down into the living quarters, and each disappeared without a word into their berth to disrobe and clean up. But despite the dirty smell of the salt water on his skin and the exhausted chill of his bones, Gideon was more interested in locating Telus first. He wasn't sure why—maybe just curiosity about whether the Raanthan had really done anything to warrant the obvious agitation in Quigly and his bondmate. Or maybe Gideon just wanted to make sure Telus was all right. Quigly had hinted that he tried to kill the Raanthan, after all. He may not have succeeded, but that didn't exclude the possibility that Telus had been injured in the attempt. Of course, Gideon didn't really know if a Raanthan *could* be injured.

He moved deeper into the bowels of the ship, careful to avoid the low-hanging beams that were set to accommodate a much shorter kind of person, and looked for anything that might pass for a holding cell.

Eventually, he came upon a locked door leading to the bilge room. He knocked. "Telus?"

"Waymaker," the musical voice replied.

"Are you all right?"

"I am pleased that you have returned safely."

"Thanks. Are you all right?"

"I am well."

"Quigly says you've been messing with his navigation of the ship. Is that true?"

"Yes."

"Why?"

"He grew weary of awaiting your return, and set sail for the East. I resisted him."

"How?"

"You need rest," said Telus. "But first you must tell Captain Quigly where you want to go."

"Where *I* want to go?" said Gideon, incredulous. "What does that have to do with anything?"

"You are the Waymaker."

Gideon laughed tiredly. "Telus, he's not going to listen to anything I tell him. Besides, I don't have any idea where I want to go. I don't even know where we are."

"Tell him that if he wishes to leave these waters, then he must go where you say."

"I can't tell him that!" said Gideon. "He'd probably toss me overboard."

"You will not die today," said Telus.

"Why don't you tell him?" asked Gideon. "I bet you know where we should go. Besides, he already hates you anyway."

"I do not know the way. I am not the Waymaker," Telus replied calmly. "You are."

Gideon sighed in exasperation. "How am I supposed to know which way we should go, Telus? Like I said, I don't even know where we are."

"You need only give him a direction."

"I don't know what direction!" exclaimed Gideon.

"Remember who you are, Waymaker," said Telus angrily. "Remember your purpose. You do know the direction."

"No I don't!"

"If you do not choose a direction, the Endurant will remain in these waters. The Council Lord Stevron Achelli will soon find us here. He will attack, and all life on board will be lost." The Raanthan issued the prophecy with no emotion, as if reading off a script.

"How do you know about Stevron?" Gideon asked. But then he thought better of it. "Never mind," he added quickly. That was a discussion for another time. Right now, he needed to figure out what he was supposed to do. "Okay," he said. "How do I figure out what direction we're supposed to go?"

"Go up on the deck," replied Telus. "Listen to your heart. And speak true."

"Speak true?" repeated Gideon. He'd heard that phrase before. *Speak true, and you will not fail.* He shook his head. "I'm really too exhausted for this," he said.

"Do this, then rest," said Telus.

Gideon rubbed his face in his hands and moaned. If he hadn't come looking for Telus, he'd be asleep by now. "All right," he said at last. "But if Quigly doesn't listen to me, I'm going to tell him you put me up to the whole thing."

"As you wish," said Telus.

"Fine," said Gideon. He turned in a crouch and started back toward the galley. But after he moved a few paces away, he turned back again. "Telus?"

"Yes, Waymaker."

"You could break out of that room if you wanted to, couldn't you?"

"Yes."

"That's what I thought."

Confused and tired, he left Telus there, trudging back up the passage reluctantly, past the sleeping quarters and into the galley. Aybel, Revel and the underlord were already there, bundled in blankets and nursing large wooden bowls of stew in their hands. The captain's bondmate was nowhere in sight.

"You should eat, sojourner," said Revel. "And drink. Your body needs to regain its strength."

"If you wish, I can speak the healing Words to help as well," he added. "But you must eat first."

Gideon waved them off. "In a minute," he said with obvious irritation. He wasn't sure what he was going to say to the Sea Folk captain, but whatever it was he might as well get it over with. He moved on past them up the stairs and stepped out onto the deck.

It was still early morning. The azure sky was wide and silent, with no sign of the storm clouds that had tormented them the night before. In fact, there wasn't a single cloud to be seen anywhere. Sunlight stretched out lazily across the dark wood planks of the forward deck as the sails overhead drooped listlessly on their masts, hungry for even a hint of breeze to bring them to life. The sea for miles around had turned to glass.

Gideon stepped quietly over to the bowsprit and climbed up to his old perch. In the background, he could hear Captain Quigly cursing the wind—or rather the lack of it—and barking orders to his bondmate to trim this or let out that, apparently in a vain attempt to catch whatever slight breeze might appear. If they noticed his presence on the deck, they did nothing to acknowledge it. Which was fine with him. He needed a few minutes to collect his thoughts.

He snuggled into a semi-comfortable position and stared out at the water. He was glad to find that his jerkin and shortpants were already beginning to dry in the morning sun, but the salt left behind in the leather chafed against his skin. He decided to ignore the irritation, and contented himself with trying to brush the remnant salt out of his scraggly beard and long curly hair, with limited success.

He felt nervous, and exhausted. What did Telus really expect him to do? How was he supposed to know which way they should go? He may have been the Waymaker in name, but what did that really mean? So far, the whole experience made him feel like an ignorant boy stumbling in the dark through a mine field.

Taking a deep breath, he closed his eyes. *Listen to your heart, Gideon. That's what Telus said. Just listen to your heart.*

At first nothing happened. For several minutes, he tried to focus on what he was feeling, but all he got was static. He was too exhausted to think clearly, much less feel anything at all. But as he continued to turn his attention inward, he noticed his heart began to beat faster. He felt himself taking short, panicked breaths, but did not know why. Everything around him looked perfectly calm. There was no threat anywhere nearby that he could see. But inside he felt his anxiety building, surging up into his consciousness like a volcano preparing to erupt. A part of him sat to the side and watched this new development with detached interest. Where was all this anxiety coming from? Where is the danger? He didn't know, but the threat of it frightened him, and he found himself instinctively looking around for someplace to run—as if, just by hiding himself, he could escape the turmoil rising from within.

Suddenly, images of his childhood abuse pierced into his thoughts like hot pokers through his eyes. He winced at the sight of them, and angrily grabbed his head to shake them away. He did not want these memories, he had never asked for these memories. They were not his memories—not *him*, not who he was now—they were somebody else's memories. It was somebody else's life—that stupid boy. He was such a stupid boy. But that's not who Gideon was anymore. What was the point of going back there?

But the images kept coming unabated—one after another, faster and faster, until they piled on top of each other like a rancid deck of cards scattered across his mind, each one reliving another time he let his father beat him, abuse him, steal away a piece of his soul. The arrogance of the man! Gideon never tried to stop him. He never once fought back. *Coward! You're nothing but a coward.* At first, he didn't know he could. And even in the later years, when he was stronger and realized he could fight back or run away, he still did nothing. By then, there was too little of his heart left to care. Or, at least, that's what he told himself to assuage his shame.

Tears ran hot down Gideon's salt-crusted cheeks. *You were wrong, Father! You were wrong to do that. You were wrong to treat me that way. How could you have done that to me? Didn't you see that I was your son?*

Unaware, Gideon slipped from the bowsprit and crumpled down on the deck in a ball. If he was moaning, he didn't notice it. All he felt was the bitter pain pouring out of him, from whatever place in his heart it had been locked away. He let the tears come freely; now that the eruption had come, he had little choice. A part of him felt he would drown in it all, that his sense of who he was now would be lost in the memory and pain. But in a deeper place, distant and calm, he knew, ironically, the goodness of this act. The purging. There was safety here, around it all, somehow. By letting it come, by letting it out, he wouldn't have to carry it anymore.

He clasped his hands around the emblem of the Pearl embroidered over the heart of his jerkin. He gripped it like an anchor—a talisman to hold him in the truth of where he was, of who he was *now*—as the pain and memory pooled around him in a flood of tears.

He wasn't sure how long he stayed that way, but eventually the eruption subsided, and he felt a quiet steadiness return to his breathing, and his heart. He sighed several times, feeling the hard wood of the deck press against his body like a hug, and thanked whatever God there was that he was here and now, and not back in that shed behind the house.

Slowly, carefully, he rose to his feet and looked around. The morning was still calm. The waters still like glass. Captain Quigly and his bondmate were busy milling about aft of the main mast, occupying themselves with various odd jobs as they waited for the wind. They apparently hadn't noticed anything that had happened to him. Or if they had, they chose to pretend otherwise.

With quiet resolve, Gideon walked aft to the upper deck where Quigly was busy recoiling some lines.

"Captain Quigly, I have something important to tell you," said Gideon.

"Aye? And what might that be?" said Quigly, glancing at the Waymaker through the corner of his eye.

Gideon pointed to the horizon off the starboard rail. "We have to go that way," he said. "That's the direction we need to sail."

Captain Quigly glanced over at Gideon again, this time with a look of suspicion around his eyes. Gideon just stared back at him, tired, but feeling peaceful for the first time in many weeks.

After a moment, the captain began to laugh. "Since you're a lander, I guess you may not have noticed," he chuckled. "But my lady here—the Endurant—she runs on the wind. If you take a look around, I think even you will see that there be none." He shook his head with a smirk.

"Yes, I know," said Gideon. "But what I'm saying is, when we do sail, we need to go that way." He pointed again.

Quigly's eyes traced the line of the direction Gideon was pointing. "Aye," he said slowly. "I'd say that's about right."

"Really?" said Gideon. "You mean, you are willing to go that way?" He didn't think it could be that easy.

"I been doing my best to take that heading for days, lad," said Quigly, again with a smirk. "You're pointing toward the Vag. That's where I mean to go. If we could just get some blasted breeze, we'd be halfway there by now."

Just then, a strong gust of wind blew across the Endurant from the west, listing the ship heavily to starboard. Quigly spun around to face the breeze, and scanned the horizon to the west. Gideon looked too. He saw whitecaps on the water as far as the horizon.

"Where the...Woman!" yelled Quigly. "Man the jib! We've got wester-lies for days." Quigly's bondmate appeared from lower deck and hobbled without comment toward the bow of the ship. Quigly, meantime, turned the wheel excitedly. "Tell your fellow misfits to get up here," he said to Gideon. "We'll need to reset the sails to catch this wind." He scanned the skies suspiciously. "It's a rare wind that blows west in these waters," he added. "This is some dark mischief of the Words, I'll warrant. Most likely your doin', unless I miss my guess."

"I don't think—" began Gideon.

"What are ya' standing there for?" Quigly continued. "I need those landers on deck!"

"Um, yeah, sure," said Gideon, and jogged down to the galley to call the others. He was struck by the Quigly's suggestion that he had caused the wind the blow, and wondered if somehow it might be true.

At Gideon's call, the others scrambled hurriedly onto the deck. The underlord had borrowed a brown woolen shift from Quigly's bondmate, which she wore instead of her now useless gown. The shift was woefully wide for her small frame, but apparently just long enough to pass for a dress, albeit a short one. She had cut out the sleeves and bound it at the waist with a strap of leather to avoid her looking like a sack of potatoes. The opening around her shoulders draped low across her chest, being designed as it was for the much larger head and neck of a Sea Folk woman. But Kyrintha had strung a narrow strip of deep green cloth across the neckline to hold the garment in place. Gideon noted with some surprise that the underlord looked more at ease in her makeshift garb than she had ever seemed in the gown.

Aybel and Revel, on the other hand, wore no garments at all. A simple blanket wrapped each of them—Aybel's being tightly bound around her chest, while Revel's was folded over twice and secured around his waist. If they were bothered at all by their lack of attire, they showed no sign of it. Though Aybel did still seem troubled; she'd hardly spoken since they fled Edor, he suddenly realized. And it was apparent she'd been crying recently. *Idiot!* Gideon chided himself. How quickly he forgot about the family Aybel had left behind at Kiki. There was no telling what Stevron might have done to them by now in his rage over Gideon's escape.

Immediately noticing the wind, she and Revel hurried over to Captain Quigly, and he quickly had them let out the sails so as to catch the strong winds as he turned the bow due East. With sails unfurled and wide, the Endurant soon caught speed and plowed gracefully through the choppy waters toward the morning sun.

For some reason, Quigly had not given Gideon any job to do on deck, so he took it as a sign that it was time to change out of his salt-encrusted clothes and get some much needed sleep. Without comment to the others, his slipped below and made his way to his quarters, where he found his staff lying across his berth along with a flagon of fresh water and a wooden bowl filled with the stew Quigly's bondmate had prepared. He couldn't guess which one of his companions had put it there, but he was thankful for the thoughtful act all the same. How long had it been since someone in his life had actually cared for him like this? In truth, prior to his arrival in the Inherited Lands, he couldn't recall a single example outside of his mother.

He carefully removed his jerkin and hung it on one of the pegs bolted to the wall. Though there were no mirrors in the room, Gideon could tell his body had changed significantly over recent weeks. He was thinner, for one thing. But the muscles on his chest and arms had grown much thicker too. Surprising, he thought, given all the days and nights of torture and deprivation he'd endured—both in Phallenar and at Morguen sounden. But the time he'd spent at Wordhaven had been extraordinarily healing for his body, as well as his soul. That combined with the hours of training with Revel on the staffs and all the weeks of travel by foot or horse had helped reshape his body into a leaner, more muscular version of itself.

Idly, he ran his finger along the scars that circled his wrists, and then the smaller one that stretched directly over his heart. His thoughts flashed back to the panicked day when he awoke from one of his nightmare rages to find he had stabbed himself deeply in the chest. He still wished he could remember the dream that had provoked such a violent act, but when he tried to recall it all that came to mind was the terrible fear he had that day that he was going mad.

After his Facing at Wordhaven finally ended and his abusive childhood had been revealed, Seer had told him that the rages would never come again. He believed that was true, though he now realized that there was still a lot of pain locked up inside his heart, and he would have to find a way to let it all come out if he was ever going to truly purge his soul of the injuries inflicted by his father all those years ago. Today's experience on the deck had been a testament to that fact, and gave him some hope that, however great the pain might be, it was no longer strong enough to destroy him.

At that moment the door swung open, and Aybel walked in, still wearing the blanket. Her gaze immediately fell to Gideon's shirtless torso, but then she quickly looked up again as if she hadn't noticed. "I came to see if you were well," she said. "The captain's bondmate suggested you might be ill."

"Ill? Me?" said Gideon, feeling suddenly self-conscious. "No, I'm fine. How are you?"

Aybel nodded lightly, but otherwise ignored the question. "I am also told we have you to thank for the wind," she said.

"Well, I don't know about that," Gideon replied, folding his arms with forced nonchalance. "I suppose I might've had something to do with it.

Only Telus really knows for sure." He felt awkward standing before her like this. But she just kept looking at him, her red-rimmed eyes as direct and unyielding as ever.

"I'm sorry about your family," he stammered at last. "I hope they are okay."

Tears returned to her eyes. But she did not look away, and she did not offer a response.

"Tell me something," said Gideon, determined to shift the focus off of the awkwardness of the moment, "Captain Quigly said we were heading to a place called the Vag. Do you know what that is?"

"Yes," said Aybel. "It is Vaganti, the principal city of the Sea Folk."

"The Sea Folk have a city?" said Gideon. "I thought they lived their whole lives on the ocean."

"They do," Aybel replied. "Vaganti is a floating city. It rides the deep currents of the Eastern Sea."

Gideon raised his eyebrows in surprise. "You mean, it's like an island?"

"In a way, yes," said Aybel, wiping her eyes as if noticing the tears for the first time. "The city is supported by vast colonies of a seafaring plant that they call Mush. I have never been there, but I am told it is a strange and wonderful place. Very few landfolk have ever seen it."

Gideon frowned. Something about going to Vaganti didn't feel right. Still, it was the right direction, wasn't it?

"You should eat, then get your rest," said Aybel. "The journey will take several days. And the Council Lord may yet try to follow us."

Gideon smiled tiredly. "Let's hope he doesn't have a boat."

Aybel frowned at him sharply. "He is a Council Lord, Waymaker," she said. "He does not need a boat."

18

RACHEL'S PRIVATE CHAMBERS

When she awakened from her sleep, she found her jaw locked shut. Her tongue felt swollen, and as useless as a water-logged sponge. Her lips were sealed together as if sewn with twine. Her entire body was frozen in place.

She knew she was helpless, but when she recognized the silhouette hovering over her, it wasn't fear that flashed across her pitch-black eyes. It was rage.

How dare you!

Lord Stevron Achelli lounged idly across her chest, as if he were her lover come home to roost after a long journey abroad. Even in the darkness, she could see him smiling as he coyly fingered the sheets that covered her breasts. The wetness of his clothes seeped through the bedding and made her skin feel clammy and chilled.

Her own sense of helplessness disgusted her. *How could this be?* she fumed. *How did he get in here?* She had wanted him in her bed; she'd made that much clear. But not like this. She always needed to be the one in control. Besides, he was filthy, and probably drunk. His entire body reeked of ocean, mud and sweat.

Where are my mon'jalen? she wondered. Surely they could sense her distress. *Why have they not come?*

He noticed her eyes glaring at him with loathing, and laughed lightly. "No shield this time, Lord Alli," he said with a grin. "As you requested."

She moaned in defiance, and angrily shook her head no. Her neck, it seemed, was the only part of her body she still controlled.

"You're probably wondering where your *mon'jalen* are, yes?" he cooed. "Don't worry, they're all well. In fact, all one hundred of them are waiting for me right now at Prisidium Square."

Ridiculous! They answer only to me!

"You see, I had to take them from you," he continued, whispering playfully. "I've corded them to me now. I apologize for not asking first, but I suspect you would not have consented if I had." He danced his finger along her throat as he spoke. "The enemy I pursue has turned out to be more intractable than I expected. I could slay him myself in time, but..." The thought seemed to wander off of is own accord. Then he looked down at her curiously, and grinned. "You know, I think you may be the first Council Lord in six hundred years who didn't have a single corded *mon'jalen* to protect her. How does that make you feel?"

Rachel grunted angrily. *Release my tongue and I'll tell you how I feel*, she fumed. She didn't believe his story, of course. No Lord could sever a cording without destroying the one corded. But his pompous attitude infuriated her. He was only barely a Lord himself. How dare he presume to use his measly Words on someone of her power and standing. And in her own chambers!

Still, she couldn't explain how he had entered her room without waking her, warded as it was, or how he managed to dissolve the shield she forged around her bed each night before sleeping. By all rights, he should be charred to ash by now.

He leaned in close and smelled her hair. His hot breath upon her neck reeked of wild game and swamp water. "I have thought about what you said to me," he breathed, "and I have decided to take your idea in a slightly different direction." He smiled warmly. "You say you wish the High Lord well, yes? Then you can help me serve him. I have need of information, you see. And I've decided that you will get it for me."

Violently, Rachel shook her head no. But Stevron took no notice. He reached up and gently stroked her hair. "I have little time," he said, "so I apologize if this is ungentle."

He began to speak to her in *Sa'lei*, softly and with ease. His Words did not sound like a command at first, but more just like a story he was telling.

She could not understand much of what he said, but as the Words took shape within her mind and heart, a part of her began to comprehend what he was compelling her to do.

In recognition of the danger, her eyes at first grew wide in terror. But soon the panic drained from her face, leaving it bland and vacant, as the venom of his whispered tale paralyzed her will.

19

CHAMBER OF THE PEARL

Wordhaven contains one hundred and forty-four portals in all. There are exactly forty-five within each of the three major rings of the Stand, two within its core near the Chamber of the Pearl, and seven situated at regular intervals within the valley along its perimeter. Each portal leads to its own unique location within the world—some close, some extraordinarily far, and some so unfamiliar that no one has yet passed through them. The majority of the portals were likely used by the Lords of old to travel to places within the Lands they had never visited before, or perhaps as a means to transport goods for trade from one part of the lands to another, or to other nations within the world. But at least two of the portals—those at its center—present a mystery that is not easily solved. We know that one of them leads to Setal Rapha. But though it is awakened, only a select few have been able to pass through its gate—most are rejected by the gateway itself, for reasons no one understands.

As for the other portal, no one has been able to awaken it at all.

—The Kyrinthan Journals, Chronicles, Chapter 18, Verses 7-13

Paladin Ajel Windrunner gazed wistfully at the shadowy scene unfolding on the facets of the chamber walls. Before him, a dark narrow corridor of weathered stone, damp and crumbling, faded into the shadows toward the east. Above him sprawled a massive stronghold, ancient and lifeless, which clung to the southern end of an island in the Northern Sea.

There was no sign of Revel anywhere. But he had been in this place, perhaps as recently as the day before, wandering through the bowels of this ancient citadel—perhaps looking for something, or running from someone.

Ajel could only guess.

Following the vision, he stepped through the lone opening along the entire passage—a barred gate leading to a fairly spacious if dilapidated prison cell. Along one side, the mossy slime—which profusely coated all the walls and walkways of the entire catacomb—had been all but worn away. *Were they imprisoned here?* Ajel wondered. *But why?* He could not fathom any reason that made sense. He knew that Aybel had been a person of some importance among her people—even though she was only a small girl at the time. Would not her family be overjoyed to see her face again after so many years? What could have provoked them to imprison her and the others?

It hardly mattered now, in any case, he realized. They were no longer there.

Stepping back into the passage, he followed it eastward, tracking the lingering imprint of Revel's presence. The walls had been recently charred with fire, and in several places along the path had been cumbled to rubble as if by explosion. Clearly, there had been a battle here, with Words stronger than any Revel would know. Guardians, he guessed. But he took comfort in the assurance that Revel, at least, had escaped unharmed, and hopefully, the others with him.

In time he came upon a small portal that opened to eastern shore of the island. He saw a charred rubble heap along the water's edge, which he could only presume had been a dock of sorts, and a smattering of footprints in the mud nearby. The trail of his brother's presence drifted out into the open sea.

Ajel sighed. *Where have you gone, brother? Are the others still with you? Do you still follow the Waymaker's quest?*

Back in the Chamber of the Pearl, his eyes turned down to the elegant script of the Book of *Dei'lo*, which lay reverently across his lap. He searched for only a moment before he found the Wording he was looking for, and gently closed his eyes as he breathed it from his lips.

Immediately, in the vision, he found himself taking the form of an eagle launching on its mighty wings from the shore of the island. He felt the vibration of the salty wind across his feathers as he turned his sharp eyes outward toward the sea. The trail of Revel's course across the waters seemed oddly arbitrary—as if he had no notion of which direction to go, or else was incapable of controlling his craft—but from the heights where Ajel flew the general heading soon became clear—Southeast, a route that, if followed to its end, would carry them to the northern shores of the Deathland Barrens.

Why would he be heading that way? Ajel could imagine nothing good coming from such a course. Undaunted, however, he followed. Eventually, the trail shifted firmly eastward, away from the Barrens and toward the open expanse of the Northern Sea.

Then, at last, he saw them. "The Endurant," he whispered aloud, watching its aged and solid shape cut across the facets of the chamber walls, mimicking the scene that played out in his spirit. Swooping down, he felt joy surge in his chest at seeing Revel there, sitting cross-legged on the center of the deck hovering intensely over a bucket of water that sat before him. He appeared to be trying to use *Dei'lo* to do something to it. From the angry frown on his face, he wasn't having much success. The Raanthan stood nearby, watching Revel in silence as its inhuman skin glistening like silver in the afternoon sun.

I found you, brother! I found you at last!

At that moment, in the vision, the Raanthan turned his gaze directly toward Ajel, and raised a slender hand in greeting.

"He sees me!" Ajel laughed aloud within the Chamber. "The Raanthan sees me! Oh, the wonder of it!" The Words of vision could carry his awareness to almost any place he wished to go, but they could never make him visible to those he encountered on the journey. For whatever reason, however, it seemed that rule did not apply to Raanthan. He laughed again, and listened as the sound of it echoed off the diamond facets of the walls, mingling with the music of the fountain bubbling at the chamber's center.

Although the burden of his new role as Paladin had brought more than its share of weariness and stress to his life, the mysteries he'd uncovered through the Book in his studies along the way had been beyond amazing. So many things he'd thought he'd never understand—about the deeper working of *Dei'lo*, about Wordhaven and the Stand, even about this very chamber—

now seemed so clear and simple in his mind he wondered why he had never grasped them before. Every day brought challenges, but also new discoveries, and with both came a deepening awe at the expanding treasure he now carried in his soul.

He knew, of course, that war would eventually come to Wordhaven—a war that brought no guarantees of victory, or even of survival. But if that was the cost of retrieving the Book of *Dei'lo*, and learning the mysteries it had to teach, then it would be, he decided, a small price to pay.

His thoughts were interrupted by sudden clanging crash behind him, and Ajel turned to see a young woman standing sheepishly just inside the chamber's golden doors. The tray of fruit she had been holding lay scattered upon the floor at her feet. Her eyes seemed filled with unexplainable horror as she looked at him.

Immediately, Ajel spoke the Words to end the vision quest. Images of ship and sea—and of dear Revel's face—all faded, and were replaced by a shifting kaleidoscope of images from all across the Inherited Lands, which was the chamber's neutral state. He frowned, noticing the change did little to soften the tension on the young woman's face.

"Don't be afraid," Ajel called to her with assuring smile. "Sarla, isn't it?"

When she did not respond, Ajel carefully closed the Book of *Dei'lo* and set it on the marble floor beside him. He stood and began moving up the ramp toward her, speaking with gentle tones as he walked. "There is no cause for alarm, Sarla," he said. "This is your first time in the Chamber of the Pearl, yes? It is a powerful place, that is true. But no one of true heart need fear it. You are safe here."

She cradled her stomach in her arms. Her face went white. "It feels so. . . ." She looked around as if the walls might eat her.

Ajel quickened his pace. "Are you well, Sarla?" he asked. "You look pale."

She tried to smile, but seemed incapable of it. "I did not realize you were studying the Book," she said. "I should not have come."

"It is no bother," Ajel laughed. "In truth, I have wonderful news! I have found my brother. He is well, aboard a ship in the Northern Sea."

But Sarla did not seem to understand. Her eyes remained transfixed on the Book at the chamber's center. "Perhaps you should sit down a moment," offered Ajel. "You seem frail just now."

"I am not frail!" snapped Sarla suddenly. For just an instant, her eyes flashed with a bitter anger that seemed incongruous with her innocent face. But it passed as quickly as it came. "I apologize," she added meekly. "Perhaps I should sit a moment, after all."

Ajel reached out his hand. "Come down to the water," he said. "It's more refreshing there."

"No," said Sarla quickly. "No, this will be fine." Hesitantly, she sunk down to the floor beneath her, ignoring the fruit that lay scattered all around. "I am sorry to be such trouble," she said. "I'm afraid the excitement of seeing such a wonder as this has made me dizzy."

Ajel knelt down beside her. "If you will pardon my saying so, but you seem more than merely dizzy. Are you certain you are well?"

"I thought you might need some refreshment," she said, looking at the floor. "I was told you were here. Kair told me the way." She smiled weakly. "It's a very difficult room to find."

Ajel grinned. "It is the heart of the Stand." He looked around. "From this chamber, the Pearl once ruled the whole of the Inherited Lands, from the largest of the soundens to the smallest blade of grass. You speak true when you say it is a wonder. I never grow tired of coming here."

Sarla smiled, but her arms still clung to her stomach desperately. "I am sorry about the fruit," she said.

"It is of no concern," Ajel replied. "Shall I walk you to your chambers?"

"No, please," she said, shaking her head dismissively. "It is just a troubled stomach. It is only a minor distraction."

Ajel reached out his hand. "Here," he said. "Let me speak a Word of healing—"

"No!" replied Sarla, her eyes suddenly full of alarm. "I could not dare to ask such a thing. It's nothing, really, Paladin. It will pass on its own." She shifted her body away from him as if his touch might burn her skin.

Ajel looked at her firmly. "The Words of *Dei'lo* need not be feared, Sarla. They are not like the Words you heard spoken by the Lords in Phallenar. Unlike *Sa'lei*, *Dei'lo* brings life and healing. Not destruction."

Immediately, Sarla's expression turned hard. "*Dei'lo* can kill, too, Paladin," she said. There was a distinct edge to her tone. "You spoke *Dei'lo* to slay the Lord that attacked here, did you not?"

How does she know about that? For a moment, he considered questioning her about it, but given her obvious distress he decided against it for now. Besides, she had most likely heard the story through idle conversation as she worked in the kitchens, or perhaps in her talks with Seer. He said, "You speak true, Sarla. *Dei'lo* is powerful and quite dangerous. It is not to be handled lightly. But though it can be fierce in its speaking, it is also good."

Sarla shifted her weight uneasily. Her expression appeared conflicted, as if she were embroiled in some internal struggle, but Ajel could sense nothing of her true feelings or thoughts in his mind. The mystical effects of Wordhaven were difficult to resist, but this delicate-looking girl had somehow managed to shut them out with such alacrity that not even one single stray emotion or thought could escape the walls she had built. In a strange way, it felt to Ajel as if she wasn't even there.

"I did not know you had a brother, Paladin," she said at last, obviously trying to shift the topic off of her discomfort. "Where has he been hiding that you must come here to search for him?"

"He travels with the Waymaker and the Raanthan who accompanies him," replied Ajel. He smiled lightly. "At least I hope that is still true. I did not see the Waymaker in the vision."

"A Raanthan, you say?" replied Sarla, her eyes suddenly curious. "That is a wonder. And who is this Waymaker?"

"He is known to many here as Gideon Dawning," said Ajel, "or the Stormcaller. You may have heard his name spoken in the Stand."

"He lives still?" exclaimed Sarla with a flash of irritation. But then, softer, "I mean, I had heard that he was slain."

"It is my deepest hope that he yet lives," replied Ajel, noticing her irritation, but uncertain of its cause. "Indeed, that is in part why I have been searching for my brother, to learn what has become of them both. I'm curious. Who told you the Waymaker was slain?"

Sarla smiled apologetically. "I'm certain I misheard," she said. "But I am...pleased to hear you have found them. Are they well?"

Ajel shook his head. "I cannot be certain. Revel seemed well enough, and the Raanthan was with him. But I did not see the Waymaker. I will need to return to the vision again to learn what more I can."

Sarla looked at him inquisitively. "Could you not go to them yourself? Cannot the power of your mighty Tongue do this for you?"

Again, Ajel noticed the edge in her tone. "The Tongue truly is an amazing power," he said. "I have gained more strength in the Words than I thought possible in so short a time. But if there is a way to transport instantly to a place I have never been, I have not yet found it."

But even as he said this, Ajel realized it wasn't fully true. Through his study of the Book, he had learned much about the Words that governed the portals scattered throughout the Stand. He knew now that they were gateways to various locations within the Inherited Lands and even beyond. With them, you could travel to any number of places you had never been before. It was a fairly simple matter to find the Words to open them—though in truth, the *Dei'lo* Word for the task was more accurately translated "awaken" in the common tongue. Ajel himself had awakened more than a dozen of the Worded passageways—opening views to distant corners of the world that he had never seen, and some he had no knowledge of at all. But more than a hundred other portals remained unopened throughout the Stand—scattered across every level of the fortress in what seemed a completely haphazard arrangement.

He hoped in time to awaken them all. He likely would have already if not for the hundreds of new initiates roaming unescorted throughout Wordhaven's halls. Since the portals allowed passage in only one direction, if one of the initiates happened to stumble through an open doorway unawares, he would be trapped at the other end. What's worse, if he were not familiar with the destination, he would have no way of knowing which route might carry him back home.

This would have been no problem for the Lords of old, of course, since they could simply speak the Word of transport to carry them instantly back to Wordhaven from wherever the portals had taken them. But most of the initiates had not been taught that Word, since it was not, strictly speaking, a phrase of battle.

Suddenly, he realized that one of the portals he had awakened led to a place he now recognized. He had been uncertain of its location before, but now he was sure—for his vision had just carried him there, displaying the castle's dull grey corridors on the chamber's multi-faceted walls. *Of course! The Domain of Domains!*

"Perhaps there is a way I could go to him, after all," said Ajel at last. He looked at Sarla, who just sat there watching him with an intense curiosity in her eyes. "I could use one of the portals to travel to the Isle of Edor. From there, I believe I could now call on a sea dragon to carry me to him."

"The Isle of Edor?" said Sarla excitedly. "You mean, leave Wordhaven?"

"Yes," explained Ajel. "The Isle of Edor lies in the northern reaches of the Hinterland. One of the portals I recently awakened could take me there." Since Sarla had been raised a slave in Phallenar, Ajel suspected she'd never heard of the Hinterland Isles before, much less the stronghold of Kiki.

Sarla's eyes came alive with interest. "These portals, can they transport anyone beyond Wordhaven's walls—even those without a knowledge of *Dei'lo*?"

Ajel nodded. "I believe so, yes. Though, in truth, I have not permitted anyone to use them as yet—Worded or otherwise. I wanted to be certain the portals were safe."

Sarla flashed him a mirthful grin. "Oh, Paladin, I would be deeply grateful if you would show me one of these portals. I would love to see such a wonder for myself!"

Ajel was surprised to feel the waves of Sarla's innocent excitement wash over him. Perhaps the girl was not so closed after all. The thought of seeing a portal—perhaps even passing through one—obviously thrilled her.

In truth, however, his own feelings about using the portals were far less clear. He was not certain that leaving to find Revel was a good idea, even if the portals could provide a way. There were many factors to consider—the most obvious being his ongoing responsibilities as Paladin of Wordhaven. And then there was Donovan, who would undoubtedly bristle at the mere suggestion of Ajel leaving the Stand for even an hour. The winter was nearly upon them, but that was no guarantee that Phallenar would not attack. And if that happened, Donovan would want Ajel close—as much for the Paladin's protection as for any strength he might lend to the battle.

Still, the Waymaker's path was important as well—perhaps even more important than protecting the Book, if what the Raanthan had told Ajel about Gideon was true. Even though Ajel had seen that Revel was alive, it still deeply concerned him that his brother had not sent any word as to the Waymaker's health or the progress of his quest since the morning the two brothers had parted ways at the Black Gorge. True, Revel had been traveling much of that time. But it was unlike him to be so silent.

"Shall we go then?" Sarla smiled at him with the wide glee of child asking for love.

Ajel returned her smile. He supposed there would be no harm in obliging her request, but her obvious physical infirmity concerned him. Despite her cheerful demeanor, her face remained as pale as gypsum, and she continued to grip her stomach as if it might escape if she let it go.

"I would be pleased to show you one," he said. "But the portal I'm interested in is a long walk from here. Why don't we go see one that is closer by? And then perhaps you should you return to your chambers and rest awhile."

She smiled slyly. "I think I will be myself again soon," she said, and genteelly proffered him her hand with the practiced elegance of a noble.

The gesture surprised him. It was an etiquette more befitting a member of the ruling caste than a former slave—but he dismissed it for now as just another eccentric expression of her rattled nerves, and gently wrapped her hand in the fold of his arm as he helped her to her feet.

Once they had passed through the gold-laden doors, he guided her down the passage to his left. The first portal he had awakened lay in that direction. He had chosen it because of its close proximity to the Pearl's chamber, which suggested that it may have carried some unique importance to the Lords of old.

To his surprise, however, the location it revealed was unlike any place he had ever seen.

THE PORTAL

In a place so full of the truth of life as Wordhaven is, how could such a deceiver pass for so long unnoticed? In any other time, perhaps she would not have succeeded. But in those days the Remnant had welcomed in well over seven hundred souls in preparation for war, none of whom had been tested in the ways of true Initiates to the Words. With so many closed and unsettled hearts roaming Wordhaven's halls, it seems little wonder that a deceiver could slip through the gates and live among them—even one as darkly saturated in Sa'lei as a Council Lord.

—The Kyrinthan Journals, Musings, Chapter 23, Verses 112-114

At last, I have him!

Lord Fayerna Baratii's eyes glared at Ajel's back with raw malice as she shuffled along meekly behind him down the narrow winding corridor of the Stand. If the portals proved true, the two of them would soon be standing face to face leagues away from Wordhaven's cursed gates, and she would at last be free to take her long-anticipated revenge.

That it had taken so long to reach this point only fueled her loathing for him, and magnified her rage. From the moment she had stepped through the golden doors of Wordhaven, her singular intent had been Ajel's deliberate, tortuous death. He had become her sole obsession; his death, her only remaining reason for living.

Until Sarlina came into her life, Fayerna had never known what it was like to be loved. She had been such a simple girl, an idiot in most respects, but it was that same simplicity that made her love so unquestioning, so free of guile. She truly adored Fayerna. She worshipped Fayerna. The girl wanted nothing but to please her.

But Sarlina was dead now—because of *him*.

There was also Bentel, of course—her dear, faithless brother, Bentel. She'd once believed he loved her as well. But he had shown his true heart when he abandoned her, leaving her to rot in Strivenwood after the battle at Morguen, running away to save his own skin while she languished in the forest alone, injured and fighting off the blighted trees night after night until she lost even the strength to scream anymore. He had never loved her. If he had, he never could have left her to suffer alone the way he did.

No. No one had ever truly loved her—no one except Sarlina.

In time, Fayerna found her strength again; not in her Words, but in the form of a dream—the dream of reaping vengeance against Ajel for the death of her dear Sarlina. That image became the singular vision that kept her alive in that cursed wood. She drank in the dream like milk from a mother's breast. She wrapped it around her body like a blanket against the cold, and it soon filled her with renewed resolve. She could not die, she would not die. Not until *he* paid for what he had done to her.

The forest had been all too ready to accommodate her hate, providing her with a thousand different Ajels, each in his turn, for her to hunt down and make suffer. She destroyed them all, in a hundred different ways with a hundred different Words. But still it was not enough to satisfy her mad thirst for revenge. Enraged by what the wood could not deliver, she soon tore her way through the trees, ripping a path of destruction with Words that eventually led her out of Strivenwood, and found her on the borders of the Hinterland. The fools who live there had found her, and even tried to constrain her, but so focused was her purpose that she barely noticed them, even as their bodies burned in her wake.

The vision of Ajel's destruction had become the only thing that fueled her will to live, and filled her with a bitterness that bordered on madness. But even in her rage, her shrewdness remained intact. She knew that she alone could not breach the walls of Wordhaven by force, and so she chose a subtler route. Using the Words to disguise herself, she took the name of

Sarla—a derivative of Sarlina in honor of her fallen sister—and made her way to Wordhaven in a guise no one would suspect. A humble maid. A slave escaped.

Each day in Wordhaven had brought the promise of vengeance. But Fayerna had not anticipated the suppressing effects of a place so saturated with the taint of *Dei'lo*. One whisper of *Sa'lei*, and she would be undone. The structure itself would likely slay her where she stood. And the presence of the cursed Book within its walls intensified the ever-deepening sickness that plagued her day and night.

But she fought through it all, she held her course, and now at last her patience was being rewarded. The time for her vindication had come.

Ajel turned and smiled at her as they walked. "We are nearly there," he said. "Are you well?"

"Yes, thank you," she replied with a smile. His smugness disgusted her.

A moment later he led her through an arched doorway on the left side of the corridor. Within, she found a simple, darkened room, barren except for an open doorway at the far end. Bright sunlight glared through the opening, making it difficult to see what place it revealed. But anyplace would do, so long as it was far from Wordhaven's effects.

"We do not yet know where it leads," said Ajel, gesturing for her to step closer. He shielded his eyes with one hand and leaned toward the gate. "It opens to a high mountain," he added, "and there is a hope nearby. But no one among the Remnant recognizes it. Not even Brasen Stoneguard, who has traveled through more of the Lands than any among us."

Slowly, subtly, she inched her way closer to him, feigning awe and timidity through her Word-wrought mask of innocence. "Is it dangerous to stand so close?" she asked.

"No," Ajel grinned. "The portal acts only on those who step beyond the plane of the door. We are safe so long as we do not cross the boundary."

"Can we move closer, then?" she asked, her false voice filled with child-like excitement. "It's so bright, and I want to see all I can."

Ajel looked at her a moment. "I suppose," he said, grinning a little. "But be careful not to touch it." Stepping to within a foot of the threshold, he reached back his hand to guide her.

She hesitated. "What do you see?" she asked.

Ajel turned his head and peered through the portal.

That was her moment.

Lowering her head, she charged at his body with all of her might.

An instant later, she tumbled to the ground upon the mountain grasses, with her doomed prey wrestling in her arms.

21

THE ENDURANT

As the weeks progressed, my former self—the girl I had known, the woman I was—slowly passed away. I did not notice it at first. But the truth of it came to light when I finally abandoned the green gown I had worn since the night Gideon first appeared. I wept as I tossed the tattered dress into the open sea, and continued my weeping well into the night. It seemed incredulous to me that I should weep. I hated my life in Phallenar, and wanted nothing so much as to leave it behind forever. And yet the experience has taught me a valuable truth of life—that even a slave must grieve his chains before he can be truly free.
— The Kyrinthan Journals, Songs of Deliverance, Stanza 14, Verses 120-122

With a flurry of frustration, Gideon threw off the covers and sat up. He rubbed his face and stared blankly down at his scarred sunburned feet. After two hours of trying to nap, he had finally decided to give up.

Standing, he peered through the small square portal near his bed. The midday sun created a sea of sparkling diamonds upon the waters, broken here and there by whitecap waves blowing past them from the west. The ocean was choppy, but no more so than it had been in the two days since their rescue. No, it wasn't the waves that had kept him from sleeping.

But something had. He felt bothered, uneasy—like he had an itch he knew was there, but couldn't quite find to scratch.

Frustrated, he sat down again and pulled on his boots. It was probably past noon by now, despite the fact that he wasn't the least bit hungry, and so he might as well go find Revel. The Wordhavener had promised him another training session with staffs this afternoon, and he hoped the fighting would take his mind off of whatever was bugging him. After throwing on his leather jerkin, he grabbed his staff and headed out the door, being careful to close it quietly behind him so as not to wake Aybel in the next berth. He glanced at her door and let out a quiet sigh. At least *she* wasn't having any trouble sleeping, he thought. In truth, after all that had happened to her in the Hinterland, she needed the rest far more than he did anyway.

As Gideon emerged from the galley, he found Revel sitting cross-legged on the foredeck, still staring at the bucket of sea water he had been fretting over for the past two days. With the ship's fresh water supply nearly depleted, Revel had taken it upon himself to use the Words to purify some sea water so they could drink it. The only problem was he didn't have the slightest idea how to do it—a fact that seemed only to fuel his resolve to conquer the challenge.

Kyrintha sat beside him, a look of intrigue mixed with concern etched on her dainty face, while Telus stood off to the side next to the railing, his bronze eyes looking on impassively as usual.

Upon seeing Gideon, however, the Raanthan bowed his head slightly. Gideon returned the nod, then stepped toward Revel, holding his staff confidently at his side. "How's it going?" he asked. But Revel's attention remained fixed on the bucket.

"He's been working with it for many hours," replied Kyrintha with compassion in her voice, "but the Words fail him so far."

"It is not the Words, Kyrintha, but the speaker," Revel corrected gently. He smiled at the underlord briefly, then looked up at Gideon. "I have churned it, boiled it, made it dance like a spirit. But I have yet to find the Words to make it clean. I feel like an infant fumbling to ask his mother for a drink."

"Then maybe it's time for a break," Gideon offered, glancing at the clear azure sky. "Unless my sundial is broken, it's time for my daily beating at staffs."

Revel nodded slightly, then smoothly rose to his feet in one fluid movement. Even after being around him for so long, Revel's grace continued to take Gideon by surprise. "Far from it, Waymaker," said Revel. "You have done well. I doubt there are many at Wordhaven who could best you at staffs now."

"Well, I don't know," said Gideon, twirling the staff in one hand. "I hear Seer's pretty good with a stick." Despite the self-effacing humor, Gideon secretly basked in Revel's praise. He had never been a fighting man, having always considered himself distinctly lacking in physical prowess of any kind. But learning the staffs had taught him to connect with his strength in a way he'd never known was possible. For the first time in his life, he took pride in knowing that he could actually step into a fight and *win*.

Revel laughed. "It is good to see your spirits rising, Waymaker."

Gideon shrugged. "Must be all the wine I've been drinking." With so little fresh water on board, Quigly's bondmate had relegated them to drinking a dark red wine exclusively with their meals, including breakfast. So far Gideon hadn't noticed much effect from the switch, other than a persistent drowsiness.

"Yes, there is that," agreed Revel. He looked down at the bucket thoughtfully. "The captain tells us it is still many days' journey to the Vag, and I have made no progress in purifying the water." He thought a moment longer, then added, "Perhaps it would be wiser to suspend our training until we reach safe haven, Waymaker. The wine may mask our thirst for now, but its effects will only heighten our need for water in the end. We should conserve our fluids as much as possible."

Gideon sighed. He was looking forward to training with the staffs, but had to admit that Revel was probably right. If he couldn't convert the water, they'd all be dangerously dehydrated by the time they pulled into the Sea Folk's floating city. Somehow, though, the problem just didn't seem important enough to worry over. After escaping Stevron's deadly attack and surviving for an entire night in the open sea, enduring a little thirst seemed trivial.

"Well, I've gotta do something," said Gideon, now tossing his staff from one hand to the other as he looked around the deck. "I feel antsy."

"Antsy?" asked Kyrintha. "I'm not familiar with that word."

Gideon shrugged it off. "Oh, it's nothing," he said. "Just a little nervous energy, that's all."

"Are you troubled, Waymaker?" asked Telus, tilting his head in a way that struck Gideon as especially peculiar, even for a Raanthan. "What do you feel?"

"Nothing, Telus," said Gideon, a little defensively. "I couldn't sleep, that's all. I just need something to do."

The Raanthan glided toward them, his white mane floating around his shoulders like a mist. "Listen," he said. Stretching forth his gangly hand, he touched Gideon lightly on the chest. "Listen," he repeated. "What do you sense?"

Gideon stepped back, feeling a little embarrassed by Telus' instructive tone. He didn't mind the Raanthan's didactic arrogance so much when they were alone, but he didn't like being made to feel like a dim-witted student in front of Revel and the underlord. "It's nothing, Telus," he said slowly. "Forget I mentioned it."

The Raanthan touched his chest again. "You must listen—here," he repeated firmly.

"I did, Telus!" Gideon snapped. He pointed his staff toward the horizon. "We're already moving toward..." Suddenly, Gideon noticed where he was pointing; to his surprise, it was not the direction the ship was going. "Wait a minute," he mumbled. "We should be going that way." He glanced toward the bow, then looked at Telus. "We're not heading the right way anymore."

"How long?" asked Telus. There was a distinct edge in his tone now. "When did you first sense this?"

"I don't know!" Gideon replied angrily. "Just now, I guess." But he realized it had actually been long before now—several hours at least. *So that's why I couldn't sleep!*

Suddenly, Telus reached out and snatched Gideon by the arm. "Did I not tell you that you must *listen*?" he snapped, his eyes gleaming brightly like molten bronze. "You are the Waymaker! Do you not realize what is at stake?"

A burst of anger flared up in Gideon's chest. Dark memories of his father rose unbidden to his thoughts. He didn't like the Raanthan's tone. Without thinking, he lifted up the staff to Telus' face, and stared into his molten eyes. "Remove your hand, Telus," he said coolly, "or I'll remove it for you."

Telus blinked and, bowing his head slightly, smiled in approval. "Good. You will need that," he said. He stepped back smoothly, then added, more sternly this time, "I am for you, Waymaker, but I cannot serve you if you fail to listen."

Gideon stared at him a moment longer, then said, "I will talk to the captain."

He stormed away from the others, leaving them to stare at his back in silence as he climbed the steps to the aft deck. Why did the Raanthan always have to ride him so hard? He knew what the stakes were, even if he didn't like to think about it. And making him feel like a child in front of the others didn't help. He harbored more than enough self-doubt about his ability to fulfill his role as Waymaker as it was. The Raanthan's constant badgering only made things worse.

Gideon found Quigly and his bondmate sitting together on a long bench near the wheel, their blockish feet dangling idly in the air as they puffed contentedly on identical long-stemmed pipes. Their gazes drifted lightly across the sails above.

"Captain Quigly," said Gideon hesitantly, "I need to talk to you."

Quigly's gaze did not shift. "Then talk," he said, puffing the smoke lazily past his lips.

"Are we still headed toward the Vag?" Gideon asked.

"Aye," he said.

"Are you certain?"

The captain's bondmate snorted derisively, and Quigly shot him a side-long glance. "That question is either daft or insulting, lander" he said. "Either way, I'd recommend you not ask it twice."

Tentatively, Gideon stepped forward. He had learned that Quigly's pride could be prickly—and that was on his good days. "I don't know how to say this," he began, "but we need to be going that way." He pointed out toward the starboard horizon.

Quigly's gaze followed his finger, then he chuckled. "Not if you're goin' to the Vag you don't, lander."

"That's just it," said Gideon. "I don't think we're supposed to be going to the Vag anymore."

"Well, that's a shame, isn't it? Since that's where you be headed."

Well, this is going well. "I mean no disrespect, Captain," continued Gideon, "but you promised to take us where we needed to go, didn't you? You made an agreement with Paladin Sky, and with Ajel as well."

The captain slowly lowered his pipe. "That contract ended the very day you failed to return to the ship as promised on the shores of the Hinterland. Make no mistake lander, you'd have seen my wake days ago if not for the dark arts of that over-tall apparition, may the waters take him. I got you safely out of the Sound. As I see it, my debt to Paladin Sky is more than paid.

"Besides, if your heart is truly set on sailing that way," he pointed with his pipe, "you might as well jump overboard and drown yourselves now. For there be nothin' that direction but death."

"What do you mean?" asked Gideon. "What lies in that direction?"

Quigly shook his head and laughed. "By the Giver, you really don't know, do ya'?" He leaned toward his bondmate and muttered, "How these landers find their way out the door in the mornin' is beyond me." She nodded her head in agreement. "The Barrens, lad!" he exclaimed, turning back to Gideon. "There be nothin' but deception and death there. No, you be better off with ol' Quigly. Not many landers get to see the Vag, you know. Tis' a rare gift, and more than you deserve after all the grief you've brought on my ship."

Gideon sighed in frustration. The Barrens? Is that where he was really supposed to go? From all he'd heard, the Deathland Barrens was nothing but a cesspool of *Sa'lei* perversions, both living and dead. Nothing good could survive there. And yet, the pull in his gut was clear. That *was* the right direction. How could he make Quigly understand? "How far is it to the Barrens from here?" he asked. "How many days' journey?"

Quigly glanced over his shoulder toward to the south. "Less than half a day, I'd say, the winds being what they are."

"Then couldn't you just take us close to shore?" asked Gideon, noticing his tone was sounding more desperate than he wished. "Close enough for us to swim the distance, or perhaps take a raft?"

"A raft?" barked Quigly "Made from what? The timbers of my ship? You're on the edge of daft, lander, you know that?"

"I wouldn't ask if wasn't really important, Captain," Gideon implored.

Quigly jumped down from the bench and hobbled over to face Gideon. Despite the nearly two-foot difference in their height, the captain still managed to look imposing as he glared up at Gideon's eyes. "I be the captain of this ship, lander. And I've said no. That's the end of it. Now go and leave us in peace before I lose my temper."

"Captain Quigly!" Kyrintha's voice rang out from the foredeck. Gideon turned to see her dashing up the steps toward them. "Captain, something has appeared on the horizon that you should see."

"Where do you see it?" asked Quigly, scanning the waters ahead.

"There," replied the underlord, pointing off the port side. "Close to due North."

Quigly shuffled to the port railing and peered into the distance. It didn't take long for Gideon to spot it as well—a lone black cloud hovering close to the waters in an otherwise cloudless sky. It looked like nothing more than a tiny thunderstorm, and Gideon said as much.

"Perhaps so," said Kyrintha, "but it just came out of nowhere. It appeared just in the last few moments, while I was looking out to sea. And it seems to be growing larger."

"Aye," agreed Quigly with a frown. "It's heading straight for us. Could be the first signs of a front comin' in from the North."

"It is unnatural, Waymaker." Telus appeared on the steps behind Kyrintha, his head towering over hers despite the fact that she stood three steps above him. Ignoring the captain's glare, he looked straight at Gideon. "It is a deathstorm, wrought by *Sa'lei*."

"You can tell this far away?" asked Gideon.

"I can see it," replied the Raanthan, as if that answered the question.

"It is Stevron, then," said Kyrintha anxiously. "He has found us."

"Can we outrun it?" Gideon asked the captain.

Quigly eyed the horizon for split second, then said, "Not without a gale of our own to pull us forward. Already its size has doubled. I reckon we have less than an hour before the front edge reaches my sails, and that's assuming the winds don't turn shifty, which they will."

Gideon nodded. He gripped his staff in both hands, taking comfort from its warmth. "Then I guess we have to fight it off somehow," he said, looking at Telus. The Raanthan gave no response.

"You cannot fight off a storm at sea, lander," said Quigly firmly. "The only way to best a storm is to batten down and surrender to its whims."

"If Telus is right then this is no ordinary storm, Captain" said Gideon, recalling the horrible malevolence he felt as he plodded through the ancient deathstorm of Dunerun Hope. "A deathstorm is created by the power of *Sa'lei* with a singular purpose. It means to destroy us. We have to fight it if we hope to survive."

Quigly waved him off. "I know nothing of such things. The Words be your domain, not mine. But I do know how to weather a gale at sea, and that's what I intend to do." He turned to his bondmate, "Woman, secure the sails. The rest of you, batten down the hatches and man the lines. Prepare to come about."

"I'll get Aybel," said Kyrintha. She disappeared down the stairs.

Gideon looked at Telus. "So, how do we fight this?" he asked.

Telus blinked. "You are the Waymaker," he said. "You must find the way."

"Don't be so cryptic, Telus!" snapped Gideon angrily. "I know you know more about this than you're letting on. Why don't you tell me something useful?"

Telus seemed unfazed by Gideon's reproach. "I know some things, Waymaker. But not all. I know that you are the Waymaker, and that you alone can find the way. That much I can tell you."

"It's not that simple," said Gideon sharply. "So what if I know the direction we should go? I can't force Captain Quigly to sail that way. And I certainly don't know how to stop a deathstorm!"

"You are the Waymaker," Telus repeated.

Gideon looked at the Raanthan in disgust. "You know what? I'm sorry I asked. Thanks for nothing." Gideon marched past him down the stairs.

"Waymaker."

Gideon paused. "What?" he snapped.

"You need only speak true, and you will not fail."

Gideon rolled his eyes. "Yeah, I've heard that one before," he quipped sarcastically. "Too bad I don't know what it means." He walked off in a huff.

The storm grew far more rapidly than Quigly had expected, covering the sky to the north with a blanket of thick darkness in a matter of minutes and resonating the air around them with rumblings of thunder. They had little time to secure the ship, but with all hands on deck, they managed to get everything tied down as best they could. Aybel had joined in the work without comment, but with one look in her sleepy eyes, Gideon could tell she, too, was afraid. There was no way for them to run and hide this time. And none of them had any idea how to fight a *Sa'lei* wrought deathstorm—least of all Gideon.

Even so, Revel and Aybel did what they could, speaking Words of resilience and strength to the timbers of the ship, especially the masts, rudder and keel. They also spoke Words over the captain and his bondmate, blessing them with peace and courage and the focus of warriors, which they received if not with gratitude, then at least with curiosity. Kyrintha clung close by their sides, perhaps in part for her own protection, but also because they were the only ones aboard who spoke *Dei'lo*, and the underlord had obviously become as obsessed with studying this Tongue as she was repulsed by *Sa'lei*. She was a pragmatic woman in most ways, it seemed to Gideon, but her passion for learning bordered on fanatical.

The Raanthan, in contrast, stayed close to Gideon, who reluctantly accepted his presence even if he didn't want it. Telus had proven himself an able teacher in some ways, helping Gideon understand more about the prophecies of the Waymaker and his critical role in the days ahead. But the Raanthan's superior attitude was wearing thin on Gideon. And he had not forgotten how Telus had displayed such deep reluctance to get involved when they fought off the viperon in the Gorge. With those kinds of pacifist tendencies, Gideon doubted the towering mystic would lend much help to him in any true fight.

Gideon took his stand on the foredeck facing the storm, with Telus hovering over his shoulder. Aybel, Revel and the underlord stood at amidships on the port side, while Quigly and his bondmate took their place on the aft deck next to the wheel. They all watched the oncoming malevolence with a silence coated in dread.

Just as the first winds of the storm front reached them, Quigly called out from the wheel, "Comin' about! Get below if you're goin'!"

"You should go below now," Revel said to the underlord. He gripped her shoulder gently. "You will be safer there."

The underlord did not respond, but Gideon could see that the look on her face made it clear that she had no intention of going anywhere. Revel sighed heavily, clearly troubled by her resolve, but he did not ask again.

As Quigly turned the wheel, the bow of the Endurant slowly shifted north until it pointed straight at the oncoming storm. Aybel, Revel and Kyrintha moved to join Gideon and Telus on the foredeck, gripping the railings to stabilize themselves against the increasing wind.

"Dragons, ho!" screamed Quigly. "Dragons, ho! Dead ahead, landers! And if my eyes don't deceive me, there be riders upon the lot of 'em!"

Gideon ran to the bow and peered into the dark canopy ahead. Amid the churning waves in the distance, he saw what looked like scores of massive snake heads bobbing in the waters. They were bright green, in stark contrast to the blackness of the sea, with what looked like wings of blood red skin fanning out behind their skulls. Even from this distance, he could see the whiteness of their dagger-like teeth, and the black dot of a rider perched upon their heads.

"*Mon'jalen!*" cried Revel. "A full company! And the Council Lord is leading them!"

"Quick! Raise the sails!" bellowed Quigly. "Wordhaveners, help the woman! Raise 'em all and lash 'em tight!"

"But we only just lowered them!" exclaimed Kyrintha.

Quigly yelled in frustration. "That was before I knew there be dragons, underlord," he said. "I'll not have those scaly beasts taking chunks out of my lady's sweet hull, and us just sitting dead in the water! Now, man the spars, all of ya. They may not be much, but it's all we got."

Gideon barely noticed the captain's bellows as he continued to stare at the surreal panorama before him. He counted close to a hundred bright green serpentine heads, looming higher and higher in the dark sky as they approached.

"How big are these things?" he called to the captain.

"Big enough that you don't want to know, lander. Now grab a spar!"

Gideon could hardly believe his eyes. The riders looked like miniature dolls compared to the beasts. How could he hope to fight something so big? And so many at once! He noticed one of the riders signaling something to his companions, and he suddenly remembered what Revel had said. *These are mon'jalen!*

"Captain," Gideon yelled out above the wind, "We have to keep them out of earshot!" He ran back toward the aft deck where Quigly stood looking at the sails. "These are *mon'jalen!*" he yelled. "They could torch this ship with a single Word. You have to steer the ship away from them! Keep them from getting close enough to hear their voices!"

"My lady's fast, but she's no sea dragon," Quigly retorted. "We cannot out pace them, even with this gale at our backs."

"We have to try!" screamed Gideon. "It might at least give us a little time!"

Quigly stared at the approaching dragons a moment, his face slowly contorting into a scowl. "So be it!" he declared. "If I'm to be food for dragons, at least I'll make 'em work for it! Get those sails unfurled! We're comin' about!"

"It's not the dragons I'm worried about," muttered Gideon. He gripped his staff angrily and shook it. "If only I knew how to fight them!" As if in response to his frustration, the staff grew hotter in his hands.

"There is a way I can help, Waymaker." Telus appeared before him, looking like a silvery specter against the gloomy dark of the clouds behind him. "But only if you request it of me."

Gideon shook the hair from his eyes. "What, Telus? What is it?"

"When the ship comes about, command me to stand at the aft rail and face them. Command me to shield you from their Words."

"You can do that?" asked Gideon incredulously. Telus inclined his head slightly. "Damn it, Telus! Why didn't you tell me that before?"

"I am but one," the Raanthan continued. "And they are many. I cannot absorb them all. But I can protect you at least."

"We all need protection, Telus, not just me!" said Gideon.

"It is all I can do," he said. "But you must request it."

"Request it?" snapped Gideon. "What have I been doing all this time?" He shoved the Raanthan roughly toward the rear deck. "Yes, yes, whatever you said, do what you can! Get back there. I'll join you in a minute."

The gale grew fiercer by the moment. As Quigly turned the ship, the sails caught wind and billowed like balloons, immediately forcing the ship to lean hard to one side. The masts creaked loudly under the strain.

"Let 'em out, woman!" yelled Quigly. "Let 'em out. Give her time to get her bearing!"

Quigly's bondmate reacted fast, loosening the lines that held the mainsails, and directing Aybel, Revel and Kyrintha to do the same on the second mast and jibs. The Endurant soon righted itself, carving a tight circle in the waters as it turned due south. Once the heading was set, Quigly ordered the sails trimmed again, and started his usual litany of prayers to the wind, interspersed with an equally colorful litany of curses.

Gideon felt the heat pulsing madly through the staff in his hand. If he could just figure out how to control it, there might be a chance. But the power in the staff was proving as elusive to him as *Dei'lo* had ever been.

Suddenly, Aybel dashed past him, heading for the jib. The sight of her jogged a memory.

"Aybel wait!" he said.

But Aybel quickly shook her head. "Follow me." She ran on to the jib and began tightening up the lines. Gideon followed.

"What was that you said once about the Words?" asked Gideon, yelling now to be heard above the wind. "About how you are able to use them?"

She did not turn around. "You must receive the message of the Words into your heart, Waymaker," she said. "You must believe in them truly."

Gideon shook his head. "No, no. After that. You believe them, you speak them, and then what? You said there was something else. What was it?"

"Pull this," she said, holding out one of the lines. Gideon grabbed the line and pulled. She locked it down on the pulley.

"There was something else you said," Gideon repeated. "Something important."

She looked at him over her shoulder, her brown eyes bright and afraid. "You must surrender," she said. "You must surrender everything, or the Words will not flow."

"Surrender!" exclaimed Gideon, remembering.

"Why do you want to know?" she asked.

He frowned in frustration as he touched her shoulder. "I'm not sure. I need to think about it. Let's get to the back of the ship. We'll need you and Revel there."

They ran to the aft deck. Revel and Kyrintha were already there, standing to the rear of Quigly and his bondmate who both stood at the wheel. Telus stood behind them all, leaning precariously against the aft rail with his arms outstretched to the sea behind them. He was humming.

"It's dark arts, I tell ya'," bellowed Quigly. "You send demons to fight demons! No good will come of this."

Gideon stepped toward Telus cautiously. Out of the corner of this eye, he could see the daggered jaws of the dragons opening and closing in anticipation. He could almost make out the riders' faces now. "Telus, what are you doing?" he asked.

"The wind favors their voices, Waymaker," he said. "Prepare yourself."

As if on cue, the attack began.

THE BATTLE
FOR THE ENDURANT

When I saw Stevron approaching with a fleet of dragons at his side, I recoiled in horror. Not because I was afraid, but because I saw in him that day the dark fulfillment of the dream my father always had for me. The great champion of Sa'lei. The most powerful lord who had ever lived. In another life, I could have been him. I would have been him, save for the desperate choice of a little girl who dared to hope for something more than the life to which she had been born.

—The Kyrinthan Journals, Songs of Deliverance, Stanza 15, Verses 20-21

D amonoi lichten vadestro shon ak Ladocreat. . ."

The chorus of Words slithered across the winds, haunting and distant, but clear enough for Gideon to feel their malevolence. Above the bobbing heads of the dragons, ribbons of lightning—black as midnight but lined with fire—danced along the bottom of the clouds toward the ship. Before Gideon knew what was happening, he was blinded by a brilliant flash, and a deafening thunderous crack rattled the Endurant's timbers from stem to stern. He opened his eyes to see Telus stumble backward, glowing like the moon.

"Are you all right?" Gideon yelled.

"They call for you by name, Waymaker," responded Telus weakly. "Stay close to me, but not too close." The Raanthan pulled himself back up to the railing and resumed his stance. "Let us hope they are not close enough to detect my presence."

"You're glowing, Telus," said Gideon. "They'd have to be blind not to see you."

"I cannot protect the ship," said Telus. "Or the others. You must—"

Just then, the Words came again, stronger this time. Three strands of lightning coursed through the clouds then leaped down from the skies, converging directly on Gideon. At the last instant, however, they arced left and blasted the full force of their fury into the Raanthan instead. The impact lit up the darkened skies and shuddered the planks of the deck as if they were made of paper. Telus stood rigid in the blast, his bronze eyes glowing with defiance as the fiery spears of lightning impaled his body. Only when it passed did he stumble backward once again, dazed but glowing even brighter than before.

"They will soon turn their Words to the ship, Waymaker," he said, pulling himself back to the railing again. "I cannot shield against that."

"They are dividing," said Revel, peering over Gideon's shoulder. He turned back toward the captain. "They mean to flank us!"

"Aye, I see it," said Quigly. "But there's little I can do for it. The sails are stretched to their limits as it is!"

"Why would they do that?" asked Kyrintha. "They've shown that they can strike with force from where they are."

"Their first two strikes were unsuccessful," said Gideon. "Maybe they're curious to find out why."

But Revel shook his head. "It's not curiosity so much as caution, Waymaker," he said. "Lord Stevron knows you have power to resist him, but he does not yet know how much. Those first two strikes were merely a test of our defenses. He will not likely strike again until he is sure of delivering a death blow."

Gideon's eyes shifted nervously from Revel to Kyrintha to Aybel. They all looked back at him expectantly, waiting. If he could not find a way to summon his power, they would all die at Stevron's Word. And they all knew it.

The almond wood staff burned like fire beneath his fingers. He grabbed it in both hands, and leaned his forehead against its gilded surface.

The heat of it seared his skin. He could feel its power seething just beneath the wood, waiting for something. Waiting for him.

Suddenly, his eyes flashed open as a rush of words flooded his mind. With one hand he reached and snatched Revel by the collar. "I have to climb the mast," he said frantically. "Come on. Help me!"

Before Revel could respond, Gideon blazed past him, dragging him by the collar as he went. They climbed the stairs to the base of the main mast. Quigly and his bondmate glanced at them curiously, but were too occupied with navigating the gale to pay them much heed.

"Climb up with me," Gideon said to Revel. "I may need you to shield me with Words as I do this."

"Do what, Waymaker?" asked Revel, clearly taken aback by Gideon's frantic behavior.

"I don't know!" exclaimed Gideon. He shook his head. "I don't know exactly. But I have an idea. Just come with me."

Suddenly, Telus' voice bellowed across the deck. "No, Waymaker!" he said forcefully. "*I* must go with you, not that one." He stepped off the railing and pointed toward Revel. "He cannot protect you from the Council Lord's Words. I can, but only if I am close by."

Gideon looked at Revel, who only stared back at him with a sort of quizzical expression. He knew Telus was probably right, but he still trusted Revel more than the Raanthan.

"All right, fine!" yelled Gideon. "Get up here then. I'm going up." With a quick slap on Revel's back to reassure him, Gideon slipped his staff under his sash and started climbing.

He'd never been afraid of heights. But then, he'd never climbed a mast in the open sea before either. And certainly not in the middle of a gale. The thing to do, he decided, was to keep his eyes on the stout wood of the mast, and not look down.

Unfortunately, that didn't stop him from noticing the dragons. They were still aft of the ship, but moving fast. Within minutes, one hundred *mon'jalen* would be flanking the Endurant, fifty on each side, perched high above the storm-tossed waves on their monstrous beasts, leering and ready to strike. But what scared Gideon most was that somewhere in their midst Stevron also lurked. The Council Lord had nearly destroyed them on the Isle of Edor, gutting the castle in the process without even breaking his stride.

During the time Gideon resisted him with the staff, he could sense the depth of Stevron's power pressing against him, and knew it was far greater than Bentel's or even Balaam's had ever been. Stevron may be new to the Council, but he was no beginner in *Sa'lei*. If Gideon's idea worked, he might be able to hold the lord off for a while again. But for how long? The ship was trapped in the wide open sea. They had nowhere to run.

When Gideon finally reached the top, he climbed tentatively into the perch and braved a glance downward. The Endurant looked frighteningly small beneath him, as fragile as a child's toy tossed about in a hurricane. But worse than that, the rocking motion of the ship was greatly magnified by his height above its decks. He couldn't afford to let go of the center post for even a second or he would be tossed from the perch like a pebble from a slingshot.

"I am here, Waymaker."

The Raanthan's narrow face appeared above the lip of the perch, his silvery hair flying madly around him. His long arm flew over the railing and locked down on it like a clamp.

"I don't think we can both fit," said Gideon, glancing at the limited floor space around him.

"It is all right," said Telus, adjusting his footing on something below. "I will manage."

Gideon nodded, and looked out toward the oncoming fleet of dragons. He could see the riders clearly now, their faces grimly focused on the decks below. They appeared to be looking for something. "I wonder what they're waiting for."

"You haven't time to wonder, Waymaker," said Telus firmly. "Be quiet and listen. Prepare yourself."

"I think I know what I have to do," said Gideon. "I just hope it works." He wrapped his arm and leg around the center pole. "Watch my back."

"By your word, Waymaker," Telus replied. "I am here."

Focusing his attention once more, Gideon lifted the staff to his forehead and pressed its smooth heat against his skin. As before, the contact evoked an eruption of words in Gideon's thoughts that he did not fully understand, though they sent hot chills of anticipation shooting up and down his spine.

"Speak true, Waymaker," said Telus excitedly. "What do you hear?"

Surrender, Gideon reminded himself. *Surrender!* He thrust the staff overhead, and cried out the words the staff spilled into this mind,

> *"Barukh atah Adonai, Eloheinu, melekh ha'olam,*
> *borei m'orei ha'eish!"*

A brilliant shaft of pure blue light severed the clouds from above and poured onto Gideon's head, instantly enveloping his body with such overwhelming presence that his own identity seemed to disappear in its wake. The power surged up through his arm and filled the staff with a resonance so powerful it hummed like a song. In that instant, all thought ceased. Now, there was only being. And from being, understanding.

He could see the riders' eyes as they glared in confusion at this new beacon of threat perched high atop the mast. He could see Stevron hiding in their midst, using the *mon'jalen* as a shield to protect him from exposure to the speakers of *Dei'lo* on board…his own eyes, blue and clear and utterly false, focused on Gideon and the Raanthan with an unbridled hatred matched only by his arrogance.

He could hear the cries of the dragons, enraged by their captivity to the Words of *Sa'lei*, straining with their great strength against their invisible bonds even as they outwardly obeyed every whispered whim of their riders.

But mostly, he listened for Stevron's voice. For he knew that, above all, was the voice he must oppose.

At that moment, three of the sails burst into flame. The ship slowed lethargically as if the bow had plowed into mud. Gideon searched the waters for the source, and quickly noticed small clusters of *mon'jalen* on either side of the Endurant closing in. Having crossed the aft line of the ship, they had veered the dragons' massive heads inward toward the sails. Listening only for Stevron, he had failed to notice them. But he saw them now, their expressions revealing their delight at the strike and their hunger for more.

"I cannot protect the ship, Waymaker," cried Telus, the smoke from the fires rising around him like a cloud. "They mean to stop our flight."

The riders called again, but this time Gideon heard. With a simple turning of his staff, he shifted the flow of the power surging through him, and the Words of the *mon'jalen*, meant to splinter the main mast, dispersed harmlessly into the winds of the storm.

Another turn of his wrist, and Words that bound the speakers' dragons to their will was severed. Three of the beasts let out a screeching roar of defiance, and in their fury hurled the riders from their backs, snatching their bodies from the air within their daggered jaws. One snap, and the *mon'jalen* were severed or consumed, and the beasts, their teeth now stained with blood, disappeared beneath the waves.

He did not have time to ponder how he did it. He simply did—or rather, the power did it through him. Quickly, he searched for Stevron among the oncoming horde. The *mon'jalen* were dangerous, as were the dragons, but he knew the Council Lord was using them all as a mere distraction. What was he planning?

Within moments the entire company of dragons flanked them on either side, keeping their distance but cruising alongside the wounded Endurant with menacing ease. The *mon'jalen* scanned the ship from atop their beasts, waiting it seemed, for some command from Stevron, who, for whatever reason, Gideon could no longer locate.

Suddenly, a second wave of dragons, at least thirty strong, veered in toward the starboard rail. Gideon turned to face them, ready to disperse whatever Words they uttered in the winds.

From below, he heard Revel cry out, "Waymaker! To port! To port! It is a ruse!"

But it was too late. As Gideon turned, he felt the ship beneath him shudder violently and plunge hard to starboard as if struck by a whale. A major portion of the Endurant's port side exploded, shooting a spray of splintered wood and iron across the stormy waves. The ship lurched once again and veered hard to port as icy waters from the sea thundered into the newly formed wound ripped along the ship's port side.

Immediately, Aybel and Revel ran to the gap and forged a shield of Words to seal the hole and hold the water at bay. The ship came upright once again, but only with reluctance. In the few seconds it took Aybel and Revel to speak the Words, a great volume of water had flooded the hold. Crippled, the ship now sat much lower in the water than it should.

Their forward progress all but stopped, Gideon swept this gaze back to starboard, where the squadron of riders, emboldened by the success of their ploy, now forced their dragons even closer to the hull.

Gideon knew he had little time. The power was with him, and he with it, but he still lacked the skill to use it to its greatest effect. It seemed he could only direct the flow toward one thing at a time. But there were simply too many of them. Even if he could stop all the *mon'jalens'* Worded attacks, he still had the dragons themselves to consider. If even one of them got close enough to strike, it could tear the ship apart in a matter of seconds— and he knew it would, given the beasts' current state of rage.

Wait. That's it! thought Gideon. *The dragons!*

Shifting his awareness away from the riders, Gideon pointed the staff at the dragon closest to the ship. As before, it required only a small shift of the energy to release the creature from its forced bondage to *Sa'lei*. The act itself felt something like slicing through a rope, but not in any way he could directly comprehend. When he sensed the bond sever, however, the dragon's reaction was immediate. Furious, it hurled its great head and neck hard against the waves, slamming its hapless rider beneath the full force of its massive bulk. When dragon reemerged, the *mon'jalen* was gone.

Suddenly, the memory of his battle with the riftmen flashed across Gideon's mind, and as if by instinct he broadened his focus to encompass the entire company of dragons surrounding the ship as a single entity. Once again, he shifted the flow, drawing far more power this time, and directing it gently toward the array of watery beasts around him.

Streamers of blue light spilled from the staff and filled the skies above the ship, undulating like a fountain of ribbons in the wind as they drifted down and lighted upon each dragon's head. A chorus of screeching roars erupted above the storm as the dragons sensed the undoing of the Words that bound them. With one mind, they quickly turned on their captors— alternately hurling them from their backs or pulling them beneath the waves to drown them. Those *mon'jalen* who were not slain instantly floundered in the storm-driven waters, their arms flailing about looking for something to hold them afloat. A handful of the riders fought back against their beasts, angrily screaming Words to set them ablaze or rip their scaly bodies asunder. But for each dragon slain, three swam in to exact a swift retribution. Within moments, the tumultuous sea was awash with a macabre array of bloody parts—some dragon, but mostly the half-eaten bodies of *mon'jalen*. For a time, Gideon feared the dragons might turn their rage toward the ship as well, but once the riders had been properly dispatched, the dragons seemed content to scream an angry warning toward the Endurant, then plow their massive heads beneath the waves and disappear.

All but one.

Lord Stevron sat atop his dragon some hundred yards off the port rail. Whatever power Gideon used had failed to undo the Council Lord's hold on the beast. The instant Gideon spotted him, a massive sphere of crackling red fire erupted to life around the lord and his dragon. Feeling a sudden panic, Gideon flung the staff around to confront the threat, but just as he did, the ship was sideswiped by a starboard swell, and the perch swung heavily to port. It was just enough for Gideon's footing to slip, and he watched in helpless horror as his body lurched across the low railing of the perch—out of control, and plummeting toward the deck.

Suddenly, a silver hand appeared as if from nowhere and latched onto Gideon's free arm like a vice, dangling his body high above the Endurant's hardwood decks. Stunned, he looked up to see Telus' phantom face hovering above him, his hair blowing wildly in the wind as his other arm coiled itself more tightly around the main mast. Without comment, Gideon gripped the Rannthan's extended arm with his own, then looked down to make certain he still held the staff. It was there, but the shimmering blue that had surrounded it was gone. Somehow, he had disconnected from the flow.

Suddenly a bolt of lightning, black as coal with a shimmering edge, impaled the Raanthan with the full force of Stevron's fury. Telus' head flew back, his eyes wide and clearly in pain. But he did not make a sound. The moonlike glow, which had faded from Telus' skin, quickly returned, and he seemed to try to move his body away from Gideon even as he continued to hold him by one hand.

"Gideon!" Aybel's voice screamed from below. "We cannot hold the shield much longer! The waters will soon take her. We must abandon ship!"

It was more than Gideon could think about. He looked around for something to grab hold of. *Abandon the ship? And go where?* There was nowhere to go.

Another lightning bolt shot from the clouds to the Raanthan's chest. And then another. And another. Each time, his body stiffened against the agony, but yet he did not utter a sound. And the grip on Gideon's arm remained strong.

Perhaps enraged by the impotence of his strikes against Gideon, Stevron roared into the clouds, his bellowing voice thick with an arrogant vengeance. Gideon could not comprehend what the Council Lord was saying, but he recognized the grating cadence of the Words. It was *Sa'lei*. Frantically, he yelled for Telus to pull him back up to the perch. The mystical, overwhelming power resonated just out of his reach. He tried to surrender to it anew, but dangling as he was so precariously above the deck proved too great a distraction. He simply couldn't focus on the power and on his own life at the same time.

Telus quickly obliged, lifting Gideon with far greater ease than any man could. Within seconds, he was back in place atop the mast.

But Stevron's Words had already done their work. The storm, which until then had hovered above them like a serpent ready to strike, in that instant came alive with madness and fury, unleashing the fullness of its chaos on the seas, and on the Endurant. Cyclones rose up from the tumult around them, spinning into the clouds above and churning across the surface as if looking for something to destroy. Lightning, like a cacophony of cannon fire, exploded from everywhere. It slashed through the remaining sails, setting them ablaze, and stabbed at the deck and rails of the battered Endurant with the ferocity of a murderer raging against his victim.

Gideon had only a moment to act before the ship would be obliterated. If he could only find the flow again, he could focus the power on Stevron, and possibly destroy him, or at least injure him enough to force a retreat. But doing that, he realized, would still not save the ship. The Endurant was already too far gone. They were going down one way or the other. What they needed was safe harbor. Or at the very least, a place to run aground.

And the only land he knew of lay to the south in the Deathland Barrens—the very place his heart still told him he must go.

Peering to the east, Gideon eyed the fiery ball of Stevron's shield as it danced upon the waters. He could not see the Council Lord's face anymore, hidden as it was beneath the crackling reactions of the sphere against the Worded storm. But he knew the lord was watching him, anxious to see a cyclone suck his body into the clouds, or lightning sever him in two. For whatever reason, Stevron had fingered Gideon as the source of all his troubles in the world, and Gideon knew the lord would be satisfied with nothing less than his utter and complete destruction.

The thought of such hatred forged a knot in Gideon's gut—not of fear this time, but deep resolve. He remembered Gideon's Fall, where he had promised himself he would see this journey through to the end, no matter where it led or how impossible it appeared. And no self-righteous power-mad lord of Phallenar was going to make him back down from that now.

He smiled. "Not today, Stevie," he said, staring at the sphere. "Today we're going to live."

Closing his eyes, Gideon let go, releasing his will to drift back into the flow. The power quickly enveloped him in a blanket of glistening blue, and Gideon consciously leaned his thoughts deeper into its warmth, allowing the strands of his own indignation and fear to disperse in the currents of its trusting strength. Fully aware but free of thought, he flung the staff up high and spun it toward the clouds. A surge of blue fire, pure and brilliant, sprang outward from the staff and, waving like a brush, began to paint a form upon the air. Lines of light descended from it and latched hold of the deck. When the last was set, the image unfurled into a mighty sail, higher than the ship was tall and wide enough to conceal all waters to the south from view.

He breathed in deep. Upon his slow exhale, a shaft of wind sliced through the storm from the north and filled the billowy sheet of luminescence dancing above the bow. The Endurant instantly lurched back to life, its creaking timbers screaming under the strain even as a cheer of hope rose up from the decks below.

Quigly let out a whoop, and cried, "Hold on, my landers! Hold on!"

But Gideon wasn't holding on at all. Once again, he lurched toward the rail, his feet askew and floundering to find purchase beneath him. By sheer luck, he managed to grab the mast tip just in time, and frantically yanked his body back to center. Even so, the mishap was enough to reawaken his fear, and he watched with sudden worry as the fiery blue cocoon around him evaporated once again. Telus leaped up to the lookout and slapped his oversized hand against the small of Gideon's back. "Stay with the wind, Waymaker," he said. "I will hold you."

But the power had already slipped away. "Stink!" he exclaimed. "I lost it again."

"It is all right, Waymaker," said Telus. "Calm yourself. And listen."

Anxiously Gideon reached for the flow again, but for whatever reason it seemed to resist him this time, resonating stubbornly just beyond his grasp. His gaze flittered nervously toward the sail of light stretched out ahead of them. To his great relief, it was still there, pulling them southward at speeds not even the deathstorm could match. He sighed. Well, at least he'd been able to do that much.

Turning his attention aft, he watched as the massive deathstorm slowly receded from their wake, thundering its anger at being denied its prey. He was surprised, however, to find no sign of Stevron's red sphere among the waves.

"He is not far," said Telus, as if perceiving Gideon's thoughts. "He will not give up so easily."

Gideon sighed. "I know." He glanced at the gaping void along the Endurant's port side. The Worded shield still held, its job perhaps made easier by the considerable lift the ship's great speed provided. But an immensity of water still pressed against it, and it was anyone's guess how long Aybel and Revel could hold it off.

"We may have outpaced the Council Lord for now," said Telus, "but his deathstorm still tracks us. It will overtake us soon after we reach the shore."

"One problem at a time, Telus," said Gideon. "Let's just hope that shield holds long enough to get us that far."

An hour later, the ship flew into a small lagoon, appearing from behind the massive sail as if from nowhere. The crew braced themselves as best they could, but when the Endurant struck the sandy embankment, the shock of the impact hurled them violently forward, tumbling bodies and loose equipment along the deck with equal ferocity. After several seconds, the grating rumble of the timbers against the gritty earth finally stopped. The mighty Endurant settled heavily on its side, and one by one, the members of the party stumbled to their feet.

At first, all that Gideon noticed was that the powerful wind he had summoned no longer blew. But when he looked at the sail, he saw that it, too, was melting away. Like a gossamer veil dissolving before his eyes, it revealed the land he had felt so drawn to find—and that might be his undoing.

The Deathland Barrens.

There were trees—beautiful and tall and arranged in clusters, surrounded by carpets of grass as rich and green as any he had seen within the Lands. Flowers bloomed in the sunny patches between the groves and a gentle breeze danced across them like a song.

It was hardly what he had expected. In fact, the scene looked nothing like the Barrens at all. At least not the way he had imagined them to be.

But then, from behind the trees, dark figures emerged. There were dozens of them, their bodies clad in a thin-spun cloth that scarcely concealed the tattoo-like markings that covered their skin from head to toe. They moved toward the ship with the slow measured pace of a lion approaching a wounded prey.

"By the Giver!" exclaimed Aybel suddenly. "They bear the Words!"

Then Gideon heard a chorus of voices singing from the trees, and everything went black.

23

SETAL RAPHA

When Paladin Ajel Windrunner and Lord Fayerna Baratii did battle on the slopes of that great mountain, they had no knowledge of where they were in the world, nor apparently any sense of the sacred nature of the ground on which they stood. Nonetheless, the portal had allowed them entrance—a fact which some have said clearly showed the blessing of providence on their fight. Perhaps. But if that is true, I find it curious that through the long hours of their conflict, the hand of providence did not also see fit to allow Ajel to reach the threshold of the great gate. For had he stood there, even for a moment, the threat of Sa'lei would have surely ended in the blinking of an eye.

—The Kyrinthan Journals, Chronicles, Chapter 18, Verses 147-150

Ajel slumped down heavily against the rough granite overhang and perked his ear to the sky.

Nothing. Just the chilling wind, singing its foreboding melody as it whipped its way around the jagged peaks. She was being quiet for now, biding her time until she found him. And she would find him, sooner or later. She always did.

He took a quick inventory of his injuries. His right arm was bleeding profusely from a gash that ran from his elbow halfway to his wrist. His legs were badly bruised, and his head throbbed like a drum from the stone he smashed against one of the times he fell. But at least he hadn't lost consciousness. At least he could be thankful for that.

Leaning back against the cold rock face, he permitted himself a quiet sigh. He still wasn't sure what was happening, or why.

He knew, at least, who it was that hunted him. He recognized her the instant her body tumbled into the portal, and her *Sa'lei*-wrought disguise melted away in the flow. One glance at her self-satisfied grin was all it took.

Fayerna. . .Lord Fayerna.

Ajel had seen her many times while he was still a child in Phallenar. The stark arrogance of her expression, framed as it was by her fiery red hair and pitch-black eyes, frightened him even then. Time had only served to make it more severe.

He remembered her, too, from the attack on Wordhaven. It was she who had snatched Gideon away from them in the valley. And it was she whom Gideon had later reported slain, lost to the trees of Strivenwood.

But here she was, very much alive, and full of a fury toward Ajel that bordered on obsession. It had been solely by the Giver's mercy that Ajel had recognized her in time. The instant his body touched the lower grasses of the mountain, he spoke the Words to vanish from her sight and ran with all his strength up the slopes and away from her treacherous voice.

Hiding from Lord Fayerna, however, had proved more difficult than he imagined. Somehow she always found him no matter where he chose to hide, and with her Words would bombard his shield with a maelstrom of fire and ice and wind and stone. He managed to deflect the bulk of the onslaughts, but not without significant cost to both his stamina and resolve. A few times he faltered, and a shower of stones or a shaft of ice would pierce through the shield and strike his flesh. But he would vanish once again and flee to a place where he could speak the Words to heal his wounds, and start the running anew.

He knew he could not keep going like this; eventually, he would have to stand and fight her. In the beginning, he had hoped that she might eventually tire of the chase, but after six hours of this deadly cat and mouse game, it was clear that she would not stop until she had her prize. She had even managed to seal the skies so neither of them could use the Words to transport away.

Her motives were a mystery to him. She was clearly obsessed with his destruction—but why? And why now? She had spent weeks masquerading as a servant girl within the Stand, with Ajel in easy reach day after day. Was that elaborate ruse designed solely for this, to lead him to a place outside Wordhaven's protected walls? Or was some larger motive fueling her deception? He frowned at the possibility. Perhaps even now, as she spun her web to trap him here, Wordhaven could be coming under attack.

"I see blood, Paladin." Fayerna's voice echoed off the rocks. "Your blood." Ajel perked his ears to the wind, hoping to pinpoint her direction. "Why not heal yourself?" she said soothingly. "Speak the Words to bring strength to your bones. I won't mind. It makes the chase more interesting."

Why does she wish me healed? As a means to keep me here? To keep the struggle going? Quietly Ajel shuffled to his feet and huddled close to the rock. He could see little from his hovel beneath the overhang, and if she stumbled upon him he would need to move quickly.

"I am close, Paladin," she said. "I could bring this mountain down on your head, you know I could. I grow weary of this game. But I want to look in your face when you die. It is only fair, wouldn't you agree?" A stream of dust drifted down from the ledge above his head. *She is there!*

"Will you not face me? Brave leader of the Remnant! Champion of *Dei'lo*," she called mockingly. "If only your followers could see you now. You call yourself their Paladin, and yet you hide from battle like a timid mouse! Are your Words so weak, Ajel? Are you truly a coward, after all?"

He held his stance, watching. He had to be certain.

"It's a pity, really," she continued. "I would have hoped for a more worthy adversary...for her sake. She deserved that much at least, and far more. More than you will ever know!"

She? He wondered. But then he remembered. *Of course! Lord Sarlina...*

"Curse you, rebel! Show yourself!" She stomped her foot on the rock, and fragments of pebbles rained down off the ledge.

It was the clear sign he was waiting for.

Raising his hands, he yelled to the stone above his head, *"Jeo rebonis alem adversum sum'patrinis! Haloquin enalem patreem!"*

The ledge above him severed from the cliff and spun as it hurled itself to the rocky soil below him. Fayerna tumbled with it, her fiery red shield blazing to life as the slab attempted to pin her beneath its weight. *"Damonoi prat!"* she screamed, and the slab instantly exploded into dust. Ajel summoned his own shield as she landed on her feet just thirty paces away.

He did not wait for her to see him. *"Adon'i'theron patrinis e'nelopar see!"* At his Word, the stone walls of the ravine in which she'd fallen instantly melted into a river of molten rock and hurled its liquid heat upon her, digging its flaming claws into the crackling power of her shield, boring its way past her defenses to wrap her body in its eager embrace.

Because of his own protective sphere, Ajel could not hear her scream. But he could see the surprise and horror etched on her hardened face. Even so, before the tendrils of liquid fire could breach the perimeter of her defenses, her sphere shot off the ground and flew toward what was left of the plateau some fifty feet above.

Ajel immediately followed, whispering the Words for flight and strength and courage to be bold. Fayerna was as well-practiced in the art of battle as she was in *Sa'lei*, he knew. Even if he brought his full strength to the fight, victory would not come easily.

He reached the crumbling ledge only a second behind her, but by then she had already spotted him and spoke again. When nothing happened immediately, he scanned the area to spot the danger her Words had wrought. Almost too late, he saw it—a jagged boulder the size of house hurtling toward him from the south behind him. There was just time enough for his lips to breathe the Words.

"Adon'i'creyis avarin delin see."

Immediately, the spinning boulder fractured and softened. From the rocky fragments, wings fluttered into life, beaks emerged from basalt, and what was cold dead stone became a flock of living blackbirds, scattering in sudden fright at the sight of their radiant shields.

For a moment, Lord Fayerna only stared—first at him, and then at the birds. *Good*, he thought. *Let her stand in awe at what* Dei'lo *can do.*

But her silence did not last long. As if to reprimand him for not dying, she screamed a curse his way, and the ground beneath him instantly shattered like glass. The force of the blast took him by surprise, and he plummeted into the cloud of dust, his shield sparking against the side of the mountain as he tumbled end over end through the murky haze. He couldn't see her, he couldn't see anything, and in the confusion of the fall the Words to soften his landing came to mind too late. His shield collapsed against the shards of shattered granite some fifty feet below. He muffled a yell as the stones, freshly sheared by her Words, sliced deep into his back. He felt the nauseous cracking of his ribs against the rocks.

"You challenge me with tricks, Paladin," her voice echoed through the haze above. "But I come to you with true power."

Ajel didn't bother to reply. Reforming the shield around him, he quickly turned his focus to his wounds, frantically whispering Words of healing to each injury in turn. He had only a moment before the dust would clear between them.

Suddenly, the air around the sphere ignited as a torrent of black lightning pummeled his shield and ripped the broken earth to shreds. Ignoring the last of his fractured ribs, he spoke the Words of flight, picturing in his mind the high ridge to the north. As his blue sphere shot out of above the dust cloud, he caught a glimpse of Lord Fayerna, her head spinning upward with a crazed glare. But before she could say anything, he was gone.

As the sphere flew toward the mist-laden peak, Ajel whispered in *Dei'lo* to his remaining wounds. He knew she would follow and find him soon enough, but for the moment that did not concern him. He kept his gaze focused toward the expansive misty peaks ahead, searching.

There! he exclaimed after a moment. *That will do.*

Guiding the sphere into the mists, he settled in an ice field nestled at the bottom of a narrow valley, just below the peak. Cliffs of solid rock shot out from the smooth white surface all around, forging a bowl of grey stone that surrounded him on three sides. The stark landscape held few hiding places, which was in part why he chose it. If he was going to stand and fight, he would do it in a place where neither of them could hide.

In truth, he did not want to battle Fayerna, though she was his enemy. Something about the way she had approached this entire scheme—stealing into Wordhaven in disguise, holding that deception in place for weeks on end with no apparent purpose, and then impulsively luring him to the portal—made him suspect her mind was unbalanced. After hearing her make reference to Lord Sarlina, he realized her attack was not guided by orders from the Council, but rather by her own lust for vengeance. She was a woman obsessed with her own pain—and he suspected that obsession, amplified as it surely would be by the trees of Strivenwood, had driven her to madness.

Even so, he realized he could deny this fight no longer. She had left him no choice.

Scanning the dead stone of the cliffs, he felt a surge of sorrow rise in his throat. He knew what he was going to say, what the Words would do, but he never imagined he'd be forced to speak them to end a life, even if it was the life of a Council Lord.

Just as he saw the first light of Fayerna's red sphere filter through the clouds, he looked to the cliffs and sadly uttered the Words to bring them to life.

"Jeo' zephi sacravelis en patrinis. Delim patrinis creyis leviatnos e'bema adversum Fayerna! Creyis leviatnos e'bema adversum Fayerna!"

The air shook as the power of Ajel's Words penetrated the cold stone of the cliffs. One by one, the rock faces crumpled, then broke away from the mountain, forging themselves into a serpentine shape even as they tumbled toward the ice. A warm glow rich with gold and purple hues exhaled from the stone, then filled it again and again like a breath, each time more brilliantly than the one before. Flashes of lightning with echoes of thunder reverberated through the ice as the stone beast took on the form of flesh, sinew, scales and wings.

Ajel turned to see Lord Fayerna hovering just beneath the low ceiling of the mist, her attention transfixed on the *Dei'lo*-wrought creation coming to life before her eyes. The speakers of *Sa'lei* had always been aware of the creative power of *Dei'lo*. But such Words as these had not been spoken, nor their effects seen, in close to two thousand years.

"You live on borrowed power, Lord Fayerna," he muttered, though he knew she couldn't hear him, "and borrowed time. The hour of your rule has ended. The power of life has returned to the Lands."

Ajel had never seen a mountain dragon before, though he'd always longed for the opportunity. They were notoriously reclusive creatures, preferring the remote heights of the tallest mountains were few humans could go. But as it spread its leathery wings and thundered its way into the sky, he could not help but shudder in awe. It was certainly the most the beautiful creature he had ever seen. But it was also, by far, the most terrible.

Filtered sunlight glittered metallically off its gold and purple scales as it swooshed overhead. Its eyes, large and golden and slit like a snake's, did not see Ajel. They were locked only on Fayerna, the target of its wrath, who hovered motionless below the clouds as if the menacing stare of the dragon had completely unhinged her will.

In the last few seconds, she recovered enough to scream at the beast—a desperate tirade of *Sa'lei* to break it, to burn it, to rip it asunder. Black lightning bolted from her chest and tore through its wings. Balls of fire exploded upon its breast and its glorious head, charring the beautiful scales with wounds of black and the thick red flow of dragon's blood.

But still it came. With one last mighty swoop of its wings it reached her, and with its steely jaws seized the Worded sphere and clamped down. As the shield collapsed, Ajel saw the spindly form of Fayerna tumble like a rag doll down into its throat. In an instant, she was gone.

Its goal achieved, the dragon raised its head and roared into the clouds in triumph, then just as abruptly dropped its wings and plummeted haphazardly toward the ice. Ajel watched in horror as the impact shook the mountain and sent thick ribbons of cracks radiating outward through the field of white.

Heartbroken to have brought such suffering to the living creature his Words had wrought, Ajel raced to its side, hoping to heal the horrific injuries of Fayerna's Words.

But by the time he reached it, the beautiful dragon was already dead.

THE AWAKENING

Rise up, sleeper, knowing the time.
It is already the hour for you to awaken
and feel the strength of your own right arm.
Rise up! Stand up! Step forward and see!
The Day of your Fear and Courage has come;
for anointing draws near to the ruthless and free.
　　　　　—From the writings of the Prophet Endimnar, in the year S.C. 1480

jel didn't know how long he wept. Perhaps an hour. Perhaps more. But by the time he finally stood—his leathers now saturated with the dragon's steaming blood—the light of the sun had fallen behind the mountain, and all the warmth of day had drained out of the air.

He had never murdered before. Sarlina had died as a result of his Word, yes. But that was an accident. It was not like this. Nothing was like this. He had ended two lives today. With clear intention and purpose, he had acted, and now they were dead, both of them lying before him in helpless accusation. The dragon, its glorious life so short-lived, now lay bathed in the blood of its own shattered heart. And the Council Lord, her own life drained by the dragon's daggered teeth, lay entombed within its belly.

All of his tears were spent now; he had no more. But in the sad calm that followed their passing, he wondered bitterly if his grief was more for himself than for those he had slain. The crusted blood on his hands glared at him mockingly. Is this the man he must be now? A killer? A wielder of Words to maim and destroy? Is this what it truly meant to be the Paladin in a time of war?

For a moment, he watched the vapor of his breath drift out over the ice and disappear into the darkness. His body had begun to shiver, but he did not feel the cold. *I should return to Wordhaven,* he thought. *They will be worried.*

He no longer believed that Fayerna's plan included any type of organized assault on the Stand. Toward the end, he realized that her madness had blocked out all stories but her own. He had been her only target. At least, with her passing, whatever threat she posed to Wordhaven was also dead.

Dead. By my Word.

Until this moment, he had never realized how much he had concealed himself behind Donovan's sword. They had fought side by side more times than he could count, but it was always Donovan who brought the death blow when no other recourse remained. Faithful Donovan—so willing to do what Ajel always feared. *I wonder if he realizes,* thought Ajel. *I wonder if he has seen it all along.*

The Paladin snatched a handful of brittle snow and, rising from the ice, rubbed it vigorously between his hands. Whatever Words Lord Fayerna had used to seal the skies had faded with her death, but Ajel wasn't ready to return to Wordhaven just yet. By now, they had probably discovered that Sarla—Fayerna—was missing as well. Donovan would put the story together quickly enough from there, and begin searching every inch of the Stand and the valley for any sign of their whereabouts. Panic may not set in immediately, but it would not be long in coming. He couldn't stay here long.

But when he did return, there would be many questions. And he wasn't ready to answer those yet. Some, perhaps, he would never answer at all.

Whispering the Words to stave off the growing cold, he turned his face toward the shadowed peak in the distance and plodded out across the ice. He needed to walk. Not long. Just enough to clear his thoughts, and settle, at least a bit, the uncomfortable sorrow in his heart. Perhaps he'd watch the moonrise, stay long enough to see it spill its silver light across the ice fields, and then speak the Words to carry him home. That wouldn't be too long, he reasoned. He could already see the faint glow of its approach hovering just beyond the highest ridge to the west.

Suddenly, his breath caught in his throat. He stopped walking, and cautiously squinted his eyes at the dim halo of light in the distance. *The moon does not rise from that direction*, he realized. Whatever light he saw was not the moon, which meant it was not natural light at all.

He did not know where he was—what part of the world. Perhaps here there were people who made their home in these desolate heights. Maybe it was only the light of a fire in the distance. But that was not likely, this high up. And the light did not waver as fires do. Whatever it was, it rested nearly at the height of the peak, on the western slope just beyond the apex. It might take and hour or more to reach on foot. But *Dei'lo* could carry him there in seconds.

He was barely conscious of speaking the Words. The sphere of blue hummed to life around him and filled his chest with a shiver of warm delight. Lifting his weary body off the valley floor, it carried him through the darkness toward the imposing shadow of the peak overhead. Even with the healing Words, he knew was too exhausted to fight any more this day. He would be careful, he told himself. He would only look, and if he found danger, he would transport to Wordhaven.

He guided the sphere to a ridge just south of the peak. Landing softly on a scree field, he let the shield disperse and carefully made his way west, ringing the peak so as to approach the light from the side rather than the more exposed vantage above. Traversing the scree in the dark was difficult, especially given the altitude and the weariness of his body. But soon the landscape leveled out and made his footing more firm.

It wasn't long before the light came blazing into view. In that instant, and without thought, he collapsed to his knees.

The image he had glimpsed, though still forming in his mind, overwhelmed him. He did not know why. At that moment, all he knew was that he did not know anything at all. Cradling his face in his still-bloodied hands, he took in several heavy breaths, and whispered the Words to center his soul.

"Go home."

Ajel looked up in shock. Two Raanthan stood before him. Their garments, as white and spindly as their hair, wafted in the night breeze like a cloud of silk. They bore no weapons that he could see, but they were none the less imposing for it. Their eyes alone, burning liquid bronze, set fear in his bones. He knew, somehow, that they were readied for war.

"I did not mean to trespass," Ajel apologized quietly. "I saw the light and—"

"Get up," commanded the Raanthan, "and go home."

Slowly, Ajel stood, and lifted his gaze to face them. The Raanthan had positioned their bodies to block his view of the light. As large as they were, it was not difficult.

"What is this place?" asked Ajel.

"Not yet," came the cold reply.

Ajel shook his head. "I don't understand."

"Not yet...Ajel," the voice repeated.

"You know who I am?"

"Yes," said the second Raanthan. "But do you?" The tone was blatantly condescending.

"This place you guard," said Ajel, matching the Raanthan's tone, "what is it?"

"It is not for you, human," said the first Raanthan. "You are not ready. Go home."

"No," said Ajel, emboldened by the burning memory of the light. "Not until you tell me its name."

"You would not understand."

"Who are you to say what I can know?" declared Ajel. Defiant, he moved to walk around them. A silvery arm—impossibly long—shot out to block his way.

"You tempt much," growled the Raanthan. "Do you not know how close you are to death?"

"Death is always one breath away for any man," countered Ajel, "This moment is no different from any other in that regard. Why will you not let me pass, or at least tell me its name?"

The Raanthan looked into each other's eyes for a moment, as if to silently discuss a curious notion that had occurred to one or both of them. Finally, the one whose hand still blocked Ajel's way pulled it back. "You have mastered *Dei'lo?*" he asked.

"I am not fluent, no," Ajel replied. "But it lives in me."

"Then know that you have stumbled upon the outer edge of holy fire. The light that shines in the darkness is none other than that of *Setal Rapha,* the Brilliant Gate."

At the sound of the name, the mountain shivered, echoing through the icy clouds as thunder. Ajel fell once more to his knees—not from the light this time, but from the naming of the place. "How...how can that be?" he muttered. "It is only a myth...a story to explain—"

"Many true things in the world seem only myth in the absence of faith," said the Raanthan. "I told you that you would not understand."

"No," said Ajel, shaking his head. "No, I do. I do." He looked up at them with newfound awe. "You are the covering."

"Go home, Paladin," said the Raanthan. "You have what you came for."

"What?" pleaded Ajel. "What do I have? I have nothing! Please, let me go closer. Let me see it!"

"You have seen the light of *Setal Rapha*, and lived," replied the Raanthan. "What more do you need before you will believe?"

"But I do believe!" exclaimed Ajel. "I believe you. I believe this is the place you say. That is why I must see it once more! To be so close..." He reached his hand out toward them as if to plead for mercy.

"I was not speaking of faith in this place, Paladin," said the Raanthan. "You have seen the light of *Setal Rapha*, and lived. What more do you need before you will believe that you are the one? Stop doubting, and go."

Ajel was undone. Collapsing to the ground, he gripped the cold earth in his crusted hands as if it was the foot of the throne of the Giver himself. Hot tears stained his cheeks as waves of grief mixed with profound relief washed over his body. The Raanthan's words burned in his soul. He did not realize until that moment how desperately he had needed to hear them.

"Why are you lying on the ground?" snapped the Raanthan. "Get up, and act like a man. You may return here someday, once the story is told. But for now there is work to be done. Be on your way!"

The Paladin breathed in deep, then slowly pushed his body up off the ground. His legs felt as if they might betray him, but when he stood, he did not waver. "Yes," he said. Then, looking in their bronze eyes once more, he added, "Thank you."

"Give thanks where it is due, Paladin," chided the Raanthan. "Not to us."

Ajel nodded with a sigh, then turned to go, being careful not to let his eyes divert toward the faint aura of the wondrous light beyond the Raanthan's backs. He would see this place again. He was certain of that, and not just because of the Raanthan's words. But the next time he came, there would be no one to block his way.

REMA

At the time of Gideon's Fall, the ancient hearted city of Broken Heart lay in the direct path of the High Lord's Word of Desolation, situated as it was behind the ridge of cliffs overlooking the Eastern Sea. But though the Word devastated the city, it did not destroy it utterly. For the power of Dei'lo was strong in that place— nearly as strong as that which rested on its sister city, Sacred Heart in the west, which endured for many centuries beyond the Fall. A smattering of Lords and apprentices at Broken Heart survived the severing of the world, and with such strength as they had, forged a beachhead of safety within the desolation that soon came to be the Deathland Barrens. Cut off from the unspoiled lands to the west and surrounded by the darkness that now assailed them, they soon lost all hope of escape, and focused their full energy upon survival. Over the years of their isolation, they came to believe that the entire world had fallen into darkness, and for whatever reason they alone had been called by the Giver to protect the truth of life. They named themselves the Cal'eeb, the "Standing Ones," in honor of Cala, the Lord of Wordhaven who led them through the first hundred years of their exile and taught them the tattooed arts that kept them alive.

—The Kyrinthan Journals, Chronicles, Chapter 16, Verses 23-32

When Gideon awoke, he found himself floating in midair, his arms and legs bound to his body with thick leather bands coated in symbols. The others hovered nearby, their bound bodies forming a large circle that hung motionless beneath the imposing ribs of what looked like massive grey-stoned cathedral. Shafts of sunlight filtered through the moist air from an elaborate mosaic of colored glass at one end, illuminating the marbled patterns of the floor, which mirrored the window's ornate circular design.

In the center of the circle stood a cluster of hooded figures robed in red. Gideon's staff lay at their feet, resting on a bed of silken black cloth. Even though their hoods obscured their faces in darkness, they all faced him in the silence as if waiting to be recognized.

Gideon glanced around. None of the others had yet awakened.

Slowly, one of the robed figures raised a pointed finger in Gideon's direction, revealing a latticework of tattoos etched across the back of his aging hand.

"What are you?" the man asked, his booming voice resonating through the chamber like a song.

Gideon was unsure how he should answer. Were these the depraved souls of the Deathland Barrens? They looked nothing like he expected. "Who are you?" he said at last.

"Evil follows you," the man said sharply. "Even now our priests hold back the ill winds that carried you here. Tell me what you are! Or I will give you to them."

"My friends and I are fleeing from an enemy," said Gideon, unsure how much to reveal. "We came to the Barrens only to escape him. We mean you no harm."

A second robed figure stepped forward, smaller and clearly feminine. "Do not presume to lie to us!" the woman snapped, her voice strong though tinged with age. "You come from the outerlands where no good dwells."

"We came from the Inherited Lands," offered Gideon.

"We are all that remains of that place," said the man. "The rest has fallen into darkness. It has been so for generations. So I ask again. What are you?"

"If you do not believe me, then ask the others," said Gideon. "We will all tell you the same. We do not mean you any harm. If you release us, we will leave you in peace, and go our way."

"Go where?" asked the woman. "Back to depravity?"

"I don't know," said Gideon. But even as he said it, he realized he did. "South. Whatever lies south of here." Even now, he felt the mysterious tug of desire singing in his heart.

"Beyond the Stays, there is nothing but living death. It would be better to lose your broken lives to the storm," said the woman.

"Awaken my friends," implored Gideon. "They will tell you. We have no quarrel with you. I don't even know who you are. All we want is to pass through."

"You are all strange, for creatures of the outerlands," said the man. "But you most of all. You bear the marks." He pointed to scars on Gideon's wrists. "Your crown is black. And you carry a staff of untainted wood." He knelt down and stroked the wood with his finger. "How did you come by this?"

Gideon sighed in frustration. "You wouldn't believe me if I told you."

"What we believe is not for you to decide," said the woman.

"If you wish us to release you, you will answer our questions," stated the man. He pointed at Telus, hanging limply in the air across from Gideon. "We know what that one is. Until today, we thought them all destroyed in the desolation. Now we see that some of them yet survive, though that in itself may be an equally just punishment for their crime. But you. What are you?"

"I'm just a man," said Gideon.

"You bear the signs!" rebuked the man. "Will you say you come with no title? That you infect our shores without intention or design? Tell me, or I will let the ill winds take you this very moment, and your companions as well."

Gideon stared down at the man, listening as his stoic words echoed through the chamber. Their captors were clearly powerful—strong enough to hold back Stevron's deathstorm, if what the man claimed was true. Gideon recognized enough of the symbols on his cords and on the man's skin to know their power stemmed from the Words, though of which Tongue he couldn't be certain. He had never seen *Sa'lei* in written form, and his knowledge of *Dei'lo* was too slight to be sure of what he was seeing. Even so, as he stared into the man's shrouded hood, he did not sense the darkness he had felt so often in the presence of *mon'jalen* or Council Lords. These people seemed as confused about him as he was about them. Perhaps it was worth the risk to tell them the truth. He hoped so. At this point, there seemed little option.

"I do have a title," he said at last, "though I don't think it will mean anything to you."

"Speak it," said the man.

"Waymaker," said Gideon. "They call me the Waymaker."

A noticeable gasp echoed through the chamber. "*Pa'bara,*" said the woman. The air resonated with the power of the Word.

"I have been sent, along with my friends, to find the Pearl," continued Gideon, ignoring for the moment the startling tremor in his bones. "We are being hunted by a powerful Council Lord who wants to stop us. Actually, he wants us dead. Me in particular."

The woman touched the man on the sleeve and whispered something in his ear. He clasped his hand around hers and nodded, then pressed her hand aside.

"My friends will verify what I'm telling you," continued Gideon. He desperately wanted them to awaken the others, especially Aybel, Revel or Telus, since they could identify which Tongue these people had tattooed on their skin, and had at least some Worded ability to fight against them, if it came to that.

The man, however, seemed content to ignore the others for now. For whatever reason, his focus remained on Gideon alone. Taking another small step forward, he raised his hands and slowly lifted off his hood. Gideon swallowed in response. Every inch of the man's skin was covered in black script, from the tip of his chin to the crown of his gleaming bald head. But the eyes were equally startling. They were clear, a brilliant emerald green— not the pitch black he'd come to dread.

"*Elo'donar see,*" rumbled the man. Gideon felt a tingle dance across his skin and with a silent grace his body drifted to the floor. He settled directly in front of the man, whom Gideon now realized was at least as tall as Donovan, if not a fair bit taller. The man peered intensely into Gideon's eyes, as if trying to recognize an acquaintance from long ago. "I will know if you are a deceiver," he said.

Gideon swallowed. "Then you will see that I'm not." He sensed the presence of the staff nearby, but dared not look at it for fear of raising the man's suspicions even more. "My name is Gideon Dawning," he said. "I am what you would call a sojourner in the Lands."

The old man raised an eyebrow in surprise. "So the prophecies of the Visitation say," he mused. "Tell me, does the sight of me repulse you?"

Gideon blinked nervously. In fact, the man's face was fairly creepy, especially when staring at it nose to nose. "It's interesting," he said. After a moment of hesitation, he added, "Which Tongue is it?"

The man did not answer. Instead he touched the cord binding Gideon's arms and said, "*Elo'epathra.*" The cord instantly snapped and slithered to the floor as if a living thing. Snatching Gideon's wrist, the man lifted it to his face. "Open your palm," he said.

Nervously, Gideon complied, and the man pressed Gideon's hand against his tattooed cheek. Those green eyes, however, remained fixed on Gideon's face.

"He does not burn!" exclaimed the woman. The fact seemed to astound her. "Could he be?"

"We dare not believe it," mumbled the man suspiciously. "Not yet."

"Dare we refuse it?" the woman replied. "He bears both sign and title. And he does not flinch at the touch of the Words."

The man dropped Gideon's hand and stepped toward the woman. "We do not know him."

"A sojourner, as the prophecy states," the woman replied. As she spoke she removed her hood as well, revealing a wizened but strong feminine face, with silver hair and eyes the color of rain. Her skin, like the man's, was covered in script. "He could be the answer to many prayers."

"I am not convinced," the man replied, looking back in Gideon's eyes. "The Words do not burn him. But neither does he recognize them. How, then, could he be the *Pa'bara*? He comes from the outerlands!"

"I can recognize a few of the letters," said Gideon. "But my friends, and the Raanthan, they know them. If you awaken them, you will see."

"You call this Raanthan your friend?" he asked.

Gideon didn't answer. The man considered him for a moment, then said, "You are in the citadel of Rema. We are the Cal'eeb, the last keepers of the Words in the world of men. My name is Galad, and this is my bondmate, Saravere. We are the *Nissim*, the stewards of the Trevail Plains and the Seven Stays."

At the uttering of the Word *Nissim*, Gideon's mind flooded with an image of a mighty shield standing upright on a hill, bearing the emblem of the Pearl in sunlight. Suddenly, he trembled.

"That was *Dei'lo!*" Gideon exclaimed. "I felt it!"

"Does the truth of it frighten you?" asked Galad, his eyes narrowing.

Gideon shook his head. In fact, it did frighten him. But not in the way he thought Galad suspected. "Not at all." He forced a grin. "In fact, it's the best news we've had in weeks."

Galad frowned. He obviously did not share Gideon's sentiment. "It has been many centuries since we faced danger from the north. The fact that you bring this evil to our shores does not speak well of your intent, whatever signs you bear. If you know our Tongue, then you know any deception will not stand long in our midst."

"I'm not deceiving you!" said Gideon emphatically. "I am the Waymaker."

"So you say," replied Galad coolly. "It is true you bear the marks, and though you come from the outerlands your soul appears to be untouched by the desolation. I confess I cannot explain this. But we of the Cal'eeb know much of the Waymaker and his purpose in the world. We have been waiting for his appearance for many generations. You are not at all what we have expected."

"Yeah, well, I get that a lot," Gideon quipped. "Listen, no one can speak *Dei'lo* unless their heart is pure, right?" Galad nodded slightly. "Then awaken my friends. I'm telling you they can speak it! They'll show you. And they'll vouch for me, everything I'm telling you!"

Galad considered him a moment. At last he said, "They will be tested. As will you. On the morrow, we will know the truth."

"Why wait?" asked Gideon, suddenly nervous. "Just wake them up, and they'll tell you now!"

"The ill wind that followed you is proving difficult to resist," said Galad, with a hint of anger in his tone. "We are needed on the cliffs. We will deal with you once the threat is sufficiently subdued."

Gideon frowned. He knew there was more than a deathstorm following them. "Listen, about the guy who's chasing us…"

"*Elo'avare see,*" said Galad, and Gideon felt his body begin floating upward toward the circle.

"No, wait," implored Gideon. "You don't know what you're up against! Don't leave us hanging up here. We can help you, really! C'mon!"

"Your help is not required," said Galad. "We will return soon."

Gideon shook his head. "No. Don't do it," he said pleadingly, suspecting Galad's intention. "You don't understand! That's a Council Lord out there! He's—"

"*Jeo'di.*"

26

PHALLENAR

The passing of Council Lord Fayerna Baratti on the slopes of Setal Rapha brought to five the number of Lords who had perished since the arrival of Gideon Dawning. Three of those had been slain by Gideon Dawning himself: Bentel Baratti on the ruins of Noble Heart, and Baurejalin Sint and Vallera Kappan-Mati in the tunnels beneath the Axis in Phallenar at the time of the Book's retrieval. The other two deaths—that of Sarlina Alli and Fayerna Baratii—came at the hands of Ajel Windrunner. In a matter of a few short months, these two men accomplished more to loosen the iron grip of the Council Lords than had been done in the previous six hundred years. They quickly gained a reputation as fearsome men of terrible power, anointed by the Giver, each in his way, to shed blood in the name of justice. The truth is that neither of them ever craved such a fierce and brutal title. They were, both of them, men of peace at heart, and free of the lust for power—which is why, perhaps, the power came to them instead of other men.
—The Kyrinthan Journals, Chronicles, Chapter 18, Verses 160-165

Lord Rachel Alli stepped quietly through the doors to Stevron's private chambers, and walked numbly to the center. The room was swept clean, dark and void of furnishings, but in her present state she did not think this strange. Indeed, nothing had seemed strange to her for days—nor interesting, nor frightening or dull. Since Stevron's visit to her chambers a few weeks before, the world had become for her a nebulous dream—a nightmare, at once horrible and vague, from which she could not awaken.

Her task was done. Beneath the folds of her gown, she hid the prize Lord Stevron's Words had compelled her to find and bring to this chamber. It had not come to her easily, or without significant cost. Several of her *ser'-jalen* were now dead, destroyed in one way or another by the powerful wards Balaam had set. But she had remained relentless; she had no choice. One by one, she threw them into the task, and one by one they perished in the attempt, some by fire, some by poison or crushing or some other bitter phrasing of the Words. But each death revealed another of the wards, and with her Words, eventually, she unmade them all, until the only obstacle that remained was Balaam himself.

He proved easier to seduce than she had anticipated. But then, he was half mad and grotesquely ill—so confused in thought that he affectionately called her Lysteria even as he willingly engaged in the betrayal of his love. Afterward, he slept like a pig, snorting and rolling his sweaty, corpulent belly around on the sheets. But he did not awaken for the rest of the night—which was precisely the end result she wanted.

By the time she left his chambers a few hours before dawn, she had replaced all the scrolls in their hovel, including those that threw her retching to the floor, and resealed it with every ward that she had removed, careful this time to allow her to return without encumbrance if she needed, and to alert her should Balaam reopen the crypt.

Now, she waited. More than anything, she wanted Stevron to be pleased. His command was the only thing that mattered to her now.

Suddenly, a shadow emerged from the darkness, lumbering toward her with the gait of an angry bear. The stench of fish and salt water spilled off his leathers even more strongly than they had before. "You have it?" he growled.

She lowered her gaze. "Yes, Lord Stevron." She produced the map from the folds of her gown and held it toward him. "No one saw. No one yet knows."

"Yet?" he asked, snatching the scroll from her hand. "Does Balaam suspect you?"

She looked at him dully. "I do not believe so, Lord Stevron," she said. "He thought me to be his bondmate. His mind is gone."

"No one else saw you? You're sure?" He sounded angry.

"No, Lord Stevron," she replied fearfully.

He stared at her a moment longer in the dark, then marched to the open door and unfurled the scroll in the morning light. After scanning it a moment, he closed the door and walked back to her. "You are certain this is the most recent map he created?"

She nodded. "It was the only map, my Lord."

He considered this a moment. Then he said, "What of the others? What of Lysteria? Have any of them learned the location?"

Rachel felt her heart jump into her throat. She knew he would not be pleased by the news she had heard, and feared he would blame her for it though it was clearly none of her doing. "All of Lord Varia's and Lord Mattim's *mon'jalen* have fled the city," she said nervously, "Other mon'jalen have followed, though their house affiliations are less clear. So many lords have died of late, it has proven difficult to identify them all.

"A handful of the High Lord's *ser'jalen* are also missing—or so claims Lord Lysteria, who is the only one in a position to know, outside of Balaam himself. She believes Varia has co-opted Balaam's *ser'jalen* to learn the location of Wordhaven, and means to usurp Balaam's rule by taking his prize for herself."

Lord Stevron growled in anger. "When?" he demanded. "How long have the *mon'jalen* been gone?"

"A week at least," Rachel replied, uncertain. "Perhaps longer. Their tracks lead southwest across the Plain of Dreams. Lord Lysteria believes the *mon'jalen* travel to join Lords Varia and Mattim at Agatharon sounden."

"Why there?"

"I'm sorry, Lord, she did not say," Rachel replied timidly. In truth, she hadn't thought to ask.

Lord Stevron frowned, then unfurled the map again, squinting at it in the dark. "If that is so, then by now they are already headed north. They will use the port west of Agatharon to circumvent the hope and enter the Heaven Range by way of Valoran." He paused a moment. "A week you say? Are you certain?"

Rachel blinked. Her memory felt fuzzy, as if she weren't quite awake. "It is difficult to recall exactly," she said sheepishly. "Lord Lysteria will know."

"What of the High Lord?" he growled. As Rachel feared, he seemed on the verge of rage. "With this news, surely he has commissioned the guardians to march toward Wordhaven!"

"Lysteria and the Firstsworn plead with him daily," she said. "But he refuses."

Stevron yelled in frustration and hurled the map to the floor. "By the Words, I do not have time for this! Must I do everything myself?"

Rachel felt her heart pounding as he paced the floor. She was compelled to serve him, to alleviate his rage, but with her own task now complete, she felt her thoughts grow increasingly jumbled and indistinct. It was difficult to hold her focus in one place.

Finally, he stopped pacing and snatched the map from off the floor. "Come with me!" he commanded, and marched toward the door.

"How may I serve you, my Lord?"

"It seems I must give Lysteria and the Firstsworn the courage to do what must be done." Stuffing the scroll beneath his jerkin, he swung open the door and stormed outside. Rachel followed torpidly on his heels.

Some minutes later, they reached the doors to Lysteria's private chambers. The four *mon'jalen* guarding the entrance bowed slightly as they approached, but made no move to step aside. One of them said something to Lord Stevron, but when he spoke back, a wall of shimmering power like a wave smashed them all like puppets against the walls and blew the doors wide open. Rachel watched the entire exchange with a disinterested stare, as if watching a memory as it faded from her mind. She followed Stevron through the doors.

Lord Lysteria stood within, her face awash with shock. Borin Slayer—the Firstsworn of the Guardians—stood directly to her left, his black gloved hand resting quietly on her shoulder.

"Lord Stevron," said Lysteria shakily. "You are here. And Lord Rachel." Her eyes were red and puffy. If she noticed Stevron's forceful entry at all, she did not show it. "Good. The Firstsworn and I were just discussing what we should do now." She lowered her head and began to weep.

"This is hardly the time for tears, Lord Lysteria," snapped Stevron coldly. "You both know what must be done! Our forces must march—now—toward Wordhaven! The treachery of Lord Varia must be stopped!"

Lysteria shook her head and waved the notion away. "Not about that," she stammered. "I can't think about that right now."

"You what?" yelled Stevron. "Have you gone mad as well, woman?" But Lysteria only wept harder.

"If I may, Lord Stevron," said Borin Slayer, his hand still resting on Lysteria's shoulder, "I have just brought Lord Lysteria grave news regarding the High Lord."

"What?" demanded Stevron, sounding suddenly anxious. "What has happened?"

"He is gone, Stevron!" Lysteria sobbed into her hands. "He is gone!" She looked up at him, her aging eyes awash with tears.

"He took a boat at first light this morning," explained Borin, "and disappeared into the Gorge. He has sealed the route so none may follow. We do not know where he is."

Lord Stevron's face turned dark with rage. "The fool!" he yelled. Then his eyes softened in the realization of Balaam's intent. He sighed heavily and stared at the ceiling. "The mad fool."

Lord Lysteria looked up at him hopefully. "You know something, Stevron? Tell me." Fresh tears sprang from her black eyes. "Please, tell me! Where has he gone?"

"I should have seen it," Stevron said darkly. "He seeks the Waymaker for himself."

PHALLENAR

Lord Varia Dasa-Rel had long craved the title of High Lord. She had, in fact, been the handpicked choice of the previous High Lord, Tamus Rel, who had meticulously groomed her for the role during the final decades of his life. But Tamus was a brutal and finicky man—not well-liked among the people, and even less so among the lords—so when he passed, the Council broke with tradition and rejected Tamus' choice in open Council, electing instead his greatest adversary, Balaam Asher-Baal, to take the title of High Lord. The affront deeply incensed Varia, and planted in her heart the seed of treason, which she faithfully nurtured in the darkness of her thoughts until, in Balaam's deranged avarice, she saw the opportunity to take the title she had longed believed was rightfully hers.

—The Kyrinthan Journals, Chronicles, Chapter 18, Verses 204-206

I tell you, though Balaam has run off on a fool's errand, his life is not in danger where he goes. But here at home his title surely is! We must act now to see that he is not usurped!"

Lysteria and the Firstsworn stared at Lord Stevron as if he were mad. But their ignorant arrogance only infuriated him all the more. Was he really the only one among them able to comprehend what was truly at stake, what must be done? Their black eyes glared at him like mindless puppets, sad and vacant and void of courage.

Marching toward Lysteria, he slapped Borin's hand from her shoulder and grabbed her roughly by both arms. "I tell you, we must act quickly!" he spat angrily. "The guardian horde must march today!" But Lysteria looked at him as if he wasn't there. Her mind was somewhere else.

"Of course I agree," the Firstsworn interjected. "But I cannot command the march without the High Lord's blessing. Besides, he alone knows the way."

Stevron reached inside his jerkin and whipped out the map. He flung it at the Firstsworn's chest. "Here is your way!" he snapped. The scroll bounced harmlessly off Borin's leathers and tumbled to the floor.

The Firstsworn raised an eyebrow in mild surprise, then knelt to retrieve the crumpled scroll. "What is this, my Lord?"

"The map to Wordhaven, drawn by the High Lord's own hand!" Stevron gripped Lysteria's arms more firmly and pulled her close. "Lysteria!" he snapped. "Did you hear me?"

She blinked a moment, then shook her head sadly. "Why does he abandon me?" she muttered. "What power does this Waymaker hold over him?" Suddenly, she seemed to notice Stevron gripping her for the first time. Her black eyes grew hard. "Why didn't you slay him as I wished, Stevron?" she demanded. "Did I not tell you it would come to this?"

Stevron unexpectedly flinched at the accusation—not because he feared Lysteria's wrath, but because her words reignited his own frustration and disappointment with himself. He was without question the most powerful Lord of *Sa'lei* who had ever lived. But three times now he had failed in his attempts to destroy the Waymaker, despite the fact that the simpleton had no knowledge of *Sa'lei.*

"My deathstorm seeks him even now," he said flatly. "And I will soon return to the Barrens where he hides to be certain the deed is done. And I will find Balaam as well, Lord Lysteria, and return him here. You know I am the only one who can."

Her eyes misted with sorrow. "I am betrayed, Stevron," she said with a hollow voice. "First my daughter. And now my bondmate. What am I to do?"

"Balaam has not betrayed us!" snapped Stevron. "He is ill, Lysteria. You know that is the cause of this madness!" Feeling his anger surge once more, he shook her violently by the arms. "I will not have you doubt him, do you understand?"

Instantly, the Firstsworn whipped his hand between them and pressed

Stevron away. "My Lord, you forget yourself," he said icily. The threat in his tone was clear. "Please, step away. We need clear minds now, not rash anger."

Stevron knocked his hand away. "You were never bonded to me, Firstsworn," he growled. "There wasn't time. So perhaps you do not realize how close to death you are at this moment. Do you think it is Balaam's will to let his army loiter in the plains beyond the western gates while a usurper marches to Wordhaven to claim his title? I should slay you now, and summon a more worthy soldier who is less a coward and more a man of war!"

Borin's face reddened. "It is not my place to predict the High Lord's will," he said coolly. "I am bonded to serve his words."

"You are bonded, yes," snapped Stevron. "And what does your bond tell you? You know full well that he is not in his right mind! The Council is breaking apart before your eyes, and you have failed to act! Your days as Firstsworn will not be long." Abruptly, he turned back to Lysteria. "My lady, you must stand in Balaam's place. You must give the order for the horde to march. Each hour we wait only serves Varia's cause."

She looked at him blankly, as if unsure of what she heard or what she should say in response. He knew he could speak the Words to compel her to do as he wanted, and the Firstsworn as well. But he did not wish to. Controlling Rachel with the Words was one thing. But to extend his power over the Firstsworn or the High Lord's bondmate, he knew, was not something Balaam would approve. Still, he decided, he would do it, if it came to that.

Finally, Lord Lysteria blinked her dark eyes and nodded her head slowly. "I believe Lord Stevron is right, Borin," she said. "I must speak for Balaam until he is returned to us, and well again." She looked at the map, still crumpled in the Firstsworn's hand. "You are certain, Stevron, that this map shows the way?"

"Yes. Balaam entrusted me with it himself," he lied. He glanced back toward Lord Rachel, but she seemed not to have heard him. In fact, the glazed way she looked at him made him doubt she was paying attention at all.

"We should summon the Council," said Borin. "Put it to a vote."

"Fool!" barked Stevron. "We here are all that remains in the Axis, save Lord Maalern Fade, and he is too old to care for anything beyond the softness of his bed!"

"We should summon Lords Elise Deveris and Sed Kappan Mati," Borin stated firmly. "They have a say in this as well."

"Do you know where Balaam has sent them? Do you?" Stevron slapped the Firstsworn hard across the face. "You are a travesty, Borin," he added coldly. The Firstsworn took the blow without a flinch, but when he looked back at Stevron, his eyes were noticeably harder.

"I know where they have gone," said Lysteria tiredly. "He sent them toward Makroth sounden, to the remote mountains north of Castel Morstal. But it hardly matters. With Balaam gone, we have no means to recall them."

"There isn't time in any case!" snapped Stevron. "The horde must march today. And you, Borin. You will see that they stop Varia and Mattim, whatever the cost to the guardians, or to yourself."

To Stevron's surprise, Borin smiled at the comment. "You forget, Lord Stevron. Five Council Lords have fallen since the Stormcaller arrived. My days, as you say, are already numbered."

"I forget nothing," said Stevron coldly. "The bonding of the Firstsworn may allow you to live a year beyond the death of a lord. But your days will end long before that appointed time if Varia is allowed to set foot in Wordhaven." Stevron shot a glance back at Rachel, who had been watching listlessly from the doorway throughout the entire conversation. He moved to where she stood and placed his arm heavily around her shoulder. "And to be certain you perform your duties to our satisfaction, Lord Rachel here will accompany you on your mission." Borin stiffened at the suggestion, but Stevron raised his hand to silence him. "She will not command," Stevron continued, "but will remain at your side continually, and report to us what you do."

Suddenly, Lord Rachel seemed to come alive, as if waking from a mindless dream. "Yes," she said emphatically. "That is what I wish as well. As Lord Stevron says, I will go with the Firstsworn."

Borin bristled at the development. "My lords, it is hardly needed for—"

"Well, it's settled then," Lysteria interjected. She patted Borin lightly on the shoulder and glided toward Stevron with more vigor than she had at first. But her face was still hollow and pale. "And you, Lord Stevron, you must find Balaam quickly. And return him to me." Her voice, though firmer now than before, still reeked of desperation. "Promise me."

Stevron smirked. He found her dramatic tone amusing. "I will, my lady," he said darkly. "As I said, I know precisely where he will go."

REMA

The tattoos themselves were a brilliant innovation for the Cal'eeb—both as a means of passing down the pure Words of Dei'lo from one generation to the next and also as a formidable protective armor against the Barrens' taint. The power of the Barrens rests in its capacity to infect with darkness all pure life it touches. But no Sa'lei-wrought aberration can tolerate the direct touch of the Words of Life. So the Cal'eeb shrewdly saw within the Words themselves their only true defense against the insidious taint that threatened to overtake them. By branding the Words upon their skin, the Cal'eeb effectively forged on their bodies an impenetrable shield against the darkness, one that allowed them to pass through the Barrens at will and without fear.

—The Kyrinthan Journals, Chronicles, Chapter 16, Verses 33-36

I t's a jewel, this place." Revel leaned into the banister and breathed in deep. The village of Rema glistened below him, its assorted white domed structures coating the jagged slopes like an alabaster cloak. "If only Ajel could see this."

"It reminds me of Phallenar," observed Kyrintha, with a hint of distaste. "All this white. Like bleached bones."

"Surely it does not!" Revel laughed, poking her playfully in the ribs. "I have never seen Phallenar in the light of day, my lady, but surely it cannot be half as lovely as what I see now." He kept his eyes on her as he spoke.

Kyrintha blushed, and averted her gaze in an unsuccessful attempt to conceal her smile. "I lived in Phallenar all my life, for the Giver's sake!" she retorted, feigning irritation. "You're hardly one to speak of what looks like what. I tell you, this looks like Phallenar!" Her gaze drifted over the sparkling white buildings, then to the glistening waters of the long, narrow lake the Cal'eeb called *Spiri'vel,* and the seven roads beyond. "Well, this is much smaller, of course. And Phallenar has no lake to compare with that one. But still..."

"I wonder what's keeping Telus," Gideon interjected—as much to remind Revel and the underlord that they were not alone as anything else. He didn't mind, really, that Revel liked her. But their flirting made him feel awkward in front of Aybel, who stood idly next to him as if waiting for him to say something. "They should be done with him by now," he added. He walked to the railing and rubbed the back of his neck tiredly. Aybel did not follow.

"The Cal'eeb are nothing if not methodical," said Revel. "They will be done with him when they are thoroughly satisfied. And not before."

"What do they think they can teach him, anyway?" asked Gideon. "I mean, he's a Raanthan. He knows more about the Pearl than all of us put together."

"For all their supposed insight, the Raanthan are a broken race, sojourner," said Aybel flatly from her place behind him. She sounded a little angry. "They came to the Lands during the Endless Age, not long after the Pearl arrived. From the time they first appeared, they swore their collective lives to the Pearl. They had little interaction with humankind, except in small ways, where the Pearl expressly wished it. Some say the Raanthans believed they were more worthy to serve than the rest of us. The tapestries record how they acclaimed themselves as the Pearl's true protectors, and looked with disdain on the human Guardians of old.

"But when the Pearl was destroyed, they quickly lost their courage. Within a mere fifty years, they had all but disappeared from the Lands, retreating to the frozen wastelands of the north where they have hidden in isolation to this day."

"I have read those stories as well," said Kyrintha, her green eyes bright with interest, "from the Black Scrolls held in the Axis. They say the Raanthans departed into self-imposed exile, as punishment for their failure to protect the Pearl from harm."

"The Roamers speak of them as well," mused Revel quietly. "Though their stories tell more of Raanthan bloodlust than their history."

"Bloodlust?" asked Gideon. "That doesn't sound right."

"My people have long hated them," Aybel continued. "They are wraiths. Demons. Abominations against lore. Their villages border our lands to the north. But even as far south as Arelis, we have captured them trespassing through our stakehold at times. And we have slain them."

"They can be killed?" asked Gideon. He had seriously wondered if it was possible.

Aybel nodded slightly, but clearly did not care to explain further. She glanced toward the lake and pretended to stop listening.

"There are many tales of death at the hands of the Raanthan among the Roamers as well," chimed Revel. "The Raanthan Plateau is rich in rare gems. But only a few of the migrant soundens will venture there. Those who do most often return in fewer numbers, with tales of violent horrors committed against them by Raanthan hands."

Gideon shook his head in disbelief. "That doesn't make sense," he said. "Telus is a total pacifist. He says his people aren't allowed to harm anything—not even a barren's beast."

Aybel stepped up to face him, her expression surprisingly bitter. "Not all Raanthans are as they appear, Waymaker," she scowled. "You would do well to remember that."

Gideon blinked in surprise. "What are you saying?"

But Kyrintha spoke instead. "The Cal'eeb tested him longer than any of us," she said soothingly. "If he were not trustworthy, they would have told us as much. They speak with him now only to test his understanding of his role as the Waymaker's guide."

Gideon sighed tiredly. "I still don't see what they think they can teach him."

Revel shot Gideon a broad smile and slapped him playfully on the shoulder. "If I did not know better, Waymaker, I would say you are concerned for him."

Gideon threw his hands up and shook his head. "Okay, that's just crazy talk," he said sarcastically. But in truth, he was. Though he certainly wouldn't go so far as to call Telus a friend, the Raanthan had demonstrated extraordinary courage and selflessness to save Gideon's neck in the sea battle with Stevron. And that wasn't the first time he had thanked the silvery giant for saving his life. Of course, he could say the same of Revel, and Aybel as well. He owed them all.

From there, the conversation drifted off into an uneasy silence. The sun had begun its slow descent toward the verdant horizon to the west, stretching the shadows of the buildings below until they kissed one another, forming a patchwork quilt of light and dark across the rolling terrain.

Gideon wondered if they'd ever get to see any of it up close. Since their arrival three days past, Galad had refused to let them leave the citadel, and given strict orders not to speak with anyone beyond the *Nissim* or the red-robed Trevail Priests, who scuttled daily in and out of the castle doors with the grim silence of military sergeants marching to and from the front lines of war. The restrictions struck Gideon as suspicious at first, until Galad and Saravere explained that news of their arrival, once announced, would cause great upheaval among the Cal'eeb.

For one thing, the Cal'eeb's long-held belief that the rest of the world had fallen under the dark taint of the Desolation would be utterly shattered. If the *Nissim's* reaction to the news was any indication, Gideon suspected the rest of their community would not take the revelation very well. Galad and Saravere said they were pleased to learn that they were not alone, of course, and seemed genuinely relieved to hear that much of the Inherited Lands was still free of the Barrens' curse. But their tattooed faces betrayed a different reaction—something akin to disillusionment...like the Pope might have looked when Galileo discovered that the Earth was not the center of the universe after all.

But the more shocking news, as it turned out, was Gideon himself. The Waymaker. Unlike the people of Songwill and Wordhaven, who for the most part considered the Waymaker a minor, obscure character in the annuls of prophecy, the Cal'eeb held him in extraordinary esteem, believing him to be the harbinger and instrument of the Pearl's return to the Lands. Because of their isolation from the mainland, the Cal'eeb had never heard about the Pearl's destruction at Gideon's Fall. Instead, they simply came to believe that the Pearl had left the Lands intentionally in order to allow the Desolation to come. It was all an elaborate test, they explained, designed to prove their faith in the truth of *Dei'lo*. The Waymaker, they believed, would appear when the testing was complete to herald the Pearl's return.

Thus, news of the Waymaker's arrival would change everything for the Cal'eeb. It was the one sign they looked for above all others.

Gideon absently stroked his fingers across the emblem of the Pearl emblazoned on his leather jerkin. The pull on his heart to move south was growing more insistent by the day. But once again, he found himself at the mercy of people who couldn't decide what to do with him. At least they weren't prisoners this time—but then again, they weren't exactly free to leave either.

A red-robed figure quietly emerged from a small door on the north side of the balcony and shuffled hurriedly over to where they stood. When she reached Gideon, she bowed. "The Raanthan awaits you in your chambers, Waymaker," she said. Her face was completely obscured by the hood, but her voice sounded young.

"Well, that's good," said Gideon. "It's about time."

The priest did not respond, and quickly turned to go. But when she noticed that Gideon had not moved, she added, "Time is short."

"Wait a minute," asked Gideon. "Is he all right?" But the priest had already scurried off.

"We should go to him," said Revel, sounding concerned.

Gideon nodded in agreement, and the four of them hurried through the large translucent doors that led to their chambers. The *Nissim* had sequestered them in a cluster of small rooms within the Citadel's main tower, a long spear of rough white stone that loomed above the village like an aging but watchful guardian. Gideon and Revel had climbed all the way to the top the first day after their arrival. From the highest windows, they could see far into the verdant hillocks of the Trevail Plains, but there was no sign of the Barrens anywhere. And no view of the sea either. The entire plain of Trevail, including the village itself, was concealed from the ocean buy a line of bleach white cliffs that ran north along the shore until they disappeared behind a knot of small mountains.

When they reached Gideon's chamber, they found Telus there seated on the floor, along with Captain Quigly and his bondmate, who were both staring at the Raanthan as if unconvinced that it was actually him.

His face was covered in cuts and bruises, as were his arms and chest. His overly-large bronze eyes looked heavy and sorrowful, as if weary of seeing, and his breathing was shallow.

Gideon immediately ran to his side. "Telus, what happened? What'd they do to you?"

The Raanthan attempted a smile. "Peace, Waymaker," he said quietly. "They found me true."

Gideon's mind struggled to comprehend what he was seeing. Telus could not *be* injured. He had stood right in the path of Stevron's Words, and barely flinched! But here he was, bleeding. *He was bleeding!* Gideon found himself a little surprised that the blood was red.

"Why did they do this to you?" Gideon stammered angrily. "How?"

Telus awkwardly raised his arm and scanned his injuries. Despite his obvious exhaustion, he seemed almost amused. "They attempted to brand me…with the Words," he said. "To guarantee my intent as your guide."

"To what? Brand you? Like the tattoos they have?" Gideon asked.

Telus nodded. "Obviously, they were unsuccessful. I am surprised they did not know it would fail." He closed his eyes and sighed. "They have held onto much of the truth. But in some ways, they are even more backward than the Remnant of Wordhaven."

"If it were not for the Remnant, both Wordhaven and the Book would still be lost, Raanthan!" snapped Aybel. "I'll not have you speak ill of it."

"She need not be upset," Telus told Gideon. He still stubbornly refused to speak directly to anyone else unless there were no other choice. "I meant only that much of what was once known has been lost. And some of what remains has become clouded by hurt and avarice. She knows this in her heart, though she is loathe to admit it."

"If you have something to say to me, Raanthan," said Aybel, "then say it *to me!*"

"Aybel, please," said Gideon soothingly. "Give him a break, would you?"

Aybel shot Gideon an angry frown, but then folded her arms and sighed in resignation.

"The Tongue of *Dei'lo* was given to humankind, Waymaker," said Telus, "not to the Raanthan. We serve the Pearl, and in serving the Pearl we serve the Tongue. But the Tongue is not for us; we do not speak it. And we are largely immune from its effects. That is why the priests could not brand me, and why their own Words could not discern the true intention of my will in serving you."

"Not all of your kind serve the Pearl," Aybel stated flatly. "I have seen proof enough of that."

"There is little time, Waymaker," said Telus, ignoring Aybel's acerbic comment. "The *Nissim* now understand the urgency of your quest. They are preparing to send us on our way at first light tomorrow. They have chosen to send seven of their priests along with us into the Barrens. That is, assuming we are still to go south?"

Gideon nodded. "Yes. But I don't understand. They're sending priests with us? What for?"

"The Trevail Priests are the keepers of the Seven Stays," replied Telus. "It is their power in the Words that holds back the Barrens from these plains."

Suddenly, Captain Quigly let out a huff. "You're all mad, the lot of ya'," he barked. "You can't seriously be thinkin' of crossing into that Giver-forsaken patch of rot! There be nothing but death there, or that what wishes for it."

"As I recall, Captain," said Revel, "you thought there'd be nothing but death here as well. Yet here we are, rested and safe under the roof of new-found friends. Surely this proves there are powers greater than the Barrens at work here."

Quigly snorted derisively. "My lady is not safe, lander. She is shattered from stem to stern, no thanks to you or your lordly 'powers'."

"Have not the Cal'eeb agreed to rebuild the Endurant?" asked Aybel. "With *Dei'lo*, it will not take long."

"*Dei'lo, Dei'lo!*" exclaimed Quigly angrily. "That's all I hear you Word-haveners speak of day and night, and now these crazed priests as well. But I want no part of it! The Tongue brings trouble to peace-lovin' folk, I've always said it was so. If it weren't for that Tongue, my sweet lady would not be lying beached like a sick whale on the shore. Now where am I to go? How am I to live? This place sickens me but deep. The ground is not right, I tell ya'! It's queer to my feet."

The group stared at him as if unsure how to respond. Finally, though, Kyrintha found the words. "Take heart, Captain Quigly," she began sooth-ingly. "I know that your people do not feel at ease on land. And I'm sure that the Wordhaveners do not expect you and your bondmate to travel with them any farther into the Barrens. And I'm equally certain the Cal'eeb will do as they have promised, with or without the Words. The Endurant will sail again."

"Make no mistake on that, my lady," snapped Quigly. "She will sail again, and soon, or that blasted Council Lord won't be the only one looking to spill your blood."

"Captain Quigly!" exclaimed Kyrintha.

"We will see to it that the Cal'eeb keep their word to you, Captain," said Aybel tersely. "You have no need to threaten us. But you would do well to open your eyes. Look where we are! We stand in the middle of the Death-land Barrens, yet the Barrens are not here. The power of *Dei'lo* did this! The deathstorm sent to vanquish us has itself been vanquished by the *Dei'lo* Word of the Cal'eeb. And your own ship would be resting at the bottom of the ocean right now if not for the power of the Waymaker, who delivered both you and your precious ship out of Stevron's hands."

"A battle that would never have happened if not for you and your mighty Waymaker!" retorted Quigly. He shook his bulbous head. "I should have let the waters take you when I had the chance."

Aybel's face flushed in anger, but Revel placed his hand on her arm to calm her.

"Enough with the ship!" Gideon commanded. "Could we please turn our attention back to the matter at hand?" He gestured toward Telus who was still sprawled on the floor and bleeding. "We've got a man down, here, in case you've forgotten!"

"Waymaker," said Telus weakly. "I am not in need. You must focus your thoughts on the path ahead."

Gideon shook his head. "All I know is we have to go south."

"The Council Lord has remained quiet since your arrival here," said Telus, "but he will come again. The next attack will likely fall on you within the tainted lands of the Barrens, where he is strongest. We must be ready."

Gideon threw up his hands in frustration. "How am I supposed to pre-pare? I'm not even sure how I held him off the last time, Telus. I'm not sure I can do it again. Beside, none of us have any idea what to expect in the Bar-rens." He gestured flippantly toward Aybel and Revel.

"You are wrong," Telus corrected. "The Priests of Trevail know much of the Barrens. As do I." He extended a long, bruised silvery arm toward Gideon. "Help me up," he said. "There is little time, and I have much to explain."

29

A SONG IN THE NIGHT

It was Aybel Boldrun who first told me of the deep schism within the ranks of the Raanthan. I confess, at first I did not believe her, thinking her judgment tainted by the stories of her youth among the Kolventu, who universally hated the Raanthan as much as any lord of Phallenar. But when I saw it with my own eyes, the bitter truth of it turned my blood to ice. How the mighty have fallen! In that dark hour, I remember thinking: If so wondrous a being could be so utterly corrupted by the Words of Abaddon, what hope remained for us?

—The Kyrinthan Journals, Musings, Chapter 15, Verses 32-34

Somewhere deep in the night, long after Telus had exhausted himself with the telling of stories and dangers related to the Barrens, Gideon was awakened by the sound of singing. The voices echoed up from the grey-stoned cathedral several levels beneath him, filling the curved stairwell of the tower with images of elegant beauty, memory and hope. The music was unlike anything Gideon had ever experienced before. At first, in fact, he thought it was a dream. Who had ever heard of a song that painted images you could never imagine across the canvas of your mind? But that was the magic of it.

He listened for several minutes before he was at last compelled to rise and seek out the source of the haunting chorus. Donning his leathers, he lit a candle, slipped out of his small chamber and padded barefoot down the cool stone steps. There was no sign that the others had awakened. Normally, he would have told Aybel or Revel before venturing toward something so unfamiliar and strange. But not this time. Something about the music touched him deeply in a way he couldn't explain. The haunting chords spoke to places within him that he had long forgotten—hidden pockets of his soul that resonated with vulnerability, innocence and fear. He felt drawn by it, but also frightened, and didn't like the idea of letting anyone else see his emotions so unguarded.

The circular stairs ended abruptly at the bottom, leading to a small, simple door of wood and iron. Gideon smirked at the sight of it. One of the *Nissim*, Galad, had told them that the tower was once home to many Lords of Wordhaven, who came to Broken Heart each season to train the novices seeking to be raised as Lords themselves. But Gideon had found the thought unlikely. The tower was quite stunning from the outside, but the chambers within it were small and very plain—too much so, he thought, to be worthy of housing powerful Lords of *Dei'lo*. The door before him followed the same Spartan theme. It was too small to pass through without ducking.

The instant he squeezed through the passage, the mystical chorus enveloped him in a warm blanket of comforting light and resolve. The resonance of voices filling the cathedral was like a sun shining at midnight. Tears came unbidden to his eyes. This surprised him, as did the laughter that followed, which bubbled up into his throat from long lost memories of meaning and hope he'd treasured once as a child.

At first, no one noticed him. Fifty or more Priests of Trevail ringed the circular mosaic on the chamber floor, their voices singing with such precision in harmony and rhythm, it seemed there was only one. Galad and Saravere stood in their midst, their unhooded faces awash with the same sort of fierce intensity Gideon had often seen on Donovan's face in the midst of battle. He could not understand the words. But he knew they were pleading.

Finally, Saravere casually looked his way and smiled as if she'd known he'd been there all along. Passing through the circle, she approached. Without a word, she clasped his arm gently and, gesturing toward a door on the far end of the chamber, led him outside into the night.

The music followed them, echoing images in Gideon's mind of things he knew were beautiful, but could not fully comprehend. After leading him several paces away from the doors, Saravere released his arm, looked into his eyes, now shadowed by night, and simply smiled.

Gideon returned the gesture, but felt immediately unnerved by her stare. It seemed somehow inappropriate to speak, but the silence made him uncomfortable.

"What's going on?" he whispered.

"It is nothing to be concerned about, Waymaker," she said, apparently sensing his discomfort. "The priests are strengthening themselves in the Words. We are in need of encouragement this night."

"Why? Is something wrong?"

She smiled reassuringly and patted his arm before speaking. "The third Stay was attacked just a few hours past. The priests prevailed, but it required five of them working in chorus to repel the attacker. This is unusual. It has never required so many before. And the enemy was not destroyed."

Suddenly, Gideon's heart began to race. "What enemy?" he asked. "Do you know what attacked you?"

"No," replied Saravere, still smiling. "We only know what it was not. It was not a horde of dark souls, nor the carrion beasts. These we are familiar with. They attack the Stays every fortnight or so, and are easily repelled by one priest alone. But whatever attacked this time, it was but one, and we have never encountered its like before. It spoke as the dark souls sometimes do, but with words of cold and malevolent power."

Gideon closed his eyes and sighed. The signs were unmistakable. "Saravere," he said sadly, "I'm so sorry to have brought this on you."

The *Nissim* looked at him curiously. "Waymaker, you know what it was?"

"Not what, but who," replied Gideon. "He's one of the Lords of Phallenar we told you about."

"Speakers of a Tongue of Power, but not *Dei'lo?*" she asked in a tone that revealed her doubt that such a thing could exist.

Gideon nodded. "His name is Stevron. He's the one we were running from when we came here. He created the deathstorm that followed us."

"That there could be such a madness in the world," she said quietly. "I confess I do not want to believe it."

"Did he get through?"

"No," she replied. "He retreated back into the marshwood. He cannot breach the Stays."

"He won't stop," said Gideon firmly. "Not as long as he knows I am here." He sighed tiredly. He hated was he was about to say, but knew there was no other way. "Saravere, we must wake the others. We have to leave now."

The *Nissim* looked surprised. "It is only a handful of hours until first light," she said. "Surely your departure can wait until then. You need your rest."

"He's found us. Every minute we stay here only increases the danger for you all," he said.

Saravere looked unconvinced.

"You have to understand," Gideon continued. "Your people are very strong in the Words, but you've never had to fight directly against someone who knows *Sa'lei*. You won't know how to fight him."

Saravere smiled. "We resisted him once already." Patting him gently on the hand, she added, "We have survived in the Desolation for two thousand years, dear one. We know well how to fight the darkness."

Gideon shook his head. "It's not the same thing." He paused a moment, searching for a way to explain it to her. "Stevron, and those like him," he began, "the language they speak caused all this. What you've been fighting against in the...Desolation, is just the effects of their Words. You've never fought against the Words themselves. Believe me. I know what I'm talking about. I won't risk more people dying because of me."

Saravere considered him a moment, then said, "I think you underestimate us. And yet, you are the Waymaker. You alone know the path that must be trod. If you believe you must leave now, then it will be done. The *Nissim* of Trevail will not stand in your way."

Gideon smiled, but it could not dispel his regret. "Thank you," he said, then added, "Will you come with me to awaken the others?"

"Yes," she replied, "but let us go another way. I do not wish to disturb the singers overmuch."

To his surprise, Saravere slipped her arm around his as they headed toward the side of the cathedral. Gideon accepted it without comment, though it renewed his feelings of discomfort.

"That song is amazing," he commented, listening to its faint melodies drifting through the shadowy walls. "I keep seeing these images in my head, like the music is showing me a story I can't quite understand."

Saravere giggled lightly. "Would you like to hear the Words?" she asked.

Suddenly Gideon felt his cheeks grow hot. "No, that's okay," he said. "I don't speak *Dei'lo*."

But Saravere spoke them anyway:

> *"Sa'Elo ya punemas meso sum pravelis*
> *E'creyis meson'pa paradis*
> *See creyis meson'sod ya'delim antelis*
> *E'avare meso en montalis*
> *Meso purvel adversum e'sezar see*
> *E'sel regalis admun endar see*
> *Elo punemas meso sum pravelis en'corin*
> *See creyis adversum bowmar meson'sod"*

A tapestry of invocative images drifted across Gideon's mind as she spoke, awakening within him a resonate well of emotions—courage, steadfastness, peace, and certain faith. But whatever specific message the song conveyed still lingered just beyond his reach, like a powerful dream he could not quite remember.

"It's beautiful," he said.

"Yes," she agreed, "because it is true."

Gideon smiled, but then walked on in silence. Silently, he wondered how long the Cal'eeb's innocent faith in the truth of *Dei'lo* would protect them from the corrupting Words of Phallenar, now that the Council knew they were here.

INTO THE BARRENS

Looking back, I find it incredulous that although I had lived near the Barrens all of my life, I had never given it much thought. In my foolishness, I believed the walls of Phallenar protected me from its influence, as easily as a solid house protects one from the ravages of rain and wind outside. It was only after I stepped foot within the Barrens' borders that I noticed the familiarity of its sickly sweet scent, and realized that the city I had called my home for years was as saturated with the taint of the Barrens as any poisoned swamp or riftmen village—only wrapped in a cloak of ordinary life to numb the hearts of the unsuspecting.
—The Kyrinthan Journals, Songs of Deliverance, Stanza 16, Verses 10-13

By the time the others had been awakened, collected their belongings and stumbled tiredly down to the cathedral, many of the priests had gathered outside the doors to see them off. Galad had hurriedly prepared several packs of food for their journey, and seemed preoccupied with making sure they knew how to keep it safe.

"You must never let it come in contact with the ground," he instructed. "If your hands become soiled, wash them in Word-purified water before handling any item of food. If you ingest even a speck of dirt from the outerlands, you will suffer infection."

By "infection," Galad was referring to the *Sa'lei*-Worded taint, which

Telus had explained permeated everything in the Barrens, right down to the smallest leaf or tiniest blade of grass. Just a touch of the vegetation on bare skin could result in serious illness. Ingestion, or direct contact with an open wound, could lead to a slow death, or in many cases, a corrupting perversion that was far worse than death. Just how they were supposed to traverse through this land without allowing it to touch them in any way remained a troubling question for Gideon—especially given that their skin was not protected with tattooed Words as the Cal'eeb were.

"We are thankful for the gift of food," Revel said to Galad. "We will be careful to heed your instructions."

Saravere appeared in the doorway of the cathedral, her tattooed face looking fresh and peaceful despite her lack of sleep. Behind her followed a huddle of men—presumably priests, though they had exchanged their red robes for brown leather skirts and long tunics of sheer spun cloth. Even in the shadows of predawn, Gideon could see hints of dozens of exotic tattoos covering their torsos and arms.

Galad anxiously waved them in. "Good, good," he said, "come forward."

The seven men paraded passed Gideon and the others, each of them bearing the same stoic, hardened expression shared by all the priests Gideon had seen since his arrival. They gathered in a line behind Galad, and faced the group.

"These are your *san'gradon*, your guard," Galad began, addressing Gideon. "They are Trevail Priests of the highest order. You will find them more than capable in battle against the darkness of the Desolation. They have volunteered for this duty, to serve as your shield and guide through the outerlands to the south. May they bear you safely to your goal."

"Thank you," said Gideon, feeling suddenly exposed as all eyes turned on him. "I'm really grateful that you're coming along," he said to the priests. "From what I've heard about the Barrens, we're going to need all the help we can get."

Galad smiled politely, and Gideon nervously wondered if he was supposed to say something more. But the *Nissim* quickly continued with the introductions.

"This is Magan, Shobi, Machir," he began, pointing to each priest in turn. "Ammiel, Terebin, Hushai, and Rojel." He turned back to Gideon. "They are good men. Seasoned. I intended you to have time to meet with them more privately. But since your need to leave is so urgent...well, I trust you will become acquainted on the way."

"I'm sure we'll do fine," said Gideon, forcing a smile. In truth, he wasn't really certain of that at all. They may have been priests in name, but their manner and bearing were more akin to that of battle-hardened soldiers. The cold ferocity in their eyes told him these men had witnessed horrors he did not want to imagine. Just looking at them rankled his nerves.

"I would have hoped for more time," lamented Galad. "We have not yet even announced your arrival to our people! I have already arranged for a gathering at first sun. Can you not wait even a few more hours?"

"We apologize, *Nissim* Galad," said Aybel. "But the Waymaker is right. If Stevron has attacked the Stays, then the Council Lords will surely soon learn of your existence within the Barrens, if they have not already. They are your enemy as much as ours, but for now their eyes are fixed on the Waymaker. It is best that we leave now, and draw their attention away from this place."

"You are a treasure in the Lands, Cal'eeb," added Revel, "a bastion of truth that we have only now rediscovered. In time, we will return and guide you to Wordhaven, should you wish it. There you will be safely beyond the reach of the Council's arm. But for now you must remain wary, and pray that your peculiar isolation within the Barrens will serve to hide you from their eyes a little while longer."

Galad sighed. "So be it, then. Saravere." He extended his hand toward his bondmate, who crossed in front of the group to take it.

"I am confident you will all do well," she said. To the *san'gradon*, she added, "Remember your oath. Remember the songs." The priests nodded, but there faces betrayed no emotion.

"The *san'gradon* will guide you through the boundary," said Galad. He gestured to the plaza directly below them. "This is the nexus of the seven roads. Each leads to one of the Stays, which are dispersed along the boundary line. You will travel on the first road, *Pa'ada*, to the easternmost Stay. Once you cross the boundary, hold as close to the shore as your quest will allow. The dark souls fear the sea, and are loathe to approach it."

"We will do as you say," said Revel.

"As much as our quest will allow," corrected Gideon. He had no wish to face the riftmen again, but the pull of his heart was strong, and growing stronger by the moment. He could not say where it might take him.

"There is one other matter, *Nissim* Galad," said Aybel. "The Sea Folk who came with us—they have risked much to help us and the Waymaker."

"We honor them," said Galad, nodding. "They are free to remain with us as long as they wish."

"Their people are not at ease on land, *Nissim*," Aybel continued. "The Captain and his bondmate will find no rest here among your people. They must be returned quickly to the sea."

Galad nodded. "Then we will see that their ship is repaired before the sun sets tonight," he said matter-of-factly. "Though I confess Saravere and I would have liked to spend more time with them. They are a curious people."

"No doubt they think the same of you," lied Revel, grinning.

"It is time, Waymaker," said Telus. "We should be going."

Gideon glanced up at the Raanthan and nodded. He was surprised to notice that the cuts on Telus' face were already mostly healed. "Let's do it, then," he said.

The group said their final goodbyes, gathered their packs and passed down into Rema for the first time, with the seven Trevail Priests leading the way.

It took only a short while to traverse the still-sleeping village, and as they passed the last of the white buildings and stepped onto the open road, Gideon felt an unexpected pang of loss. He wondered if he'd ever get the chance to return here and explore it all in the light of day.

A short distance from the city, the road veered left and rose steeply toward the white cliffs that walled the rolling plains of Trevail from the Eastern Sea. After a lengthy traverse, the group summitted upon a narrow plateau—just in time to see the sun peek above the watery horizon to the east, casting its warm glow across the stark limestone cliffs and spilling its rich, red light into a smattering of clouds that hovered tentatively over the Eastern Sea. The distant roar of the ocean could be heard rising up from below.

"It's quite beautiful," commented Kyrintha to no one in particular.

"Beauty is true within Trevail," said on of the priests gruffly. "But only a fool would trust its lure beyond the Stays or upon the open waters. Best keep your eyes on the road."

The admonition passed without comment. But the priest's words hovered worriedly in Gideon's ears. How could they protect themselves in the

Barrens if they couldn't even recognize what was dangerous? Perhaps the staff would warn him somehow. But if it didn't, he realized grimly, their survival would rest fully in the hands of the priests—men they hardly knew.

They walked on, following the stone road as it wended its way southwest along the cliffs. In time the sun expanded their view on the landscape, revealing the verdant, rolling plains of Trevail, and, to the south, a narrow inlet cutting a swath of angry ocean into the land. Beyond the inlet there were no cliffs—only a wide tongue of sandy loam fading lazily into the sea.

"Behold the Desolation," announced one of the priests, pointing toward the beach.

Gideon scanned the shore worriedly. To his surprise, it looked much like any other beach. There were no riftmen, no vile perversions he could see. Some eighty yards from shore, a wall of short twisted trees and viney shrubs wafted lightly in the morning breeze. The green of life stretched lazily down the coast, as tranquil and at ease as if it had been there since the beginning of time.

"It doesn't look all that dangerous," said Gideon at last.

"The land deceives, Waymaker," replied the priest without turning around. "It sees us even now, and hungers. It will show its teeth soon enough."

Soon after, the road drifted inland, and the view of the Barrens faded from sight. The group followed the stone path down the diminishing slopes of the limestone cliffs until they emerged on a level field of grass smattered with trees just north of the inlet Gideon had seen from above. As they entered a wooded knoll, they were met by two red-robed priests standing patiently upon the road as if they'd been expected. Upon seeing the group, the two priests bowed to toward Gideon, then turned and walked ahead of them. They said nothing, and their shrouded faces gave no indication why they were there. But the *san'gradon* followed them as if it were all a part of the plan.

Minutes later, they rounded one final bend of trees and came at last in view of the Stay. The *Nissim* had said little about them—except that they somehow worked in concert to hold back the Barrens from the Trevail Plains. But the sight of it stole Gideon's breath away. The massive head and shoulders of a cloaked and hooded giant rose out of the ground before him like a mythical warrior, its stoic form staring off into the Barrens like a messenger of death.

The statue, carved completely of white stone, towered at least fifty feet above their heads. Gideon marveled at its artistic beauty and the imposing quality of its presence. Despite its obvious stone composition, it seemed quite alive. He could even hear the deep resonate hum of its breath wafting on the gentle breeze of morning.

It wasn't until they walked to its side that Gideon realized the monument had no face. Instead, the hooded carving formed an empty cavernous dome. The red-robed priests who had accompanied them ascended the shoulders of the giant by way of a narrow line of steps carved into the stone, and quickly disappeared beneath the deep shadows of its hood.

"The priests will watch our way as far as they are able," said one of the *san'gradon*. He pointed south across an open field to a line of low trees in the distance. "But once we cross into the marsh, their Words will no longer reach us."

"The way appears clear for now," said another of the priests. "It may be that the land ahead does not yet suspect what we are doing. But we must not linger here long." Removing his pack, he placed it on the ground and pulled from it a wad of brown cloth embroidered with green markings. Tossing it toward Kyrintha, he barked, "Put this on."

The underlord lifted the cloth off the ground and let it fall open. Its entire surface was embroidered with *Dei'lo*.

"What is it?" asked Aybel.

The priest pulled out a second garment and tossed it toward her. "A Worded cloak," he said. "It cannot guard you fully against the Desolation, but it will help."

The underlord delicately traced the Wording on the garment, her eyes alight with interest. "Does it work like the tattoos on your skin?" she asked.

"In part," said the priest gruffly. "You will see. Now put it on. We must go."

This was all moving too fast for Gideon. He stepped toward the priest. "Now, hold on a minute," he said in frustration. "What's your name?"

"Terebin." The priest reluctantly stopped what he was doing and stood to face him.

"Well, Terebin, don't you think we should know a little more about what we're walking into here?" asked Gideon firmly. "It seems foolish to me for us to just waltz in there without having some idea of what to expect."

"Your pardon, Waymaker, but there is no time." The priest sounded impatient.

Revel stepped toward the pair. "Let us work together, Terebin," he said gently. "Aybel and I have the Words as well. You need not carry this burden alone."

Terebin stood quietly for a moment, his piercing green eyes shifting back and forth between Revel and Gideon. Finally, he said, "Scouts from the dark souls may have already spotted us from the marsh. If they have, then they will leave and soon return with a host of their brothers. We must be far from this place before that happens. The Desolation is weakest along the boundary. The Waymaker and the rest of you will be safe enough in our care until we reach the brown fields beyond the marsh. Once there, there will be time for talk. But right now, there is none." He reached down and pulled out two more cloaks from his pack. Thrusting them toward Revel and Gideon he said, "Now please, don your cloaks and let us be gone from this place."

Several of the other priests grunted their agreement. Gideon considered Terebin for a moment. His tattooed face betrayed no fear, but he was clearly anxious to leave. Finally, Gideon took the cloak from Terebin's hand. "All right, Terebin," he said slowly. "But we will go where I lead. You understand?"

The priest lowered his eyes in a quick bow. "We will follow the Waymaker," he said firmly. "But you must trust us to lead you beyond the boundary."

Gideon nodded reluctantly. "Fair enough," he said. "But we'll stop at the first opportunity, and you will answer our questions."

"As you say," the priest replied. He quickly snatched the pack from the ground and tossed it onto his back. "Stay behind us until we reach the trees," he commanded. He turned to go, but then paused and turned toward Revel. Pointing toward Aybel, he said, "You and the dark-skinned woman, you say you know the Words?" Revel nodded. "Then do not speak them within the marsh," he instructed. "They will draw the attention of the dark souls."

Revel looked surprised. "But how then will we protect ourselves from the land?" he asked.

"You will not need to," Terebin replied flatly. Then he turned to go. The other priests quickly fell in line behind him.

"Wait," said Gideon. "What about Telus? Don't you have a cloak for him?"

"The Rannthan has no need of a cloak," one of the other priests replied without turning around. "The Desolation does not see him."

Gideon looked at the Raanthan in surprise. "Is that true, Telus?" he asked.

Telus nodded slightly. "Yes," he said. But then his bronze eyes suddenly turned sad. "And yet, there is evil within the Deathland Barrens that even I cannot evade."

"What do you mean?" asked Gideon.

"A discussion for another time, Waymaker," he said. "Quickly, put on your cloak. And keep your staff close."

Gideon grunted in frustration. Why wouldn't anyone give him a straight answer? Irritated, he clumsily tossed the cloak around his shoulders and fastened the cords at his neck. The brown cloth felt rough as burlap against his skin, but the embroidered lettering of *Dei'lo* that covered it glistened in the morning light with the smoothness of refined silk. He touched the letters as the underlord had, half expecting to feel a surge of power from the script. But there was nothing.

Once the others had donned their cloaks, they left the comforting presence of the Stay behind and headed out into the open field. The priests were already some distance ahead of them, marching in a line toward the distant trees. Gideon considered trying to catch up with them, but then his thoughts were interrupted by the sound of singing. Looking back, he saw the two red-robed priests standing in the shadows of the Stay's faceless hood. Their baritone voices, amplified a thousand times by the resonate chamber in which they stood, joined together in a haunting chorus that saturated the air with a power and presence so palpable that Gideon could sense the weight of it pressing against his body, and urging him courageously forward.

Elo'creyis pa'see paradis!
Rebonis shadoom e'punemas far!

The priests sang the Words over and over as Gideon and the others marched toward the trees. He had no idea what the Words meant, but so long as he heard them, he knew they had nothing to fear from the Barrens.

The farther they walked, however, the fainter the song became. By the time they reached the far end of the field, it was reduced to a faint whisper carried weakly on the breeze. And when Gideon took the final step and passed beyond the trees, all memory of its comfort instantly disappeared.

WORDHAVEN

For a woman of such obvious avarice, Lord Varia was nontheless masterfully adept at keeping her plans well hidden. No lord in Phallenar had the slightest insight into what she had devised, nor did any soul in Wordhaven foresee it. It came on them all like a tempest at midnight, like a towering wave from the sea at low tide.
—The Kyrinthan Journals, Chronicles, Chapter 19, Verses 40-44

I s she certain?"

"She is always certain, Paladin, even when she is not." Donovan Truthstay stepped toward the platform. "She insists that you and I join her in the Chamber of the Pearl immediately."

Ajel frowned. The news was not unexpected, but he had hoped it would not come for several months yet. "Very well," he said. Rising from his seat behind the Servant's Call, he bowed to the other members of the Wordhaven assembly. "Katira, Teram, Saria, forgive me. I will return as soon as I am able."

"Seer's message is urgent," noted Teram Firstway. "Do not worry yourself. We can complete the work here ourselves."

"I pray the news is not as bad as she fears, Paladin," added Katira Peacegiver.

"Yes," replied Ajel. "As do I." But he knew otherwise.

Donovan followed him out of the Servant's Hall, his fitted warrior's garb a mirror to Ajel's own. An assortment of workers, fighters and volunteers scurried past them in the meandering corridor, their faces for the most part barely noting the passing of the Paladin or the Head of Arms. Their presence together had become commonplace all across Wordhaven since Ajel's return from *Setal Rapha*. The preparations had been intense, and had pushed both of the leaders to their limits more than once. But if Seer's information proved true, everyone at Wordhaven would need every ounce of the training he and Donovan had given them. Even then, it might not be enough.

"Did she say how long?" asked Ajel briskly.

"Paladin?"

"How long they have been marching. Did she say?"

"No."

Approaching the golden doors of the Chamber, Ajel whispered the Words to swing them wide, and strolled passed them without a glance. Once he entered, however, the scene displayed across the facets stopped him cold.

A writhing sea of black-garbed soldiers filled the diamond-shaped mirrors overhead, moving like a living plague across the plains. There were thousands of them. Tens of thousands. In their midst, dozens of pondarin plodded along, each armed with a sound cannon that on its own could blast a hole through Wordhaven's cliffs. Every few seconds, a swarm of juron swooped in and out of view.

"They are still on Plain of Dreams," said Ajel. "How far west have they come?"

"They are beyond the ruins of Noble Heart," Seer replied. She stood at the base of the Ring of Bright Water, leaning tiredly on her staff as if she no longer trusted her legs. "They travel both night and day, taking rest only when they risk collapse. At this pace, they will reach the edge of Dunerun Hope within another two days."

"Let us hope the Dunerun slows their advance," sighed Ajel. He turned to Donovan. "Why do they push themselves so?"

"I do not know, Ajel," the big man replied. "We are now well into the Season of Memories. The snows of winter have arrived upon the range." He shook his head thoughtfully. "In truth, this battle force is coming too late. They should have begun their march in the Season of Omens, when their forces first formed on the fields beyond the Wall."

"And yet they come now instead, and in haste," observed Ajel. "Why?" He marched down the sloping path toward the fountain. "Something is driving them."

"The route they follow leads to Sacred Heart," suggested Seer. "Perhaps they mean to winter there."

"Sacred Heart will not see snow for another month at least," answered Donovan. "There is no need to move at such a pace just to reach those ruins. Besides, it is not a place *jalen* would willingly choose to go. And it is too small, besides. Only a fraction of their forces could be housed within its walls."

"No," agreed Ajel. "They cannot leave their forces exposed in the open for the winter. They would lose too many." He rubbed his chin thoughtfully. "Donovan, can they breach the snows? Can a force that size actually reach us in winter?"

Donovan considered a moment. "Perhaps," he said finally. "But not without leaving a scar of Word-wrought devastation in their wake. Even then, they will lose many guardians with such an effort." He shook his head. "Still, most of the pondarin would survive, so long as they are fed. They are built for cold."

Ajel pursed his lips thoughtfully. "Then that must be it. They are coming here—now," he said. "But why in such a hurry? It is not for winter's sake; it has already come. There has to be another reason."

Seer frowned at him. "Did that sniveling Lord Fayerna reveal nothing of this, Ajel?" she asked, her voice dripping with suspicion. "You were together on that mountain a long time."

"We did not engage in pleasantries," replied Ajel curtly. "Besides, I do not believe she knew anything of Phallenar's plans. They thought her dead, same as us."

Seer sniffed. "Too bad you couldn't have questioned her before the end. But then, it was a quick death, as you say."

The prophetess clearly still bristled at Ajel's decision to keep most of the details of his experience on *Setal Rapha* to himself. It was a thing unheard of in the Stand; no member of the Remnant had ever willingly withheld so much from its leaders—much less the Paladin himself.

But Ajel had chosen not to reveal most of what had happened there. He told them nothing of the shameful way he hid from Lord Fayerna for hours before finally summoning the courage to face her. And though he did admit to slaying the lord in the end, he revealed nothing of how the deed was done.

More than anything, however, he meant to keep secret his encounter with the Raanthan, and his brief glimpse of the Brilliant Gate. That moment had transformed him, awakening within his soul a renewed confidence in his purpose and a bold fierceness that was clearly evident to all the moment he returned to Wordhaven. But though they all wanted to know what had brought about this change, he had no desire to explain himself to anyone anymore—not even to Donovan.

He would tell someone eventually. He knew that. But not yet. For now, the gift was his alone.

"I still cannot believe I did not recognize her," grumbled Donovan with disgust. "I knew something was not right about that girl, but..."

"It is a testimony to how far you have come, Donovan," said Ajel. "You were once bonded to Fayerna. Your tie to the lords is all but forgotten."

But Donovan only laughed bitterly. "My eyes are still black with the taint of Sa'lei, Paladin," he said darkly. "I still see the lords' memories every night in my dreams. Some shadows of my past will never be erased."

Ajel prepared to argue the point, but his thoughts were suddenly interrupted by a voice calling out in his mind. *Paladin! Paladin!*

"Do you sense that?" he asked Donovan. But from the look of concern that suddenly flashed across the big man's face, Ajel knew that he did.

"It is Brasen," said Donovan. "He calls for me."

"And me as well," said Ajel. "Where is he now?"

At that moment, Brasen Stoneguard ran through the doors, breathing heavily. The worried look on his young face turned immediately to shock as he took in the dark scene sprawled across the Chamber walls. He pointed to the panels emphatically. "They are here?" he demanded.

"No, Keeper," said Donovan. "Not yet."

Confusion flashed across his face, but he quickly shook it away. "You must come," he said breathlessly, "to the inner gates. One of the scouting parties has been attacked."

"Where?" demanded Donovan.

Brasen shook his head. "We do not know. Only one made it back, and he is badly injured." He shook his head in disbelief. "The healing Words had no effect!"

"Are the gates secure?" demanded Ajel.

Brasen nodded. "You must come now, Paladin. He has said little, and I do not think he will last."

Ajel turned to Seer. "Keep watch over them," he said, gesturing toward the dark scene above. "Inform me if anything changes."

Seer nodded stoically, but Ajel did not see it. He had already disappeared.

The Paladin materialized along the valley road not far from the inner gates of Wordhaven. The midmorning sun cast a field of diamond sparkles across the snow-laden fields. But the thin warmth of its rays barely reached him. He shook off the sudden chill and looked toward the gates.

A smattering of Wordhaven scouts huddled on the road up ahead, shuffling toward him in a panic. They carried the body of a young man in their arms. Steam from his open wounds drifted idly across their worried faces.

Just as Ajel headed toward them, he noticed Donovan's imposing form take shape beyond the huddle, just inside the gate. An instant later, Brasen Stoneguard materialized at his side. They locked eyes on Ajel quickly, and ran in his direction.

The group, meanwhile, had only just recognized his presence.

"Paladin Windrunner," said one of the scouts breathlessly. "We have been attacked."

"I know. Let me see," commanded Ajel.

They stopped and made room for him to approach the wounded man. In truth, he was just a boy—barely twenty years if that, with freckled skin and curly reddish hair. His body was split wide open along one side, from the waist to a pocket just beneath his arm. Beyond this single surgical gash, however, there were no other signs of injury. He was not bleeding.

"We spoke the Words, but nothing happened," said the scout in amazement. The thought clearly unnerved him.

Ajel placed his open palm against the young man's chest. Instantly, he felt a pang of repulsion in his gut. "The taint of *Sa'lei* lingers on him still," he exclaimed. "This Word was not meant to slay him quickly. He is being tortured."

"He is of Jessa Greenbearer's team, Paladin," announced Brasen breath-lessly as he and Donovan reached the group. "His name is Tomas con-Meridith, of Makroth. Their team scouts the southern quadrant."

"Is there word of Jessa?" asked Ajel. "Or any of the others?"

Brasen shook his head. "Only him. I was just about to go looking for them when Tomas stumbled through the gate. He mumbled that they had been attacked, then he lost consciousness.

"The *Sa'lei* Word continues its work on him," said Ajel. "Get him inside, quickly! Take him to Seer, in the Chamber of the Pearl. She will know what to do."

The men nodded sharply, and hurried passed him on down the road. Ajel turned his attention to Brasen. He sensed the young man's anger, and recalled Donovan mentioning that Jessa and the Keeper were close. "We do not yet know the fate of Jessa, Keeper Stoneguard," he said. "She may have escaped the attack and be waiting for a safer time to return to us."

"There were five on that team, Paladin," replied Brasen stonily. "It is my duty to see that they are all returned safely. And their attackers, whoever they are, will be brought to justice."

"It is not so simple as that, Keeper," said Donovan. "This is the work of *mon'jalen*, or worse. I have seen this technique before. They captured the boy and interrogated him. When he would not tell them what they wanted, they cut him wide and allowed him to escape."

"But why would they do that?" asked Brasen.

"In the hope that in his desire to save himself from death, he would lead them to the gate," said Ajel. He looked up at the crisp blue sky, and took in a heavy breath. "And so it seems he has."

"But where did they come from?" asked Brasen angrily. "The horde I witnessed in the Chamber is not yet here! You said so yourself."

"An advance guard, perhaps," said Donovan, "come to scout the best route for the Council's main force."

"How many would Balaam assign such a task?" asked Ajel.

Donovan shrugged. "As few as six. No more than twelve."

"Then we must find them and stop them before they can return to their master," said Ajel firmly. "Keeper Stoneguard, assemble your scouts. Your teams will depart within the hour—"

Suddenly, the ground beneath their feet began to tremble. A few seconds later, Ajel heard the rumblings of a distant explosion echo over the cliffs.

The sound sent a chill of alarm shooting up his spine. He wasted no time. "Donovan," he commanded. "Go to the Stand and gather the assembly. Tell them to prepare to awaken Wordhaven's defenses."

Donovan nodded as he spoke the Words, and immediately disappeared.

"Come with me, Keeper," said Ajel. "Quickly!"

Grabbing Brasen by the arm, he summoned a shield around them both, then spoke the Words to lift them into the air.

"Where are we going, Paladin?" asked Brasen, looking somewhat unnerved as his body lifted effortlessly off the road.

Ajel pointed toward a narrow ridge glistening darkly in the sun, a thousand feet or more directly above the inner gate. "There," he said. "We must see what is happening beyond the gates."

They flew to a narrow outcropping ten feet below the ridge line. As Ajel's boots touched down on the rock, he whispered away the sphere, and glanced at Brasen. The young Keeper mounted the ledge without comment, but his nervous expression conveyed his obvious discomfort at Ajel's chosen mode of transport.

"My apologies, Brasen," said Ajel quietly. "I should have realized you have not yet learned the Words of flight."

"It's nothing," he replied briskly, and turned away abruptly to scan the ridge. "I think this way will keep us hidden from view," he said, pointing. "They may have juron. Or worse."

Ajel nodded in agreement, and the two men scrambled quietly up the ridge, with Brasen taking the lead. Once they slipped to the outer rim of Wordhaven's cliffs they laid flat on the protruding rock and looked down the slope. The cliffs of Wordhaven were profoundly steep, but not vertical enough to allow a clear view of the bottom. They would have to climb farther down.

Ajel let Brasen choose the route, while he kept his attention focused on the surrounding skies. While well-hidden from any searching eyes on the distant slopes below, they were hopelessly exposed to the air above. If they were spotted by mon'jalen on juron, the riders could burn them off the mountain with a single Word.

A few moments later, Brasen arrived at a large granite outcropping some hundred feet below the crest. He gestured to Ajel, and the two of them dropped onto its surface and crawled cautiously to the edge of its sloping face. Peeking their heads over the ledge, they looked down.

"By the Giver!" whispered Ajel.

A thousand feet below, several massive fires ringed the small lake that marked the entrance to Wordhaven. The plumes of destruction scorched the mountainside, producing thick shafts of billowing black smoke that licked the grey stone cliffs before following the breezes to the north. Felled trees lined the snow-cleared meadows as well, strewn like corpses on the blackened earth. Their great limbs were severing and hurling about as though raped by an unseen storm. Beneath the turmoil of limbs and smoke, Ajel could see a small swarm of guardians rushing about like ants, though to what end he couldn't tell.

"Paladin," whispered Brasen, "to the south."

Following Brasen's gaze, Ajel spotted it. A large pit topped with a makeshift covering of tree trunks and boulders. He knew instantly what it was for.

"Juron. From the size of the pit, a large number." Ajel frowned at the implications. "There are far more than a few dozen guardians here."

"More like a hundred," agreed Brasen, his voice tense. "This is no scouting party."

"Just so," said Ajel. "Whoever they are, they are quite unconcerned with being discovered. But what is their purpose here? Why all this industry?"

"I cannot say," Brasen replied. "But whatever it is, they mean to stay a while."

Suddenly, the realization hit, and Ajel felt his heart sink. "Great Giver, Brasen," Ajel said quietly. "They are laying siege."

THE DEATHLAND BARRENS

Though we never spoke of it on the way, the memory of Stevron was never far from our thoughts. I never admitted it openly, but I had believed that Stevron's restraint with us prior to his most recent attack was due in large part to my presence among the rebels. After all, I thought he still wanted to bond with me; and that my father, on some political level at least, still cared for my life. After Stevron's attack upon us in the northern sea, however, I became convinced that both he and my father had at last discounted me as a reasonable loss in their endeavor to stop the Waymaker. With that barrier removed, and with Stevron's pride injured on the seas as it was, I knew it was just a matter of time before the world at our feet exploded with his rage.

—The Kyrinthan Journals, Musings, Chapter 25, Verses 7-9

Upon entering the marsh, the Trevail Priests immediately stripped off their tunics, exposing their densely tattooed skin to the sickly sweet air. Though this seemed to be standard procedure for them, none bothered to explain it, and with no further word of comfort or instruction, they forged ahead—sifting out a path through the marshwood like dancers through a minefield.

After a moment of uncertainty, Gideon and the others quickly fumbled after them, rattling off questions about where they were headed and why the priests seemed so intent on quickening their pace. Their reproachful glances, however, made it clear that they would tolerate no discussion. They moved silently and close to the ground, slinking through the trees like serpents on the trail of prey only they could smell. The only sound they made was the occasional hiss—a warning to stop Gideon or the others from wandering too close to a dangling limb or a black watery pool concealed in the mud.

Even with their considerable focus, however, progress through the marsh was excruciatingly slow. The knotted branches of the trees curled around the group like a menagerie of clambering hands, and they had to navigate past them all without grazing so much as a twig. They also had to contend with the mud itself, which had the troubling quality of being both sticky and slippery at the same time, and with each step sucked hungrily at their boots as if eager to swallow them whole.

But all of that was nothing compared to the stench. It didn't take long for Gideon to realize why Galad had so often used the word "infection" to describe the taint of the Deathland Barrens. The sickly aroma of the Worded blight saturated everything within the marsh—the mud, the grass, the bark of the gnarled black branches hovering above his head. The land itself reeked of disease. It was more than enough to set his stomach to churning in revolt.

But then, an hour or so into the trek, a new wind blew over them all, and everything changed.

The stench wafted away, and in its place came a scent so sweet and alluring that Gideon not could help but look up from the mud to search out its source. To his amazement, his eyes saw a chorus of brilliant trees—not the dead twisted limbs of the boggy marsh, but a rich, verdant orchard laden with glorious sweet fruit—extending far into the wood. The mud had like-wise vanished, replaced by a soft pelt of grass so lush that he could hardly think of anything more desirous than to lie down in its welcoming hollows and stretch out for a much-needed nap.

However, though it took considerable effort, he resisted the urge. Telus had warned them all that this would happen. The Barrens, he explained, had but one insatiable hunger—the consumption of souls—and it would employ whatever powers it held to satisfy it. Concealing its true nature beneath a veil of beauty was but one of the many tactics the Raanthan had described, and it was far from the worst of them.

Still, resistance was bitter indeed. Gideon never expected the illusion would seem so real. But he did resist, and after a long passage of time, as if awakening from a dream, the veil fell away, and everything became as it was at first—no orchard, no grass or sweet brilliant fruit—only the dark web of gnarled branches brooding overhead, and the thick smell of death everywhere.

It continued this way for several more hours. With no illusion to mask the stench, a vomitous nausea eventually overtook them all. All of them, that is, except the Trevail Priests. They seemed immune; or perhaps they'd been exposed to the Barrens so many times that they'd long since lost their sense of smell. Either way, they ignored the travelers' distress. Even when the underlord accidentally retched on Terebin's boot—grabbing the priest's arm for support as she did it—he kept his gaze stubbornly riveted on the trees ahead as though she wasn't even there.

As sick as they all felt, however, it was Revel who got the worst of it. Gideon had never seen the man's strength so completely drained, nor his face lost in such thoughtless agony. He clung to himself, tentatively hunched over, and stumbled repeatedly as he trudged through the mud. Even Strivenwood had not taken him so low. But when Gideon whispered his concern, the Wordhavener only pushed him away, muttering something about the trees not being right.

Somewhere around mid-afternoon—though with the sun obscured by the lattice of the marsh it was difficult to tell much about the time—the seven priests, who had been marching in advance of the group, suddenly redistributed themselves, enveloping Gideon's party like a cocoon.

"What's going on?" Gideon asked aloud.

The priest closest to him gripped his arm angrily. "Be quiet!" he whispered. "They will hear."

"Who?" asked Gideon, this time in a whisper.

"The dark souls are known to traffic through this portion of the marshwood," the priest explained. "We have learned to see them."

Gideon pulled his arm away. "I've seen them myself. They're a little hard to miss."

"Not so in the marsh, Waymaker," whispered Telus—an act which seemed to require tremendous effort for the Raanthan. "The riftmen take shape only as it serves them. They lurk in the muds nearby even now."

"They are here? Where?" asked Gideon.

"I sense them," Telus corrected, "to the west. The priest senses this as well."

"But how could they hide in the mud?" protested Gideon. "I thought they hated water."

"Pure water, yes," said Telus. "But the defiled muds of the marsh present no obstacle to them."

The priest made a sharp gesture with hand, as if slicing off a head that wasn't there. "Enough talk!" he snapped. "There is little they cannot hear."

Despite the priests' fevered warnings, however, no riftmen appeared, and the group's progress through the marsh, though always slow, was largely uneventful. Toward day's end, after sifting through one final cluster of branches they found themselves on an expansive clearing that stretched on for what seemed like miles to the east and south. In stark contrast to the marsh, the field was dry as bone, and coated with the brittle remains of tall grasses that looked to have died of thirst decades before. The sun's heat, formerly obscured by the trees, suddenly felt smothering and unnaturally close.

Revel was the last to emerge from the jumble of gnarled limbs, leaning on a priest for support. Fumbling into the field like a drunkard, he mumbled, "By the Giver...by the Giver...", then rested his hands on his shaky knees and let out a low, grumbling moan. Kyrintha moved to his side to offer what comfort she could—though, in fact, she herself looked far from well.

"We will make camp here," announced Terebin, not quite whispering this time. Aside from the thick sheen of sweat on his tattooed torso, the priest showed no signs of the trauma the rest of them were experiencing.

"Why here?" countered Gideon. "It's completely exposed here, and we still have a long way to go." He frowned even as he said it. What was this pull burning in his heart? He was exhausted, as were they all. He knew they needed rest. Surely the priests could see this too. But just the thought of stopping shot a hollow pain through his gut—like hunger, only more so. Despite his better judgment, he needed to go on.

"We need not stop on my account," muttered Revel, still bent over and looking conspicuously pale. "I need only a moment."

"It is not on your account," noted Terebin flatly. "The Fallen Wood stands to the south, and is no place to be in the evening hours. And to the east lie the shattered lands, where far greater dangers than even the dark souls live." He reached down and slapped the dead grasses with his open palm, as if to mock their inability to harm him. "Once darkness falls, this place will be safer than most, though that means little here. After we make camp, we will plan the route the Waymaker would have us take on the morrow."

"I see no woods to the south," countered Aybel. "The way seems clear enough for us to at least find shade from this sun." She blocked the harsh light from her eyes.

For some reason, upon hearing Aybel's comment the priests all broke out laughing. It was a shocking sight; the first indication that any of them had a sense of humor. The nature of the joke escaped Gideon, however; though it was obvious that Aybel was the brunt of it. And that, he didn't like at all.

"The Fallen Wood is closer than you imagine," grunted Terebin with a grin. "It lures you even now. When you finally do see it, you will believe it is the most beautiful place your eyes have ever beheld. But by then you will have already wandered too far into its darkened heart."

"How does it lure me?" snipped Aybel, her eyes indignant. "There is nothing here but dead grass as far as the horizon."

But Terebin only grinned at his fellow priests and shook his head. At last, he said, "No more questions until after we've made camp." He quickly swept his gaze across the fields. "Stay close. The land will not sit idle for long."

"No, Terebin," announced Gideon coolly. "There will be questions. Right now. And you will answer them." Ignoring the churning in his gut, he marched toward the priest, deliberating thudding his staff into the hard earth with each step. Terebin watched his approach, but continuing removing his pack along with the other priests.

"Waymaker," cautioned Telus. "The priest is right."

But Gideon did not stop. "No, Telus," he countered, "the priest is not right." When he reached Terebin, he planted the butt of his staff firmly on the priest's pack. Terebin stood quietly before him, his green eyes meeting the Waymaker's with a cold calm that almost concealed the anger behind them. This time, however, Gideon did not look away. "Your leaders sent you here as our guides, not our keepers," said Gideon. "You know this place better than we do, I don't deny that. But this is our quest—*my* quest. If you can't get in line with that, and start answering the questions that you are asked—whether from me or anyone in my party—then leave us now, and we'll go on alone."

Terebin blinked, but his face remained impassive. "I am *san'gradon*. I have sworn my life to your protection, Waymaker," he said, nodding to the group, "as have we all. That is why we must make camp now. Any further delay increases our chances of attack."

"From what? The woods we cannot see?"

"That is but one threat among many." The priest's eyes softened a bit. "Please, allow us finish setting the perimeter, and I will explain."

Suddenly, Gideon felt the heat of the Raanthan's oversized hand resting on his shoulder. "Let them finish, Waymaker," he said quietly. "There will time enough for reprimands later."

But Gideon held his gaze on the priest. "You are here to follow. Not lead. Do you understand?"

"We are here to serve," granted Terebin. But his eyes remained defiant.

Turning toward Aybel, Gideon shook off Telus' hand and let out a sarcastic snort. "I don't know if this is going to work out," he told her with a shrug.

"I am not offended, Gideon," said Aybel calmly.

"May we continue setting camp now, Waymaker?" said Terebin. That's when Gideon noticed that all the priests had stopped their work, and were watching him with bland irritation.

"By all means," growled Gideon with dismissive wave, "do your thing." He strode toward the edge of the group, being careful not to meet Aybel's gaze.

Terebin smirked. Then, kneeling among the grasses, he waved his hand over the brittle stems and began to sing,

> *"Elo pur'im sera lugaramel*
> *Sezar alem'shadoom aquel*
> *e'punemas sum yan'sacravelis*
> *e'shamar sum yan'far"*

The grasses before him shuddered and stirred beneath the Words as if breathed upon by unseen winds. And as they quivered they transformed—

from brittle brown to vibrant green, the color flowing up their stems as if drawn from some deep place in the earth beyond the reach of the Barrens' shattered crust. Within seconds a patch of ground some ten feet wide and nearly as long sprung into life, its grasses waving lazily as if awakened from a long bleak sleep.

"Now," instructed Terebin. "Stand in the green."

The group complied, hurried along by the priests, who prodded them impatiently into a huddle in the center of the small island of life. Forming a ring around them, the priests then mimicked Terebin's act, each kneeling along the edges of the newly living grass and singing in unison to the dead grasses beyond. The miracle repeated itself seven-fold. Within moments, the group stood at the center of a circle of green that stretched eighty feet or more from side to side.

When the deed was done, Terebin turned to Gideon and said, "You are safe within the green." He almost smiled. "But using the Words within the Desolation is a two-edged sword. For though this ground is now free of the infection, the dark souls are now certainly aware of our presence here. We will soon be attacked."

"What?" cried Gideon. "You mean we just spent hours avoiding the riftmen only to turn around and announce our location?"

This time, Terebin didn't smile. "They will not breach our perimeter. The priests will see to it. But the purification is necessary. Without it, you and your companions cannot rest."

"How long will the transformation last?" asked Kyrintha. "Is it permanent?"

Terebin shrugged. "If left alone, a day perhaps. No more." He turned to one of the other priests nearby. "The Bitter Pond is not far. Best we refill the skins before dark." The priest nodded, then quickly gathered the water skins from everyone present and headed off to the east. Two other priests trailed after him in silence.

The remaining Trevail priests moved to stand along the edges of the perimeter—not looking outward toward the Barrens, as Gideon would expect, but inward toward him and the other travelers.

"Please," said Terebin, "removed your cloaks. We must check your skin for injuries while there is still light." He bowed his head in deference to Gideon. "By your leave, Waymaker, of course."

"I'm not injured," Gideon stated flatly. *Is he mocking me?*

"You would not know it if you were," explained Terebin. "It is the nature of the Desolation to hide its infection until it has taken firm hold. Please." He offered his hand toward the Waymaker.

Gideon sighed grudgingly, and obliged the priest's request. The others—Aybel, Revel, and the underlord—did likewise, each handing off the cloak to whatever priest stood closest. Telus, who had no Worded cloak, seemed to observe the activity with practiced indifference.

"Your boots and leathers, too," said Terebin. "We must be certain."

"My leathers? Certainly not!" objected Kyrintha. "My boots you may examine all you want, but my britches are my own concern."

"It's all right, Kyrintha," soothed Aybel. "We can have them hold up a few cloaks as a curtain. We will be each other's eyes." She smiled gently.

The underlord considered this a moment, then nodded reluctantly. "All right, if we must," she said. Looking askance at Terebin, she added, "But it seems a lot of fuss for a scratch."

"It takes only a scratch. A scrape. A flip of a twig to lance the skin," insisted Terebin, "and tomorrow you'll be dead. Or worse. There can be no secrets between allies in a place like this. We either trust each other, or we die."

Gideon let out a mocking laugh. "Well said, Terebin," he chortled. "You know, you should really listen to yourself. Maybe heed your own advice." He stared defiantly at the tattooed man.

"Extend your arms, please," requested Terebin. He did not meet Gideon's gaze.

"Trust goes both ways," Gideon continued. But Terebin said nothing. He bent over to scan Gideon's arms.

"For this to work, you must be willing to extend to us the same trust you're asking us to give you."

"Now your feet and legs," said Terebin.

Gideon knelt to unlace his boots, but Terebin gripped his hand as he reached for the knot. "Wait," said Terebin. "There is mud."

Using his fingers as spades, the priest stripped off the mud that had caked itself to the sides and top of Gideon's boots, whispering in *Dei'lo* as he worked.

"You're purifying it?" Gideon asked.

Terebin nodded. "You may now handle them without concern."

"Thanks." He wrenched one boot off, and then the other. "Sorry if my feet stink."

"Please, sit, Waymaker." Gideon obeyed. Terebin grabbed one of Gideon's feet and started probing it for signs of cuts or blisters. He glanced up with a mild grin. "I don't smell anything," he observed blandly.

Gideon chuckled. "Yeah. Well, coming from you that doesn't mean much."

Terebin glanced up at him quizzically. "I don't understand."

Gideon smirked "Never mind."

Terebin gently placed one foot on the grass, and lifted the other. As he began to scan it, he said, "It isn't that we do not trust your heart, Waymaker. You or your companions." He glanced furtively toward the others. "It is that you are ignorant."

"Ignorant?"Gideon nodded, trying not to sound defensive. "Really? How so?"

"You yourself, though you are the Waymaker, have no knowledge of the Words. And your companions," he lowered his voice even more, "those commissioned to protect you, are not much better." He shook his head. "You are like children here, in this place."

"Well," Gideon quipped, "we are lucky to have you then, aren't we?"

Terebin frowned. "You misunderstand." He placed Gideon's foot back on the ground. "I need to check your legs."

Without comment, Gideon untied the cord that bound his leathers and shuffled them down to his ankles. He was thankful that his linen undergarments looked and fit more like ordinary shorts than anything resembling underwear in his world.

"Will you stand?" asked Terebin. Gideon obliged. "We Priests of Trevail," Terebin continued as he surveyed Gideon's skin, "we are trained soldiers. We fight against the infected creatures of these broken lands. In the years since the founding of the Stays, we have never allowed the uninitiated to cross beyond them."

"What are you trying to tell me, Terebin?" Gideon asked.

"You are uninjured," said Terebin. He stood.

"Thank you." Gideon pulled up his pants, feeling hopelessly undignified in the process. But when he stood again, Terebin was staring him in the face.

"What?" Gideon asked.

Terebin nodded, as if he reached agreement with his own thoughts. "It is not that we do not trust you, Waymaker," he confessed. "It is that we do not trust ourselves to protect you. We are not...accustomed to having people like you here." He lowered his head. "There is so much you and your companions do not know, so many dangers," he sighed, "so many ways to die. You are vulnerable here. Your skin..." He glanced at Gideon's arms with a frown. "And I am afraid we will not be able to stop all of the dangers from reaching you."

Gideon pursed his lips. He hadn't expected the sudden show of vulnerability in the priest. "I see," he said awkwardly. "Well."

Terebin lifted Gideon's cloak from the ground and offered it to him. "We only ask that you trust in our knowledge of this place, even as we entrust our lives to you." He nodded deferentially, then walked away.

It took the priests only minutes to finish securing the perimeter, and setting up the camp. A blue fire burned in the circle's center by the time the sun set in the west, fueled by branches collected from the twisted marsh. The priests returned with water from the Bitter Pond at dusk as well—just in time for supper, which consisted of dried beef, nuts and knots of hard bread.

"Tell us more about the dangers of the Barrens, Telus," Gideon requested as the group reclined on the grass and ate. Telus wasn't eating; but then, he never did, as far as Gideon could tell. "What can we expect tomorrow?"

"Same as tonight, Waymaker," Telus told him. "Deception. And fear."

"C'mon, Silver, don't be cryptic," Gideon chided playfully. The relief of finally getting the chance to rest—and to eat solid food without concern for the Barrens' nauseous effects—made him giddy.

"Silver?" inquired Telus.

"Your new nickname," offered Gideon, smiling.

Telus seemed unsure how to respond.

"A nickname," repeated Gideon. "A pet name, you know" Telus still did not seem to understand. "Don't worry about it," Gideon laughed, gnawing on a chunk of bread. "If I call you Silver, you just answer like always."

Telus blinked passively at the explanation, then quickly seemed to dismiss it in favor of other matters. "How does the land deceive?" he began,

"How does the land provoke fear?" His large eyes glistened like pools of bronze in the light of the fire. "Sometimes by means of deep terror. Sometimes by twisting good desire to evil. Sometimes by showing you only what you want to see. Sometimes by haunting you with the thing you most dread."

"Tell us something useful, Silver," demanded Gideon. "How will we be attacked? And when? Will we have to fight, or is the Worded perimeter enough?"

"The riftmen will likely come tonight," Telus acknowledged, "but they will tire of the barrier long before morning."

"They need not push themselves overmuch," added Terebin. "They know this place better than any priest—or Raanthan. They need only wait in the shadows for the Barrens to claim us, then feast on the spoils."

"You don't sound very hopeful of our chances, Terebin," observed Gideon angrily.

"I say only how the dark souls perceive it," countered the priest. "It does not mean I agree. Though, as you well know, I have concerns of my own."

Gideon watched Terebin a moment longer, then laid back on the grass. Resting his right hand lightly on his torso, he ran his finger along the subtle ridge of the scar protruding from beneath the Worded cloak. He chuckled at the irony. The scar that once mocked his life as a symbol of deadness and shame now marked the spot where his heart most hotly burned. He let his arm stretch out in the direction of the pull—south, ever south. "I wouldn't count us out just yet, Terebin," he said. "There are powers at work here that the Barrens cannot begin to comprehend." Leaping to his feet, he snatched up his almond wood staff from the ground nearby, and displayed its glistening surface for Terebin to see. "Besides," he quipped, "you haven't seen me use this yet."

THE DESOLATE FIELDS

The smell of the trees burned both nostrils and eyes alike. The stench of it turned our stomachs, and never abated, even long after all food in our bellies had been emptied on the ever-rotting grass. You could not sit, regardless of how exhausted you became. Nor could you lean or rest your arm, save on one another's shoulders. The heat clung to your body like hot tar, and the wind, when it came, gave no relief. I honestly do not know how the Trevail priests endured it, day after day in their forays into the Barrens. And that is to say nothing of the creatures that lurked in the shadows behind every blighted shrub or tree, waiting for the moment when you might not be looking, and stumble into their claws.

—The Kyrinthan Journals, Musings, Chapter 25, Verses 30-34

The attack came in the middle of the night. No one saw what they were—just the crackling bluish outlines of invisible howling mouths that pounded against the domed shield the priests had raised. The *san'gradon* stood defiant along the perimeter, but none of them said nor did anything to chase the beasts away. The others—Kyrintha, Revel and Aybel— watched the affair for some time with great curiosity, but none of them seemed the least bit afraid either. Gideon, however, did not share their confidence in the priests or their shield.

His staff was cold throughout the entire event. He gripped it tightly, willing it to sense the danger, but to no avail. How could he hope to protect them if the staff failed him like this? In the northern sea, it had burned hot like fire in the face of Stevron's attack. Gideon had found a way to surrender to its power then, and channel it. He could do that again, he believed. But not if the staff refused to awaken.

After an hour or so, the beasts apparently tired of the attack, and disappeared into the night. The priests remained vigilant for a few minutes more, whispering in their harsh way to the ground and to each other. Then they, in silent unison, relaxed their guard and promptly laid back down to go to sleep.

"Is that it?" asked Gideon, turning toward Telus, who had been sitting impassively behind him the entire time. "Won't they come back?"

"It is not likely," replied the Raanthan quietly. "The Barrens will try another way to breach the perimeter, or else wait until a time when we are less protected."

"You keep talking about the Barrens as if it were a person," noted Gideon. "Are you suggesting that the land itself has some kind of intelligence?"

But Telus shook his head. "Not intelligence as you or I possess," he said. "But instinct, yes. A keen instinct; yes, it has that."

"Is it alive?" asked Gideon.

Telus blinked his large bronze eyes in surprise. "Is it alive? Now, that is an interesting question, Waymaker. I shall have to think on that." He seemed pleased at the prospect.

Gideon leaned in toward Telus, close enough to whisper. "Telus, do you trust these guys?" He nodded toward one of the priests nearby.

Again, Telus seemed surprised by the question. "I neither trust nor distrust them," he said at last. "I trust the Giver, who has directed my path here. That is all I need to know."

Gideon thought a moment, then said, "What about me? Do you trust me?" Without thinking, he pulled the staff close. It was still cold.

"You are the Waymaker," Telus replied. "I trust that you will make a way. You feel it now, do you not?"

Gideon let his gaze drift to the ground. "Yeah," he said. The pull felt like a hook imbedded in his chest. South—ever south. "But I don't know. I'm not sure I'm up to this." He looked into Telus' orb-like eyes as they glistened in the blue light of the fire. "When those beasts, or whatever they were, attacked, the staff was stone cold the whole time. If the priests weren't here…"

"The power does not reside in the staff, Waymaker. It rests in you," explained Telus.

But Gideon shook his head. "No," he said, "that's not how it works. It comes from the sky, or the staff gets all hot and it comes from there. Somehow the staff…well, when it's hot, it gives me confidence. Like I'm connected to something that's bigger than me, and I can use it."

Telus nodded thoughtfully for a moment. Then he said, "Does the glory of a diamond lie in the diamond, or in the light that shines upon it?"

Gideon grimaced. "What?"

"Think on that, Waymaker," instructed Telus. "Stop fretting, and get some sleep." With that, he rose to his feet and glided away.

The next day they headed south by Gideon's command, toward the Fallen Wood. As they departed, Terebin announced that the forest edge stood less than a league from the camp, but for reasons no one could divine the wood remained invisible to all eyes but the priests'. Gideon reckoned the *san'gradon* were right about the forest being there, but it wasn't until Revel stepped past threshold of the first line of trees that Gideon fully believed it.

"Incredible," breathed Revel. His face, tilted up toward the empty sky, was awash with wonder. "I do not see it. But the wood is here. Yes, and it's vast!"

Terebin called the party to a halt, then gathered the other priests to the front of the procession.

"Do not marvel at such a forest as this, traveler," quipped one of the priests as he strode by. "Its enticements cannot be trusted."

But Kyrintha touched Revel lightly on the arm. "What do you sense?"

"Vast," he repeated, still looking up. "Ancient. And…" he perked his ear up toward the sky as if to catch the song of a bird that no one else could hear, "something else."

"The Desolation will soon tire of the mirage," advised Terebin, "once it realizes you will not easily stumble into its waiting arms. For now, each of you choose one of the *san'gradon* to follow, and walk directly in his steps. We will guide you around the trees and other dangers. Keep your cloaks pulled close."

"Would that I could touch the trees," said Revel, still distracted by whatever sensations the forest awakened in him. "This wood is not like the marsh. Its roots run deeper than the Barrens."

"It deceives you, woodsman," warned the priest just ahead of him. "Now come, follow me. You and the woman both. It's not good to tarry long anywhere in the Desolation."

"Forgive me, *san'gradon*," Revel replied. "I do not recall your name."

"What matters in a name?" the priest grunted cynically. "But since you ask, it is Shobi. Now, follow." He turned and marched off into what seemed a field of brittle grass.

"I am called Revel," he replied, grabbing the underlord by the hand, "and this fair woman is Kyrintha." Gently guiding the underlord ahead, he fell in line behind the priest. "I can tell that you and I will have some wonderful talks, Shobi. For I do not see these woods as you do."

Shobi laughed bitterly. "You do not see these woods at all," he mocked. "Besides, talk in the common tongue is a waste here. Only what is spoken in *Dei'lo* matters."

Gideon watched this whole exchange from his place behind Telus a few paces away—and noted with curiosity the underlord's blush when Revel took her hand. How could anyone think of romance in such a place as this? The notion seemed ridiculous. Still, that was a discussion with Revel for another time, if it ever came at all. Right now, it was Revel's comments about the forest that interested him more.

"Keep talking, Revel," instructed Gideon. "How is this forest different from the marsh?"

The Wordhavener shook his head curiously. "I'm not certain, Waymaker. Only that it is not as corrupted as Shobi believes." He listened to the silence for a moment, then added, "It is almost as if the wood is struggling within itself. And there is something more here...a light." He shrugged, as if that was the best description he could give.

"The only struggle these woods know is the struggle to ensnare any who enter its lair," spat Shobi. "I tell you true, I have trafficked in these woods since the year I took my vows, and I have never in all that time seen anything but evil come from these boughs." He chuckled. "You wait. You will see."

But Gideon took in Revel's words. Through his experiences with the Wordhavener in the Hinterland and in Strivenwood he had learned to respect Revel's unique sensory abilities. He wondered what his impressions might mean.

The way soon grew hilly, and with the added exertion required of them, Terebin decided to have them all stop at midmorning to rest and take water from their packs. But no one was allowed to sit because the ground had not been purified.

Telus, as was his custom at such times, strolled to the edges of the group and watched the way ahead impassively. But Aybel found her way to Gideon. She said nothing as she removed the water from his pack and handed it to him. Gideon nodded his thanks. "It's weird, isn't it?" he said, leaning on his staff. "Hiking through an invisible forest."

"Just so," she agreed, but she did not meet his gaze.

Gideon took a swig from the skin. "Are you all right?" he ventured.

She nodded. But then added, "These woods trouble me. It is hard to guard against an enemy you cannot see."

Gideon nodded. As lovely as Aybel was, it was easy for him to forget that she was a warrior at heart, trained from her youth to assess the world through a warrior's eyes. She was, in fact, much more like Donovan than he cared to admit.

"The priests seem able to see it easily enough," Gideon offered.

"You trust them after all, then?"

He smirked. "It seems we have little choice for now."

"The priests are not the only ones among us who can see the wood," she said darkly.

"You mean Revel?"

"No. Him." She nodded toward the Raanthan. "If it is a 'him.'"

"Telus?" Gideon whispered. "He can see the forest? How do you know?"

"The priests do not guide him," she said. "They know he sees it as well."

"Well," Gideon shrugged, "so what if he does? Frankly, it wouldn't surprise me." He took another swig from the skin.

"Does it not strike you as strange that he did not tell you, Gideon?" she asked, her tone crisp. "Even as he hovered near you all these hours that we've hiked through this invisible wood? He saw it yesterday, too, just as the priests did. Yet he said nothing to verify their word, even when you accosted Terebin for not answering our questions regarding it."

Gideon sighed. "What are you suggesting?"

At last, she let her eyes find his. "If he hides this from you, Waymaker, such a small thing as it is, then what other knowledge might he be hiding?"

Gideon grinned. "Telus probably hasn't told me close to half of what he knows about all of this, Aybel. He's cryptic. That's his way. It doesn't mean he can't be trusted."

She raised her head and took him in. "I hope your faith in this Raanthan is not misplaced, Waymaker. I, for one, doubt his intentions are pure."

Gideon nodded. "I know." It was no secret that Aybel disliked the Raanthan. But Telus wasn't like the violent Raanthan that made war with her people when she was a child. He was a pacifist, forbidden to harm any living being—even the *Sa'lei*-cursed viperon that had attacked them in the waters of the Gorge. Gideon seriously doubted that Telus would even swat at a wasp as it stung him for fear of causing it harm.

As he saw it, the real question Aybel should be asking is why the Giver would send a pacifist to serve as the Waymaker's chief bodyguard. But then, she probably didn't believe the Giver had sent him at all.

Suddenly the atmosphere all around them began to shimmer in waves like water falling from the sky. And just like that, the trees appeared, so many and so tall that they all but blocked out the sun. All across the rolling hills verdant mounds of ferns and flowering vines materialized, shifting lightly in a cool late-morning breeze, which was also new. They found themselves in a modest clearing, where several large trees had fallen all in a line as if shocked from the ground by a blast from the north. Gideon immediately recognized the smell of jasmine and honeysuckle.

"I told you," said Shobi, chuckling at Revel and the underlord, "you would see."

But Terebin let out a disapproving sigh. "It is hardly good news, brother, and you know it. Now our way becomes harder than ever."

THE FALLEN WOOD

The wood was as I imagined heaven to be, especially in contrast to the rancid fields through which we had hiked for what seemed like weeks without end. But here, suddenly, the air was cool and lush and dusted the skin with a clean mist, fine and subtle and tingling with life. The trees, like the spires of grand cathedrals, cradled us in a calming embrace unlike anything I had ever known. The birds in this place were luminent in flight; I know no other way to describe it. It was a paradise. And, if the Trevail priests were to be believed, every square inch of it was a poisonous lie.

—The Kyrinthan Journals, Musings, Chapter 25, Verses 50-54

Revel threw back his head and laughed with such pure delight that Gideon could not help but chuckle a little himself, just to see it. "Stunning!" declared Revel, grinning like a boy. "That I am blessed to see such a wonder!"

Truly, it was a wonder to behold. For beyond the grandeur of the wood itself—which Gideon likened to the beautiful rain forests of the Pacific Northwest—the atmosphere was filled with tiny birds of every hue and song that Gideon could imagine. Some—a few—even seemed to glow in flight, but he figured that to be a playful trick of the hundreds of sunbeams that broke through the canopy in a scattered array. For some reason, though he knew this was still the Barrens, the birds did not alarm him. They seemed innocent, and perfectly content to ignore the travelers as they flitted about high overhead.

"Speak no more of it," commanded Terebin. "Do not comment on anything you see, nor invite it closer. That is what it seeks."

But Revel did not stop smiling. "Respectfully," he said, "I agree there is deception here. A dark Wording, yes. But that is not all. Some of what we see is true."

"You especially, then," said Terebin, pointing a tattooed finger at Revel, "must not speak of it." He glanced at Shobi. "Watch him."

"Why does it reveal itself now?" asked the underlord.

"Who can divine the thoughts of the desolate?" Shobi declared in reply. "The Fallen Wood is all hunger and hate, whatever face it shows. What does it matter?"

"I have seen this before," said Terebin, scanning the trees. He spat on the cursed earth at his feet, then turned to the group. "We must be on our way. Quickly now. Keep your gaze directly ahead of you, on the back of the *san'-gradon* you follow. Continue to walk in his steps, even though you now see the path. Do not look about, nor respond to any enticements you see."

Gideon had Aybel slip his waterskin back into his pack, then moved to join Telus on the fringes of the clearing. "What sort of enticements is Terebin talking about?" Gideon asked quietly.

The Raanthan flinched in surprise at Gideon's approach, which Gideon noted with surprise of his own. But Telus quickly recovered himself, and confessed, "I am not certain, Waymaker. Something is amiss. I have never seen the Fallen Wood like this before."

"Like what, exactly?" Gideon pressed.

But Telus only shook his head and glided away, following the priests who had already resumed the trek south.

"Like what?" Gideon repeated, trailing after him. But Telus seemed not to hear him. At that moment, Gideon noticed Aybel at his side. "Your friend seems distracted," she noted in a whisper, then shot him a cautionary look as she passed on by.

Gideon plodded along behind her for a time, saying nothing. So what if Telus was distracted? That didn't have to mean anything, did it? Eventually, Gideon found his way to Terebin, who was at the front leading the way for them all, and settled in behind him. Telus, he noted, had now wandered to the back of the group, well behind Revel and the underlord.

"The pull is getting stronger," noted Gideon, addressing Terebin's tattooed back. "Before long, we'll need to be turning a little more east."

"As you say, Waymaker."

"What lies ahead?" asked Gideon.

"To the south, more forest, for many leagues yet," Terebin replied without turning around. "To the east, there is the shore, about a day's journey. It is somewhat safer there, should we reach it. The dark souls fear the ocean and don't often approach it."

"I'm not sure we'll go that far east," said Gideon. "It's hard to tell. Still, it doesn't seem all that dangerous here either. Just where are all the dangers you warned us about?"

"Are you in a hurry to face them?" Terebin scolded. "You should be thankful that they tarry for now."

Gideon stabbed the dirt with the butt of his staff, pulling himself closer to the bald-headed priest. "I'm not in a hurry," he said gruffly. "Just curious. What are the enticements you spoke of?"

"Some beauty in the world is true, Waymaker," grunted Terebin. "But here, it is all deception. You must look beyond the surface. Things are not as they seem."

As usual, Terebin's answer did not satisfy him, but he had grown weary of always having to prod the priest or the Raanthan for more detailed information. He let it go for now.

They continued on in relative silence for several more hours. The woods provided shelter from the Barren's hot sun; the air was moist and cool, and there was a constant light breeze that made the journey pleasant. The priests were clearly unnerved by the agreeable climate; it was apparently not the norm. Their eyes continually darted up into the canopy or through the thick clusters of tree trunks and vines that flanked the group on either side. Their anxiety hovered over them all like a dark cloud, leaving everyone with the nagging feeling that attack was imminent—though from what or from where no one could tell. If the priests themselves knew, they certainly weren't telling.

Things seemed to calm a bit once Gideon turned them east, but still the priests would not allow any frivolous conversation, and even talk they considered essential was restricted to a whisper. Though Gideon remained close to Terebin at the front of the group for most of this time, he grew increasingly bothered by Telus' absence at his side, where the Raanthan had stubbornly remained throughout most of their journey. Instead, the Raanthan now clung to the rear of the group, and seemed to be falling farther and farther behind with each league they traversed. Even with the distance between them, Gideon could tell that he, too, seemed jittery. His liquid bronze eyes flashed about nervously—eyeing the wood, and then the sky, then the wood again. He didn't even notice that Gideon was watching him.

With a tap and a nod, Gideon gestured to Terebin to keep forging ahead while he stepped away. As nonchalantly as he could, he made his way to Telus, passing by the curious stares of Revel, Aybel and Kyrintha without comment. The silvery Raanthan did not notice his approach until he was only a few feet away.

"Waymaker," he whispered. "You should be in the lead."

"Terebin knows the way for now," whispered Gideon in reply. "What's wrong with you?"

Telus looked up to the trees, but then quickly made his reply. "I hear them," he muttered nervously. "They whisper in my spirit. It is as I feared. I am for you, Waymaker. But if I remain with you, it may bring danger to us all."

The staff immediately grew warm at the sound of the Raanthan's words, sparking Gideon's pulse to quicken. "Who do you hear, Telus?"

"My brothers," he whispered, "but not my brothers."

"Raanthan? Here, in the Barrens?"

Telus nodded slowly, his face at once fierce and profoundly sad. "They are not of my tribe."

"What do they want with us?" demanded Gideon.

But at that moment, the Raanthan screamed. "Stand clear!" He snatched Gideon by the arm and hurled him away. It was all Gideon could do to avoid tumbling headlong onto the deadly grass. "Telus, what the...?"

But when he looked up, he saw them. Leaping through the trees like silvery specters of death, twenty Raanthan or more approached from the west. They moved like cloth in the wind, graceful as music and foreboding as a burial shroud.

"Why come you, brothers?" yelled Telus to the trees. His voice, booming like the sound of a thousand trumpets, forced Gideon to cover his ears. He had never heard Telus sound this way before. "You are lost, and have no place in the world of men. Go back to the shadows that you have chosen to love."

But they came on, dancing through the limbs like a whirlwind of doom.

"These before you are charged to me," proclaimed Telus. "You know the authority by which this charge is made. You know the power that makes it. Turn back, my brothers. Perhaps you may yet gain mercy."

"There is no mercy for us," howled a voice from the trees. "Or for you, Telus of the Brilliant Gate. We come for you."

The staff burned hot in Gideon's hands—so hot it began to glow like the blue fires of *Dei'lo*. Gideon knew he must center himself to use the flow—to surrender to its will within him—but the shock of what he was seeing kept him teetering on panic.

The Raanthan descended from the trees like free-flowing sheets of silver and white. The beauty of their movements haunted his eyes, and froze him to the ground in wonder and fear.

Just then, a mighty blue shield sparkled to life around the perimeter of the group. The priests had formed a ring around Aybel, Revel and the underlord, and stood in angry defiance of the assault from above. But the Raanthan did not take notice of them; their large molten eyes remained fixed on Telus alone. And on Gideon, too, if only by default of standing too close to Telus. For the two of them had fallen far behind the group, and now both stood beyond the perimeter of the shield the priests had erected. As soon as the priests realized that Gideon was not among them, Shobi, who stood closest to the pair, broke rank and burst through the shield toward them, yelling commands in *Dei'lo* as he went.

"He cannot help us," muttered Telus. His voice was so horribly sad it made Gideon's heart ache.

But then a scream from above ripped away the pain and replaced it with terror. A shimmering blast, like the shockwave of a bomb, hurtled toward them from mouth of the Raanthan as their feet touched the ground. Somehow, in that instant, Telus matched it, bellowing out a screech of his own. The two waves, barely visible but palpable in their strength, collided, spewing energy to the sides and into the canopy above. Trees like matchsticks splintered in the blink of an eye. Ground that had been covered in lush vegetation was instantly stripped bare. A broad swath of barren earth appeared to either side of them, with just a meager patch of green still standing at their feet. It was as if the hand of God had come down and simply swiped it all out of existence.

The shield around the priests still held, though they were not in the primary line of the blast. Shobi, however, was no where to be seen.

"The Words have no power over these, Waymaker," Telus half whispered to Gideon, "but you do. Fight them!"

The Raanthan approached at a pace that seemed almost languid and carefree. Their mouths, which on Telus had always seemed almost nonexistent, gaped open so wide and long they looked like portals to hell itself. Still they did not look to the priests, but kept their bronze stares fixed on Telus.

Undeterred, the priests sang out—first one, then another, then all of them in chorus. Gideon immediately recognized the invocation as *Dei'lo*. The power of the Words resonated thickly in the air, then coalesced into a cloud above their heads—so black it turned the day to night before his eyes.

A storm of deliverance! he thought in amazement. He knew that's what it was, though how he knew he could not say. Still, he marveled at the sight of it, and at the knowledge that a storm like this had heralded his arrival in the Lands.

As if on cue, shards of lightning bolted from the cloud—first red, then green, then blue and yellow—each striking at the heart of a different assailing Raanthan. But, to his horror, the bolts passed right through them, striking harmlessly on the ground below.

Another screech—this time a chorus—erupted from the silvery forms, and burst directly against the shield the priests had erected. The cloud quickly vaporized as the priests turned their attention and their voices back to shoring up the shield. It came ablaze in blue fire and crackled in the strain. Trees all around shredded like tissue at the sound of the blast and disappeared into the wind. But the shield held true, holding the patch of green intact like a small island in a flood of devastation.

The staff burned in Gideon's hands, hotter now than any time before. But it did not cause him pain. Its glow was new to him—not like before when the lightning came down from the sky and consumed it. This time it burned as if from his touch. Blue fire danced along its edges like the heat of a desert mirage. It was ready, as was he. But how do you fight against a Raanthan?

"Tell me what to do!" he cried to Telus, but his own mouth now gaped as wide as his brothers. The screech that issued forth from him unhinged the very air around them, making the trees turn to liquid and piercing Gideon's ears with thousands of painful tiny needles. Six of the Raanthan closest to them sailed up into the clouds like rag dolls on the wind of his breath. In a matter of only a few seconds, they were blown too far to see.

But a dozen or more remained, and they came on, more quickly and with new anger in their judgmental bronze eyes. Telus lacked the time to take in a breath before the first of them was upon him. With mouth agape and narrow fingers extended like claws, he gripped Telus around his narrow throat and squeezed. Telus struggled against his brother's grip, but the alarm in his eyes told Gideon that his friend was in danger of losing the fight. As if by instinct, Gideon raised his staff high and raced to meet the attacker. Gripping the staff like a bat, his swung hard and straight at the Raanthan's midsection, which stood roughly at a height with Gideon's shoulders. The staff swung through with no perceptible resistance, as if through air, but the Raanthan screeched in agony as the force of Gideon's blow hurled it skyward into the trees, several of which cracked and shattered under the strain of the impact.

At this new development, the remaining Raanthan stopped dead in their tracks, then slowly began to back away. Telus gripped his own wounded throat, then bellowed after them, "I told you, did I not? The authority here is too much for you. Who dares to send you on this fool's errand?"

"Who else, brother?" came the mocking reply. "Surely you know!"

"Take what you have left, and leave now," Telus demanded. "Tell your lord his days in these lands are few and numbered!"

"You can tell him yourself, when we drag your shattered body to his great mountain." Suddenly, the Raanthan all leaped from the ground and floated airily into the trees. But instead of fleeing, as Gideon expected, they turned back toward Telus. "Attack!"

Again, a chorus of screeching descended from the heights, and was quickly—but weakly—matched by Telus' own voice, which had clearly been damaged in the assault.

But this was not all. From the fringes of the wooded hills around them, a carpet of black oozed forth from the shadows, beckoned forth by the Raanthan's command. It came upon them from all directions, and Gideon immediately knew what it was.

"Waymaker!" cried Terebin, "Quickly, run to the shield!"

"Do as he says," echoed Telus. "I cannot protect you from both my brothers and the riftmen."

But Gideon drew up his staff, still glowing with blue fire, and stabbed it into the cursed earth at his feet. "Protect me?" he asked incredulously. "Last time I checked, I was protecting you."

"But I am for you, Waymaker," Telus protested.

"Shut up," said Gideon. "Save your voice for them."

Another shockwave blasted from the trees, but this time Gideon raced forward to meet it, with his staff held before him like a shield. And in that instant, a shield it became, as blue waves of light like the ripples on the shore flowed out to meet the scornful cry of the Raanthan. As the shockwave touched to leading edge of Gideon's blue fire, it simply vanished, evaporating into nothingness as if it never was.

This happened just as the first wave of riftmen reached the shield of the *san'gradon*. Its crackling fires broke out against the black horde, and the first few shrank back in pain. Words from the priests sang out, and Gideon could hear the proud voices of Aybel and Revel sing out as well, issuing commands in the Tongue of Life. All around blue fire erupted until it seemed the entire expanse of blasted earth surrounding them would be scorched black. And those riftmen the fires touched were quickly undone.

But there were so many. Too many. They just kept coming, pouring out of the woods like a sea of black lava, taking human form only as they neared the shield.

They came toward Gideon and Telus from the rear as well, but, perhaps ironically, the blasts from the attacking Raanthan's voices prevented them from approaching too close.

Another screech, and once more Telus matched it with his call. The sky thundered at the impact of their dissonant cries, and more trees were decimated, this time to the south. Gideon stabbed the ground with his staff in frustration. He had called forth lightning from the staff before—why not now? All he could do was block their screeching attacks...or knock them to high heaven if they came close enough for him to take a swat at them. But they clung stubbornly to the tops of what few trees remained.

"Why do you hide in the trees like cowards?" Gideon yelled in frustration. "Come down here and face us on the ground, and we'll see what you're really made of!"

"This cannot go on," Telus whispered hoarsely in his ear. "They know my voice is failing. They need only wait until I can no longer cancel their cries."

"I can fight them," countered Gideon. "I just need to get close enough."

"Your battle will come, Waymaker," warned Telus, "and when it does, you will long for the days when you did not have to wield the staff. But this fight is not for you. It is mine."

"C'mon, Telus," Gideon snapped. "We're in this together and you know it. Now help me figure out a way to get to them!"

But Telus only smiled. "Your friends need you," he said, and pointed a silvery finger toward the priests.

Gideon looked, and drew in a breath in shock. The shield was gone. Or rather, it was covered in a thick black sheen, and crackling as if on fire. *How could the riftmen endure its touch?* he wondered. But on they came, more and more, each new wave toppling over the vaguely human black forms ahead of them, piling up and over themselves, coating the priests' shield in a blanket of corruption. There were simply too many of them for the priests and Wordhavers to repel. It would not be long before the shield would collapse.

"We have to help them!" Gideon yelled. But when he turned, the Raanthan was no longer there. He caught sight of him, just a flashing glimpse, as he flew to the trees where his brothers awaited. His silvery hair flailed in the wind of his passing like the wings of death itself. "Telus!" he cried. But the Raanthan was already there, and in that instant a whirlwind of silver and white and the sound of screeching filled the skies overhead like a storm.

What was he to do? Telus could not hope to overcome a dozen or more of his kind all at once—could he? Gideon's first instinct was to chase after him, but he had no way to reach them in the trees, and his staff still refused to answer his call for lightning or wind or any such power that might be used to strike them down. And the riftmen's pressure on the shield was growing.

While trapped in indecision, he heard a noise behind him, like the slithering of a snake, and turned just in time to see a carpet of glistening black on the ground rise up to take the form of a man. Then two. Then six, and more. Raising the staff in battle stance as Revel had taught him, he immediately advanced on the black line. He had no time for this; he needed to help his friends! Swinging the staff like a scythe, he sliced through the riftmen—first one, then two, then eight and ten. The blue fire of his staff severed their bodies, and at the same time somehow turned them solid, so that they crumbled at his feet in chunks of charred coal. He barely took notice of what he was doing; his thoughts were on Telus, and the shield behind him with his friends trapped within. The riftmen fell in droves. They offered no cry, no protest. But still they kept coming. It was as if they wanted to die.

A moment later, Gideon heard a loud crack behind him, and a hiss. Daring to glance, he saw the dome of the shield buckling under the strain of the thick layers of riftmen upon it. It would take only a crack, he knew. The riftmen could seep into any opening, and in no time flood the dome. If he was going to make a move, he would have to make it now, or lose them forever.

Taking one final sweep at the encroaching riftmen, he turned on his heels and raced off toward the glistening black mound. The silvery storm cloud still screeched overheard, but the movement of the Raanthan was too fast for Gideon to discern Telus' whereabouts or condition. He could only pray that his friend was able to hold his own. Upon reaching the dome, he wasted no time. Grasping the staff once more as a scythe, he swung at the blackness with all of his might.

The spray of dark forms that filled the skies shocked even him. Dozens of riftmen splintered off from the mound, flung skyward by the power of Gideon's thrust. They were said to have voices, though Gideon had never heard them until now. Thick and dark and full of fury, the riftmen moaned at Gideon's attack in agony and hate. But their cries quickly faded as they shot off into the distance.

Another swing, and another spray of riftmen splattered through the air. But with every dozen he knocked away, another twenty oozed in to fill their place. He heard a scream beneath the dome, and recognized it as the underlord's. The riftmen had breached the shield. Perhaps it was already too late.

But he could not give up; he was so close, mere inches away. The priests were within. And Revel, and Aybel. They would know how to fight them, make new shields, set them ablaze with the Words, something. All he needed to do was get to them, to make a way out.

He swung once more, then again and again and again—each time more frantic and angry than before. More and more riftmen flew off the mound in a wail, but it was like digging a hole in a vat of hot tar. Why couldn't he use the staff in some other way? Why couldn't he burn a hole through the mass of them, or purify them as he had done on the slopes of Heaven Range? It was maddening! Deep down, he knew he could do any of those things. He'd done it before. He *should* know how! But for whatever reason—inexperience, fear, some hidden working of the riftmen or the Raanthan or the Deathland Barrens itself—he could not find the way.

And now, because of his failure, his friends within the dome were dying.

Suddenly, he felt something grip his cloak from behind. Turning too late, the hand of the riftman yanked hard on the cloth, even as the Words embroidered on them burned into its dark taloned flesh. Gideon teetered off balance, tumbling roughly to the blasted, barren ground. The riftman followed his fall and drew close, hovering above him in what seemed like a combination of hunger and trepidation. He barely had time to raise his claws before Gideon thrust the butt of the staff into his face. There was a sound of churning mud and cracking bone, and the creature flew into the air and out of sight—only to be replaced by two more. Again Gideon thrust, first at one then the other, and again they flew. But then another two came, and then a third. He kept knocking them away as quickly as they appeared, using the fiery staff to hold them away from his body just enough to avoid their claws. But as long as he remained stuck on his back, he could do little to fight them, or better his position—which, he quickly realized, was their primary intention. If they could keep him down long enough, it was just a matter of time before one of them could slip in and strike him before being hurled away. All it would take is a scratch. And the Worded cloak, invaluable as it was, offered no protection for his hands or face.

More and more came—four, then six, then more than he could count. He swung madly, furious in his desperation to gain his footing. He could hear the underlord screaming again, and more cries as well. The priests! The priests were falling. But no matter how desperately he fought off the riftmen, they just kept coming. The staff flared brilliant blue in his rage as he swung it, and the creatures wailed at the sight of it. But still they came, inch by inch drawing closer to his body, their sharp claws patiently gauging the distance to his unprotected skin.

"Telus!" he screamed. "Help me!"

A rumble, a thud, and the sound of a cry. It was a human cry. Suddenly, an arm of flesh reached through the circle of riftmen surrounding him and snatched one away. It was human, but not tattooed. Unprotected by even a cloak. Who was it? Revel? Whoever it was would be dead in minutes.

Another arm appeared, and then another, both just like the first. They strangled the dark menacing forms about the neck and jerked them hard away. The riftmen moaned as if it pained them to be touched by the untainted skin. Soon, a dozen more arms appeared, but not all were like those that came first. Many, perhaps half, were grotesque, misshapen and scarred—in one place quite obviously human while in another charred black and shriveled, and coated with an oily sheen.

Whatever they were, the riftmen seem genuinely terrified of them. They quickly recoiled as the new threat appeared within their ranks. It wasn't long before the field cleared away enough for Gideon to get a look at one from head to toe.

His face was mostly human. But the lower left jaw was distended and twice the size it should have been. Teeth like daggers shot out from the jaw line, and the skin all around them was black and bubbling like hot tar. His eyes were blue, and clearly human, as human as his right arm and both of his legs. But not his torso, for it bore the same cold black sheen of the riftmen he had just chased away. He wore loose-fitting leggings of tan-colored cloth, rough like burlap and shredded at the hem. His hair was short and probably red, but so caked with mud it was hard to tell.

He couldn't be sure if the creature or any of his companions had spotted him yet, sprawled on the ground as he was. The screaming had stopped, and all signs of the riftmen had vanished into the shadows. He desperately wanted to look south to see if the priests' shield still held, or if the storm cloud of Raanthan still raged against Telus in the trees. But he dare not risk it; not yet. He lay still as death with the staff lain across his chest, waiting to see whether these new creatures also meant them harm.

The half-humans milled about for some time, scraping at the soil or peeking under the remnants of shattered trees as if to make certain no riftmen remained hidden underfoot. Some of them looked mostly like riftmen themselves, with only a few parts—a hand and forearm, the side of the face—human. But others seemed completely human, with no aberrations visible at all, though they might have been concealed beneath their ragged clothes.

It was one of the human ones, a woman, a teenager by the look of her face, who finally locked her gaze directly on Gideon and approached. She did not come quickly, however, and seemed as concerned about his intentions as he was about hers.

Her hair, like all the others, was short, but it was blond and free of mud, as was her skin and garments. She had clearly not participated in the fight.

"You are the Waymaker," she said. Her voice sounded odd, deeper than it should have, and gravelly.

Slowly, Gideon sat up, being careful to keep the staff free in his hand. He noted worriedly that the blue flame no longer danced along its length. "Who are you?" he demanded.

"We are the people," she said. "The teacher sent us to find you, and bring you."

"Bring us where?" Gideon rose up on one knee. The girl scuttled backward nervously.

"He has words for you," she said.

"Are you here to capture us, then?" he asked.

"No," she replied. "No."

"I need to see to my friends," he said threateningly. Stabbing the butt of the staff into the ground, he pulled himself up to his full height. She was short by comparison, still just a girl. "If you try to stop me, I will fight you."

"We..." she stammered. "We...will not stop you. We will wait." She bowed her head lightly and forced a polite smile.

He didn't take time to respond, but immediately turned to look for the remnants of the Worded shield surrounding his friends, or the whirlwind of Raanthan in the air above. He found neither. Instead, he saw Aybel and Revel running toward him. They looked worn from battle, but otherwise appeared unharmed. "Are you well, Gideon?" called Aybel worriedly. "Are you well?"

Gideon raised his staff. "I'm fine," he called. "Where are the others?"

They waited until they reached him to respond. "Four of the priests are slain," said Revel. "The three that remain are tending to Kyrintha. The riftmen struck her down when the shield gave way, but her Worded cloak protected her skin from their poisoned claws. Terebin says she will be fine."

"Terebin is all right?" asked Gideon. "Who else is left?"

"Ammiel and Magan," Aybel replied.

"What about Telus?" Gideon asked. "Have you seen him?"

"No, Waymaker," said Revel. "The last we saw he was standing at your side."

"Once the riftmen covered the shield, we could see nothing of the Raanthan battle," explained Aybel, "or of you. What happened?"

But Gideon was already storming past them. "We have to look for Telus," he declared. "The last time I saw him he was fighting with the Raanthan, over there." He pointed up to the place where the trees had been. Now, there was nothing. "He could be injured."

"Wait, Waymaker!" Revel followed behind and caught him by the arm. In his ear, he whispered, "What of these creatures that saved us? What have they said to you?"

Gideon wrested his arm away. "Later! Right now we have to find Telus. Come on!"

Revel and Aybel reluctantly followed, and said no more. Marching past the remaining priests, Gideon summoned all but Terebin to follow him as well. He knew they must be grieving the loss of their comrades, but there was no time for that now. Take care of the living first, right? Then deal with the dead.

They searched the shattered landscape for the better part of an hour, with random clusters of the half-human creatures standing on the sidelines, still as statues but watching their every move. The ground everywhere was coated with a fine wood dust. Every so often, there'd be a splinter of a tree limb or the flattened remnants of a vine or fern. But nothing beyond that. Nothing. No blood. Not even a stray silver hair.

"He must have fled south, deeper into the wood to draw them away," Gideon announced in obvious frustration, "or east toward the shore."

"That is possible, Waymaker," said Aybel softly. Too softly. Why was she looking at him like that?

"What?" he demanded. "He's not here, that's all. We'll just have to keep looking."

Aybel stepped closer, within arm's reach. "We have been searching for more than an hour," she said. "It is more likely that they took him."

Gideon backed away. "Oh you'd like that, wouldn't you?"

"I know their ways, Waymaker," she said, with more edge this time. "Once they attack, they do not retreat until they achieve their objective, or perish in the attempt."

"So?"

"So they are gone," she said, "which means they either achieved their goal, or your one Raanthan managed to destroy them all."

"You underestimate Telus," Gideon said hoarsely.

"Aybel is right, Waymaker," said Revel, who had been listening to the whole exchange from several feet away. "You know if Telus had prevailed, he would be here, close to you, regardless of any injury he received at the hands of his brothers. He is not here. I fear they have taken him. Or worse."

"What, you just want to walk away, then?" Gideon sneered sarcastically. "Just walk away! Never mind what happened to him! Let's just move on. Is that what you want to do?"

"He is gone, Waymaker!" snapped Aybel. "What would you have us do?"

Gideon scowled at her and turned to storm away. But he felt Revel's hand catch him roughly on the arm. He pulled him in close. "Telus was not the only one who was lost this day, Waymaker," he whispered scoldingly. "Is this profound demonstration of grief not also for the four Cal'eeb priests who fell this very hour defending our lives, or for Kyrintha who lays injured not fifty paces away?" His grip tightened. "And what of these humanlike creatures that stand around us staring as if waiting for your word? They too saved us today, and not without cost. And what do they want of us in payment? We do not know, for they will speak to no one but you—or didn't you know that? Open your eyes, Waymaker! There is more going on here than merely your pain." He shook his hand loose and walked away.

For a moment, Gideon just stood there, staring at Revel's back as he plodded off toward Terebin. The words of the hawk-faced man stung him deeply, but the instant he heard them he knew they were true. He had gotten so wrapped up in his grief over Telus that he lost sight of anything else. Of anyone else. There was a time when he would have gladly shut out all concerns but his own. But he couldn't afford such a luxury anymore. He was the Waymaker, and these people were depending on him. Only he could lead them out of this.

Gathering himself to full height, he walked past the two Trevail priests, who were still searching for signs of Telus in the debris. "Enough," he said. "Let's go." He led them back to Terebin, who was still hovering over the underlord, checking the skin of her arms for cuts or scrapes. Revel and Aybel were there as well.

"Is she well enough to walk?" he asked Terebin.

"I am," replied Kyrintha, "thanks to the priests." She offered Revel her hand, who quietly began to help her to her feet.

But Gideon had already moved on, toward the far end of the meadow, where he'd stood with Telus for the last time. The girl was still there, standing with her hands clasped, watching him with a curiosity too intense for her years.

When Gideon reached her, he planted his staff firmly into the ground between them, and said, "Do you have a name?"

To Gideon's surprise, she blushed. "I do," she replied. "I am called Grace Lightfoot." The name fumbled awkwardly off her tongue as if she were not used to saying it.

"Well, Grace. My name is Gideon Dawning. And as you apparently know, I am the Waymaker."

"Yes," she said.

"Tell me," said Gideon, "in which direction does this teacher of yours live?"

Pointing eastward, she replied, "The teacher's house lies that way."

Gideon sighed. Her answer did not surprise him. "Well, you're in luck, Grace," he said. "For that is also the direction I must travel." Her face brightened at hearing Gideon's words. "But let's be clear," he continued, more sternly now. "We will only agree to go with you on two conditions. First, that no harm will come to my any of my companions or me while in your company—"

"Agreed," she said quickly.

"And second, should we decide to leave your company for any reason, you and your people will not attempt to stop us."

"Yes, of course," she said, just as quickly as before. "But I do not believe that will happen. The teacher is expecting you."

Gideon grinned, but said nothing. Instead, he gestured for the girl to follow him back across the meadow to where his company waited.

"Gather your things," he announced as he approached the group. "We're going." He gestured to the girl. "And Grace, here, will lead the way."

WORDHAVEN

By the time of Wordhaven's siege, the Paladin and Head of Arms had managed to form two full divisions of Worded warriors, each numbering between twelve and thirteen hundred strong. The vast majority of these were Wordhaven's own; all but the very old and very young were suited for war. The rest, around seven hundred souls, had come from the soundens. These were brave men and women, as well trained in the Words as any could be in the short weeks they had since the Book's return. But even with the Book of Dei'lo in their midst, and the strong walls of Wordhaven standing at their back, they all surely knew—from the least to the greatest—that they were far too small to resist for long the hordes of Phaltenar marching inexorably toward them, carrying certain death in their cloaks.

—The Kyrinthan Journals, Chronicles, Chapter 19, Verses 133-139

This choice is borne of arrogance, Paladin, and you know it!" Seer rapped Ajel on the shin with her staff as she spoke as if to emphasize her point. "This is no time to be thinning our ranks in the Stand!"

"What would you have us do?" asked Ajel firmly. "Agatharon suffered greatly at the passing of the two Council lords and their *mon'jalen*. The sounden is all but stripped of supplies, and has lost most of their able-bodied men. They will not survive the winter without help."

"Why must it be us that helps them, Paladin?" countered Seer. "Why not have Agatharon seek aid from the other soundens nearby? Or have you forgotten that we are currently under siege by the very force that struck them down?"

"The other soundens will do their part," replied Ajel, "but for now we are Agatharon's best hope. Makroth cannot reach the need as quickly as we can, and Valoran is dealing with shortages of its own." He nodded toward the portal on the far wall of the chamber. Several dozen leather-garbed warriors huddled around the shimmering door, each with a canvas pack resting on the floor beside them, waiting impatiently as volunteers carried in last-minute supplies for them to carry. "Besides," added Ajel, "it is only one hundred warriors, and they will return within a few days' time. The guardians will not breach the walls of Wordhaven in that time."

"We have already been attacked seven times by mounted juron, Paladin," snapped Seer. "You know full well they do not need to breach the walls to reach us."

"The juron are too few in number to be a significant threat, especially now that Wordhaven's defenses are awakened. Besides, those *mon'jalen* are scouts, nothing more."

Seer thumped her staff against the floor. "You are foolish to discount the threat they bring. There is more than scouting at work here."

"Are you Head of Arms now, Seer?" asked Ajel with a wry grin. "Even Donovan does not think the force at our gates has come to wage war on us directly, or even to starve us out by siege. They are here only to prevent us from fleeing the Stand before Balaam's main force arrives. They do not realize that we have no intention of fleeing this time. And even if we did, they could not stop us. They know nothing of the portals."

"There are at least a hundred *mon'jalen* outside our gates—twenty or more mounted on juron," countered Seer, "and at least two lords as well, who have yet to show themselves. Tell me, Paladin, why would the lords hide their presence from us except in hope of catching us unawares?"

"I fully expect Varia and her bondmate are devising some sinister work against us from the shadows where they hide, Seer. I have instructed Donovan and Brasen to form teams to search the ridge along the heights of Wordhaven for any sign of activity by the lords or their minions. If they mean to enter Wordhaven by stealth, that is the only way. But while we wait to hear what they may find, Agatharon will be helped."

"I have an ill sense of this, Ajel," said Seer. "I tell you, we are spread too thin—"

"The matter is settled, Seer," said Ajel firmly. "But you need not fret the absence of these fighters. With the Words now fully at our disposal, our voices have more than enough strength to resist Varia's attacks. Her mounted juron will gain no footing here."

"Lord Varia knows that as well as you, Paladin," chided Seer. "You would be wise to consider that."

36

SOLIDARI SOUNDEN

I took the quiet road in those days. In truth, I had never felt so helpless. Being the only one in our party with no knowledge of the Words and no power to wield save my own wits, I had no sense of my purpose for being included in this quest. I was a child among giants, ignorant and deaf. I judged myself a burden, a fool, and in the way. I dared not even speak for fear of awakening the beautiful dread of the Fallen Wood.

But when I came at last to Solidari sounden, and beheld the miracle of its people, I began to perceive the role reserved for me in this grand story. For I was a witness to wonders that the prophets in all their wisdom had never foreseen. Could it be that I was called, not as a prophet of what is to come, but as proclaimer of what has come to pass? From that day on, I set my heart to watch everything, to listen to it all, and to remember.

— The Kyrinthan Journals, Songs of Deliverance, Stanza 17, Verses 93-95

I t was like a leper colony. Or at least, what Gideon imagined a leper colony would be.

Hundreds of hands clambered for them as they entered the village, each attached to a body in its own unique stage of grotesque transformation. Few of the "people," as Grace called them, were recognizably human, though all had some quality of a human form emerging from their black, glistening hide—a human hand to counter the claw on the other arm, a pair of human feet on a body as amorphous as steaming tar, or eyes of brilliant blue drowning in a swirl of black oozing putrescence. Deformed smiles greeted them, some dripping an oily mucous on the pine-needled earth, a few full of daggered teeth that made the smile seemed more a sneer. But there was no animosity in their movements. If anything, there was awe.

The mass of deformity touched them all, reverently stroking their hands or pinching their hair between their fingers. They giggled and gurgled in amazement and delight, and no one in Gideon's party seemed to feel the least bit threatened by any of it, not even the Trevail priests. Not even Gideon himself.

The ruins surrounding them indicated that this place had once been a sounden—and a beautiful one at that. Like all soundens Gideon had seen, the village was laid out as a sort of amphitheater. There was a large clearing in the center, marked by four ornate wooden towers that reminded Gideon of the stone towers of Calmeron. The shelters closest to the village center sat on the ground, while those farther away were constructed up in the trees, each row of buildings higher than the last as one moved farther from the clearing. Wooden bridges dangled from house to house in a pleasing array like garlands on a Christmas tree.

Much work had clearly been done to restore the sounden to its original glory, but like its inhabitants, the structures themselves seemed locked in a struggle between horror and beauty. Many were dilapidated; some were festering with a living rot that looked like something akin to maggots. A number of the bridges were dangling unattached, their ropes frayed and rotting as they swayed in the breeze. But those structures that had been restored glistened with a vibrancy that seemed almost palpable—as if, somehow, the buildings were alive and humming.

Eventually the mob herded Gideon and his party toward the clearing in the sounden center. Grace remained faithfully at his side throughout the curious onslaught, but said nothing until they reached the towers. Only then did she raise her hand to quiet the crowd. Small as she was, it was a wonder to Gideon that anyone saw her hand raised in halt, but as soon as she did it, the clambering stopped and the cacophony of voices faded to a murmur.

"You are only the second trueborn they have ever seen up close," she said.

"Trueborn?" asked Gideon. "I don't understand."

"You were not born in the Waste," she said. "They long to be like you."

"What about you, Grace?" Gideon asked. "Were you born here too?"

She nodded, clearly a little ashamed by the admission. "It is easier for the young to shed the corruption, if they begin the journey early enough. I have been among the people since my fifth year of life."

Terebin was apparently listening in on the conversation, for he pressed his way toward them and said, "What do you mean, girl? Are you saying these are all dark souls?"

"We know you, priest; you and your brothers and sisters of the pure land to the north. You could have helped us, but you never invited us in. Instead, you shunned us. You killed us." Grace's words did not sound angry; merely sad.

"The dark souls never came to the Stays looking for help; only to destroy," said Terebin. "Besides, you are only a girl. What would you know of it?"

"The teacher teaches us many things," replied Grace. "He knows you, too, just as he knows us. He says we are brothers, that we are to love you as brothers, even though you have slain us. He says you do not yet understand about love."

"Where is this teacher, that I may hear his words for myself?" demanded Terebin.

"Perhaps you will see him," said Grace, "though it is the Waymaker he has summoned. First, the speaker will come. He will say whether you can see the teacher or not."

"It will be dark soon, Terebin," Ammiel broke in. "The day has been long and trying for us all. We need rest, and food. We should go outside the sounden to set up our camp. We can meet this teacher in the morning."

"Nonsense, my friends! Nonsense!" A man's booming voice thundered toward them through the trees. When Gideon looked to where the voice originated, he saw a grey-bearded man bounding toward them with arms spread as wide as his generous grin. He wore robes of grey and white that draped all the way to the ground—and spun of a far nicer cloth than any Gideon had seen here. His face was clear and pleasant; he was fully human as far as Gideon could tell. "I won't hear of it! You will stay here this night, and dine with us!"

"Waymaker," said Grace, "this is the speaker."

"Yes, yes, Grace, thank you," said the speaker, still bounding toward them with a glee in his step as if on a mission to bear hug the lot of them all at once. "Well done. Well done, all of you. Now give our guests some room to breath, would you? Let us talk a moment without the whole sounden listening in, hmm?"

Begrudgingly, the mob began to move away, murmuring as they slinked toward the trees in all directions. Many of them appeared to ooze more than walk, a fact that Gideon hadn't really noticed until now, and which he suddenly found unnerving.

"Grace, go and tell the teacher that our guests have arrived, would you?" asked the speaker.

The young girl immediately lit up. "Yes, speaker. I will. Thank you!"

"That's fine, then. Now off you go." He patted her on the head as she scampered away, acting like a child for the first time since Gideon met her.

"Now," bellowed the man, "let me take a look at you." He gripped Gideon by the shoulders and squared himself before him. "Ah," he said, "the staff, the hair, the scars on the wrists—that's just wonderful. You are the one! Welcome, Waymaker! We've been waiting many seasons, many seasons indeed."

"And you are?" asked Gideon.

The man laughed, loud and deep and full of delight—the same way Revel laughed when he entered an unfamiliar wood for the first time. "I am so sorry," he said. Thrusting out both hands, he latched onto Gideon's right hand and shook it vigorously. "I am called Darind Reach. I am the speaker of this sounden."

Gideon stared solid down at Darind's hand in amazement. No one in the Inherited Lands had ever shaken his hand before. He had long ago assumed that the custom was unknown to them. The speaker must have noticed Gideon's confusion, however, for he suddenly stopped and let go. "Forgive me," he said, "am I doing it wrong?"

"No," said Gideon. "It's just that no one's ever shaken my hand before. No one here, I mean."

Darind beamed with delight. "The teacher taught me to do it. It is a curious custom, I must admit. Tell me, what is it you hope to shake off by doing it?"

"Forgive me, Darind," said Gideon, "but I have a lot of questions of my own. This is all very confusing for us."

"And you are tired, yes," added the speaker. "And you have suffered a great deal of loss today. I know." Darind smiled warmly at Terebin and patted Gideon on the arm. "Come, let's eat. I can answer your questions at the table we have prepared. And you, priests, do not worry. Our food is free of the taint of this land. Of course, you are welcome to purify it again for yourselves, if you like." He pulled Gideon forward, and gestured with his other hand for the rest to follow. "After the meal, you can rest. On the morrow, the teacher will see you."

He led them to a sizeable building not far from the center—hewn from dark logs with long and high walls—and hurried them inside.

The great hall was lit with dozens fire sconces along the walls, each backed with thick resin to guard the flames from the wood. The entire building was this single room. And the meal set out for them within it was an extraordinary banquet. A single gilded-wood table, long enough to easily seat fifty or more, was arrayed at one end with an assortment of flowers and decorative cloths, and set with plates of fired clay, glazed in the colors of the forest, with a goblet of pewter arrayed next to each, and utensils forged of exquisite beaten silver.

But the food was what really took Gideon's breath away. Huge silver platters stacked high with grilled salmon, along with mounds of steaming vegetables and assorted sweet breads. Pewter pitchers sat at regular intervals along the table. Gideon wondered with anticipation if they might contain wine.

"By the Giver!" exclaimed Aybel. "How did you come by such extravagance?"

The speaker laughed. "By the Giver, indeed! But then, you already knew that. Come now, be seated. The fish won't stay warm forever."

The speaker sat on a stool at the head of the table. Following his lead, Gideon seated himself at the speaker's right, on one of the many gilded-wood benches that lined either side of the table, and rested his staff against the bench at his side. Terebin, Ammiel and Magan took the seats to Gideon's right, while Aybel, Revel and Kyrintha seated themselves directly across from him, to the speaker's left. Gideon was struck by how much smaller a group they had become in the past few days. The Barrens had claimed so many of the priests. And Telus.

"Don't be sad, Waymaker," commanded the speaker with a warm grin and a glint in his eye. "This is a night to rejoice!" He raised his goblet as he stood to his feet. "Thanks be to the teacher," he bellowed to the room, "who has brought the Waymaker and his friends safely to us. This is a new day. A new day, indeed!" He swung the goblet around in delight and sloshed its contents on the decorative display, then swigged it down like a sailor before retaking his seat.

Gideon reached to take a drink, but was stopped by Terebin's hand. "Wait," he said, and took the goblet from Gideon. Whispering Words over its contents, he quickly passed it back. "We sense no taint," said Terebin quietly, "but it is best to be certain."

Gideon nodded. "What do you make of this, Terebin?" he whispered. "A place like this, these people, this food. How can these things be here in the Barrens?"

"I cannot say," replied Terebin. "I've never seen its like. All I can tell you is that the Desolation is never to be trusted. Especially not here, within the Fallen Wood."

"Are you saying this is all a deception?" asked Gideon.

Terebin shook his head. "The food is clean, Waymaker. That much I know. But I do not understand it. As for these 'people'—"

"What has you two whispering so intently?" the speaker broke in. "Come, Waymaker, tell me, won't you? There need be no secrets here."

But it was Terebin who replied. "We were wondering how you came by the fish? We have always known the dark souls to loathe the waters offshore."

The affront was blunt, even for Terebin. The speaker lips twitched into a subtle grin. "There are no dark souls here," he said.

"That is not possible!" exclaimed Terebin. "Do you not know where you are? Where we sit at this moment? What surrounds us on all sides?"

"Yes, priest. I know what this place is," said Darind, his voice suddenly hard. "But I wonder if you do."

"Forgive me, speaker," Revel interrupted, "but I have a question of a personal nature." Gideon recognized that Revel was trying to diffuse the tension in the room, and breathed a sigh of gratitude.

"It's about your name—Darind Reach," Revel continued, "and that of the girl Grace as well. I can't help but wonder if your naming traditions are similar to our own. If you don't mind, how did you come by your name?"

The speaker's smile returned bigger than ever. "Darind is the name the teacher gave me. I didn't have a name before that."

"And Reach?" asked Revel.

"Reach is the name given me by the sounden, once there were enough of them to decide such things."

"It's an unusual name, Reach," said Kyrintha. "What does it mean?"

"They named me 'Reach' because I was the first among us to reach out to the teacher for help. And because, after I came to know him, I reached out to many others to bring them to him as well."

"Then the naming process is quite similar," said Revel. "In the Remnant, our first names are given by our parents, as a prophecy and a hope of who we might become. Our second name is given to us by the community, but not until our fourteenth year, so the people have sufficient time to experience our true nature, and call it forth in the naming."

"Yes," said Darind, "it is much the same for us. But here, the teacher is the parent of us all."

"Where did the teacher come from?" asked Revel. "How did he get here?"

"I don't know," replied Darind. "He simply appeared one day in the midst of the wood. At first, we all feared him. We sensed he was very powerful. Even the land itself dared not challenge him. But wherever we fled, he pursued us. He never attacked, but he was never far. Finally, one day, he came to me in a field of thorns, and I did not run away. I am not sure, even now, why I didn't run. Something in me, or perhaps something in him, told me I didn't have to. In any case, without really thinking about what I was doing, I reached out and touched him." A sudden swell of tears filled his eyes. "My life, my true life, began that day."

"I do not think we can wait until tomorrow to see the teacher," said Gideon. "We need to know who he is, and if he really is the one who drew me here."

The speaker smiled. "I understand completely. Believe me, I do! But you see it is not up to me—or you, for that matter!" He laughed, and took another swig of the wine. "The teacher will see you at first light on the morrow, after you are rested. That is the way of it." He shrugged, as if to say there was nothing more to discuss. "For now, eat! Enjoy. And once you are filled, you will sleep the sweetest sleep I dare say you have had in many years."

37

WORDHAVEN

How lonely sits the city that was once full of light!
She has become like a widow, a sojourner weeping bitterly in the night.
She dwells among the heights, but she has found no rest.
Her pursuers have overtaken her in the midst of her distress.
Her roads are in mourning; her gates, desolate.
Because her adversaries have become her masters, and her lovers have gone away.
— From the writings of the Prophet Silmar, in the year S.C. 1320

They're coming in for another strike!" Brasen Stonegard yelled to his men, his voice amplified by the Words to carry across Wordhaven's valley. "Hold staffs at ready, warriors. Wait for earshot, on my command."

From his vantage high on Wordhaven's glistening black walls, Ajel watched as the distant squadron of warriors—a few dozen strong—raised their focus staffs in unison toward the approaching squadron of juron. There were nine this time, more than any previous attack, each mounted by one of the Council's *mon'jalen*, flying in from the north.

In the beginning, the siege force outside Wordhaven's gates had sent only a handful of juron over the ridge. They would appear every few days, soaring in from the heights to the east or north where the ridges were lowest, and attacking a different region of the valley each time. They were not earnest attacks, Ajel knew. The *mon'jalen* were merely looking for weaknesses, probing the Remnant's defenses for possible gaps where Balaam's larger force might be able to gain a foothold within the valley once it arrived. Only one such probe had dared approach the Stand itself, and had learned too late that the Stand would tolerate no utterance of *Sa'lei* within earshot of its walls. All three *mon'jalen* were vaporized before their captain had finished forming the Word on his tongue.

In recent days, however, the attacks had grown more frequent and more aggressive, though they remained small in number, and were still careful to stay on the far end of the valley away from the Stand's Worded walls. Even so, they were no longer merely probing. They're objective had changed.

"They mean to draw out more of our forces," said Donovan as he stepped out on the balcony. No doubt, he had read Ajel's thoughts. "The lords want to see what they're up against before Balaam's horde arrives."

Suddenly, Brasen Stoneguard's voice echoed across the valley. "Now!" A chorus of voices rose up from the valley floor in response to Brasen's command, all yelling in unison the sweet and terrible sounds of *Dei'lo*. Instantly, dozens of lightening bolts, white as pure gypsum, erupted from the tips of the warriors' staffs, each targeting one of the nine mounted juron swooping in from above. *Sa'lei* shields erupted to life, crackling red with fire and rage, then just as quickly collapsed under the strain of the Wordhaveners' attack. Within seconds, nearly half of the juron were either blasted to oblivion or else dropping like dead birds from the sky. The remaining *mon'jalen* quickly retreated back up to the heights.

Ajel grinned. "That's why you've limited Brasen to only one squadron of fighters."

Donovan nodded. "No more than three dozen warriors are allowed out in the open at any one time. If our enemy wishes to spy out our strength, let them see as we want them to see. I mean them to believe our force is many times smaller than is actually true."

"If only our forces were truly as large as we had hoped," sighed Ajel. "I am thankful for the seven hundred who answered the call of the Sacred Path, but in truth I had expected many more. Do the soundens not see that we are fighting for their freedom as much as our own?"

"Courage is abundant in the heart of a man until it he is called upon to show it," Donovan snipped. "We must make do with what we have been given. Besides, it is not all up to these volunteers. We also have eighteen hundred ready warriors of our own. That is more than a match for Varia and her one hundred *mon'jalen*."

"But not nearly enough for the horde that follows in her wake," said Ajel. "Even with Wordhaven's defenses fully awakened, we cannot hope to hold back an army of *jalen* ten thousand strong. Their sound cannons alone could shatter this mountain within a day's time."

"*Dei'lo* is powerful," countered Donovan, "and the Stand is a fortress more secure than any I have known. I believe we can successfully resist them...perhaps for a long time."

Ajel frowned at the prospect. "I'm not interested in resisting them, Donovan. I'm interested in defeating them. And what we have now, however good it is, is not enough for that."

"What do you propose?"

"We need a new strategy," said Ajel. "One that Balaam cannot foresee. One that calls for new allies."

"Speaking of new strategies," replied Donovan, pointing to the distant skies "look there."

Ajel squinted toward the late morning sun. "What is Varia up to now?"

What appeared at first as a dark shadow on the sun gradually fluttered beyond its glare and took the form a flock of birds. Ajel had seen them a dozen times before in recent weeks, and recognized them instantly as juron. But never before had there been so many.

"I see at least two hundred," said Ajel.

"More like three hundred, I'd say," corrected Donovan. His black eyes glistened with sudden intensity. "Where have they been hiding so many *mon'-jalen*? We never counted more than a hundred in their camp. And what of the beasts? Of them, we've never seen more than twenty!" He spit and slammed his fist against the black stone rail. "Varia has been playing me for a fool!"

"A discussion for another time, Head of Arms" said Ajel sharply. "Brasen and his squadron are still in the meadows. Go to him, now! Summon a full division of warriors. I don't want a single *mon'jalen* to fly out of this place alive."

"By your word, Paladin," Donovan bowed, and whispering the Words, disappeared.

Moments later, over a thousand warriors appeared on the meadows, materializing out of the air in waves as if uncovered by a succession of invisible veils. They quickly formed into regiments and squadrons, each one stationing itself on the meadow according to Donovan's predetermined plan. The ominous cloud of black juron shifted its course in response, like locusts on the hunt, bearing down on the Wordhaven fighters below. Shields flared to life both above and below, each side anticipating the instant when the sound of their voices would be close enough to kill.

What does she mean to gain by this? wondered Ajel. *Perhaps she aims to thin our ranks in advance of Balaam's arrival. But if so, why now? Balaam's forces are still several weeks away.*

Again, considerations for another time. For now, Ajel needed to go prepare the second division for battle, should their voices be called for to defend the Stand. Picturing the Outer Hall in his mind, he breathed the Words to carry him there, and disappeared.

Down in the meadows, Donovan surveyed the mass of leather-garbed warriors surrounding him on all sides, their staffs raised and eyes trained on the approaching cloud of *mon'jalen*. More than half were Wordhaveners—many of them friends he had known for years. The rest came from the soundens, distinguished only by the deeper fear he sensed from their hearts. But few, even the most seasoned of Wordhaven's elite, had ever experienced open battle on this scale before. By the end of this day, even if the battle ended in victory, he knew those who survived would be forever changed. And not for the better.

As the cloud of juron approached the line beyond which the Words' of death could be dealt, he lifted his sword toward the late-morning sun. "To the Words!" he bellowed, his voice magnified by the whispers of *Dei'lo*. "Let these vermin feel the power of your united voice!"

Instantly, a thundering chorus rose up in the air, and more than a thousand shafts of white lighting bolted toward the skies—each one targeting a specific rider, just as the warriors had been taught. The red hue of three hundred *Sa'lei* shields crackling to life dimmed the skies, and the walls of Wordhaven moaned in response to the presence of *Sa'lei* so close to its chambers. Dozens of *mon'jalen* plummeted from the sky, their unmounted juron beating their wings skyward in blind panic. Those that were not slain by the lightning were maimed by the fall. But a few managed the Words to land without injury, and were quickly encircled by the warriors on the ground.

Unlike in previous attacks, however, this time the *mon'jalen* who remained aloft did not retreat. Instead, they lashed out with black lightning and wind, seeking to corral Donovan's forces closer to the forest to the south of Wordhaven's gate. A haze of blue light gleamed above the mass as the fighters fought to stave off the wind.

"Hold your ground!" commanded Donovan, his booming voice carried on the winds of the attack. Brasen Stoneguard quickly echoed the command from his position on the eastern flank. But on the northern front of the division where the black lightning struck hardest, many shields buckled and screams arose to fill the air with sorrow and dread. "Hold your ground!" Donovan commanded again. *They mean to push us south against the mountain!*

As if to disprove the thought, however, several scores of *mon'jalen* suddenly broke formation with the main Council force and dived straight for the western flank. White lightning flared in waves from the ground below, setting several of the juron and their riders ablaze in mid flight. Yet many of the red shields held. As the *mon'jalen* neared the ground, they leapt from their beasts and drifted on Word-wrought winds to the earth. The juron, however, plunged on, slamming into the front line of warriors with the crazed ferocity of bears protecting their young. The creatures tore through the shields as if they were paper, rending the flesh of many before their fellow warriors could come to their aid. These summoned new shields to guard from physical attack, then dispatched the beasts with fire or earth or some other Word-wrought weapon of death.

By the time Donovan reached the line, the juron had all been destroyed. But the damage was done. Dozens of warriors lay splayed across the field, many of them severed in two from the swath of the juron's powerful claws. The line was weakened and confused, just as the *mon'jalen* had planned. Screaming their hate at the disheveled line, dozens of the Remnant fighters still alive turned to flame, and set off running in every direction in the madness of their pain. The Word was not the usual one employed by *jalen*; the Remant warriors did not turn to ash. Rather, it was a slow, suffering burn, like falling into fire and not being able to rise. They were being cooked alive.

"Water! Call forth water from the stream! Douse them! Douse them!" cried Donovan to the warriors. He did not wait to see if they heard him or understood. Instead, he turned his angry stare upon the *mon'jalen* themselves. Brandishing his sword, he charged through what line remained and barreled toward the cluster of Council warriors, summoning a throng of shields as he ran. They must have recognized him, for a few stepped back as he approached, hesitant. But they were at least thirty strong, perhaps more, and their numbers emboldened them to stand their ground. They had no need to run, even from a former Firstsworn.

"Elo adversum nepolar'en patreem!" Donovan's Words rumbled like thunder from his angry throat. The earth beneath the feet of the *mon'jalen* rose like a sheet from the ground and, closing like an open hand clenches to a fist, enveloped them all. Their shields could not bear the strain of it, and quickly shattered one by one. But a few called forth Words to blast holes in the earthen tomb, and escaped, fleeing to the north toward the Stand. Donovan let them go. Ajel would deal with them, or if not him, the fortress itself, if they were foolish enough to venture too close to its walls.

Turning back to the fray, Donovon caught site of Brasen floating in the air within a sphere of flight, along with several other captains on the eastern line. *Mon'jalen* had apparently landed there too, though no sign remained of the beasts that carried them. A fury of fire and tempests of wind swirled around the battlefield, but Donovan could not see exactly where the *mon'jalen* were, or how many of them remained on the ground.

The rest of the attack force, still nearly two hundred strong, remained in the skies above, pummeling the ranks of Wordhaven warriors with barrage after barrage of dark power—be it fire or acid or wind or stone. Their attacks varied, but each one was met head on with equal power from below, and even greater fervor. Donovan could feel the swell of courage in the ranks of his men, and taste the pride with which these green warriors now fought. The battle's end was far from certain, but at last the fighters of Wordhaven could see with their own eyes that the Tongue of *Dei'lo* was every bit a match and more for anything the *mon'jalen* could throw at them. Until this moment, Donovan realized, it had all been merely hope. Only now, in the desperate work of battle, was their faith made real.

Along the northern front, from the river that divded the valley, a water-spout rose, quickly towering some three hundred feet into the air. It had the sense of *Dei'lo* about it, though Donovan could not say who had summoned it. A Wordhavener, for sure, for such a feat was beyond the language of any sounden warrior. Its funnel turned like a gaping mouth toward the ranks of *mon'jalen* circling above, and lunged toward them like a snake.

The *mon'jalen* veered to avoid the strike, but some were drawn inside the vortex and torn apart, right along with their beasts. Circling away, the main force summoned winds from above to try to push the funnel back toward the Remnant battle line. But the spout's own winds intensified in response, and continued unabated, forcing the line of juron back toward the north, away from the main body of the Wordhaven division.

We are here, Donovan. The thought was Ajel's, and the echo of it drew Donovan's gaze to a lone, blond-haired figure standing along the river bank. With arms extended, the man was directing the breadth and movement of the windstorm with the graceful focus of a sculptor shaping a mound of clay.

Ajel, said Donovan in his mind. *You are here?*

Let us be done with this.

The funnel continued to press against the line of juron, pushing them back until there was a substantial distance between them and the Remnant force. Then, in the open space between them, the entire second division of Wordhaven's forces began to materialize. The instant they appeared, they raised high their focus staffs and with their voices launched a fresh barrage of white lightning into the skies. A cheer arose from the ranks of the first division, who quickly joined their kinsmen in a chorus of white death, thunder and storm. More than two thousand bolts of lightning shot skyward all at once. It appeared as a brilliant sheet of raw energy, so thick with power that it outmatched the sun. The sound of it deafened Donovan's ears, and shocked his vision so he could no longer even tell if the bolts were reaching their intended marks. Indeed, he could no longer see any juron at all.

Ajel, who guards the Stand? Donovan demanded, shielding his eyes. *We agreed your division would remain at the walls.*

Do not fret, kinsman,, came Ajel's voice in his mind. *These* mon'jalen *are not here to defeat us; merely to thin our numbers in advance of Balaam's arrival. I do not intend to let them take even one more life this day.*

This is not wise, Ajel. You have exposed our numbers. If but one of them escapes to inform Varia of our strength—

None shall.

Donovan slammed his fist in his palm. *Why appoint me Head of Arms over Wordhaven if you will not follow my counsel! This is not wise, Paladin.*

Look up, Donovan, came the calm reply. *The battle is nearly done.*

Donovan did look, and saw the smoke of white fires clearing from the sky. The waterspout dispersed, dissolving into a misty vapor that drifted in a cloud above the battlefield. Behind the mists, he saw scores of juron ablaze, darting in circles in madness and pain, their riders clinging to their backs as if frozen to them. Their skin was as black as their uniforms, and their expressions, those few Donovan could make out, were locked in a state of agony and shock. Meanwhile, others, many others, lay sprawled on the meadows below aside their juron, scorched and smoking and as still as death.

Only a few *mon'jalen* remained untouched, by luck perhaps. But they were panicked and confused. There was no cohesion among them anymore. They ran or flew this way and that, and the Remnant warriors were quickly pursuing them, with both Word and body. Soon enough, they too would be cut down.

"You see?" Ajel appeared beside him, grinning as if he'd just won his first race. "It is better this way. We are rid of Varia's pestering attacks once and for all. She should never have sent in her full force all at once. She got arrogant and overreached herself."

"I would say the same to you, Paladin!" Donovan snapped. "There was no need to commit our full force to this battle. It is luck that saved us this day, not strategy. We must never allow our enemy draw our forces completely away from the Stand. Protecting the Stand is our highest objective—in this battle or any other!"

"You are lecturing me, Donovan?" asked Ajel, his tone decidedly more sharp. "Look around you. The battle is won."

"You rule Wordhaven, Paladin," said Donovan coolly. "Let no one question that. But this I ask: Do not call on me to defend these gates or lead the charge against the Council Lords unless you are willing to abide by my counsel in matters of war!"

Just then, the ground beneath their feet began to rumble and shake. From the bowels of the mountain a tremendous explosion sprang forth, shattering the entire cliff face north of Wordhaven's walls. The sound of it was ominous and hard, like that of a hundred thousand mounts galloping on stone. A second equally malevolent explosion followed, farther to the east—then a third, and fourth, quickly encircling the valley in a cacophony of destruction, rubble and dust. Great plumes of rock and smoke billowed upward on all sides, filling the skies in a matter of seconds with a black cloud of foreboding.

"It is an eruption!" exclaimed Ajel. "We must lead the forces back to the safety of the Stand. Quickly!"

"No, wait!" said Donovan, gripping Ajel's arm. "This has the feel of something far worse. Look!"

From out of the ash of the first explosion, a wind began to swirl. Within seconds, it grew to a height and breadth far greater than the funnel Ajel had summoned. Then in the blink of an eye, it turned to fire, and began to billow forward, cutting a swath of fiery desctruction as it roared into the valley. Three more of the firestorms appeared soon after the first, each rising from the ash and rubble of destruction the explosions had left in their wake, until they all towered over the valley like fiery sentinels of death.

Behind the advancing cyclones of fire, swarms of guardians poured forth from the darkness, raising a thunderous cry of Worded blight upon the rich earth of Wordhaven's valley as they ran.

"There are so many of them!" exclaimed Donovan gravely. "A thousand, perhaps more. Where could she hide thousands from our eyes?"

"A question for later, Head of Arms!" Ajel snapped, slapping Donovan squarely on the back. "However she did it, Lord Varia is here. War has come to Wordhaven! Come!"

SOLIDARI SOUNDEN

His vesture was like white snow and the hair of his head like pure wool.
His throne was ablaze with flames, a single Word of burning fire.
A river of fire was flowing and coming out from before him;
Thousands upon thousands were attending him,
and myriads upon myriads were standing before him;
He sat, and the Book was opened.

— From the writings of the Prophet Shikinah, in the year S.C. 1610

Gideon's sleep may have been sweet, but on first light, he awakened with a start. His heart pounded in his chest as if confronting a great battle. But slowly then, the memory of where he was flooded back into his mind. Reaching for the staff nestled beside him in the bed, he rose to peer out the open window near the door.

The speaker had escorted them to separate quarters—small one-room cabins side by side, arrayed in an arc next to the clearing in the sounden's heart. Each cabin contained only a bed and a small lamp that sat beside it on the wooden floor. But the bed was large and more comfortable than anything Gideon had experienced since his brief stay with Galad and Saravere in the citadel of the Cal'eeb priests.

Despite the early hour, the sounden was already alive with activity.

Scores of soundenors slithered and scurried here and there across the clearing, carrying wood or food or tools of various kinds in their mishappen arms. Some gathered in clusters and spoke in hushed whispers, which sounded to Gideon a little too much like the hissing of snakes. How could a place like this be safe for him and his team? And yet the staff was as cool as the morning air, and he felt no fear.

Suddenly, Kyrintha appeared outside. His presence at the window clearly startled her. "Waymaker," she said, composing herself. "I came to see if you had risen."

"I have," said Gideon. "Good morning."

"I wanted you to know something," she said, sounding matter of fact. "I didn't want to say anything about it last night."

"What is it?"

"This place...this sounden," she said. "I think it is the sounden once known as Solidari. It is included on many of the older maps I have studied, the ones from before the time of Gideon's Fall."

"What of it?" asked Gideon.

"If my memory serves, Solidari had a large port, from which the sounden drew its livelihood. If some portion of the port still exists, or if they have rebuilt it—"

"Then they might also have ships," Gideon broke in.

"Yes," said Kyrintha. "The fish we ate last night sparked my memory of it. They must have boats to draw in a catch of that size. Still, their boats may not be suited for long journeys on the open sea."

"But if they are, then it sure beats the thought of going back the way we came," added Gideon, grinning.

Kyrintha nodded. "I thought you should know."

"Thanks."

"The others have already risen, and have gathered with the speaker at the teacher's house. I have come to bring you to them."

"I'm ready," said Gideon, feeling suddenly anxious. "Let's go meet this mysterious 'teacher.'"

Gathering his staff, Gideon followed as the underlord led him across the clearing and into the woods on the west side. As they walked, Gideon's heart started pounding so hard that it quickly began to ache. The pull within him, which had diminished somewhat when they first entered the sounden, now erupted within his breast like a living fire. He could not tell if it was a sign of danger, or merely anticipation. Could it be that this "teacher," whoever he was, had somehow managed to locate the Pearl, and now harnessed its power to rule these riftborn souls? Since arriving in the sounden, he had tried hard not to dwell on the possibility for fear of raising his expectations. But he couldn't block out his hope any longer. The ache in his heart was undeniable.

Suddenly, Kyrintha stopped.

"Are you lost?" asked Gideon.

"The girl was to meet us here," replied Kyrintha, looking around, "beside this old *bian'ar* tree." She glanced at Gideon. "No one is permitted to approach the teacher's house without an escort."

Gideon nodded. "Oh." Anxious to get on with it, he busied himself surveying their surroundings. The old *bian'ar* tree looked to be more than twenty feet across at the base, and stretched so far into the sky that its height was obscured by the clouds that had blown in that morning from the sea. Its dark chocolate bark looked mottled and worn, and tough as old leather. He reached out to touch it, but then thought better of it. "Is it safe for us to be out here without our cloaks?" he asked.

"Yes," said Kyrintha, "or so say the priests. The speaker claims that the region all the way to the shore has been cleansed of defilement."

"By the teacher..." said Gideon.

"I suppose," said Kyrintha. "The speaker didn't say."

Gideon decided not to touch the tree, just in case. He had felt the bark of many *bian'ar* before anyway, in Strivenwood. But he was too preoccupied with surviving back then to pay them much mind. Brushing past Kyrintha, he wandered around the base to a small clearing on the other side. The tree's size was certainly notable, but it did not lack for company. Dozens of other *bian'ars* surrounded it, each nearly as large. One could not help but feel like an ant in such a wood. High above them, just below the misty clouds, bridges draped the high branches like elegant decorations, linking tree to tree and hut to hut. He wondered what means the soundenors used to climb up and down from such a height.

"Waymaker."

The girl stood before him, appearing as if out of nowhere. She looked much younger and more fragile than she had the day before when she silenced the crowd.

"Hello, Grace," he said.

"This way," she replied, gesturing west toward the sea. She turned and walked off without waiting to see if he would follow.

"Kyrintha," Gideon called, but by the time he said it, she had already appeared from behind the old tree. They trailed after Grace without further comment.

The treed houses continued to climb in height as they passed deeper into the wood, until becoming obscured entirely by the mists. Gideon wondered just how high a tree they would have to climb to reach the teacher's dwelling. But upon skirting one of the massive trunks, Grace led them into a clearing large enough to allow a clear view of the sky, veiled though it was at present by the clouds. In its center sat a tent of woven *bian'ar* leaves, about twenty feet wide and half as high. Stationed in a half circle around it stood Aybel, Revel and the Trevail priests, all looking somewhat wary and tense. The speaker stood much closer to the tent, leaning toward the draped entrance as if listening to whatever was going on inside.

"Your teacher lives in a tent?" asked Gideon. But Grace did not turn around. Approaching the entrance, she called for the speaker, who beamed with delight at the sight of Gideon and the underlord.

"There! There you are," he said in a loud whisper. "Come, come. Wait here with me. The teacher will be with us shortly."

Gideon's heart began to pound even more fiercely than before. He couldn't help but worry that this feeling was a warning of danger. But the staff, for the moment anyway, remained cool. "What's he doing?" asked Gideon.

"Oh," grinned the speaker and shaking his head, "The teacher's business is his own. It's not for me to tell. Most of the time, truly, I'm not sure at all." He sighed quietly as if the thought were somehow comforting.

Terebin approached, nodding curtly toward the speaker before addressing Gideon. "Waymaker, may I speak with you privately?" He did not look happy. But then, he never did. They walked some distance from the speaker before the priest felt secure enough to talk. "There is something unnatural here," he said. "I do not think we should remain."

Gideon gripped the staff a little more tightly. "What is it?"

"I do not know," said Terebin, clearly unnerved by the fact. "Neither can the others say with certainty what it is. But something is not right. There is…a presence."

"A presence?" Gideon felt a rush of adrenaline as memories of Kiki and the Isle of Edor flashed through his mind. That horror, too, had begun with the sensing of a presence. "Has Revel felt this as well?"

"He most of all," affirmed Terebin. "It was he who noticed it first." His tattooed jaw tensed in frustration. "We have surveyed in every direction for a quarter league or more. The land has been purged clean, right down to the soil. I cannot explain how. And yet, something is not right. We should leave. Now."

"We can't," said Gideon, shaking his head. "Not yet. Not until we see this 'teacher.' Just give it a few more minutes. Keep a sharp eye. We'll leave as soon as we can."

Terebin nodded, but was clearly not pleased. "Stay close to me," he said, "and the other priests."

"You there, priest, stop coddling the Waymaker," called the speaker, now not whispering at all, "and come back over here now. It's time, it's time!" He stood at the tent's entrance, bouncing in an excitement that bordered on dancing. "Come here now, get ready!"

Gideon and Terebin walked cautiously toward the entrance. The rest of the group gathered around them as well, including Grace. Her presence gave Gideon a vague sense of reassurance. If this was a trap, surely they wouldn't have the little girl here. Would they?

Gideon's gait was apparently too slow for the speaker, for he marched out toward him and latched onto his arm. "That's right, this way. Come stand at the entrance. You want to be ready when he appears."

Gideon shook his arm free of the speaker's grip. "Ready for what?" he asked suspiciously.

But right then the drapes at the entrance of the tent flew wide, and a portly man came bounding out, his fat hands raised in anticipation. He locked Gideon into a smothering bear hug before the Waymaker knew what was happening. "Dear boy, dear boy!" The muffled voice rumbled into Gideon's leather jerkin. "Thank you! Thank you! By the Giver, I thank you!"

"Gideon, away!" cried Aybel. "It is a trap!"

Suddenly Gideon felt a mass of muscle slam against his side, tumbling both him and the man to the ground. He saw Revel's elbow jam between them and plunge hard into the fat man's throat, forcing him to relinquish his hold on Gideon and roll away from the strike.

"*Adoni shamar'sus!*" cried Revel, and a shield of brilliant blue crackled to life around both him and the Waymaker. The man lay stunned on the ground a few feet away, his fingers gingerly touching his throat. It took only a moment to recognize his face.

"Balaam!" cried Gideon in disbelief. *The High Lord. But how?*

Shields materialized around them all, including the priests, though they had never seen the man before. The speaker, meanwhile, rushed over to the High Lord of the Council and covered him with his own body as if to protect him from further harm. He raised his hands and screamed something at them, but the shield prevented Gideon from hearing it.

"This is your teacher?" Gideon spat. "Don't you know who this is? This man has no interest in helping you or your people. He is nothing but a tyrant and a sadistic beast! Move away from him, speaker, or you will share his fate!"

But the speaker shook his head no, his hands still raised pleading for mercy. Words poured fervently from his lips, but Gideon couldn't hear them.

"Aybel and I do not have the strength to resist the High Lord, Waymaker," said Revel. "The priests may, but I cannot say that for certain. We must strike him now before his throat recovers, or else retreat from here with great haste. Which shall we do?"

"I don't know, Revel!" snapped Gideon. "It doesn't make sense. What's he doing here?"

"If you mean to stay and find the answer, you must prepare to fight him," said Revel. "What of your staff?"

Gideon ran his hand along the gilded wood. "It's cold," he said. "It doesn't sense the danger for some reason."

"The staff has nothing to do with that!" exclaimed Revel. "Look within yourself, Waymaker. What do *you* sense?"

For a few moments, Gideon just stood there, staring at the High Lord, who was still lying on the ground gripping his neck in obvious pain. The speaker knelt beside him, trying to help him sit up, but Balaam was having none of it.

"You nailed him pretty good," said Gideon finally.

"Waymaker!" exclaimed Revel. "There is no time—!"

"Lower the shield," said Gideon.

"What?"

"Lower the shield." He turned to Revel. "It's okay. Really, lower the shield."

Revel sighed worriedly. "As you wish—"

"But..." Gideon raised a finger.

"Yes?"

"Be ready," said Gideon, "just in case I'm wrong." He grinned.

Revel rolled his eyes, then spoke the Words to dissolve the shield. Aybel and the priests, however, continued to let theirs stand. With the shield down, Gideon could hear the sound of Balaam's labored weezing as he tried to draw air through his damaged wind pipe. His eyes were wide in panic. The speaker had given up trying to get the High Lord to stand, and was now attempting to drag his bulbous body back toward the tent.

"This man is evil," said Gideon to the speaker. "Whatever he has said to you about who he is or what he wants—it's a lie. He has tried to kill me and my friends on many occasions—"

"As you just now tried to kill him?" snapped the speaker, still tugging feverishly on the High Lord's cloak. Even for a big man like the speaker, the High Lord's size was proving to be a challenge. "Priests, why do you just stand there?" he barked. "You can heal his injury with a Word, can you not?"

"I don't think they can hear you," said Gideon. "Those shields around them are probably blocking out everything."

"Then what of you, Waymaker?" bellowed the speaker. "Will you not prevent this man's death? By the Giver, at least help me drag him to the tent!"

But Gideon's face remained set like stone. "The world would be better without him," he said. "He is not a worthy teacher for your people."

"Teacher?" bellowed the speaker. "Teacher?! This man is not the teacher! He is a trueborn soul from beyond the Desolation, same as you."

"If that is so," Revel interjected, "then why is he here?"

"Same as you," repeated the speaker. "Same as you all. He came in the night while you were sleeping. To see the teacher. He is no danger to you. Though you clearly are to him!" With one last heave, the speaker finally pulled Balaam's body to the threshold of the tent. The High Lord was gasping loudly. His face was starting to turn blue.

"Wait," said Gideon. He walked over to the High Lord and cautiously knelt beside him. Balaam's eyes followed his movements, but his face remained locked in an almost childlike expression of shock and alarm. "You know he could destroy us all with a single Word," Gideon said to the speaker. "He could destroy your whole sounden."

"He has as much right to be here as any of us, Waymaker," the speaker replied. "I do not fear him, as I do not fear you, nor the priests, nor any of my people."

Gideon smirked. "Well maybe you should start. A little fear might just keep you alive."

"No," said the speaker, grabbing Gideon's wrist, "you do not understand. Where fear rules, there can be no love. And love is the only way." He squeezed Gideon's wrist. "Please," he said. "Heal him."

Suddenly, a voice of authority resonated in the chamber of Gideon's thoughts. *Do not be afraid. He will not harm you.*

Images of the fiery man in the forest from Gideon's dreams flashed across his mind. He saw the white robe, torn at the breast. He remembered the echo of his final words. *Speak pure, and you will not fail.* The impact of it left him stunned and shaken.

"Waymaker, what is it?" Revel leaped to his side, ready to pull him away from the High Lord.

But Gideon raised his hand to stop him. In that moment, he suddenly knew what he had to do. "Heal him, Revel," commanded Gideon. "Quickly."

But Revel shook his head. "No, Waymaker, this is not—"

"Do it!" commanded Gideon again. "The others are shielded and ready, should he try anything. But he won't."

"How can you be certain?" demanded Revel. "You of all people know what he is capable of!"

"Stop arguing with me, Revel!" snapped Gideon. "I don't know how I know. But I am the Waymaker, right? And I'm telling you, this is the way. Heal him!"

Revel stared at him a moment, then slowly nodded his head. He looked to Aybel and Kyrintha, and then to the priests, as if to warn them of what he was about to do. Their shields hummed quietly in the morning air as they looked on, their faces each reflecting a mix of readiness and confusion. But no one said a word. Finally, Revel let his gaze fall on Balaam's tortured face, and spoke the Words to undo the injury he had caused.

A flood of color rushed into Balaam's cheeks, and he sucked in a series of full, noisy breaths, replenishing his depleted lungs. The speaker whispered his thanks as the High Lord's breathing slowed to normal. Finally, he blinked and swallowed, and rubbed his throat. And then he smiled. "I suppose I should have expected that," he said. "The Giver knows I deserved it."

"Measure your words carefully, Council!" warned Revel. "You are still only a breath away from death even now."

But Balaam didn't pay him any heed. Instead, he looked at Gideon. "Finally," he said. "Finally, I have found you! Thank you, my boy. Thank you."

"Don't thank me yet, old man," said Gideon. "I may yet let them kill you."

"You have nothing to fear from me, my boy," said Balaam, smiling. "I'm free, you see. You set me free."

"*I* set you free?" asked Gideon, stunned by the suggestion. "Free from what?"

"From the grip of *Sa'lei*," he replied. "You showed me the path. Forced me down it, really. Tell me, is it all right if I get up? This is an uncomfortable way to carry on a conversation."

"Of course, of course," said the speaker, interjecting himself between them and smiling once again. Grabbing onto Balaam's arm, he began to help him to his feet.

"Waymaker, what is happening?" cried Aybel, clearly distressed by what she was seeing from behind her shield. The rest of the group looked equally panicked.

"Revel, go explain to them what's happening," instructed Gideon. "Tell them to adjust their shields so they can hear the common tongue. But warn them not to act unless Balaam begins to speak *Sa'lei*."

Revel nodded and rose to his feet. "They will be quick to strike you down, Council, should you try anything—as will I. Move slowly, and let your words be few." With that, he walked away.

Balaam frowned at the warning, but said nothing, and let the speaker help him to his feet. As he stood, Gideon readied his staff to strike, targeting Balaam's throat once more. "Now, explain yourself, Balaam," Gideon commanded. "Why have you really come here?"

"To find you, of course," replied Balaam, almost happily. "You began my journey, and I knew you were the key to its end."

"What are you talking about?" warned Gideon. "I only want you dead."

Suddenly, Balaam looked sad. "Yes, I understand," he said. "I am truly sorry for all I have done to you. It was…it is…inexcusable. But I am free from that now. I am changed! Don't you see? There was a bigger purpose at work all along."

"You are talking nonsense," said Gideon. "Your lust for power has finally driven you mad."

"It was the Book, you see," continued Balaam unabated. "When your friend struck me with the Book, in the chamber beneath the Axis, it…it did something to me. It awakened something within me. The war it evoked within my soul made me gravely ill. I nearly died. And it did, in fact, very nearly drive me mad as well.

"But in my struggle against the madness, I searched the prophets of the Grey Ages, for I knew somehow that only in them would I find a way to heal the injury to my soul. And in their writings I finally found my way. Or rather, I found you. I know who you are, you see. It's all there, for anyone willing to seek it out. You are the Waymaker. The moment I realized it, I knew that only you could lead me to the answer."

"What answer?" asked Gideon incredulously.

Balaam smiled broadly. "The only answer that matters, my son." He reached for the tent, and slowly pulled back the drape that covered the entrance. "The answer to everything."

On the floor within, resting on a bundled cloth of shimmering purple, sat a glimmering orb of impossibly beautiful light.

Just one glimpse of it forced Gideon to his knees, as if, in that brief exchange, the weight of all creation had lighted upon his shoulders, and kissed him. His body crumpled under the burden of it, but his soul burned hot, instantly seared to the quick by the indescribable thickness of life. Why had he never seen this before? He suddenly felt as if he were standing on the sun. Absolute brilliance. Raptuous awe. And above it all, the icy gaping gulf of separation between the darkness and the light that should not be; that must be breached. It all burned him with a pain sweeter than any grace or beauty he had hoped to behold in his short miserable life.

"Come," said the Pearl in Gideon's thoughts. *"Come and see."*

Without hesitation, Gideon hobbled into the tent. The flap closed behind him with an unexpected resounding boom, sealing the entrance with the finality of thunder and heat.

THE TENT

I kept looking, and behold, a new beast arose,
dreadful and terrifying and extremely strong.
It had the eyes of a man
and a mouth uttering great and unbearable Words.
It devoured and crushed and trampled down.
And it was different from all the beasts that were before it.
— From the writings of the Prophet Shikinah, in the year S.C. 1610

Gideon!" Aybel cried, rushing toward the tent as she watched the flap seal behind him. "What deceit is this, Council?" she railed at Balaam. "What have you done to him?" Balaam quickly raised his hands and smiled as if in appeal, but his smug expression only enraged her more.

In the seconds it took to reach the tent, Revel had already shoved the High Lord aside and was running his hands along the seam of its entrance, looking for some way to grip the sealed curtain. A moment later, he looked at Aybel and shook his head no, his face etched with the same anger and fear that she herself felt.

Without hesitation, Aybel charged Balaam straight on, all fear of his considerable power forgotten, slamming him against the tent wall with her shield. Blue sparks crackled against his bulbous skin, but despite the obvious pain it caused him, he did not try to wriggle away. "You will tell me what you've done here," she spat, "or as the Giver lives, I will end you now!"

Despite the pain, Balaam's expression turned curiously soft. "I am the same as you," he whispered. "The same as him. The same as you all."

"Come now, lady, come now!" exclaimed the speaker, who once again found himself attempting to tug the High Lord away from harm. "What's all this?"

But then Revel's hand appeared at the High Lord's throat. He had slipped past the speaker's fumbling bulk as deftly as passing through an open door, but his expression looked as panicked as she felt. He had summoned no shield, which she thought foolish. Revel rarely did have the good sense to be wary of danger, even when it was staring him down the nose. At least the three Trevail priests still held their shields, and had gathered around them all in attack stance. They expressions were unreadable, but their eyes were clearly locked on Balaam's lips.

"If you so much as sigh except in response to our direct questions, I will crush your throat," growled Revel, "And this time I will leave it that way."

"Why are you all doing this?" Grace cried out suddenly. The girl stood to the side, clearly distraught by all the commotion. "He hasn't done anything! Speaker, why are they doing this?"

"I don't know, dear, I don't know," replied the speaker, his tone equally full of exasperation. He continued to try to pull the High Lord away from Aybel's shield, but to no effect. Revel's grip held him firmly in his place. "What fear has possessed you all?" demanded the speaker. "Why do you attack this man with such hate?"

"Release the Waymaker, Council," commanded Aybel. "Now."

"I am not holding him," rasped Balaam quietly.

"Liar!" cried Aybel.

"No, he speaks the truth!" exclaimed the speaker. "The Waymaker is in council with the teacher. The teacher summoned him, not his man! Did you not see him go in of his own accord? Now please, stop this!"

"Why is it sealed?" demanded Revel.

"I don't know!" the speaker replied. "That is the way of it sometimes. It is the teacher's choice, or the choice of those with whom he meets. It has nothing to do with anyone out here! When they are finished, the Waymaker will emerge. There is no need for concern. Now please, dear woman, won't you step away? Please." Darind seemed genuinely worried that the High Lord might suffer permanent harm from her shield. He clearly knew nothing of this pig's true nature, or of the true danger of this moment. His ignorance repulsed her.

"Your eyes are still as black as midnight, High Lord," Aybel said icily. "You are a slave to your Tongue. No word you speak will convince me otherwise."

"Everything I said to the Waymaker is true," Balaam replied hoarsely. "Your own Donovan Blade still bears the marks of his dark past. Why could it not also be true for me? Am I really beyond the Giver's mercy in your eyes?"

"I should strike you down even for speaking his name!" sneered Aybel. "Tell me, Council. What is your true purpose here?"

Balaam looked away, his lips tight and quivering as if her question had reawakened some deep tumult within him. He closed his eyes and tried to breath deeply, but the pressure of Aybel's shield cut him short. When he finally looked at her again, his black eyes were filled with tears. "Redemption," he whispered. "I am here to find my redemption."

At that moment, a small flock of birds appeared over the clearing, soaring in from the forest. They had the look of ordinary black gulls, but something about them seemed indistinct to Aybel, as if her eyes refused to focus on them directly. The sight of them left her feeling uneasy.

"I thought you said the teacher had purified the forest here," said Aybel to the speaker.

"He has, of course," the speaker replied. "It has been so for many years now."

"Those birds bear the taint of the Barrens," said Revel. "They are marked with darkness."

Aybel leaned into the High Lord, forcing fresh sparks to burn on the seared skin of his face. "Is this your doing, Council?"

"Lady, please," pleaded the speaker, still tugging on the High Lord's arm "They are only birds. If they are tainted by the desolation, they will not find rest here. Let them fly on by. You will see."

But the birds seemed in no rush to depart. Instead, they began to circle above them, playfully catching the updrafts of the morning thermals rising from the clearing.

"Revel, signal the Trevail priests to dispatch them," said Aybel. "Quickly!"

Revel nodded and begrudgingly released his hold on Balaam's throat. But just as he raised his hand to signal the shielded priests, the atmosphere in the clearing inexplicably darkened. Aybel looked up just in time to see the birds tuck in their wings and dive.

They were unnaturally fast. She had barely time enough to think of a Word to speak, but by the time she formed it on her lips, one of the birds was already upon her. It passed right through her shield as if it wasn't even there, and latched its claws upon her white hair. Furious, she flung up her hands to bat it away, but the moment she touched it the bird dissolved into ash and smoke, and its vapors floated wispily into her ears.

"*Lusifen hechton et shtek.*"

She recognized in horror the Words as *Salei'*, but in the hearing it was already too late. Her shield instantly vaporized. Her feet froze to the ground, immobile as if sealed in stone. And in that moment, she became mute.

Her piercing gaze locked accusingly on Balaam, whom no bird had attacked. But he shook his head no. In fact, he looked almost as alarmed as she felt. Revel's condition was no better than hers. Unable to speak, he could only glare his outrage at her through his golden eyes. The speaker and the girl were both equally immobile, looking up at the sky as if afraid more birds might come and do far worse. But Aybel did not expect that would happen. If whomever spoke the Words had wanted them dead, they would be already.

The Words had rendered her arms useless to her as well. They dangled from her shoulders like dead meat on a hook. But she could still turn her torso, and swivel her neck. Apparently, whoever immobilized them wanted them to retain the ability to watch. But watch what?

She turned to check on Kyrintha and the priests, and quickly confirmed that they suffered the same fate as she. Shieldless and immobile, the priests stood dumbfounded, glaring at their skin in horror. No doubt they wondered how the *Sa'lei* Words had slithered past their shields and tattoed defenses. How indeed?

Turning back, she glared at Balaam with renewed disgust. *Undo this!* she screamed at him in her thoughts. But he only stared at her vacantly, with a curious hint of fear touching his black, soulless eyes.

"Now," said Stevron, "we won't be bothered."

Aybel turned to see Lord Stevron Achelli arrogantly marching toward the tent, and frowned. She wasn't surprised. The young lord had been Balaam's attack hound from the beginning, hunting them since the night of their escape from Phallenar. He and Balaam had probably been setting this trap for Gideon for some time. No doubt he would be smug about it all, as would Balaam, who excitedly leaped out in front of the tent entrance to meet him.

"My son," he said, his voice nearly a whisper.

"Do not presume to call me son," said Stevron sharply. His harsh tone took Aybel by surprise, prompting her to examine Stevron's demeanor more closely. His expression remained calm, but his eyes were full of fury. "I've been listening, you see. I've been listening for some time. Yes, High Lord, even before these rebels found their way to you. I've heard every word that has spilled from your treacherous lips." His chin began to quiver, like a volcano on the verge. "Why, Father? Why have you betrayed me? Why have you betrayed us all—even your own bondmate?"

"Stevron, my son..." the High Lord stammered.

"The Waymaker is your son now!" bellowed Stevron. "Not me! From now on you will call me Master."

"Hear me, Stevron," Balaam pleaded. "Listen! I'm not mad! Not anymore. And I've not betrayed you. What I've done, I've done as much for you as for myself—and for Lysteria. Let me tell you what I've discovered."

"Traitor!" The word echoed through the clearing, booming with a force that shook the trees, and knocked Balaam back on his heels. "You have nothing of value to say to me," sneered Stevron. He clenched his fists. "I excelled beyond you a long time ago," he whispered. "But you were too busy using me to see it. You thought I was only your pawn. Your prize student! But now look at you. You're like a worm to me now. So small. So weak. The mere sight of you disgusts me!"

"Then take me," said Balaam, his voice suddenly hard. "I will go with you willingly. No doubt you wish to parade me before the Council, and name for them my many crimes, and thus claim your rightful place as my successor."

"Oh, I will take you," nodded Stevron. "But not before I finish what I came here to do."

"Stevron—" Balaam raised his hands.

"Master!" Stevron's voice boomed. "You will call me Master!" His scream forced Balaam to his knees. Aybel watched as he went down, but did not understand what she was seeing. Stevron was speaking in the common tongue. No *Sa'lei* had spilled from his lips that she could discern. And yet, somehow, his words still carried a palpable force. She did not understand how that could be.

"No, Stevron. No," Balaam pleaded, his black eyes spilling tainted tears upon the pure green grass. "Please don't make me! Please don't..."

"Make you what, High Lord?" asked Stevron mockingly. "Make you beg for your life? Make you grovel on the ground like the worm you really are?"

Balaam looked up. "No, my son," he said, tears streaming down his face. "Forgive me. *Damonoi hacht trell!*"

The Words grated against Aybel's ears, but she knew they were not aimed at her. But whatever they were meant to do to Stevron, they did not. For he merely laughed. The High Lord quickly stood to his feet, stunned.

"How like you, Father," said Stevron coldly. "Arrogant to the end."

Suddenly a shield erupted around the High Lord. Stevron, however, did not flinch, nor summon his own shield in response. Instead, he extended his arms, as if inviting the High Lord to attack him once again.

And, with tears still streaming down his face, that's just what the High Lord did. The abrasive tongue of *Sa'lei* poured out from Balaam's lips like blood gushing from a freshly-cut wound. He launched a tirade of destruction against Stevron, a barrage of Words so forceful and vile that the earth itself began to shake and the trees tremble at the sound of them. The world itself seemed to try to lean away from the sound of it as if desperate to escape a raging fire. But Stevron, still unshielded as far as Aybel could tell, remained unmoved. With his own outburst, he matched Balaam's onslaught Word for Word, somehow cancelling out every attack from Balaam's lips before it could take hold. He grinned maniacally as he railed against Balaam's booming voice, each of his own Word's seeming to fill him with greater and greater rapture and satisfaction.

Finally, Stevron raised his hand, and Balaam's shield collapsed. His body rose into the air. He was clearly exhausted, and shivering in the panic that comes on many in the moment they finally realize death is near. He stopped speaking in *Sa'lei*, and turned again to the common tongue.

"There is no profit in this road for you, my son," he said raspily. "In the end, it will not take you where you want to go."

Stevron closed his eyes. "Be quiet!" he murmured. "When, oh when, will you be quiet? You could have learned from me. You could have learned. But you were always too drunk with the sound of your own voice. Well, it's time for you to listen to *my* voice now, Father...and weep! *Abaddo detovestro ak curpecht!*"

The High Lord screamed. His body, like a morbid balloon, began to swell. And then, he simply exploded. His body, what little was left of it, splattered on all of them, and on the tent as well. But mostly, it landed on Stevron. His face and shoulders were now coated in a sickly red sheen.

As the mist of vaporous blood and bits of body still lingered in the air, the tent flap quietly unsealed. A hand gently pulled back the curtain until a face appeared. It was Gideon's face; but at the same time it wasn't. Something about him had changed. Then, beside him, Aybel saw the reason why. Immediately, she wept.

Gideon took one look at Stevron, still drunk with the Worded power that had blasted his adopted father out of existence, and said, "*Skandalos.*"

Stevron's eyes suddenly grew wide—flashing his surprise. But then, like a feather captured by the winds of a cyclone, he was gone.

EPILOGUE
SACRED HEART

Lord Rachel Alli stood expectantly, shivering as she pulled her wool blanket tightly around her shoulders. A massive fire pit blazed beside her—one of dozens dotting the ancient terrain, casting morbid shadows over the ruins of Sacred Heart—but no matter how high she made them burn, no fire seemed able to soothe the chill of dread that now clung to her soul. Feeling a rush of panic, she realized what a frightful mess she must look. She hadn't bathed or even washed her face in days, perhaps even weeks. She sighed, running cold fingers through her matted red hair. There was nothing for it now. Perhaps it would be better if he killed her for it anyway. Perhaps it what she deserved.

Resigned, she stared off into the darkness, and waited.

His form emerged slowly like a smokey apparition coalescing from the shadows of the cold dark. His movements seemed sluggish and somewhat strained, as if resisting his own approach, resentful of the fact that he had to be there at all. It wasn't until the light of the fire reached the contours of his face that she recalled her fear of the power locked within his deep blue eyes. But she did not blink at its return. She no longer resisted her own terror anymore.

Bowing low, she said, "Lord Stevron, you have come to us at last."

Something wasn't right. He looked unnaturally weary, and his face was crusted with streaks of dried blood. The sight of his injury served only to heighten the undercurrent of her unease.

336

"Is everything prepared?" he growled.

"Yes, my lord."

"Then summon the Firstsworn," Stevron commanded. "At first light, I will take a contigent of his best guardians and head back to the east."

"East, my lord?" Rachel stammered, suddenly dismayed. Had she misheard his command? Had she displeased him? "But what of the forces here? Have I missed your will in some way? Will you not take Wordhaven?"

Stevron struck her hard across the face; his eyes alight with contempt. The impact knocked her to the ground. "You will take Wordhaven!" he spat. "You and these dogs will hold it for me until I come to claim it. For now, a new enemy in the east has arisen, and has dared to challenge me. He is expecting my return. And I will not disappoint him."

GLOSSARY

Abaddon (Ahb-bah-DAAN)—True name of the force of evil in the Land. Formless and untouched by age, his origin is not known. Millennia ago, the Pearl subdued him and locked him away in Castel Morstal. There he remained for thousands of years, guarded by the Kah and the powerful Words of the Old Lords. Nevertheless, at some point in the distant past he escaped (it is not known how), and set his heart toward the destruction of the Pearl, and the people along with it. After accomplishing that dark deed through Gideon Truthslayer, Abaddon's whereabouts became a mystery. Although he is no longer commonly believed to be an actual being, he is nonetheless referred to in most cultures as the legendary enemy of the Giver. In this present age, his common name is the "evil one," but in past ages he has been called Destroyer, Father of Ruin, Spirit of the Age, Corruption, Deathfear and Pearlslayer.

Ajel Windrunner (AH-jil WIND-run-ner)—Son of Laudin and Danielle Sky, and nephew of Jesun (Paladin Sky), Saria and Seer. The new leader of the Remnant.

Alielis of Celedriel (AH-lee-EL-iss)—Second daughter of Shal'adum Celedriel by Kaligorn; younger sister to Aybel Boldrun, and twin to Tyragorn.

Aybel Boldrun (AY-bel BOLD-run)—A member of the Remnant and trusted warrior apprentice of Donovan Truthstay. In the land of her people, the Kolventu, she is known by a different name: Aliel, First Daughter of Celedriel by Kaligorn, and heir to the shal'adum of Arelis.

Balaam Asher-Baal (BAY-lum Asher-BAYL)—High Lord of the Council of Phallenar, a man of great power and even greater ambition.

Barrier Wall, The—Also called the Memorial Wall, or simply the Wall. An expansive stone barrier on the edge of Phallenar built by Palor Word-wielder, supposedly as a memorial to his own greatness. Historians who have examined the Wall, however, suggest its purpose may have been as a defensive shield against some unknown threat west of the city.

Batai (Bah-TYE)—From the High Tongue, meaning "Right Hand of the Pearl." In ancient times, it was a common reference for the High Lord of Wordhaven.

Baurejalin Sint (Bar-REJ-a-lin SENT)—Lord on the Council of Phallenar. A pragmatic supporter of Balaam, who saw himself as the natural successor to the High Lord. He was slain by Gideon Dawning in the Chamber of the Pearl beneath the Axis.

Bentel Baratii (Ben-TEL Bar-a-TEE)—A young, ambitious Lord on the Council of Phallenar. Along with his sister, Fayerna, they were once a powerful team that only a few on the Council would openly oppose. He was slain by Gideon Dawning at the ruins of Noble Heart.

Bian'ar (BYE-an AHR)—From the High Tongue, meaning "the light of life." A white putty-like substance found as a solid layer between the outer bark and the inner hardwood of the trees in Castellan Watch. The *bian'ar* is harvested through a complex mystical process known only to the people of Calmeron sounden. The process collects the *bian'ar* while leaving the trees undamaged. *Bian'ar* harvested in any other way rots within an hour or two after it is collected.

Bian'ar eyes—Waking visions that sometimes occur after prolonged exposure to unrefined *bian'ar*. Although these visions, which can last for days, are often mysterious and difficult to interpret, they always indicate a major event looming on the horizon. The greater the magnitude of the event, the greater the frequency of *Bian'ar* eyes. These visions had so consistently warned the Calmeron soundenors of guardian attacks, for instance, that the guardians became convinced they had an informant in their ranks. The "eyes" also foretold Gideon's arrival, and of the death of Cimron's daughter in Gideon's arms (see Cimron te'Mara).

Black Ages, The—The period from the first year of the Slaughtering (S.C. 1605) to the present day. In S.C. 1650, the Council Lords forbade the use of the title "Black Ages," calling the times the "The Council Age." This new title, however, is rarely used except in Phallenar, or whenever the ears of the government may be near.

Black Gorge, The—A long, narrow water-filled canyon that marks the major boundary between the Deathland Barrens and the rest of the Inherited Lands. Commonly called the Gorge.

Book of *Dei'lo*—A sacred tome containing the knowledge of *Dei'lo*, a language of power taught by the Pearl during its time in the Inherited Lands. Only those whose hearts are free of *Sa'lei* may touch the Book, open it, or learn the Words within it. Almost all others who try instantly perish. Immediately following the destruction of the Pearl, the book disappeared from Wordhaven. It was recently rediscovered and returned to its proper home.

Borac conMata (BOOR-ac con-MAAT-ta)—High elder of Songwill sounden. See "*Nissirei.*"

Borin Slayer—Firstsworn of the *mon'jalen*, and chief commander of all guardian forces under Council rule. His succeeded Donovan Truthsayer (Blade) in the role, who was his mentor for several years leading up to Donovan's capture, and subsequent conversion, by the Remnant.

Brasen Stoneguard—A young but capable member of the Remnant. A master of woodlore, Brasen's spent close to ten years living in the wilds after both his parents were slain for their outspoken opposition to Council oppression in Agatharon sounden. In his 21st year, a Remnant warrior encountered him on the outskirts of the Barrier Mountains, and convinced him to come to Wordhaven. He now serves as the Keeper of the Sacred Path.

Broken Heart—The second in a series of ancient training centers designed to test Initiates who aspired to become Lords of Wordhaven. Now thought to be located somewhere in the Deathland Barrens.

Cal'eeb—From the High Tongue meaning "Standing Ones." The descendants of the original Wordhaven lords and novitiates who were at Broken Heart at the time of Gideon's Fall. Isolated for generations by the Deathland Barrens and the sea, they have developed into a unique society based upon the principles of *Dei'lo* and their neverending battle against the desolation of the Barrens.

Calmeron sounden—A village on the edge of the Castellan Watch. The soundenors of this village are the only people in the Inherited Lands skilled in harvesting *bian'ar*, which they use to create glowood or Worded breads that can be exchanged for goods they need to survive. They also regularly give the Worded breads as tribute to the Lords of Phallenar, in exchange for the Council's "benevolent protection."

Castel Morstal (kaas-TEL moor-STAL)—From the High Tongue, meaning "Death's Inner Chamber" or "Death's Breaking Place." A vast mountain keep created by the Pearl as a prison for Abaddon. Though watched over by the Kah for centuries, no mortal has ever entered it.

Castellan Watch—A great forest stretching from the Barrier Mountains in the West, to the Scolding Wind Hills in the North, and to Calmeron sounden in the East. It was named by the Kah, who, legends say, once lived in the heights of the great trees. The massive trees in the Watch are similar to those found in Strivenwood Forest, though it is not known whether the trees of Strivenwood also produce *bian'ar*. Other than the people of Calmeron sounden, few are willing to venture into the Watch for extended periods. Those who do often never return.

Chief Mentor—A title given to the head scholar responsible for educating the underlords at Phallenar in the ways of government and Council life.

Cimron te'Mara (SIMM-ron TE MAAR-ah)—An informant of the Remnant who lives in Calmeron sounden. Through the *Bian'ar* eyes, Cimron and his bondmate both predicted Gideon's arrival, and foresaw that his appearance would mean the death of their daughter, Kira. Nevertheless, they chose not to interfere with the vision, because they believed Gideon was indeed the Kinsman Redeemer. And without their daughter's presence with him, they feared that he would have been killed instead.

Cording—The practice used exclusively by Council Lords to bond their *jalen* to them using the Words of *Sa'lei*. Once corded, *jalen* become Wordsworn to protect their lord from any injury. If their lord is attacked, they are instantly aware of it. If their lord is killed, they too will die, within one month's time. Although it is possible for Council Lords to become corded to each other, their mutual distrust has thus far prevented it.

Council of Lords—The ruling body of the Inherited Lands, presently made up of thirteen Lords who have been granted the right of succession by their elders. Succession is granted only to direct descendants of the original twenty-five families whose members formed the first Council in S.C. 1610 (after the death of Palor Wordwielder). Although officially all members of the Council except the High Lord are equals, in reality those members who can claim ties to the greatest number of Council bloodlines hold the greatest power in the Axis. This ranking system has resulted in significant inbreeding among the Council Lords, and has caused several serious medical problems to arise over the centuries. Not the least of these is barrenness. In the present Council, all the women of child-bearing years are barren, and only a few of the female underlords are capable of bearing young. So far, this knowledge has been kept from the public.

Darind Reach—Speaker for Solidari sounden. The designation of "Speaker" is apparently similar to that of *Nissirei*.

Deathland Barrens—Commonly refers to all land east of the Black Gorge. This land became both desolate and dangerous as an immediate result of the Word of Desolation spoken in ancient times by High Lord Gideon Truthslayer.

Dei'lo—A powerful language that has in its speaking the capacity to transform both the physical and spiritual world, and the individuals within them. The heart of *Dei'lo* is the power of life and creation.

Donovan Truthstay—Originally Donovan Blade, the former Firstsworn of the Council Guardians. Donovan was captured by the Remnant after he was mortally wounded in a battle with Laudin Sky (S.C. 2139). Not long after being restored to health, the Remnant severed his cording to the Council Lords and convinced him to abandon his former office and join the rebellion against Phallenar. He now serves as the commander of Wordhaven's battle force, the Head of Arms.

Edor—From the Kolventu tongue meaning "mist." An obscure island located in the northern reaches of the Hinterland off the coast of the Raanthan Plateau. It is the location of Kiki. (See "Kiki.")

Elise Deveris—Lord on the Council at Phallenar. A woman of great cunning and even greater ambition.

Endimnar—A highly-esteemed prophet from the Grey Ages. Endimnar prophesied the coming a Kinsman Redeemer, a warrior-teacher who would reclaim the power of the Pearl, and restore the hearts of the people in the Inherited Lands. He also foresaw the coming of the Slaughtering, calling it the starting point of a Black Age in which hatred would rule without mercy. Palor Wordwielder claimed to be the Kinsman Redeemer Endimnar had foretold, but his rule actually brought on the Black Age. Since that time, many people associate the coming of the Kinsman Redeemer with a second, more horrible Black Age, instead of the prosperity Endimnar foretold.

Endless Age, The—The period dated from the arrival of the Pearl in the Inherited Lands until the time of Gideon's Fall. The actual length of this age is not known.

Endurant—The name of Captain Quigly's ship. With an overall length of eighty-seven feet, dual masts eighty feet high, and three thousand square feet of sail, the Endurant is built to carry a full load of cargo at top speed through difficult waters. She is a solid work of construction and grace.

Fallenwood—A corrupted forest located in the eastern part of the Deathland Barrens. Before Gideon's Fall, the forest supported several soundens established within its borders. Nothing is known about what became of them.

Fayerna Baratii (Fa-IR-na Bar-a-TEE)—Lord on the Council of Phallenar. Older sister to Bentel, who together shared a common love interest, Lord Sarlina Alli. Fayerna was slain by the Word of Paladin Ajel Windrunner on the slopes of Setal Rapha.

Fel'adum—From the Kolventu tongue, meaning "protector of lore." Title for trained warriors within each Kolventu tribe.

Galad—*Nissim*, or "Shield of the Pearl," for the Cal'eeb, along with his bondmate, Saravere.

Gideon Dawning—An unwitting sojourner in the Inherited Lands. A man of great wounding, and great promise.

Gideon Truthslayer—Ancient High Lord of Wordhaven responsible for the Pearl's destruction, and the creation of the Deathland Barrens. Originally named Gideon Truesworn, his devotion to the Pearl became clouded by personal greed. Seeing the opportunity to destroy the Pearl through the High Lord, Abaddon offered to teach him a Word so powerful it would destroy the Pearl and transfer its power into Gideon himself, thus making him the supreme force in the Inherited Lands. At a place now known as Gideon's Fall, the High Lord spoke the Word that destroyed the Pearl. The High Lord was never heard from again after that, but the resulting earthquakes and firestorms ravaged the land continuously for three days and three nights, resulting in the creation of the Black Gorge and the Deathland Barrens.

Gideon's Fall—The final act of High Lord Gideon Truthslayer, which destroyed the Pearl and created the Deathland Barrens. Also refers to the place where Gideon spoke the Word, a knobby blackened hill north of Phallenar along the cliffs of what is now the Black Gorge.

Gilding—A wood-treatment process that involves encasing wood in the sap that bleeds from the trees of the Castellan Watch. Once hardened, the sap forms a lightweight shield that has the appearance of crystal but is hard as steel. The process was originally created for use on glowood, to seal the wood against moisture and thus prevent it from glowing.

Giver, The—Common name for the Creator, who sent the Pearl into the Inherited Lands to subdue Abaddon and establish the Endless Age. Although his ways are often viewed as mysterious, he is still believed to take an active part in the lives of the people.

Glowood—A common name for wood that comes from the Castellan Watch, or any other wood that has been infused with *bian'ar*. Unprocessed *bian'ar* has the effect of causing the wood to glow when saturated with water. The effect lasts as long as the wood remains wet.

Grey Ages, The—The period from the end of the final Sojourn in S.C. 867, until the first year of the Slaughtering in S.C. 1605. It was during this age that Wordhaven was abandoned, and eventually forgotten.

Guardians—In the present age, Worded soldiers responsible for enforcing the Council's will throughout the Inherited Lands. Though they are sworn to follow the will of any Council Lord, the wishes the lord to whome they are corded generally take precedence over all others. In ancient times, the guardians were life-sworn servants of the Pearl, whose primary task was carrying out the Pearl's wishes.

High Tongue, The—An ancient language derived from *Dei'lo*. Many remnants of the language remain in present everyday life, but most of the language's original power has been lost.

Hinterland—A narrow strip of lush greenlands isolated between Silence Sound and the Raanthan Plateau. Populated by a proud people called the Kolventu.

Ja'moinar (ZHA-moy-NAR)—From the High Tongue, meaning "bread of the living." Only the breadmistresses of Calmeron sounden are able to make this bread, using an ancient ceremonial process in which the women recite a litany in the High Tongue while mixing *bian'ar* with their own human tears.

Jalen (zha-LEN)—The common title for all personal bodyguards and spies belonging to a specific Council Lord. There are two specialized orders of *jalen*, according to their primary function. *Ser'jalen* are information gatherers. Their task is to spy on other Council Lords, or anyone else of interest to their master. *Mon'jalen* are of greater importance. They act as personal bodyguards for their lord, or as commanders in the Council warcors. While *ser'jalen* are taught rudimentary fragments of *Sa'lei*, *mon'-jalen* are trained in a full arsenal of Words, even more than guardians. Because any Council Lord may kill another simply by speaking a Word, *mon'jalen* are sworn to immediately avenge any injury, however slight, that's inflicted on their lord. All *jalen* are "corded" to their lords by the Words of *Sa'lei*—so that in the instant any lord is injured, his or her *jalen* will know it; and if any lord is killed by unnatural means, all of his or her *jalen* will also die within one month's time. This delay before their deaths allows the *jalen* time to avenge their lord's murder. As a result of this cording, all *jalen* tend to be highly-motivated protectors and servants.

Juron (ZHUR-ON)—Black, winged lions that nest on the heights of the Barrier Mountains. Although naturally fearful of people, they can quickly become vicious if threatened.

Kah, The—From the High Tongue, meaning "Watchers." A legendary race of tree-dwellers whose sole purpose was to stand watch over Castel Morstal to make certain that Abaddon could never escape. Legends claim that the Kah were endowed with mysterious talents, and the ability to sense the movements and intentions of the evil one wherever he roamed.

Kaiba—First of Mahdwin, a designation that distinguished him as the favored bondmate of his tribe's shal'adum, Melindra of Cestra.

Kair of the Songtrust (KYE-EYR)—A member of the Remnant whose mother is from Calmeron and whose father is from Songwill. Because of the enmity between these two soundens, she can claim neither as her home. She is especially adept at the healing Words.

Kaligorn—Aybel's father. His title as "First" of Ki'Arelis designates him as the most favored bondmate of the shal'adum Celedriel, and places the female offspring of his loins first in succession to the seat of shal'adum.

Katira Peacegiver (Kah-TEER-ah)—Servant of the Pearl at Wordhaven. She and her husband, Teram Firstway, are among the last of the original Remnant who fled from Phallenar during the Sky Rebellion.

Ki'Arelis—From the Kolventu tongue, meaning "domain of Arelis." The title refers to the land controlled by the tribe, as well as the primary settlement within that land where the shal'adum holds office. Ki'Arelis is the ancestral land of Aybel Boldrun and her tribe. With the death of Aybel's mother, Celedriel, the role of shal'adum for Ki'Arelis falls either to Aybel or her younger sister, Alielis.

Ki'Mahdwin—From the Kolventu tongue, meaning "domain of Mahdwin." The title refers to the land controlled by the tribe, as well as the primary settlement within that land where the shal'adum holds office. The current shal'adum of Ki'Mahdwin is Melindra of Cestra.

Kiki—From the Kolventu tongue, meaning "domain of domains." It is an ancient fortress built by the Lords of Wordhaven during the Endless Age as a summit hall for all the tribes of the Kolventu. Also known as the "Holding."

Kinsman Redeemer—A mysterious figure mentioned in many prophecies recorded throughout the Grey Ages. Some prophecies speak of the Kinsman Redeemer as a mighty warrior who will defeat the evil one and return the language of *Dei'lo* to the people as it was in the beginning. Other prophecies describe him as a champion of peace, who will be overthrown by evil authorities and sacrificed to somehow preserve the land. Since the time Palor Wordwielder claimed the title for himself, all people have associated the Kinsman Redeemer with tumultuous change—whether for good or for evil.

Kolventu—A proud, tribal people living in the Hinterland north of the Inherited Lands.

Kreliz'adum—From the Kolventu tongue, meaning "hater of lore."

Krell—Large flightless birds native to the marshes of the Hinterland. They have been largely domesticated by the Kolventu, who breed them for various uses, including food and transportation.

Kyrintha Asher-Baal—Underlord of the Council in Phallenar; daughter of Balaam and Lysteria. Though approved for succession onto the Council, she rejected it. After being sealed up in the Tower of the Wall for three years for her rebellion, she joined forces with the Remnant and escaped her parents' clutches. She now travels with Gideon Dawning on his quest for the Pearl.

Lairn conCimron (LAYRN con-SIMM-ron)—Teenage son of Cimron, who was to become one of the first real Initiates into Wordhaven in over 2,000 years. He perished protecting Gideon Dawning from a horde of riftmen.

Laudin Sky—Instigator of the "Sky Rebellion" against the Council Lords in S.C. 2060. Once Chief Mentor of all the underlords in Phallenar, Laudin later escaped with over one hundred companions in search of the fabled Wordhaven. After a 35-year sojourn, he found it, and became the first leader to sit within its walls in over 1,000 years. Rather than equate himself with the ancient Lords of Wordhaven, however, he chose the title "Mentor," as a constant reminder of the bondage from which he had been freed. After he was killed by Donovan Blade in a guardian ambush, the mantle was passed on to his younger brother, who changed the title to "Paladin." That title is now held by Laudin's son, Ajel Windrunner.

Lysteria Asher-Baal (Liss-TEER-ee-ah Ash-uhr BAYL)—Lord on the Council at Phallenar. Wife of High Lord Balaam. A great patron and fierce defender of the glory of Phallenar.

Maalern Fade (MAY-lern FAYD)—Oldest member of the Council Lords. He represents the last of his family line.

Mara ta'Cimron (MAAR-a TA SIMM-ron)—Bondmate of Cimron, and a breadmistress of Calmeron sounden.

Mattim Dasa-Rel (Matt-TEEM Das-a-RELL)—Lord on the Council in Phallenar. Bondmate of Varia Dasa-Rel.

Mon'jalen—see *"jalen."*

Morguen sounden (morg-YU-en sounden)—A village located on the southern end of Silence Sound near Strivenwood Forest.

New Ages, The—The period from Gideon's Fall (S. C. 1) to the end of the last major Sojourn (by Lord Kih, in S.C. 867). This period was marked by successive generations of lesser Wordhaven lords, who launched mammoth sojourns to try to locate the lost Book of *Dei'lo* and reclaim the glory of former days. So obsessed were they with finding the Book that they neglected to protect the knowledge of the Words they still retained. Consequently, the strength of their society steadily declined as the knowledge of *Dei'lo* and culture of Wordhaven were gradually lost. Not long after the end of this period, Wordhaven was abandoned.

Nissirei (Nis-seer-AYE)—From the High Tongue, meaning "First song of the people." The title belonged to the High Elder of Songwill sounden, who was hand-picked from birth by the previous High Elder, and raised solely to fill that role for the people.

Noble Heart—The first in a series of ancient training centers designed to test Initiates who aspired to become Lords of Wordhaven. Thought to have been located somewhere in the Plain of Dreams.

Pact, the—An ancient agreement struck between the old Lords of Wordhaven and the Kolventu. Its substance and terms have been long forgotten by all but the Kolventu.

Paladin—Title given to the First Servant of the Pearl at Wordhaven. Currently the title belongs to Ajel Windrunner.

Palor Wordwielder—The only person who ever sought the title of king over all of the Inherited Lands. His attempt failed, but not before killing hundreds of thousands, and shattering the soul of the people.

Palor's Finger—A point on the edge of the Delving Ocean where Palor apparently destroyed himself after failing to overthrow Songwill sounden. Legend claims Palor killed himself by summoning a mighty ocean serpent that dragged him out to sea.

Pearl, The—A fantastic living orb sent by the Giver to teach the people of the Inherited Lands the Words of *Dei'lo*, and show them how to live in peace with one another.

Phallenar (FALL-en-NAR)—Capital city of the Inherited Lands, seat of power for the Council Lords for over 600 years. Its founding by Palor Wordwielder led to the Slaughtering in S.C. 1605.

Plain of Dreams—A Worded plain of singing grasses that stretches from the Dunerun Hope to the outskirts of Phallenar. The region is Worded so that anyone who sleeps within the plains will dream of actual events from his or her past, present or future. The origin and purpose for this Wording are unknown.

Pondari—A large sloth-like creature with long reddish fur and a peaceful disposition. Though dull-witted and often stubborn, its immense size and strength make it a favored beast of burden for roamers and other travelers carrying large loads. Though largely domesticated, wild pondarin can still be found in the high mountains as well as many parts of the Raanthan Plateau.

Portal—A Word-wrought doorway enabling instantaneous, one-way travel from Wordhaven to a specific location far away.

Priests of Trevail—Male warriors among the Cal'eeb who take a life-long vow of celibacy and poverty so that they might fully commit their lives to the protection of the Cal'eeb and the defense of the Trevail Plains.

Proftel sounden—The original name of Phallenar. In ancient times, the sounden's Trust was the knowledge of interpreting prophecies and dreams. It is where Palor Wordwielder was born.

Quigly—Sea Folk captain of the Endurant. Once a trading partner of Paladin Sky, he and his bondmate aided the escape of the Remnant from Phallenar after they retrieved the Book of *Dei'lo*.

Raanthan (RON-thun)—From the High Tongue, meaning "To Cover." A mysterious race said to live north of the Heaven Range in the Raanthan Plaueau. Few facts about them are known, but legends and myths abound. Some of the more prominent beliefs are that Raanthans have no gender, can speak only in song, and are able to wrap their bodies in light like a blanket.

Rachel Alli—Lord on the Council at Phallenar. Older sister of Lord Sarlina Alli.

Rema (REY-ma)—A little-known settlement near the northeastern coast of the Deathland Barrens. Built directly on the ruins of Broken Heart,

Rema is now the home of the Cal'eeb, direct descendants of the Word-haven lords and novitiates who once lived in the hearted city at the time of Gideon's Fall.

Remnant, The—Originally called "The Society of the Remnant." A clan-destine organization within Phallenar, whose members believed the Council Lords had indeed found the Book of *Dei'lo*, but had not been able to destroy it. The Remnant's original purpose was to infiltrate the government in order to discover the Book's whereabouts. Their ultimate aim was to steal the Book, and use its language to overthrow the Coun-cil's rule. After the Sky Rebellion, most of the Remnant fled Phallenar, or were killed. Though the organization was thought to be shut down within borders of Phallenar over 600 years ago, it does, in fact, still exist. (See "Sky Rebellion.")

Revel Foundling—An orphan boy adopted by Laudin Sky after a guardian raid on Morguen sounden. His origins are a mystery, as are the source of his unique abilities, which come alive whenever he enters forested lands.

Riftborn—Humans or other creatures born in the Deathland Barrens. Also can refer to any creature that's been mutated by the Barrens' effects.

Riftmen—Humans who have been perverted by the effects of the Death-land Barrens. Riftmen can assume any shape they wish, and hold a human form only by choice. Their skin and body fluids carry the plague of the Barrens. One touch can cause serious illness; a scratch will cause death. So feared are they that contact is avoided at all cost.

Roamers, The—The common name given to nomadic soundens of travel-ing merchants. Essentially, they are smugglers, often stealing from one sounden in order to sell the goods to another. Their existence is offi-cially forbidden by Council Law, though the law is rarely enforced.

Sa'lei—A powerful language that has in its speaking the ability to pervert both the physical and spiritual world, and the individuals within them. The heart of *Sa'lei* is the power of death and destruction.

Sacred Heart—The last in a series of ancient training centers designed to test Initiates who aspired to become Lords of Wordhaven. Located on the eastern slopes of the Heaven Range.

Sacred Path—The Remnant designation for an aggressive and some would say foolhardy program for bringing sounden volunteers to Wordhaven to study *Dei'lo* so they might fight alongside the Remnant against the Council Lords and their forces.

Saravere— *Nissim*, or "Shield of the Pearl," for the Cal'eeb, along with her bondmate, Galad.

Saria Sky (SAH-ree-ah SKYE)—The quiet eldest sister to Seer, Laudin and Jesun (Paladin) Sky.

Sarla Ferin—A slave girl from Phallenar who carries secrets and a past she is not willing to reveal.

Sarlina Alli (sar-LEEN-ah ah-LEE)—Lord on the Council at Phallenar. She perished in an attack against Wordhaven orchestrated by her companions, Lords Fayerna and Bentel.

Scolding Wind Hills—A Worded region of verdant hills stretching from the Barrier Mountains in the West to the border of the Deathland Barrens in the East. Named "Scolding Wind" because of the unique and terrible power they unleash against anyone who speaks a Word of *Sa'lei* within their borders.

Sea Folk, The—A race of squat, gnome-like people who make their home upon the seas. Also called the "Wondrojan," they instinctively distrust solid earth and prefer instead to live in floating cities out on the open ocean.

Sed Kappan-Mati (SED KAP-an MA-tee)—Lord on the Council at Phallenar.

Seer Sky (SEE-ur SKYE)—Elder sister of Jesun (Paladin Sky). Especially gifted in the interpretation of dreams.

Ser'jalen—see "*jalen.*"

Setal Rapha—From the High Tongue meaning "Seat of Healing." An ancient holy mountain beyond the Arid Hope where legend claims the Pearl first appeared in the world, arriving through a massive portal called the Brilliant Gate.

Seven Stays, The—Seven towering "sound chambers" constructed along the border of the Deathland Barrens south of Rema. Day and night the priests of the Cal'eeb cry out from the chambers the Words that hold the Barrens at bay.

Shal'adum—From the Kolventu tongue, meaning "Keeper of lore." The title belongs to the chief matriarch within each Kolventu tribe.

Shikinah (Shi-KEY-na)—A highly-esteemed prophet from the Grey Ages. Her prophecies foretold of the coming of a second High Lord of the Pearl, who would be betrayed as the Pearl was, and hung to die on a Great Wall in Phallenar. So great was public reaction to this prophecy that several factions in Songwill demanded she retract it. When she would not, Skikinah was forcibly taken to Castellan Watch, beaten, and hung there to die. Oddly, just as she died, she looked toward the sky and laughed, saying, "It is torn! The heart is torn! At last I understand!"

Sky Rebellion—Named for its instigator, Laudin Sky, the rebellion was actually more of an organized escape from Phallenar. The rebels were all members of the Remnant who fled the city on a quest to locate the fabled Wordhaven.

Slaughtering, The—A three-year war led by Palor Wordwielder and his armies of "New Guardians." During that time, many soundens were completely obliterated, their inhabitants killed or taken as slaves to Proftell sounden (now Phallenar). The war represented the first time the Words of *Sa'lei* were used in open combat. The war ended with Palor's suicide, which came at the end of an unsuccessful siege of Songwill sounden. Until recent events, Songwill was the only sounden in the Land that was still officially free from Council rule.

Sojourn—A private journey taken by individuals who seek spiritual renewal or intellectual enlightenment. Once a sojourn begins, it does not end until a person either finds the enlightenment he seeks, or dies in the attempt. In ancient times, the Lords of Wordhaven led entire armies of people on sojourn together in search of the Book of *Dei'lo*.

Sojourner—A title of respect bestowed on any person who leaves home on a quest for spiritual enlightenment. In ancient times, the title referred to those who traversed the Inherited Lands in search of the Book of *Dei'lo*.

Songwill sounden—Located in the heart of the Scolding Wind Hills. Their original Trust under the Old Lords involved the power and beauty of music and art.

Sounden—A community of people within the Inherited Lands.

Stevron Achelli (STEV-RAHN ah-KELL-ee)—A Lord on the Council in Phallenar. Handpicked by Balaam and Lysteria as bondmate to their daughter, Kyrintha, and secretly chosen by Balaam to be his successor as

High Lord. In defiance of Council law, Balaam schooled Stevron in the language of *Sa'lei* from the time of his early youth, intending that Stevron would be his living legacy, succeeding him as the most powerful Council Lord who had ever lived. Little did Balaam realize how successful his training of Stevron would be.

Strivenwood Forest—A vast forest stretching from the Heaven Range in the West to the Black Gorge in the East. The forest is Worded, though the exact nature of the Wording is unclear. All that is known is that anyone who enters the forest never returns.

Telus—A Raanthan of unknown origin. Sent to guide and protect Gideon Dawning in his quest to locate the Pearl.

Teram Firstway (TARE-uhm)—Servant of the Pearl at Wordhaven. One of the few original members of the group that escaped from Phallenar in the Sky Rebellion.

Trevail Plains—A small region of land on the northern tip of the Deathland Barrens, inhabited by a people who call themselves the Cal'eeb, which in the High Tongue means "Standing Ones."

Trust, A—An endowment of hidden knowledge. In reference to soundens, a Trust is a unique application of the Words of *Dei'lo* known only to the people of the sounden to which it was given and to the Wordhaven Lords themselves. The Trusts gave each sounden its identity and purpose, and so naturally each sounden held its special knowledge in the highest esteem and guarded it with utmost secrecy. The knowledge of each Trust was complementary rather than competitive, creating a society in which each sounden contributed equally to the success of the others, thus binding the soundens together in a rich tapestry of culture and industry. It was an easy symbiosis, but one that could be maintained only so long as each sounden played its role, and guarded its Trust, with diligence.

Tyragorn—Second son of Shal'adum Celedriel by Kaligorn; younger brother to Aybel Boldrun, and twin to Alielis.

Tyrenon—Beloved older brother to Aybel Boldrun and first son of Shal'adum Celedriel by Kaligorn. His disgraced expulsion from the Hinterlands when Aybel was a child prompted her to run away as well in the hopes of going with him. She tracked him as far as Phallenar, but then lost his trail. His current whereabouts are unknown.

Underlord—An honorary title given to a son, daughter, nephew or niece of a Council Lord. Although underlords have no official authority, nor any access to the Words of *Sa'lei*, they still manage significant influence in the affairs of the government in Phallenar.

Vaganti—More commonly, the "Vag." A floating city that has served as the principal home of the Sea Folk since the time of the Endless Age. (See "Sea Folk.")

Vallera Kappan-Mati (va-LEHR-ah KAH-pan MAH-tee)—Lord on the Council at Phallenar.

Varia Dasa-Rel—Lord on the Council at Phallenar. Bonded to Mattim Dasa-Rel. A woman of extraordinary power and conceit.

Visitation, The—A common reference to the prophesied arrival of the Kinsman Redeemer.

Warcor—A military unit of guardians or other soldiers, consisting of exactly 1,300 fighters—100 for each of the thirteen Council Lords.

Wordhaven—Home of the Pearl and ancient center of power during the Endless Age. Except for the Remnant, no one knows its location.

ACKNOWLEDGMENTS

I owe an enormous debt of gratitude to a great team of heroes whose help has been invaluable in getting this story out to the masses. Many thanks go to my editors and friends, Karl and Lisa Lauffer, whose invaluable feedback and suggestions helped shape the manuscript into the final form you now hold.

I am equally grateful to the many friends and allies whose skilled assistance in the production of this book was as invaluable as it was gracious. Among these great champions of Gideon's cause are Josh Tilton, Kristin Goble, Marcy Bojrab, and my sister and brother-in-law Stephanie and David Meadows, without whose help this project would still be floundering in dreams.

And of course, to all those fans of Gideon's Dawn who stayed with me through this crazy and often frustrating journey—THANK YOU! I'd love to hear from you! Feel free to visit me on my website: www.michaelwarden.com.

HELP SPREAD THE WORD...

If you have been inspired by *Waymaker* and its characters, you may have already thought of some people you'd like to recommend it to. That's great—please do! In addition, here are some other ways we would really appreciate your help in spreading the word about this series:

- If you have a website or blog, consider sharing a bit about the novel and recommend it to others.
- Write a book review on Amazon.com
- If you own a shop or business, consider buying some of the books to resell to your customers.
- If you know people who are in a position to influence a wider audience, buy them a copy and encourage them to consider promoting it to others.
- Go through the book together in your book club or writers circle.
- Encourage your local radio station to interview the author.
- Buy a set of books to donate to prisons, church bookstores, libraries, youth groups—anywhere people might be entertained and encouraged by its message.
- Talk about the book on email lists or online forums you belong to, or other online communities you frequent.

Thanks! As we are not a big publishing house, word of mouth makes all the difference in helping a book like this gain visibility to a wider audience.

The story continues in...

THE WORD WITHIN
Book 3 of the Pearlsong Refounding

"In the end, only one Word will rule"

War has come to the Inherited Lands. Though the Remnant now wield the life-giving power of *Dei'lo*, their numbers are still too few to stand against the staggering might of the *Sa'lei* Lords and their armies. Besieged and weakened to near collapse, the Remnant rebels are forced to leave Wordhaven and flee to the four corners of the world. Isolated from one another and unable to find help for their cause, their defeat is all but certain.

And yet, within the dark shadows of the Deathland Barrens, one thread of hope remains. Gideon Dawning, the prophesied Waymaker from another world, has recovered the Pearl, a holy sentient orb that holds within it the full knowledge and power of *Dei'lo*. If Gideon can bring the orb to the fight, it may be enough to turn the tide. But time is short, and many dreadful enemies stand in his way.

But beyond all this, the Pearl itself is not what he expected. It resists his will, compelling him to follow an unexpected path—one that seems set on bringing about the doom of the world.

Coming Spring 2009!

For more information, visit us on the web:
www.thepearlsongrefounding.com